Maisey Yates is a *Ne*  of more than seventy-... coffee habit she has m... Pinterest addiction. S... children in the Pacifi... writing she can be fo... shopping for shoes or... ... pu...... ...g dishes. Check out her website, maiseyyates.com.

USA TODAY bestselling and RITA® Award– nominated author **Caitlin Crews** loves writing romance. She teaches her favorite romance novels in creative writing classes at places like UCLA Extension's prestigious Writers' Program, where she finally gets to utilise the MA and PhD in English Literature she received from the University of York in England. She currently lives in the Pacific Northwest with her very own hero and too many pets. Visit her at caitlincrews.com.

THE SPANIARD'S UNTOUCHED BRIDE

MAISEY YATES

MY BOUGHT VIRGIN WIFE

CAITLIN CREWS

MILLS & BOON

First Published in Great Britain 2018
by Mills & Boon, an imprint of HarperCollins*Publishers*
1 London Bridge Street, London, SE1 9GF

The Spaniard's Untouched Bride © 2018 by Maisey Yates

My Bought Virgin Wife © 2018 by Caitlin Crews

ISBN: 978-0-263-27323-6

Printed and bound in Spain
by CPI, Barcelona

THE SPANIARD'S UNTOUCHED BRIDE

MAISEY YATES

To romance novels.
Which have been my inspiration as a writer,
and my comfort as a reader.
I'm grateful there's an entire genre devoted to love.

PROLOGUE

HE DOESN'T HIRE WOMEN.

Camilla Alvarez looked into the mirror at her decidedly plain reflection. She was a woman, that much was true. Though, she had never been considered a beauty. Even so, she imagined that as far as Matías Navarro was concerned, she was a woman.

Her cheeks were still wet with tears, her eyes glittering with more. It was unthinkable. Losing her father suddenly as she had to a heart attack, and then losing the ranch, as well. And all the horses...

It was her heart. And, shattered though it was, fractured as it was now, she couldn't lose it. She could not.

But the horses, the *rancho*, everything was being sold to cover her father's debts. Everything was going to Matías Navarro.

He had been one of her father's fiercest competitors. His racehorses were the only steeds that could compete with those of Cesar Alvarez.

And now Matías owned them.

Because apparently, their *rancho* had been in debt, the supposed millions of dollars that her family possessed nothing more than smoke and mirrors. All mortgaged to extremes and behind on every payment.

Her father had been an idealist. A man completely

laser-focused on his ranch, his animals, his workers. With little time or thought given to anything else. She didn't even have to ask herself how it had happened. She knew. Her father hadn't liked the situation, and so he had ignored it.

Collectors had been hounding Camilla ever since Cesar's death. And her mother—predictably—had gone off to France, taking shelter under the wing of one of her many lovers.

She had always flaunted them in the face of her husband, but Camilla supposed that now that Cesar was dead, her mother felt it was all justified seeing as she clearly had an insurance policy.

Camilla had nothing. Nothing but the *rancho*. The place she had grown up in, grown wild in. Her mother had rarely been in residence, and for most of Camilla's life, it had simply been her and her father.

And he had allowed her to do whatever she wanted. To run barefoot. To ride until she reached the end of the property, and then beyond. Roaming all over the Spanish countryside as she pleased.

Her mother, an American heiress who had never settled well into the rural country life, had seen it all as beneath her.

Camilla had seen it as everything. And now it was gone.

She had begged, pleaded, as her horses had been led away from the property by members of Matías's staff for them to let her go, too. If she was going to lose the *rancho*, as long as she could be with the horses, as long as she could be with Fuego, she could survive it.

She had told them she would do anything, any job.

But the stone-faced man guiding her favorite black

stallion into the trailer had simply shaken his head and told her that Matías Navarro did not hire women.

And indeed, the evidence had been all around her that it was the truth. There was not a single woman among Matías's staff present at the *rancho*.

Her father was gone. Her horses were gone. Soon, she would be evicted from the *rancho*, with nowhere to go. There were no provisions made for her. She had nothing. Nothing and no one. She had never been able to count on her mother during good times, she had no illusions that she would be able to count on the woman now that things were difficult.

Camilla knew one thing. She knew horses.

She knew *those* horses. She loved *those* horses.

Fuego was going to be the next champion on the European racing circuit, she was confident in that. But no one else could handle him. No one else could ride him, and he had some way to go before he was ready for anyone else to try.

Matías Navarro would find out soon enough that his new acquisition was essentially useless to him. If the horse could not be broken, then he was worthless.

And without the horses… Her life felt worthless.

She looked back in the mirror, examining her face. She was not classically beautiful. Her mother had always despaired of her heavy bone structure, the angular nature of her jaw and chin. Not feminine, her rather spindly mother had declared.

For the first time, though, Camilla was completely pleased with this assessment of her looks. Because it was going to be an asset to her now.

She opened up the drawer in the vanity and pulled out a pair of scissors. Then she touched a lock of glossy, black hair, and ruthlessly stretched it tight, cutting it close to her ears.

Yes, she had found her solution.

Matías Navarro did not hire women. But perhaps he would hire a new stable boy.

CHAPTER ONE

CAMILLA STRAIGHTENED AND wiped her brow, looking out over the now familiar fields of the Navarro *rancho*. In the two months since she had come into Matías's employ, the place had become close to home. Of course, it couldn't compare to the Alvarez *rancho*. She had lived there for twenty-two years, and she couldn't imagine anywhere feeling like home the way that it had.

Sometimes she ached with the desire to walk through that familiar front door, to feel the red stone floor beneath her feet, the places where it was imperfect. Where it bowed and cracked from years of wear. It was like a familiar friend, and it was gone. She could never have it again.

But at least she had the horses.

It was a tricky thing, though, getting access to Fuego. Matías had refused to allow anyone but his most trusted handler and himself to get anywhere near him. Of course, he was proving to be difficult. Camilla had known he would be. Because he was a difficult animal.

But she had opted to keep herself mostly out of Matías's vision. She had not seen the point in drawing attention to herself, but it was becoming clear that if she wanted to have anything to do with Fuego she was going to have to assert herself.

A difficult thing, since the assumption was that she was a fourteen-year-old boy, simply doing work in exchange for board on the property.

Very few questions had been asked, and for that she was grateful. She had done a bit more digging about Matías and had discovered that he was generous with his employees. That he had a soft spot for troubled youth and made putting them to work something of a mission.

In spite of his family's difficult reputation, Matías himself seemed to be a good man. When she ignored that little *doesn't hire women* thing.

But she had found a workaround. She had decided to play the part of a troubled youth, fallen through the cracks and likely to end up sleeping on the streets if not for the kindness of the Navarro estate.

It was true enough. She had very few options available to her at the moment. She had no money.

And she was, in fact, qualified for the job she had been hired to do.

All in all, her solution was a reasonable one. So, perhaps concealing her gender might be considered less than reasonable.

But with her hair cut short, and baggy clothes over her rather straight up and down figure, no one questioned it.

In part, she imagined, because very few people looked directly at her. Much less Matías Navarro.

Or his beautiful, birdlike fiancée, who had come to live at the estate just last month. She was a lovely creature and reminded Camilla very much of her mother. She had cascading waves of curling blond hair, pale blue eyes and alabaster skin. Anytime she went out onto the *rancho* she took extensive breaks to stand in the shade and slather her body with sunscreen.

Matías seemed solicitous of her, often putting his hand on her lower back, or taking hold of her arm, as if the woman would fall onto her face on the uneven terrain if he did not hold on to her in some fashion.

Camilla wondered what it might be like to have someone treat her like that. No one had ever been gentle with her. Her father had treated her as though she were the son he didn't have. Had allowed her freedom, had encouraged hard labor. Her mother had treated her like an irritation. She had preferred the former.

But no one had ever made her feel precious. No one had ever made her feel fragile.

She sniffed and shrugged her shoulders upward, going back to the task of shoveling manure.

She would rather have this than be cloistered away in that giant manor house. Would rather be out in the sun, out where it smelled like hay and horse and grass.

She looked up and squinted. Judging by the position of the sun, it was about time for Matías to make his rounds. That meant he would be coming out to the stables, likely attempting to take Fuego into the arena to be lunged.

Historically, that had not gone well.

Camilla had watched through a crack in the door of the stable, whenever she had the opportunity. Whenever she wouldn't get caught by the foreman and scolded for being idle. She wouldn't do well at all to get fired.

She scampered over to the end of the stable and took her typical position. And then her breath caught.

There was Matías, walking into the arena with Fuego on a lead. Fuego was as beautiful as ever, his coat glossy beneath the late-afternoon sun. He tossed his head, already telegraphing his irritation with the situation, his ears listing backward.

Then her eyes slid to Matías. And everything inside her seemed to freeze.

He was stunning in his own right and reminded her in many ways of the animal he was attempting to tame. His black hair was pushed back off his forehead, his skin bronzed and gleaming. His chest was broad, his white shirt unbuttoned down to the center of his chest, the sleeves pushed up past powerful forearms. He was wearing tan breeches that molded to lean hips and powerful thighs, to say nothing of…other parts of him.

Camilla had been around jockeys her entire life. Typically, they were slightly built, all the better to ride quickly. And she knew that Matías did not race for that very reason. It wasn't practical. A man well over six feet tall with such a heavy build could never compete with other racers.

No, Matías was not a jockey. Therefore, the sight of him in those breeches was…a different experience. And one she was not accustomed to, no matter that she had grown up at a stable.

Matías and his foreman switched out the horse's lead for a lunging rope, and Matías stepped backward, moving to the edge of the arena, a whip in his hands, which would be used, not to harm the animal, but to signal changes in what he desired Fuego to do. When he wanted him to change his gait, when he wanted him to stop, or turn.

But, as had happened every time in the past couple of months, Fuego balked. He more than balked. He reared, nearly turning himself over onto his back. Camilla felt a spike of rage, and before she knew what she was doing she was tearing out of the stable and heading toward the arena.

Her face was on fire, her heart beating quickly, and this time it had nothing to do with Matías's breeches.

"Tonto!" she shouted. "You know he doesn't like it. And you insist on doing it. He's going to injure himself."

It took her a moment to realize what she had just done. That she had just shouted at the master of the domain, while in his domain. That she had just undone two months of attempting to go unnoticed by rendering herself as conspicuous as possible.

"I see," Matías said, taking too long strides across the arena and heading toward her. "You fancy yourself a great trainer, do you?"

Those dark eyes pinned her to the spot, her feet nearly growing down into the grass as he moved to the edge of the fence. She took a step backward, with great effort, trying to put some distance between herself and her formidable boss.

"Not great, perhaps," she said, attempting to keep her voice low and steady. "But I know the horse."

"What do you mean?"

"When I came here…" She desperately tried to improvise. "I did not lie when I said that I would have no home if I wasn't hired." She cast a look at the *rancho* foreman just to be sure that he was listening. So that he could corroborate at least that part of her tale. "I came from the Alvarez *rancho*. I'm familiar with Fuego. I can work with him."

"You're only just now telling us this?" Matías asked, shooting his foreman an appointed glare.

"Don't blame Juan. I didn't tell him. I was afraid to draw attention to myself. But now I see that Fuego is not going to acclimate to this new environment. Or to new trainers. I could ride him."

Matías leaned over, resting those strong forearms

over the top rail of the fence. "I am to believe that Cesar Alvarez allowed a scrawny boy to ride one of his most prized horses? That this beast responds to you?"

"That's right," she said, tilting her chin upward. "I have a way with him."

She had always had a way with difficult horses, just like her father had. It was a gift. One that Cesar Alvarez had believed you either had or didn't. He had told her it was in her DNA, as it was in his.

It had been their sole point of connection. Her father had been entirely invested in the *rancho*, and anyone who loved him had to love that place just as much. And she did. She very much did.

"I'm not letting you anywhere near that animal."

"Why not?" she asked. "What do you have to lose?"

"It's not so much what I stand to lose as what I don't want to have to cope with. I would rather not have to respond to an inquiry over a foolish boy breaking his neck on my *rancho*."

"I'm not going to break my neck," Camilla said. "But Fuego might snap a limb if you continue to handle him like this. I hear that you're very good with horses, Señor Navarro, but I have not yet seen it."

"You think insulting your boss is the way to long-term employment?"

"I assume that you are a man who would appreciate honesty. You are allowing your pride to get in the way of making the most of your animal, and I daresay I have seen it many times before."

One of Matías's dark brows shot upward. "Many times?"

"Yes. During the year I was employed with Cesar Alvarez. There were a lot of rich men with animals they could not handle."

"I'm a horseman," Matías said. "Not simply a rich man."

"You are a businessman primarily. That is nothing to be ashamed of, but it does mean that your focus is split."

Then Matías did something she did not expect. He laughed.

"All right then, boy. Come into the arena and show me what you can do."

Matías could not believe the unmitigated gall of the youth standing rooted in the grass only a few feet away from him. He could not be older than fourteen, and he spoke with the kind of boldness that grown men did not have in his presence. Although, in many ways that made sense.

Fourteen was that sort of age. When a boy could have all the bravado in the world, and not be aware of what consequences might befall him.

Matías was certain he had been similarly brash at that age. In all actuality at thirty-three he was still as brash, it was just that when you were a billionaire with limitless funds and no small amount of power, it was not considered brashness. It was simply considered reasonable.

He was a man of responsibility also, and one who—unlike the rest of the men in his family—cared about doing what was right. He cared about the ranch. About the village the ranch supported.

His *abuelo* was currently playing games with it. But Matías wasn't to be trifled with. The old man had pitted Matías and his older brother Diego against each other, saying they had to comply with specific terms, and whichever of them managed in an allotted time frame would get their share of the ranch and the family assets upon the old man's death.

If they both complied, they would get half each.

But if only one did...to the victor went the spoils.

Matías had no doubt he would be the one to win. Marriage was one of his grandfather's stipulations, and Matías had secured his union to Liliana Hart a couple of months earlier. He had known her casually for years. Had seen her at various functions with her parents, and her father had indicated he wouldn't be opposed to the union and Matías had seen it as an opportunity.

That was the sort of man he was. Decisive. Not opportunistic in the way his grandfather or brother were. He did things right.

And he reaped rewards for it.

He had expected the youth to back down the moment he had realized the manner of the man he was coming at. But he had not. Which Matías could only grudgingly admire.

The boy followed his command, moving closer to the arena, a scowl on his face.

Matías looked over at Fuego, his tempestuous new acquisition. The horse possessed the ability to be great. Matías knew it. He was an excellent judge of horseflesh. He was also an extremely skilled trainer. But the animal had refused to come to heel, no matter how long and hard Matías worked with him.

Though it galled him to admit the boy was correct, he was. Matías was also a businessman, and his work often demanded that he spend time away from the *rancho*. That meant having others work with the horses in his stead.

His family was an old one in Spain, and had been breeding champions for generations. But it had long ceased to be their primary source of income. And Matías was involved in various retail conglomerates across the world, his business centered in London, not in Spain.

Though he had achieved a level of status that allowed him to work from wherever he wanted, as various other business associates and dignitaries would meet with him wherever he chose, it still required a fair amount of travel.

So yes, in that way, this urchin boy was correct. The fact that Matías was a businessman did keep him from dedicating everything he had to the animals.

Matías regarded the boy as he walked over to the animal, who immediately seemed to still in his presence. If he had not, Matías would never have allowed the boy to get any closer. He hadn't lied when he said he was not going to subject himself to an inquiry over a teenage boy's stupidity.

Completely unafraid, the boy lifted his hand and brought it to Fuego's nose. The horse sniffed his hand and seemed to find him familiar. For he stilled, almost immediately. The boy grabbed the rope, close to the bridle, and then looked over at Matías, nodding his head once, in a clear bid for Matías to drop his end.

Matías complied.

The boy leaned into the horse, pressing his face against the horse's nose, stroking him gently and speaking to him in soft tones that Matías could not readily understand.

As if by magic, the horse quieted.

Then the boy turned to look at Matías. "I didn't lie to you. Fuego knows me. Now, he's not going to perform perfectly right away. He didn't always obey me. But I can ride him. I can work with him. And I can make it so that someone else can ride him, as well. Which is what you need if you want him to be able to race. As it is, his temperament is too hot. And the fact that no one can manage it makes it impossible. I can make him manageable. I will never make him well behaved, but manageable I can accomplish. And I assume your jockeys are strong enough riders to go from there."

"This is unprecedented," Matías said, looking over at Juan. "I do not allow children to train my animals."

"And yet," Juan responded, "clearly Cesar Alvarez did."

Matías looked back over at the boy, who was regarding him with rather hopeful eyes. "Fine. Whatever your duties are, you're relieved of them. Fuego is now your responsibility. Fernando Cortez is going to be the jockey that we use for him, so eventually you're going to be working with Fernando. But you may start by yourself."

"Good," the boy said, tilting his face upward.

He suddenly looked a bit older than Matías had thought originally. But perhaps that was the bravado again.

"Then it is good," he responded.

He moved over to the edge of the fence. Matías nodded once, signaling the boy to proceed.

The boy paused, then stared at him. "Don't you want to know my name?"

"If I know your name will you become a better horse trainer?" Matías asked.

"No," the boy said, blinking. "I don't suppose."

"Then I do not care to know your name."

The boy said nothing but set about silently moving Fuego through his paces. The horse was jumpy, skittish, but not completely immovable as he had been when Matías had attempted the same.

There was no denying that the boy had a way with the horse. And if Matías wanted him trained in time, he was going to have to allow the boy to step in. The last thing he wanted to do was mishandle such a magnificent creature.

Acquiring Cesar Alvarez's stock had been a boon for him, and he was not about to waste it.

"What about the other horses from the Alvarez *rancho*?" Matías called. "You are familiar with them, as well?"

"All of them," the boy said, not looking over at Matías. "I have worked with all of them."

"You will work with all of them here," he said, decisive now. "My trainers keep logs. Juan will show you the proper way to do this. That way I can read about your progress without having to speak to you. As I prefer it."

"Of course, *señor*," the boy said.

"It is because I'm a businessman, and not simply a horseman," Matías said.

He could have sworn he saw a smile curve the boy's lips. "Of course, *señor*."

Matías turned away, smiling. It was possible that now he had the break he needed to make this animal profitable for him. It seemed as though everything was finally going his way. His engagement to Liliana was cemented. Though she was staying in her own quarters, rather than coming into his.

She had found the transition in their relationship to be a fast one. From a business associate of her father's to his fiancée. And it was clear she required a bit of time to adjust.

He didn't mind. He was a patient man, in all things.

He began to walk back toward the ranch house.

He would fulfill his grandfather's requirements, and the control of the vast family estate would be his at last. A wife. A champion racehorse.

The old man should have known better than to challenge Matías Navarro. Because with him, challenges never went unanswered.

Matías would win this battle with the old man. He knew no other way.

CHAPTER TWO

CAMILLA COULDN'T REMEMBER the last time she'd had a chance to shower. It was an awful thing, but there was no shower in her personal quarters. She had to make do with the shared one in the stables, and it always felt a bigger risk than was strictly necessary.

Still, she was dying for one, especially after spending all day working in the intense heat. She had worked with Fuego until they were both nearly exhausted. But it was the happiest she had been since her father died. Being on the back of that horse again. Riding through the olive groves on the property, the hot, dry wind burning its way across her cheeks.

If her mother could see her now, she would truly despair of her. Reddish face, chapped lips, her hair cut close to her skull and just long enough now to stick up at strange angles when she ran her hands through it in frustration, from when the horses failed to do what she asked of them.

She did indeed look like a boy, and it was easy to feel fully immersed in the role. Until she needed something like a shower, in which case she became terribly aware of her body.

The other time she became terribly aware of her body was when Matías would stride across the grounds, wearing those problematic breeches. It made her feel hot, and it made her feel strange. And so much of the feeling centered on the parts of her body she tried to disguise, that it was impossible for her not to hyper-focus on them.

It was late, the sun having gone down a good half our earlier, a chill starting to wrap itself around her body. Hot days like that always left her skin feeling tight, as though there were an invisible layer of dust over every last inch of her.

Most of the staff had gone home, very few of them living in residence as she did, and the others either had private bathroom facilities or would be showering in the morning. At least that was what she was going to go ahead and bank on tonight.

She scampered into the stable, moving through to the tack room, and heading into the shower. She locked the door behind her and stripped her clothes off quickly, unwinding the precautionary medical wrap that she had around her chest.

It was such a slight chest, she probably didn't have to bind herself, not really. But it was a precaution that she took seriously. Along with these clandestine show-ers. Just in case. Just in case someone had a key to the room she was in. Just in case somehow, right after her shower, having just been naked, she looked somehow more female.

That was the one good thing about the dirt. It pro-vided an extra layer of coverage. She smiled at that, stepping beneath the hot spray of water and scrubbing each inch of her body as quickly as possible.

That was one asset to short hair, as well. The fact that it took much less time to manage. To wash. And in the morning, she did nothing with it at all.

She hummed as she scrubbed and then shut the water off, much sooner than she would like. But really, she didn't have the luxury of lingering.

She dressed into the fresh clothes she had brought inside with her—nothing more than baggy sweat-pants—and was just about to pull her tank on when the doorknob rattled.

She froze, her heart fluttering like a frightened bird trapped in her chest.

"Occupied," she said, doing her best to keep her voice low and husky while panic raced through her.

The doorknob quit rattling. She wrapped her chest quickly with the bandage and then gathered up her dirty clothes, taking care to hide the old bandage that she had been wearing.

She unlocked the door, fortifying herself for who she might see on the other side, and stepped out. "I'm sorry," she said, the words dying on her lips as her eyes made contact with Matías Navarro's.

"Sorry," she said again, mumbling.

"I was taking a walk," he said, his voice hard. "And I saw that there were lights on in here and I came to check."

"I just needed a shower," she responded.

"There is no crime in that."

She shook her head and then attempted to scurry past him. But she ran into the edge of that heavily muscled arm, stumbling forward and dropping the armful of clothes in her hand.

"Easy," Matías said.

Then, much to her horror, before she could act he bent down and collected her clothing. And that pale, taupe-colored medical bandage had somehow risen to the top. Obvious, she thought.

Matías frowned. "Are you injured?"

"I…" She cleared her throat, her head spinning, her cheeks hot. She was grateful that he had supplied that question. Because of course that was the much more logical thought to have. Not that she had been binding her breasts for the past two and a half months to conceal her gender. "My wrist was feeling tender. Just… Fuego pulled a little bit harder and in the opposite direction than I expected when I was lunging him earlier." It was amazing how easy the lie came. Camilla had never been put in a position where she'd had to lie.

She had always done exactly what her father expected. Which had suited her just fine as it had all centered around the *rancho*.

Her mother had never required a lie. She was disinterested in her only child and did not care what Camilla was up to so long as it did not interfere with, or embarrass, her.

She had never known whether or not she was a good liar, because the opportunity had never presented itself. Apparently, she was proficient.

"The swelling has gone down now," she said. "And I'm feeling fine. I was afraid it might be sprained, but it is not."

"That's very interesting. Because I went over the logs earlier and did not see that in there."

"It didn't matter to me," she said, feeling the heat mounting her cheeks. "I mean, it didn't bear noting to me."

"Do not mistake me, boy. It is not your health that concerns me. If Fuego is not responding to training…"

"He is," Camilla said hurriedly.

Matías shifted, rubbing his thumb across the bandage. Something in her stomach grew tight, and then the whole thing flipped over. Her breasts suddenly felt heavy. Even bound beneath the fresh tape as they were.

"If he is a danger to you…"

"He isn't," she insisted, reaching out and snatching the clothing out of his hand. She couldn't bear him touching it. She didn't know why. It made her skin feel warm.

Idiot. That's because you just took a hot shower.

"As long as you're certain."

She nodded. "I am."

Matías nodded once in return, those well-sculpted lips turning down slightly. She felt…immobilized by them. Just for a moment. She didn't think she had ever seen such a handsome man. Not in her whole life. And here she was, dressed as a boy. And even if she wasn't, he would never look twice at her.

No man ever had. Matías Navarro would hardly have been the first. But even if there had been a possibility, it was rendered completely impossible by two things. He thought she was a boy, and he was engaged to his counterpart in beauty.

Liliana was the human version of a meringue. A confection of a woman. All light, airy and pastel. Sweet and beautiful.

Standing anywhere near her made Camilla's bones feel heavy. Made her shoulders feel broad, and her height absurd.

The sad thing was, she had a feeling that even if she was presenting as a woman she would show much the same way in the petite American's presence.

Her one consolation was that Liliana's Spanish was fairly atrocious.

Though, Matías never seemed to indicate that he thought so. And he often spoke to her in English, which

Camilla thought sounded lovely and cultured coming from his lips. She had grown up with both languages, because of her mother, and she was familiar with the way native speakers sounded.

She preferred it from Matías's lips.

"Be careful," Matías said before turning away.

And Camilla was left standing there, her heart thundering hard. And she knew that it was not beating quickly because of adrenaline anymore. That it was something else. Something impossible and terrible. Something that had to be ignored at all costs.

Fernando Cortez was going to have an introduction to Fuego today. Matías had arranged to watch the meeting, and he had also managed to get Liliana to agree to come watch, as well. They drove in an air-conditioned truck across the property to the arena, and then he set them both up in the shade at the edge of the arena.

Liliana's blond curls tumbled over her shoulders and down her back, half of her hair caught up in a row of pink flowers. Her cheeks were a pleasing, matching pink, as were her lips. She wore no makeup. Liliana often did that. He had a feeling it was, in many ways, to highlight just how beautiful she was.

She would make a beautiful wife. A very suitable wife. One that would make him the envy of many men. Certainly of his brother.

But Diego was disgraced, and he was on the verge of being disinherited. He would never marry in time to fulfill their grandfather's will, and, as a result, it would leave Matías in charge of everything. The whole of the Navarro *rancho*, and all the stock.

Plus, it would eliminate the opportunity for his brother to get his hands in Matías's business. That was actually his primary concern. That Diego would end up part owner of Matías's company, even if it was a minority share. Because when Matías had started his retail empire, it had been with money from the Navarro family trust. Which would technically be half Diego's were he to find a suitable bride.

But his brother was a villain. And out of the country after the death of his first wife, with rumors swirling around him.

He had gone on to amount to...nothing much. Gambling and whoring his way through Europe, managing to amass a fortune via misdeeds as far as Matías could see.

He and Diego had never been close, but after their mother's death they had only gotten more distant. His older brother, growing darker, had withdrawn into himself. He had begun to act out, destroying furniture and art pieces. Setting fire to a shed on the property. For his part, Matías had built a taller wall up around himself.

Their methods for surviving a childhood with a violent father who tended toward insanity had been vastly different. For his part, Matías had kept his head down. He had stayed the course that no one had set out for him. But one he had set out for himself.

Diego, meanwhile, had seemingly drunk his father's poison. He moved through life delighting in his wickedness. In his depravity.

Matías would not allow him to have control here. This land had seen enough suffering and cruelty.

Matías would marry Liliana and that would be the end of it all.

"He's a beautiful horse," Liliana said, leaning back in the cushioned chair that had been brought up to the arena for her comfort. She picked up the glass of lemonade that had been delivered for her, as well, and took a delicate sip, her pink lips on the straw captivating his attention.

He suspected his future bride was an innocent. Either that or she was quite good at acting the part of virginal maiden. It made no difference to him, in all honesty. But it was the reason he held himself back from her now.

"He is," Matías agreed. "But a temperamental one. So far, he only responds to that stable boy."

Liliana wrinkled her nose. "Well, that seems rather inconvenient, considering the stable boy can hardly compete in a race. Age limits, I should think."

"Yes. But that's why Fernando Cortez is coming today."

As if on cue the jockey strode out of the barn and into the arena. He had a brief exchange with the stable boy, who seemed somewhat agitated. But then, the boy was easily excitable when it came to the horse. In many ways, Matías appreciated that. The boy was passionate about the horses, it could not be denied, and while he found it somewhat unorthodox to have one who must be quite inexperienced handling such things, he could not deny that the horses responded to him.

Fernando took the lead rope out of the boy's hand, and Matías gripped the sides of his chair, sitting upright and leaning forward. "I hope he doesn't do anything stupid," Matías said.

"The boy or the jockey?" Liliana asked.

Matías glanced over at the boy, who was looking downright angry now. "Either one."

The boy crossed his arms and watched as Fernando approached Fuego, and abruptly swung himself up onto the horse's back.

Before Matías could react, the boy was crossing the

arena, flinging himself into the path of the horse, who was beginning to panic.

"Dios mio," Matías said, moving as quickly as he could.

The horse threw Fernando, and then his hoof clipped the boy in the side of the head. It opened up a gash on his forehead, and he went down to the dirt.

Liliana was standing, a look of horror etched across her lovely features, her pink lips gone waxen.

"Stay back!" he shouted back to his fiancée. The last thing he needed was for her to get in the path of that animal. It was certainly not good for a boy to be anywhere near that animal when it was in a rage. He was not going to allow a woman in there, as well.

Fernando was already standing, backing away from the angry horse. Matías was going to fire the man, and make sure everyone knew he was irresponsible. But first, he had to make sure his youngest employee was alive.

He bent down, holding his hand in front of the boy's nose. He was breathing. So there was that. But he was bleeding, and he was unconscious. Matías tore his shirt-sleeve and pressed the cloth up against the boy's forehead, lifting his slight form into his arms and carrying him toward the truck.

"Medico!" he shouted, putting the boy inside the truck.

Liliana had mobilized, and he knew that she was ensuring that a doctor was called.

Then he began to drive back to the house, hoping that his initial prediction of the horse killing the boy did not prove to be true.

CHAPTER THREE

CAMILLA FELT WOOZY, and when she came back to herself, she felt first a shot of anger, followed by one of pain. She groaned, putting her hand to her forehead. "What?"

"You were kicked," he said. "Not fully."

She opened her eyes and the light hurt. But she saw that she was in a truck, and Matías was driving. "Well, yes. I imagine my head would hurt even worse if the horse had gotten me directly."

"What's your name?" he asked, his tone infused with urgency.

She could hardly process the question. He had never asked her that before, and somehow it made her feel... warm. But then she realized he wasn't asking her.

At least, not her, Camilla Alvarez. He was asking his stable boy. And still, it felt significant. Even though he was only asking to make sure she didn't have a traumatic brain injury.

"Cam," she said, giving the name that she had given to everyone else here.

"Well, do your very best to stay awake, Cam. It won't do to have you falling asleep and not waking up, right?"

She tried to shake her head, but it hurt. "Yes," she said.

She tried to hold her eyes open for the rest of the

drive across the property, and then he put the truck in Park, getting out quickly and rounding to her side of the vehicle, opening the door and grabbing hold of her, pulling her into his strong arms. Holding her against his broad chest.

She suddenly felt weaker, but it wasn't because of the lack of blood, or from the hoof to the head. No, this weakness was squarely related to the fact that Matías Navarro was holding her close, like she mattered. Like she was special.

No, fool, he's holding you close like you're an injured child. Because that's what he thinks you are.

"I sent for a local doctor," he said, laying her down on the couch in the sitting room.

She took a moment to take in all of the details, as best she could. It was one way to try to keep her eyes open. One way to distract herself from the heat and strange tremors that were rolling over her.

Shock.

It had to be shock.

"Calling for emergency services would have taken too long. If we need to send you to a hospital, we can do that. But I would feel better if we brought someone directly to look at you now."

Just like that, she felt suddenly much more awake. Because being examined by a doctor would be problematic, all things considered. And going to a hospital, even more so.

But she couldn't say that. Anyway, she was in no fit condition to spring up off the couch and do anything. Much less run away and deny that she needed any medical attention.

She lay back, looking around the room. At the ornate scrollwork on the crown molding, at the way that it was mirrored in the wood carvings on the plush, pale blue upholstered chairs.

"Not my design choice," he said. "My flat in London and my penthouse in Barcelona look different."

"I... Nothing seems strange about it."

"Of course not," he said, his expression opaque. "Tell me, how long were you homeless?"

She shook her head. "I wasn't. I mean, I was certainly in danger of becoming homeless once Cesar died." Her heart clutched with grief. Because, after all, even though she was playing the part of a stable boy from her father's *rancho*, she was not. It was her father, and she still couldn't speak of him without feeling pain.

"And before you came to work for Cesar Alvarez?" he asked.

She bit her tongue. Because she was simply going to have to fabricate from here. They had a boy that had worked at the *rancho* for a while before her father had paid for him to go away to school. His parents had died, and he had fallen through the cracks of child welfare. It felt wrong to steal his story, but it was also the easiest thing to do under the circumstances.

"I never knew my father," she said, the line tasting like acid, particularly as she had just been thinking about the loss of her father. "My mother died when I was only nine. I was on my own for a while, but then I wandered onto Cesar Alvarez's ranch. He gave me work. He gave me purpose. Education. But horses are what I love. They're what I know. I followed the horses."

Matías nodded. "I love them, too. It is in my blood. My family has had this *rancho* for generations. It means a great deal to me."

"If this is your place, why don't you redecorate?"

Matías crossed to the armchair across from her, picking up a crystal decanter full of sherry. He poured some into a glass. He did not offer any to her. But then, that was because he thought she was fourteen.

Well, probably also because he didn't want her to fall asleep.

"It is not mine," he said, taking a sip of the liquid, then swirling it slightly. He set it down on the table with a decisive click. "It will be. But as it is now, my grandfather is very ill and he has laid out terms. Depending on what my brother and I do before he dies, that is how he will decide who gets what. If both of us comply, we will split it down the middle. If only one of us does, then to the victor goes the spoils."

"What are his terms?" she asked, blinking.

"It's good that I'm keeping you awake with my story, but it might be a little bit too much information. Suffice it to say, I have low expectations that my brother will be able to complete said terms. My brother is not a good man."

"They say…"

He tilted his head to the side, his expression no longer passive. "What do they say?"

Immediately, she regretted starting that line of conversation. "I know about your brother."

Everyone did.

"Of course."

"They say he was responsible for the death of his wife."

"Yes, they do."

She tried to straighten. "Do you believe it?"

"When it comes to Diego it is difficult for me to disbelieve much of anything. Except…" He frowned, hesitating for the space of a breath. "I don't believe he murdered Karina. I will not say he didn't have some level of responsibility for it. But he has also never tried to clear his name. Which is also just very like him. And difficult to apply a motive to."

"They talk about you, too," she said, realizing that this perhaps was not the best line of conversation. But she blamed her head injury. Also, the fact that when he was near it was difficult to breathe. And it made her feel dizzy.

"Do they?"

"They say you don't… That you don't hire women to work for you."

It was a deadly game that she was playing. At least, it felt that way to her. But Matías never looked at her closely. He looked at her the way he did the rest of his staff. Dismissively, though, not unkindly. He was energetic, and always seemed to be looking around, his focus never bound to one place for too long.

She had a feeling that if he was to ever truly look at her he would see much more than she wanted him to.

"It's true," he said, inclining his head, his arrogant mouth curving upward.

"Wh-why is that? You don't think women are good with horses?"

"Of course not," he said, waving his hand. "The problem is, they always fall in love with me."

The words hit Camilla in an uncomfortable space. Because she wasn't neutral to him. Of course, she wasn't in love. That was ludicrous. But she certainly wasn't immune to him, and she could see how it was possible that women might position themselves to get a job at the *rancho* simply to gain access to him.

"Perhaps," Matías said, "it is something you will understand when you're older."

Irritation prickled her face. "I understand it well enough now."

Matías chuckled. "Of course."

"That's very closed-minded of you, actually," she said.

Matías arched a brow. "Is it?"

"Yes," she insisted. "There are some men who might fall in love with you, as well."

He laughed at that. "I suppose that is a possibility, given that I am replete with charm. However, I have never gone up to my bedroom to find one of my male employees naked in residence."

Her mouth dropped open, her cheeks growing warm. "Oh."

"Indeed."

She was starting to feel dizzy, and she let her head fall back to the arm of the settee, staring up at the ornate ceiling. The room was beginning to swirl around her. A confection of gold, blue and white.

"Cam," Matías said. "Stay with me."

She jerked upward. "Stay with you?"

She was feeling confused again. The differences between Cam and Camilla beginning to seem fuzzy. The reason for him asking her to stay becoming ambiguous in her mind.

"Don't fall asleep," he said.

She blinked. Of course. Of course that was what he was asking her to do. He wasn't asking her to stay with him. As in…to stay in the house. As in, to be Camilla with him.

He didn't know who she was. And frankly, she didn't know who he was.

It had been much easier when he was nothing more than the faceless villain who had purchased her father's horses. Who had taken advantage of the state of the *rancho*, and of her father's debts.

He did not seem like a villain now. He was kind. And he cared about the horses. Also, surprisingly, he seemed to care whether or not she died. Though he had made it pretty clear that it was an investigation he wanted to avoid. But perhaps, he also cared whether or not she was dead.

It was strangely warming.

But then, that perhaps could also be the head injury.

Suddenly, the doors opened and the doctor and Juan came into the room. She was caught up in a flurry of being checked over, examined. But thank God, it seemed as though she wouldn't have to go to a hospital. The doctor looked into her eyes and deemed them clear.

And then he ushered Juan and Matías from the room. The older man looked at her with a strange glint in his eyes.

"Your name?"

"Cam," she responded.

"Age?"

She looked away. "Fourteen."

"Have you any parents?"

She shook her head. "No."

"Are you going to tell me the truth?" The older man looked at her with eyes that were far too piercing, far too knowing.

She shook her head, her throat growing dry. "That is as much of the truth as I can tell you."

"I must tell you," the doctor said. "I care a great deal for Matías. I treated him when he was a boy. When that father of his would injure him, give him a black eye, I was the one the staff would call to care for him, and I care for him still. I will not have him taken advantage of."

"I don't want to take advantage of him," she said.

"I believe you. I'm not sure why. Only that I spend a great deal of my time taking care of people. Looking at people. That is the only reason your ruse has worked so far. People like Matías… They train themselves to never look at anyone too closely. But that is what I do. Examine people."

"My head is all right?" she asked.

"Yes. Though I recommend you do not sleep outside. And that you don't work out in the sun for a few days. I will speak to Matías about this."

When the old doctor left the room her stomach twisted. What if he was lying? What if he was going to betray her? Tell her secret? Clearly, he had recognized that she was a woman and not a boy. He had no actual reason to trust her, no matter what he said. Except for some reason she also had a feeling that he would not lie when the truth would serve just as easily.

Because he'd had no reason to placate her. None at all. He could have raised the alarm immediately when he had realized that she was a woman, but instead he had sent Matías and Juan from the room.

Still, she picked at her fingernails, twisted her fingers, nerves overtaking her as she waited.

Matías came back in, his expression dark, stormy. "The doctor has recommended that I set up a room for you inside the house, at least for the next couple of nights. To make you more comfortable, and to ensure that you aren't by yourself."

"Thank you," she said, feeling guilty now. Because this was becoming more than simply taking care of the horses. This was becoming something more.

He was extending hospitality to her now, and she was lying to him.

But it wasn't to hurt him. It wasn't to take advantage of him. It was for Fuego.

Yes, for Fuego, but also for her own damaged heart. Because she had lost so much, and she hadn't been able to bear the idea of not having the horses, too.

She discovered fairly quickly that, in fact, a great many members of Matías's household staff were women.

She looked quizzically at the elderly woman who led her to the bedroom. "He told me he didn't hire women," she commented.

"He does not hire young women," she replied. "Particularly not to work with the horses. He is rarely home, but he is often out at the stables when he's here. So, those are the people he interacts with most often." She shook her head. "He had quite a few girls make appalling fools of themselves for him some years ago."

Camilla took some sense of relief in that assurance as she put on the sweats that had been brought to her from her quarters. At least she hadn't engaged in this ruse because of a false rumor.

That would have been truly untenable.

But she wasn't going to concern herself with that. Not now. She settled herself into the bed—the softest thing she had felt against her skin in months—and tried to stay awake, simply because she felt comfortable, truly comfortable, in the way she had grown up for the first time in so long she wanted to bask in it.

But she couldn't stay awake. And eventually, she gave in and let sleep pull her under.

CHAPTER FOUR

IT WAS THE screams that woke him up. Then at first, he was convinced that he was dreaming. Dreaming of that day that was buried back in his mind, so deep, so far, that his waking consciousness would never dare dredge it up. But in his dreams…his dreams were all women and horses screaming.

But it took only a few moments for him to realize that it wasn't screaming in his head. But in reality.

And he had one thought, only one thought, that the screams were coming from Liliana.

He tore himself out of bed and ran across the house, feeling a jumble of emotions, mixed memories combined with the reality of what was happening. Of course he should never have brought a woman here. Not one so delicate as she was.

Of course he should have known that the curse of the Navarro men—or rather, the women that they took as their own—would come to pass.

Ridiculous. She was having a nightmare, or, she had seen a spider. Something easily explainable. He was telling himself that as he made his way down the hall. But then he heard the screams of his housekeeper, and that was when true fear overtook him.

Heart raging, sweat beading on his back, he raced to

Liliana's room, only to discover that the door was flung open wide, as was the window, her lacy curtains blowing in the breeze. They were three floors up.

Surely, if Liliana wasn't happy she wouldn't resort to flinging herself out a window to escape him. All she would've had to do was ask.

That absurd thought wormed its way into his mind as he ran to the window and looked down below, half expecting to see her inert, white nightgown-clad form crumpled in the grass. But she was not there.

He looked across the broad expanse of lawn and saw her. That white, flowing figure—her nightgown and her pale blond hair—whipping in the breeze. But she was not alone. There was a black shadow that seemed to be consuming her, holding her fast.

Diego.

He knew it. Deep in his bones, he knew. His brother had stolen his bride.

And then, just like that, they were gone. Disappeared completely. Diego had Liliana.

He issued orders to his staff in rapid-fire Spanish, and only after a few moments did he see the boy standing there in the hall, his eyes wide, fear etched over his youthful face.

"Go back to bed," he commanded.

"What happened?" he asked.

"Liliana has been taken," he responded, not seeing any point in being dishonest.

The boy swore. "By who?"

"By my brother."

Camilla still wasn't allowed to go back to work because of her injury, and that meant that she was currently tied to the house, wandering the halls and feeling far too conspicuous.

But if anyone had been even close to looking at her before, they were not doing so now. Everyone was consumed with the search for Liliana Hart, who had been—it appeared—kidnapped out of her bedroom window by Matías's older brother.

Diego Navarro.

And as that search waged on, Camilla had far too much time to simply sit and think. To wonder about the manner of man Diego was, and to attempt to piece it together with what kind of information she had gotten from the doctor. About what kind of man Matías's father had been.

The old doctor had said that Matías had been injured by his father, and he had spoken of it as though it had been routine. Camilla could scarcely wrap her mind around that. Around such horror.

She tried to remember if she had ever heard anything about Matías's father, but she couldn't remember, as all of those rumors were obscured by those about his brother. People did talk about Diego. About how his pregnant wife had died, and how the circumstances had all seemed quite suspicious.

But of course, all of this had been done under the guise of saying prayers for the family, careful bits of gossip wrapped in concern.

Matías, for all that he had a reputation of being hard, also had a reputation for being good.

She had the feeling that none of the other Navarro men held such a claim.

She heard footsteps and scampered deeper into the library, where she was currently attempting to waste some hours. She settled into an armchair near the fireplace, grateful that the only light in the room came from the flames there and a small lamp positioned across the room.

Then she heard voices outside the door.

"Any word at all?" It was Matías's voice.

"None," came an unfamiliar response. "The grounds were searched thoroughly, but somehow, they seemed to have disappeared by the time we got to where the car was abandoned."

Matías let out a derisive snort. "I imagine, knowing my brother, a helicopter was involved."

Camilla raised her brows, putting her hand over her mouth to keep from making a sound that might give her away.

"You are certain it was your brother?"

"Oh, I am certain. There is little I would put beyond his boundaries."

"I am sorry," the other man said. "But if they are not in Spain any longer there isn't much we can do. We have no leads."

"And my brother has not resurfaced anywhere else in Europe yet," Matías said. "I've been keeping watch on his various haunts. Or rather, having certain people in my employ do so. Diego seems to have gone underground."

"We will do our very best. He will not be able to come back into the country without us knowing. That is certain."

She heard footsteps, then she heard Matías muttering about the fact that he had likely gained entry into the country without their knowing this time. She could see that he had little confidence in law enforcement at the moment.

The door opened a crack, and Camilla sank farther

back into the armchair, wishing that there was something she could hide behind. She didn't want to be alone in a room with Matías again. It had been confronting enough when she had been lying there with a head injury. At least then he had been concerned for her well-being and had likely only been looking at her to figure out how injured she was.

She just didn't want to encourage any more moments where he saw her clean, where he saw her in a domestic setting, without the sun in his eyes. Anything that might reveal her to him.

Plus, there was the simple fact that whenever she was in a room with him he made it feel so much smaller. And somehow he felt large. Something about that magnetism filling her chest, making her feel hollow, all at the same time.

She felt aches in places she was not normally conscious of, aches that she didn't know a remedy for.

He made her aware that she was a woman. Much more aware than she had ever been in her life, and certainly more aware than she wanted to be when trying to pass for a boy.

"Cam," Matías said, "I didn't expect anyone to be in here."

"Sorry," she said, starting to stand. "I can go somewhere else."

He waved a hand. "It doesn't matter."

"I am sorry," she said, "about Liliana."

She was sorry. Sorry that the other woman had been taken, that she was likely afraid. No matter what Matías said she supposed it was entirely possible that Diego actually was a killer, in which case Liliana might be in actual danger.

But in many ways she wasn't actually sorry that the

other woman was gone. Which was awful. Except that he made her feel funny. Made her feel light-headed. Made her bones feel heavy.

"So am I," he said, his tone fierce. "I must find her. There is no other option."

"You will," she said, "of course." She knew that it was an unearned confidence, but it was clearly what he needed to hear. She wanted to tell him what he needed to hear. Wanted to make that arrogant mouth curve up into a smile again. Wanted his dark eyes to look at her with approval. Even if it could never be the kind of approval or appreciation that part of her seemed to crave.

It was such a strange thing. Being caught between the urge to avoid him and to seek him out. To build a connection between the two of them and to keep their interactions limited. She wasn't sure that she would ever understand what she wanted from him.

"I'm certain this has to do with the estate. I should have known that if Diego had no intention of complying he would ensure that I could not."

"Surely your grandfather will…"

He shook his head. "My grandfather is not a nice man. You must understand…the men in my family believe in taking what they want without asking. I am from a long line of villains, Cam." He smiled, a dark, feral smile, highlighted by the flames in the fire. "No matter that I've tried to aim for something better. My grandfather doesn't care about scruples. I'm not sure that he will be impressed with my story. In fact, I suspect that he will take Diego's side. A man must take what he can. If he must take the *rancho* this way, I assume my *abuelo* will find this a creative solution."

"I don't see how that's possible," she said.

"Because you do not know my family. Truthfully,"

he said, "I should have seen this coming. Historically, women who marry Navarro men never come out of it well."

"You're speaking of your sister-in-law?"

He looked at her, clearly trying to decide how much to say. And then he surprised her by taking a seat. His large hands gripped the ends of the armrests, and she found herself fascinated by them. By their strength, their sheer masculinity. She had been around men all of her life, and yet somehow he was something separate. A different kind of creature. So much more than anyone else had ever been.

"I am speaking of my sister-in-law," he said, pausing for a moment. "And my mother." He shifted in his chair, those powerful legs spread wide. There was something gripping about that posture. It was casual, nearly lazy, and yet she knew that at a moment's notice he could spring into action. All of that leashed strength.

To say nothing of how boldly masculine it was. The way he spread his legs as if to draw attention to…

She blinked. There was no way she was looking there. She just wouldn't.

"My grandfather," he continued, his voice bringing her back into the present. Bringing her back to sanity. "Is…an eccentric. But my father… He had a dark soul. Always. If he was ever any different I certainly didn't know him to be. He was violent. He had periods of extended rage. He could never be pleased. And he took all of that out on Diego and myself. And our mother. Always our mother. Who was so pretty and delicate, a Spanish rose. She was miserable. All the years until she died. Until she fell off a horse and broke her neck." His eyes were blank, horribly flat and black, and she had a feeling that he was leaving out part of the story.

But she also knew that he was only saying these things for his own benefit. Here in the near dark library to a boy who didn't matter.

She was no one. He might as well be speaking to a mirror. And she understood that. At the moment she was grateful she could fulfill that for him.

She heard a buzzing sound, and then he reached for his pocket. He lifted his phone and frowned.

He answered it. "Hello?"

"Matías?" It was a woman's voice, clearly audible in the relative silence of the room, and Camilla recognized the American accent immediately. "I'm so glad that I reached you."

"Liliana? Where are you? Where has he taken you?"

"I can't say," came the reply, stilted, robotic.

"Why? Because you don't know? Are you injured?" He issued the questions rapid-fire.

"I'm not injured. I'm perfectly safe. In fact, I need for you to stop looking for me." The words were thick-sounding, sad. "I didn't mean to deceive you, and I never meant to hurt you in any way. But I cannot marry you because Diego is the man I really want. I left with him of my own free will. The only reason that I screamed is because he startled me. But it was always my intention to waste your time and make it difficult for you to complete your task, and then marry him. I was not kidnapped. You don't need to look for me."

"Liliana…"

"It's okay, Matías. Truly. I regret my behavior, but there is nothing to be done. Diego and I have already married. And that means… You know what that means. All of it will be his. If you fail to marry, then all of it will be his. It's too late. We have paperwork. Everything is legally binding. We're married. It's too late."

"Liliana…"

And then the phone line went dead, and Matías was left there glaring ferociously at the phone in his hand as if it were a snake.

"You can't possibly believe her," Camilla said. "She sounds as if she's in distress."

"She has married him," Matías said, the words falling heavily in the room. "My brother is a terrible villain, but what he is not is a monster. And what he is not capable of doing is forcing someone to say vows. Even he would not hold a gun to her head."

"He kidnapped her out of her bedroom window."

"Or not. If she is to be believed she went with him of her own volition." He threw his phone down onto the coffee table, the light from the fireplace reflecting off the planes and angles of his face. "I was fooled. I thought that my brother would fade into his own dissolute lifestyle. That he would not attempt to please my grandfather. But I was looking at it through my own eyes. I was going to engage in a real marriage. My brother would think nothing of taking a wife simply to fulfill the terms of the will. A wife he will probably casually discard in the end."

"But you were marrying her because of the will, weren't you?" she asked. She didn't know why she was asking that. Matías clearly cared about Liliana. If he didn't he wouldn't be so distressed. And something about that galled her. But she hoped that he didn't love her. Which was small, and terrible, and she had no right to think such a thing.

"But I intended to make it real," he said. "I'm not a man given to love. You must realize that. Or perhaps, at your age you do not. Love was never part of the equation for me. But a wife, children, all of that I would have.

Why not?" He shook his head. "It was all too easy, and that I should have realized."

"How long do you have?"

"Only a couple of weeks," he responded. "Diego is smart. Because by whatever means he accomplished it, he has married her."

"Perhaps he hasn't. Maybe all of it's a lie."

"No. He would have no reason to lie about that. Because he would know that it would only spur me into action. Better to keep quiet if he hadn't made arrangements to marry her."

For some reason, she didn't know what she was thinking, she reached out across the space between them and touched the top of his hand. And then she drew back as though she had been burned.

Scrambling out of her chair, she stepped toward the fireplace, trying to move herself into the darkness, as if that response wouldn't make all of this even more out of the ordinary.

That he wouldn't see the effect he had had on her. That was the last thing she needed. To introduce something so horrific into the equation. He was coping with the fact that his fiancée had been taken by another man—whether by force or by seduction, she felt at this point either was devastating—and eventually they would have a horse to train, to make it to the races.

If she ruined it now by being so stupid...

"Dios mio," he said, his voice harsh.

She looked over at him, and his face was frozen, a mask of rage, his dark eyes glittering in the firelight.

He stood, gripping her by the arms and drawing her close. "What is your part in this? All this time... Were you a part of this treachery that was committed against me?"

CHAPTER FIVE

MATÍAS CURSED HIMSELF. He called himself every kind of fool imaginable.

She was a woman.

It was so clear now that he was looking at her. Now that she was standing there, bathed in firelight.

How could he not have seen it? How could it have escaped his notice until now? It was all painfully clear, here in the firelight, in this quiet house with shock coursing through his veins. With that soft touch echoing over his skin, a ripple on the surface of the water that should not have been there.

Then Cam had taken a step backward, and something about the way the light had caught that stubborn face, that strong bone structure, had suddenly revealed what he had missed all this time.

His stable boy was not a boy at all.

And he had spoken to her so openly, freely. As though she were an extension of the wallpaper in the room, because to him she might as well have been. A boy who worked for him was beneath his notice. But this…a liar. A treacherous woman.

He would not have spoken to her so.

"Answer me," he said, tightening his hold on her arms. Definitely *her* arms.

It was so apparent now. She did not possess the frame of a young boy, not really. But of course, when he had held her yesterday after her injury he had been thinking only of her safety, not of the way that she was built.

She was strong. Of course she was. She had become so working with horses, he assumed, but it was not the strength of a rangy youth.

She was soft. And no amount of hard labor could disguise that.

He examined her face, and it struck him with full force. As though he had been looking at one of those trick images and had seen one version of it, only to be shown the other. And now he could not go back to seeing the first. Her face was square, her chin strong, her dark brows thick, and in a very basic sense those things lent her a masculine quality.

Combine that with baggy clothes and the disguised female figure, and he supposed at a glance anyone could be forgiven for mistaking her for a boy.

But not now that he was looking at her. *Really* looking.

Her cheekbones were too fine. That strong bone structure in her face the kind that supermodels would envy, the kind that with makeup would give a dramatic effect of hollows and angles.

It was not a soft beauty. And in many ways, perhaps it would not be considered beauty by most.

He had no idea what to think as he felt like she had just sprouted a second head. Anger. He felt anger. Because he could not cope with being tricked by two people, not in the same moment. Three, if he counted the treachery of his brother, who did not even have the *cojones* to make a phone call himself.

Of course, if anyone but Liliana had been on the other end of the line he simply wouldn't have believed it.

"Did you help my brother gain access to this place? Are you a spy? Is that why you were sent here?"

Suddenly, it all made more sense. The way the boy—no, she was not a boy—the way she had asked him questions. About why he didn't hire women. About why he needed to marry. She had been gauging the situation. Of course she had been.

He had been infiltrated. And everyone involved would pay.

"I was not," she said. Her eyes were glittering now, and he noted that she denied nothing. He had leveled no specific accusations against her beyond the possibility of her being a spy, had said nothing of her gender, but it fascinated him to see her nearly transform beneath his touch. It seemed as though her face had softened, her voice slightly higher now. "It had nothing to do with your brother or Liliana. I had nothing to do with that."

"If that is so, then why are you here?"

"I came because of the horses. That much was true." She swallowed hard, looking up at him, those dark eyes filled with unshed tears now. "I'm Cesar Alvarez's daughter. Those horses were mine, and I would do anything to be back with them. Surely you must understand that. It had nothing to do with you. It was all for them. All for me."

He wasn't sure if he believed her. If she was truly motivated by her love for the horses. Because what he knew about Cesar Alvarez was that the man had been in incredible debt.

His daughter would have no money to her name at all and would most definitely be susceptible to a man like his brother.

"I swear to you," she said, her expression getting desperate, "I had nothing to do with Liliana or Diego. I don't know your brother. I've never interacted with him. I came here for my own purposes. Because I would do anything for those horses. To make sure that Fuego's purpose isn't squandered. The horses are all I have left. My mother has gone off to Paris. You can check on that and see that it's true. You can check my phone records, anything that you want, and they will prove that I never spoke to your brother. I have been in contact with no one since I came here, and nobody knows that I'm here."

She seemed to regret making that admission to him. Seemed to regret letting him know that were she to disappear here on this mission, no one would be any the wiser as to where she had gone. He wondered then if he looked as frightening as his father used to look when he was in a rage.

That should make him back off. Should make him move away from her. And yet, he didn't.

"How old are you?" he demanded.

"Twenty-two," she responded, trembling in his arms now.

"A woman. Not a boy. And not a girl."

"No," she said.

"You want the horses. You want to train them."

"I *need* them," she insisted, "and they need me. You know that you can't handle Fuego without me. You know it. You have seen him, and you have seen what happens when others try to work with him. You're going to have that fool Fernando ride him?"

"Of course not. He was fired directly after what happened yesterday."

"You know that I'm the only one who can work with him right now."

"It is so important to you? Because if I don't manage to defeat my brother then all of this goes to him. Including your horses. That isn't what you want, is it?"

"No," she said.

"You have deceived me," he said, leaning closer to her, relishing the moment when she shrank away from him. Because dammit all, someone should be afraid of his wrath. His brother certainly should be, but the fool wasn't here.

"I'm sorry. It had nothing to do with you. Or rather, it did. If you would only hire women…"

"I have one use for a woman in my life at the moment. And now I wonder if you and I have a common enough purpose that you might serve me well."

She shrank back, her expression one of confusion. "I don't understand."

"I think you do." He released his hold on her and took a step back. "It is convenient, in many ways. As a boy you only served one purpose. But as a woman you can serve many. What is your name?" He felt a smile curve his lips. "Your real name."

"Camilla," she said. "Camilla Alvarez."

Camilla Alvarez. Of course. He'd heard about her, though he'd never met her. A spirited horsewoman said to have a near supernatural way with the animals, just as her father had.

A fine match for a man like him, in many ways. Though he had no intentions now of making a permanent arrangement. And yet…that did not negate his need for a bride.

He needed one, and he needed her quickly.

Camilla, it turned out, needed something, too.

That mutual need could be his salvation.

Holding the horses hostage didn't bother him in the least. He needed to gain control of the family *rancho*, of the family fortune. Diego had kidnapped his fiancée, and there was no way in hell Matías was going to allow his brother to win.

His path was clear. And the solution to his problem was standing before him, delivered to him at just the appropriate moment.

"Well, Camilla Alvarez. If you want your horses, then I expect something in return. If you wish to remain here, if you wish to train Fuego, then you will be my wife."

CHAPTER SIX

CAMILLA WAS IN a state of shock. One that superseded the *previous* shocked state that had accompanied being kicked by the horse.

Because somehow in the last moment her entire ruse had unraveled around her, one thread at a time. And not only had Matías discovered her identity, but he had also asked her to be his wife. His wife.

She, Camilla Alvarez, who had not done so much as kiss a man, who had never been held so close to a man as she was being held by Matías now—in anger, rather than in passion—was being proposed to by that same angry man.

"I don't understand…"

"I need a wife," he said, his voice hard as rock. "My brother has acquired a wife, and if I do not then the entirety of this estate goes to him. You are one with a stake in this, as well. Because the horses will go to him. You don't want that. Trust me. You think he's going to keep you on? You think he's going to care about the well-being of your beloved animals? Murderer or not, Diego is not a man given to caring."

"Not forever," she said. "I mean, I won't be your wife *forever.*"

He shrugged. "Of course, there will be no reason for

the marriage to be more than paper. But it must be legal. My grandfather will not live forever, and once ownership has been established, once everything has been settled, then you may have your divorce."

"An annulment," she said, "surely."

"No." He waved a hand decisively. "There will be nothing that shall call into question the validity of the union. I shall not take any chances of Diego contesting this in court. I put nothing past him, as I already stated. He stole my fiancée. He would think nothing of challenging the legality of this union, as he cannot take more than one wife. Otherwise, I feel he would steal you, as well."

Camilla felt edgy, unsettled, a raft of emotion and heat careening through her. "How would he set about stealing me?"

"I assume via seduction," Matías said. "As I assume this is what he did with Liliana, who had an extreme aversion to sharing my bed, and this makes it all the clearer."

Those words tangled up in her brain. "Liliana didn't…"

"I was not sleeping with her. Does that matter to you?"

"No," she said, shaking her head. "Only that you intended your marriage with her to be real. To be lasting, I mean. So, naturally I assumed…"

"Liliana presented herself as being quite the sheltered virgin," he said, his voice dripping with disdain. "She said she did not know me well enough."

"Oh."

"I suspect, however, that the real issue was that she had given herself to my brother already."

"Or," Camilla said softly, "she really might have been

taken, and he could have been forcing her to say those things."

"I suppose that's possible," he said. "But either way, I do not have the time to wait and find out. I have two weeks to marry. And if I engage in some kind of public national search for a wife, no doubt I will find one. However, I'm not sure my grandfather will find it compelling."

"But he'll appreciate your brother stooping to kidnapping and subterfuge?"

Matías chuckled. "Because that is Diego's way. He's the gambler. The black sheep. I… I am the *good* one, and I suspect my grandfather would like to see me accomplish his task while sticking to my personal code of honor. More to the point, I imagine he would find it amusing if I could not. Which is why I would have him believe this relationship is real."

"You have no trouble violating your code of honor so long as nobody knows?"

"Am I forcing you, Camilla?" he asked, her name dripping with disdain. "I believe that rather than force, what I have done is offer you a mutually beneficial deal. You want the horses, you want to be able to stay here and train them, and I will allow it, as long as you help me in this. I must be able to maintain control of the *rancho* in order for it to be so. I must be able to maintain control of my business. If Diego takes over the family assets in their entirety, then it is possible he will end up with a stake in the company I built myself. I will not allow that. However, if we are able to split the assets, then we can draw up an agreement that keeps him out of it. That means that half is mine. I feel very much that Diego wants to win more than he actually wants to control anything that happens here at the *rancho*. I, on the other hand, care very deeply about it. I am the one who has spent years here. I am the one who has cultivated a relationship with the animals, with the land. I should think that you of all people would understand that."

She did. His passion, his need for this place, resonated inside her. It reminded her of the way she felt about the place where she had grown up. The *rancho* that she missed with all her soul. Those familiar grounds, the worn entryway tiles, that she once again ached to feel beneath her feet.

"I agree," she said. "On one condition."

"And what is that?" he asked, his expression dark.

"When we divorce, return my father's *rancho* to me."

He said nothing for a moment. "That is a rather large ask."

She crossed her arms and gave him her fiercest glare. "As is demanding I marry you."

"You think you're worth millions?"

"Yes," she said, not blinking. "Or at least I think the demand that we marry is worth that."

He arched one dark brow. "You expect to be my wife in name only and come away with a grand estate?"

"And some of the horses. Not Fuego. I understand that you won't relinquish control of him. But the others. The ones that will never make champions for you. I want them."

"And additionally, you would like to continue to see Fuego. Am I right?"

"Of course. Do you have anyone else who can train him? Who can counsel a jockey on how best to handle him? No, I don't think you do."

"That is quite a hard bargain that you're driving, but I have to tell you that I'm inclined to refuse. You are not offering me enough in return."

"I am offering to be your wife for however long a term you need."

He appraised her slowly, and it felt like a flame held close to her skin and drawn over sensitive, vulnerable areas. A thorough burn that made her feel restless and helpless.

"If you were offering use of your body, then perhaps you would be in a greater position to demand such a thing."

Everything inside her recoiled, curled up into a ball, not out of disgust, but fear. That he had identified her shameful attraction to him, that he could see inside her. And that he was mocking her. Because surely, a man who had wanted to marry that birdlike blonde beauty would not find her attractive. Particularly not standing there in ragged boy's clothes, with her hair cut close to her skull and sticking up at odd angles.

"No. You need a wife. And that's all. If you want a prostitute, buy one." She tilted her chin upward, attempting to radiate defiance, attempting to radiate confidence.

She was banking on the fact that his options truly were limited or he never would have approached her with this in the first place.

If he was shocked by her words, he didn't show it.

"Fascinating," he said. "You truly do possess a remarkable amount of boldness. I assumed it was because of your youth, back when I thought that's what you were. Fourteen-year-old boys are often imbued with a sense of self-confidence that is undeserved. However, it is rare to find a woman who is the same."

"I cannot tell if you're flattering me or insulting me," she said.

"Neither," he said simply. "It is what you make of it.

I am merely observing. I find it inconvenient, as a great many people would be cowed by me, and you clearly are not. However, if you will agree to be my wife, then I will give you all that you have asked for."

Heart pounding, she stuck her hand out and met his gaze. "I agree," she said, "I will be your wife."

He looked down at her hand. "You expect to close this deal with a handshake?"

"Yes," she said. "As I see it as a business transaction, and nothing more. You're right. I am bold. And I'm feeling quite confident in my position."

She hoped she wasn't overplaying her hand. Because she had nothing. Nothing at all, except her person. Her gender had been the barrier to what she had wanted before, and now it was the key. She would not hesitate to use it. She could have her home back. Something she had never thought possible. All she would have to do was be his wife, and that was nothing. A simple legal matter. Then she would be free. She would be free to ride through the olive groves again, to run barefoot on hot, sundrenched grounds that spoke to her of happiness.

She had known, had felt driven and compelled to get work on this *rancho*, because she'd had nothing else, but she'd had no idea it might lead to this level of salvation. That it could well and truly solve all her problems.

"Then you have yourself a deal." He reached out, taking hold of her hand and shaking it hard, the strength and heat in his grip making something tremble deep inside her. But she ignored it.

She wanted the ranch. She wanted her freedom. Wanted something more than facing a life of potential homelessness should the whims of someone else dictate it.

"Perfect," he said. "Tomorrow I shall call my grandfather and explain there has been a change of bride. And then… We shall work at making you suitable."

Matías was still feeling the sharp, hot effects of rage as he picked up the phone the next morning to call his *abuelo*.

Liliana had been perfect. And now he was to be tasked with turning this…this *urchin* into a silk purse. Something he doubted was even possible. She was… He imagined in some ways she could be lovely. At least, he was hoping so.

But she was not Liliana. She would never be. Also, there would have to be a way to take the story and turn it into something that didn't sound salacious. That he had fallen for a woman dressed as a stable hand on his property during the course of his engagement to the lovely heiress would be a difficult one to spin, though not impossible.

Particularly given Liliana's defection.

The fact that she was now with Diego made that part easier, at least. In no way would he come out of it looking the cad. Not when she had been seduced away from him.

"*Hola*, Matías," came his grandfather's rough, cultured voice over the other end of the line. The man sounded yet more ancient with each passing day, and still, he spoke with an air of authority that made Matías grind his teeth.

The old man was a puppet master. Not overtly cruel in the ways his father had been, but he had been the creator of Matías's father, after all, and it was clear to see how a lifetime of those machinations had dulled Matías's father's senses to right and wrong. To any sense of human kindness.

The Navarro family had a legacy that seemed to be born of spite and nourished by blood. Matías wanted no part of it.

But his grandfather didn't want the *rancho*. And he didn't want to maintain control of his company.

"Hola," Matías responded. "I assume by now Diego has been in touch with you to inform you that he has taken a bride."

The old man chuckled. "Indeed. He has. Though I think in his case he has literally *taken* a bride. Your bride."

"Yes. However, it was convenient for me in many ways, as I did not have to shatter Liliana's heart," Matías said, each word decisive.

"Really, Matías," his grandfather said.

"Really. I have met someone else. Don't you see? I was trapped because I needed to honor my commitment to Liliana," he said, knowing he was spitting out a tale that gratified his grandfather's sense of what roles he and Diego played in their lives. Good and evil.

There was never a question as to how far Diego would go, because he lacked scruples, and it was well-known. But he knew that his grandfather would be incredibly amused to see how the scrupulous grandson dealt with this.

"Is that so?" his grandfather asked. "That seems a bit convenient."

"I suppose it is. But then things in life so seldom are, so it is nice when it all falls into place. There has been a girl working for me, taking care of the horses, and I found myself quite compelled by her skills with them. I find I had quite fallen for her before I realized what was happening. I never violated my commitment to Liliana, because of course I would never break my word. But things are clearly changed, and now Camilla Alvarez is going to become my wife. You may have heard of the Alvarez family. I know you knew Cesar Alvarez, from back in the days when you dealt in horses. From when you worked at the *rancho*."

His grandfather chuckled. "Yes. Cesar. Didn't he recently die?"

"Quite so. And I ended up taking in quite a few animals from his *rancho*. And that is how I met Camilla."

"A fascinating story. One I'm not entirely certain I believe."

"I do not require your belief. I simply wished to inform you that I am marrying Camilla within the time frame you have dictated. She will be the perfect wife for me. She will run the *rancho* with a great deal of skill, and with passion. She loves the horses."

"And you?" he asked. "Does she love you?"

"Perhaps not as much," he responded.

That made his grandfather laugh. "I do appreciate your honesty, Matías, as you are the only one of us who seems to feel bound by it at any given time. It is endlessly amusing."

"I do live to be a punchline, Grandfather. I'm glad that my engagement can provide you with some levity."

"You will have ample opportunity to present her to the world as your bride next week at the charity ball in Barcelona, will you not?"

"I suppose I will," Matías said, grinding his teeth together.

"Excellent. You know, because of my health I will not be able to attend, but I will look for the photographs in the paper."

"I should expect nothing less from you, *Abuelo*."

"I should hope not."

And with that, they ended the call. Matías felt a sense of triumph, in many ways, as he was certainly transcending the roadblocks that had been set out before him. He was not going to allow Diego to win. But at the same time, there was an element of manipulation he was having to capitulate to, and that, he would never find acceptable.

But he had work to do. A stylist to hire, a ring to procure, and he was not going to linger on anything unpleasant in view of that. There was far too much to be done.

And he would do what he always did. He would see it done.

CHAPTER SEVEN

WHEN CAMILLA WOKE UP, she was immediately yanked out of bed and into some kind of alternative reality.

She was sent straight into a lavish bedroom much different than the one she had been staying in when she had been Cam, the stable boy. This one was sumptuous, frilly and quite a bit more feminine than the one she had existed in back at home. It didn't take long for her to realize that she had been installed in Liliana's old room.

That she was being used as a direct replacement, even down to being sent to the same lacy surroundings full of flowing curtains and billowing canopies.

If the housekeeper found it strange that she was making this transition, she didn't say anything. If she found it strange when a rack filled with clothing was brought in, and a basket of lush toiletries was provided, she said nothing to that, either.

"You are to bathe," the woman said, her tone brisk. "Use the bath salts, and all of the scented washes. And then there is an appointment with a stylist later."

"Oh," Camilla said, feeling slightly dizzy. Reeling over how quickly things were changing.

"You want to know why I'm not surprised," the woman said. "It is because I knew the moment that I first saw you, that you were not a boy."

"But Matías…"

"If he truly did not see," the housekeeper said, "it is because he rarely pauses to look around him, not at the things he considers beneath his notice. It is why he hires people, you see. To deal with matters he finds unimportant."

"I see," she said.

"I'm not sure you do," she responded. "But I think you will."

After the other woman left, Camilla padded into the bathroom and took stock of all the finery there. The body washes, salts, soaps and scrubs. She opened the tops and smelled a few, setting aside some in lavender and some scented like warm brown sugar and honey.

Camilla stripped her clothes off slowly, relishing the lack of binding on her breasts. Enjoying the thought that she wouldn't be binding them again today, or ever.

The tub itself was pale blue with gold claw feet, deep enough to submerge in, she thought. She turned on the golden tap and poured some bath salts beneath the churning water, scent blooming upward, wrapping itself around her.

Then when it was full, she stepped inside. She sighed. She could be free to linger in the warmth, to sink in to the bottom of her chin and lie back, letting the lavender-scented water carry her to another moment in time altogether.

Letting it take the weight from her shoulders, if only for a moment. The months of grief and stress, the heavy cloak of sadness.

When she went back to reality she would have to face the fact her father was still gone. But at least her own fate was secure.

At least there was that.

When she finally got out, she wrapped herself in the softest towel she had ever felt in her life and padded out into the bedroom where there was silk underwear laid across the bed and a simple summer dress. She felt so strange putting them on. Stranger still, when she looked in the mirror and saw that billowing fabric resting gently over her curves.

She felt… Well, even there in the isolation of her bedroom she felt hideously self-conscious.

If Matías imagined that she was going to have some great transformation where she became even half the beauty that Liliana was with a little bit of polish and a pretty dress, he was going to be sorely disappointed.

Her hair was still short, and her face was still…well, her face.

Angles and hard lines much more suited to a man than a young woman, and no hair to disguise or soften it.

She didn't have time to ruminate on this, however, because shortly after, breakfast was brought to her room.

Coffee and homemade jam on fresh bread. *Huevos rancheros* and bacon.

Now, that made her feel spoiled beyond anything. She had been existing on much more meager offerings and it was wonderful to fill herself completely.

As soon as she had finished the last sip of her coffee, her room was invaded again by three different women all talking at once. There was much clucking over her hair, and discussion about color palettes and various other things.

One of the women took out a pair of scissors and Camilla was appalled when she approached her and began to run her fingers through her hair.

"There's not enough hair left to cut off!" Camilla protested.

"Trust me," the woman said, "you will want me to smooth out this hatchet job, and once I do it will look like there's more there."

She began snipping, shaping what remained of Camilla's dark hair. She left the top slightly longer, clipping the sides and the back shorter, and teasing it a little bit so that it looked much more like an artful, purposeful pixie cut then exactly what it was—exactly what the stylist had called it—a hatchet job. Something that Camilla had done to herself in a panicked rush with a pair of dull scissors.

Then the second woman began to get out various pots of makeup. An array of different colors that reminded Camilla of summer, sunsets and somehow, of candy.

Warm tones, golds and oranges were swept over her eyelids, her cheekbones, the hollows of her face, adding a sculpted look to her that she hadn't known was possible to achieve. By the time her eyes had been lined and mascara added to her lashes, she felt that even her mother would be hard-pressed to say she had a masculine appearance.

It was strong, certainly, quite a bit more angular, perhaps, than many women would consider ideal. But she was shocked to discover that she found the woman looking back at her in the mirror to be beautiful.

"The short hair is quite nice on you," the hairstylist said.

Camilla nodded, looking at herself, leaning in to try to get a better idea of everything. She was shocked.

"I didn't know I could look like this."

"It's all about finding what works for you," the woman said.

"I just… I was always told I wasn't…"

"What?" the makeup artist asked.

"I was told I wasn't beautiful," she responded. "Too dark. Not petite enough. In my figure…"

"Your skin is such a beautiful golden brown," the makeup artist said. "And you can wear gold tones that would make a paler woman look sallow. You have a strong beauty. Which means it will not always agree with everyone around you, but those who appreciate it will never find another woman to match you."

"And as for your figure," the woman who had done nothing yet, and therefore Camilla assumed was the stylist, "it is the kind many would envy. We simply need to find the right dress to show it off."

"But why do I need a dress?" She knew that she would need a wedding gown, and the very idea of that made her stomach turn over.

"Because," the woman said. "You have a ball to attend."

By dinner that night Matías was in a foul mood. He had not seen Camilla at all, and in many ways he supposed that was for the best. They were going to dine together tonight, but she was late. He didn't like tardiness. Not in the least.

He tapped his fingers on the table, still marveling at the changes that had occurred in his life in the past twenty-four hours. What had begun with a stable boy getting kicked in the head by a horse had ended with a kidnap, a shocking revelation and a marriage proposal.

Or more a marriage *demand*, he supposed.

But in the end, the semantics of it didn't matter. Not really.

The door to the dining room opened and he looked

up and was utterly stunned by what he saw. The woman walking in wearing a bright orange dress, her short, dark hair styled neatly, with the gold band around her head like a halo, looked like no one he had ever met before. And yet, at the same time, he recognized her.

There was no question that Cam was indeed a woman.

Her curves were slight, her body toned and athletic, but most definitely female. Her breasts were small and high, her waist slim, her hips sturdy, which was an odd descriptor, perhaps, but not a negative one.

It made a man want to test that strength. She was like a warrior goddess. All gold, bronze and a kind of glowing beauty that seemed nearly supernatural.

He curled his fingers into a fist and tried to gather his thoughts. She was a tool to be used to spite his grandfather, to thwart Diego. She was correct. If he wanted a woman for sex, he could easily acquire one. There were ways to go about keeping things discreet. He did consider himself a man of integrity, a man who would honor commitments once they were made. But so long as Camilla knew about the other women, as long as they were clear about the general state of their marriage, he saw no real issue with taking lovers. It was, indeed, a business transaction, sealed with a handshake as she had suggested. Then it shouldn't matter.

"Hello," she said, her shoulders slightly stiff, her expression difficult to read.

"So this is who you really are?" he asked.

"No," she said, making her way down the side of the table, her fingertips brushing against the glossy surface as she did so delicate. If he had ever truly looked at those hands he would have known immediately that she was all woman. "This is a very polished version of me. Though it is the one you will see for the duration of this ruse, I have no doubt, so long as I have that team readily available when needed. I cannot accomplish this on my own."

"Can you not? You are an heiress. I was under the impression that women like you learned these things from the womb. Isn't your mother a great socialite and beauty?"

"I am the heiress of nothing but debts, as I'm sure you're well aware. Meanwhile, my mother had little interest in a daughter, whether or not it was to raise her, or to teach her to use eyeliner. I was raised by my father."

She took a seat with two chair spaces between them. "I spent my life with horses. My father let me run wild, I think because he felt bad for the way my mother treated me. For her disinterest in me. Or perhaps, it was simply because he was lonely, as she was equally disinterested in him. Whatever the reason, it meant that I had a rather unconventional upbringing, as they go."

"He must have instilled a certain amount of boldness in you."

"Cesar Alvarez was nothing if not bold. A man who continued to run his empire as though he possessed millions when he was, in fact, in debt, that amount could be expected to be nothing less, I suppose."

"Did your father lie about a lot of things?"

She lifted a bare shoulder, and his eyes were drawn to that sleek, golden skin. She was a fascinating creature. To transform the way she had, from such a brown little sparrow beneath his notice, to this vision of gold and fire.

It didn't matter, of course, not really. He needed a wife to appease his grandfather, and he needed a woman on his arm for this gala because dammit all, he had his pride.

He might not have loved Liliana, but losing a fiancée to his brother was not acceptable, regardless.

Having another woman on his arm to replace the one he'd lost suited him. The fact that Camilla was a rare beauty was a bonus.

"Not that I knew. But then I had no idea about the state of his finances, so I suppose it's possible. I suppose it's possible that I never knew him. That he concealed a great many things from me. But I do think that I knew his heart. He loved me. And he loved his horses. It's why I feel so compelled to make sure that both are taken care of."

"And self-interest, I would imagine."

She nodded. "Self-interest certainly comes into it. I would like to not be homeless. And I miss the *rancho*. It was…in many ways my second parent. It raised me. The people on it raised me. It's part of who I am. In my blood. I would do…nearly anything to be restored to it."

"That, I think I can understand. I love this place," he said, looking around the ornate dining room.

"Did you have a happy childhood here?" She looked away from him when she asked that question, almost as if she already knew.

But then he wouldn't be surprised if she did. Rumors of his father's temper certainly weren't contained only to his village.

"I did not," he responded. "My mother died here. My father was a tyrant. My grandfather before him was no better. I suppose you could say what I love about this place is that it endured. That it remains beautiful in spite of the ugliness that has bled itself all over the grounds. There are very few honest things in this world, and I think you and I agree on what they are. Horses, and church. These things… They will not fail. I wish to make this place something it should have been all along. Something better. Something that is not about serving the egos of the men in control of it."

"And if Diego ends up with it…"

"He will be no different. He is not a man capable of love."

Her brows creased at the center. "And you?"

"There are things that I love. Or, if not love, then things that I feel a sense of obligation to. I have never understood the benefit of caring only for myself. I would rather invest in what is around me. Make no mistake, I am a difficult man, and I know you have seen this. My reputation speaks to that. But I consider myself a man of honor. Because I have seen what happens when a man turns away from it. When he has no code. No allegiance to anyone but himself. I will not be that man."

"Do you want to have a family here?"

He looked around, a strange tightness in his chest. "I had imagined I might. I felt it was the way to secure my hold on this place. Now I wonder if there is something else. It is perhaps best if I don't marry."

"You don't want children?"

The very idea of something so small and helpless in his care made him feel a sense of unease. "If I had a son," he said. "I believe he would spend most of the time in the company of his mother and also being raised away from me here on the *rancho*. I am here now because of the circumstances, but my primary obligations are in London."

"I understand," she said.

"But you do not approve."

"I know what it is," she said, raising her dark gaze to meet his, "to have a parent who's not at all interested in your existence."

"Sometimes that disinterest can be a kindness," he said. "What was your time spent with your mother like?"

She ducked her head. "Difficult. She did not… She didn't have the patience for me. And she despaired of my lack of beauty."

"The only thing, I think, worse than being neglected by her would have been to spend more of your time in her company."

She surprised him by laughing, her shoulders jolting forward as she lifted her hand to cover her mouth. "I suppose that's true. And a much more honest assessment of the situation than I have allowed myself to, given the past. She's terrible. And she's gone off to Paris to live with a lover, and I hope she stays there."

"She abandoned you? What were your prospects if you had not followed the horses here?"

"Homelessness. In that regard I did not lie to Juan when he hired me. I would have been tossed out onto the streets. There was no money. There was nowhere for me to go. No provision was made for me at all. I know that my father didn't expect to die so young. I know he thought that he was going to fix everything. That there was still time. And I think he didn't want me to know how difficult things were. How dire it had all become. He wanted to protect me."

"Sadly, his version of *protecting* you left you vulnerable," Matías said.

She nodded. "Yes."

They paused in their talking for a moment when his household staff came in and delivered large bowls of paella.

Then they ate in silence for a moment before Camilla lifted her head and treated him to another look from that luminous dark gaze. "What ball are we going to next week?"

"It is a charity gala," he responded. "It is where I will present you formally as my fiancée. Likely, it will be bigger than our actual wedding."

"Well, yes. I can see how difficult it might be to get together a large wedding ceremony in the amount of time we have."

"Well, the venue is already selected, and people have already been invited. It's just that the bride has changed."

She frowned. "That feels quite…reductive."

"Well, the bride is not important to me. Only the marriage."

She lifted a brow. "Well, in some ways I'm glad that Liliana escaped you in that case."

"Liliana did not love me, either. She would hardly have been heartbroken by this."

"I suppose she didn't," Camilla responded. "But she seemed… She seemed very sweet."

He bit back an acidic laugh. "Apparently not."

"Did she hurt you?" she asked.

"No," he said, then again, more definitively. "No." He had planned on marrying her, and he didn't like his plans being upended. But hurt? No. That would necessitate that he'd had feelings for Liliana that went beyond vague appreciation of her beauty. And he did not. "I felt…protective of her. As she did seem sweet. Sheltered. But it always made me feel as though I was trying to corral a baby chick. One that was fragile and delicate and might break at any moment."

Camilla squared her shoulders. "I am not so breakable."

He appraised her for a moment. "I did not think you were."

She lowered her head and he examined her features. Long, elegant neck, her strong jawline and the sweeping curve of her lips. She was actually quite the beauty. Her brows were dark and bold, her eyelashes no less so. She was the kind of woman a man would find himself hard-pressed to look away from once she had caught his attention.

The kind of woman who would stand out, a regal, steady creature in a room full of butterflies.

His gut tightened, and he had to acknowledge that he was beginning to find himself attracted to his fiancée.

"Do you know how to dance?" he asked, the question, and the need for an answer, suddenly occurring to him.

"A bit," she said, hesitating. "I mean, we would dance at *fiestas* at the *rancho*. Informal gatherings. Always attended by all members of the staff. My father was… generous. Egalitarian."

"You will find this gala to be anything but. It will be appallingly formal, and every woman in residence will be ready to pick you apart. Especially given the nature of our engagement. It would perhaps be best if you were as prepared as possible. I get the sense that while you grew up with a certain amount of privilege, it was not the same sort that Liliana possessed."

A challenge lit her eyes. "I would suggest that my upbringing produced a much stronger person. My father allowed me to work. He allowed me to fail. He taught me to take chances. And he allowed me to work with the horses. It's in our blood."

"Having seen you with the horses, I believe it. But that is not going to help you when it comes to fending off attacks of a rather more feminine nature."

"Why would these attacks be of a feminine nature?"

"Because jealousy is an ugly thing," he said.

She frowned. "You're quite obsessed with the idea that women are in love with you. Or, rather, on the verge of falling in love with you if the breeze blows in the wrong direction."

"It has nothing to do with me," he said. "Rather, my money, or the mystique of the Navarro family. The Navarro men."

"I was under the impression that the men in your family did not have the best reputations."

He shook his head. "That adds to it. Often. Good-looking men with dark pasts, desperately in need of reformation and something to spend their billions of dollars on."

"That's quite bleak."

"You consider yourself above that temptation. Obviously. And yet, here you are, prepared to marry me for your financial benefit."

She tilted her head to the side, her expression remaining steadfast. "And yet," she said, "I am not in love with you. And I think it would take quite a bit more than a breeze to propel me in that direction."

"Fair enough."

"Furthermore," she said, pressing her palms flat on the table and standing, "I do not want your money. Not in the generic sense. You know about my father's estate. You have ownership of the horses. You are the clearest path to having my family assets restored. I have a very specific need of you, not just some generic billionaire."

"Careful," he said. "I'm likely to fall in love with you. As that was a very specific bit of praise."

"I imagine you'll do just fine."

He stood then, closing the distance between them

and reaching out, grasping hold of her fingers, lacing his through them and pulling her forward. He had been correct in his assessment of her. She was strong. But he had caught her off guard. Her dark eyes widened, her full lips dropping into a rounded oh.

Heat flared in his gut, an intense, visceral need to draw her in to his body. To close all the space between them. "Perhaps not," he said, gripping her chin and tilting her face upward. He could see her pulse throbbing at the base of her throat, watched as her eyes grew even darker. As the slender brown rings around her pupils slimmed. He wanted to see if her mouth tasted as ripe and sweet as it looked like it might. *Dios*, how he wanted to sample that surprise that shaped her lips just so.

But he would not.

This was about the *rancho*, not about his own selfish desires. He did not use women. He never had. And he wouldn't start with her.

He straightened, bringing her into a close hold. "We shall see how the dance lesson goes."

CHAPTER EIGHT

CAMILLA HAD BEEN hoping for a nice slice of cake after the paella. Instead, she was ushered into the ballroom with the assurance that coffee would follow. She hoped there would be chocolate. For certain, there was going to be a dance, and she was not sure how she felt about that.

Her whole body still burned from when Matías had grabbed hold of her in the dining room.

He was teasing her. She knew that. He was not going to fall in love with her, and he was not so compelled to touch her that he had no choice but to take hold of her back there.

She had no idea what he thought about her. What he assumed in terms of her level of experience. Likely, he hadn't thought about it at all.

As he had said, the bride in this equation was completely interchangeable with the one that had been scheduled to appear before. So why would he give a single thought to whether or not she had ever been held in a man's arms before? Why would he care that she had never danced with a man, had never been held close, had never been kissed?

She felt restless and edgy, and she kept catching sight of herself in random mirrors and various reflective surfaces and getting a shock.

She didn't recognize the woman she saw there.

It was like she was inhabiting a stranger's body. Strange, because it had felt less like that when she had been masquerading as the stable boy. Plain. Nondescript. She was much more comfortable that way. Identified much more closely with those adjectives than bright or fiery or any of the other words that might be used to describe her as she looked now.

"Are you ready?" Matías asked, turning toward her and holding his hand out. She knew from experience that it was strong, hot and rough. That even though he was wearing a suit, looking every inch the businessman, he had the hands of a working man.

She admired that about him. Because for all that he might seem mercenary, for all that he was a hard taskmaster, he was not above doing the work himself. He held himself to the exact same standards that he held everyone around him to.

Her father had been like that. A man who had valued hard work and had also expected that he would partake in it, no matter how wealthy he became.

"There is no music," she said.

"It's all right. You won't need music. You're going to follow my lead, not a song."

She sniffed. "I think dancing without music would be quite boring. Whenever we dance at the *rancho* somebody plays guitar, and someone plays tambourine. And we all just…move. The way that it feels good to move."

"Yes. Because you are using dance as an expression of joy." He began to step toward her, his face that of a predator. "At a gala like this, dance will not be used in a similar fashion. It will be used to gauge relationships. Used as an opportunity to assess someone's upbringing. Their importance. Everyone will be watching. And they will wonder why your hands did or didn't linger when they touched my shoulder. Why I did not steal a kiss when the music slowed and I had ample opportunity. Why my hand was positioned just a bit too high at the center of your back, rather than taking the opportunity to flirt with impropriety by drawing it down just a bit lower."

Her face flushed, her entire body growing warm. "I don't think anyone will be watching us that closely."

"You mock me for saying that women fall in love with me, but I am a man of status, and I have recently been abandoned by my fiancée. No doubt my brother will arrange for there to be headlines about his recent nuptials as early as tomorrow. With plenty of time for rumors to be swirling by the evening of the gala. People will be watching to see—is our relationship real or are you simply a stand-in? Are you nothing more than a Band-Aid that I have put over my wound? A trick, a salve for my pride."

She looked away from him. "Well," she said, "aren't I?"

"I refuse to allow you to appear to be such. I refuse to allow Diego to control this, or for my grandfather to have his way in manipulating us."

"He is rather succeeding in manipulating you into marriage." That last word ended on a squeak as she found herself pulled back into his arms, his iron fingers wrapped around her own, his arm curved around her waist. Her breasts were pressed up against the hard wall of his chest, and she tried so hard to keep her breathing regulated. To keep herself from panicking and taking in air so deeply that it forced those vulnerable parts of her into contact with him.

But she failed. Sensitive, aching breasts brushing

against him helplessly. She looked up at him, and their eyes clashed. Then she looked away, and regretted it immediately, because he must know she was only reacting that way because of the effect that he had on her. And she didn't want him to know that he affected her at all.

If she could only find a way to resemble the woman that she saw in the mirror. If she could only find a way to play the part of glorious sophisticate. Of course, it was probably difficult to convince anyone that you were a glorious sophisticate when they had originally seen you as a teenage boy.

Still. She wanted to try.

Because Matías Navarro was a whole lot more man than she had ever encountered in her life, and she was only just barely a woman by anyone's standards.

She had been cosseted in many ways. She would never have described herself as such before now. But though she hadn't been kept in an ivory tower, though she hadn't been pampered or treated like a princess, she had been held apart from the rest of the world.

Running around barefoot on the *rancho* had been like living in a fantasyland. It had had nothing to do with real life. Nothing to do with survival. And she had been placed in a survival situation after her father had died.

She hadn't known how to take care of herself. Hadn't known how to go out and get a job. Because she had never needed one.

And she did not know the ways in which women operated in this part of the world. She had very purposefully looked away from the way her mother moved through life, because it both enraged her and made her feel small. Inadequate.

Because truth be told, though she might like to pretend she didn't hold beauty in high regard, it had always felt futile to want to be beautiful when she was always destined to be outshone by her own mother.

But now she wished she had learned a little bit more of the world. Now she wished that she knew more about controlling her own body, her own femininity. At the moment she felt as though it was all controlling her. It felt as though she was at the mercy of all of this. Of him, of her own self.

That strange, glowing woman that she had seen in the mirror with a luminous face and an enticing figure wrapped tightly in an orange dress.

And then they began to move.

As he had said, he led, his confident steps somehow dictating her own. He made her feel like she was flying, floating, his strength the only thing keeping her from collapsing onto the high-gloss marble floor.

It was like magic. The closest thing to freedom she had felt that wasn't on the back of a horse.

She was lost. In the effortless way he manipulated her body, and that handsome face of his, all those glorious planes and angles.

He held her so tightly, and yet somehow she still felt like she was flying.

Her heart was beating so hard she thought it might burrow its way out of her chest, but it wasn't because of exertion, or because she was tired. It was a strange, exultant spike of adrenaline that was unlike anything she had ever experienced before.

The closest thing to it was the first moment she had seen him. The way her body had reacted that very first time she had spotted that strong, masculine form walking across the stables. And now he was holding her. Now he was going to be her husband.

That thought made her pounding heart jerk forward suddenly, slamming it against her breastbone.

Her eyes flew to his, and he looked down at her, clearly unaffected by this. Of course, for him, this was routine. For him, there was nothing different about dancing with a woman. For him, at this point, there wasn't even anything different about being engaged.

She was a replacement. That was all. A tool that was being used to aid him in acquiring this estate.

She meant nothing to him. Less than nothing. If she left him tonight he would have her replaced tomorrow by an unwitting maid.

And for her, this would always be dangerous. Because for her, this was singular. This experience of being held by a man. This experience of wanting. To touch him. To kiss him.

That thought took root in her mind, skittered down her spine like an electric shock.

Kiss him. Did she really want to kiss him?

She looked at that dangerous, sculpted mouth and imagined what it might be like to press her own against it. To test the shape of it. To test its strength.

It made her melt, dissolve at her core, and when he tried to sweep her into the next step, she stumbled, and found herself pressed yet more tightly against him. She had to wonder if this had been a bit of calculation on the part of her body.

If this was some kind of latent feminine instinct propelling her toward the things she desired.

It was certainly not a decision she would have made consciously. She would be too frightened to do it. Too timid. She was bold in so many ways, but not in this.

The fear of rejection, of being told she wasn't enough, of him laughing at her even, asking why a woman such as herself would imagine she might have some impact on a man that women fell in love with every other day...

Yes, that would have held her back. But here she was, pressed tightly against him, her mouth but a whisper away from his.

The world seemed frozen, even though she knew they still moved.

But then they did stop. He lifted his hand, warm and rough against her cheek as he drew his forefinger along the edge of her jaw, down to the center of her lower lip. She felt her eyelids begin to flutter closed, helpless to do anything but lean into his touch.

His eyes were so intense as they looked into hers. So very purposeful. She could feel the tension between them like a physical band, drawing them together.

She waited. Waited for the press of that mouth against hers. But it didn't come. Instead, he released his hold on her and left her standing there, shivering in the sudden chill of his withdrawn heat.

"I have a ring for you," he said, walking across the room, his footsteps slow and steady, echoing in the vast, empty space.

It was so quiet in there. Then she realized that it had been silent except for their footsteps the entire time they were dancing. It had felt like there was music.

But there hadn't been.

Not ever.

It had all been in her head.

She looked at his dispassionate face and felt foolish. Felt as if a magical spell had been lifted and suddenly she could see clearly again. And it was clear that this was nothing to him.

He moved to an ornate side table and opened the drawer, producing a small, velvet box.

"Were you able to convince Diego to overnight your engagement ring?" she asked, feeling the arch, brittle tone in her words and not able to do anything to modify it.

She felt hideously exposed. As if he could read every last one of her insecurities. As if he could see her disappointment. The thwarted desire for a kiss that she should never have wanted.

"Liliana's ring would not have suited you," he said. "It was classic. Quite delicate."

She bristled. Of course she was not delicate. Of course she did not rate the sweet little antique design that his fragile American flower would have.

"For you," he continued, "I thought I might select something stronger."

She was awash in shame. In embarrassment. She felt as though he was just as likely to produce a ring made of Teflon as he was an actual engagement ring.

But then he opened the lid on the box and her breath caught. It was gold, and it was brilliant. The diamond in the center was yellow, and it glowed like the center of the sun.

"You are not a traditional woman," he said. "You are unique. And you are fiery. I thought you deserved a ring that reflected that."

She clenched her teeth tightly together, trying her best to look unaffected. "You think you know me?"

"You are bold. Bold enough to go undercover to gain a job here. To risk everything to be near the horses."

"It's easy to risk everything when you own nothing," she pointed out.

"Perhaps. But a great many people in your position would have simply sat down and bemoaned the unfairness of life. You were not prepared to cope with your loss. Not the loss of your father, not the loss of the *rancho*. And yet, you have done so admirably. And perhaps your actions were unorthodox, but I find that I respect that all the more. It is rare that someone is able to fool me, Camilla," he said. "I should be angry, but I find that I only respect what you have done."

He thrust the ring box toward her and she took it, still feeling slightly stunned.

"There," he said. "It is done."

"I haven't put it on yet," she said.

"But you will," he responded, his tone maddeningly certain.

"Perhaps," she said, snapping the box shut just to spite him. She had a feeling he'd expected her to go all silly over the piece of jewelry. She had a feeling he had expected her to slip it on her finger immediately. To see how it might fit.

Driven either by some magpie instinct he imagined all women must possess, or by some sense of avarice that someone like her—someone impoverished—might be expected to demonstrate.

The truth was, she felt both of those things stirring in her chest, but she would not give him the satisfaction of it.

She had expected a kiss. She had not received it.

She was not going to give him what he expected.

"Do you suppose my dancing will suffice?" she asked, letting her hands drop to her sides, her fingers curled around the ring box.

"So long as you don't trip over your feet," he returned.

She sniffed. "If you lead correctly, I don't suppose there is a danger of that."

A slow smile spread over his face, and he chuckled. "Then I will endeavor to lead, *mi tesoro*."

CHAPTER NINE

MATÍAS SPENT THE next few days avoiding Camilla. He told himself that was not what he was doing, because he was no coward. Particularly not where women were concerned. He was a man who'd had ample and early access to the female form, who had never much seen the point in denying himself physical feminine company when the need arose itself.

However, he felt it best not to engage himself physically with Camilla Alvarez. Their fates were too linked. Their lives far too intertwined at the moment for his peace of mind.

When all was said and done, he wished to part with her as business partners might.

But that did not stop the yawning ache in his gut from making itself known.

They would get through tonight. Through the public presentation of them as an engaged couple. And then he would find himself a woman to deal with his physical desires.

As he had suspected, his brother had ensured that his marriage to Liliana became a headline the world over. In the days since her defection, it had become headline news.

And so he had to replace it with the headline of his own, and he was determined to do so tonight.

Another reason he could not afford a distraction.

He had to maintain control of himself. Even though the attraction that sparked between himself and Camilla was convenient when it came to presenting a front as an engaged couple, he could not afford to be anything but in absolute control of himself and his body.

He thought of the way she had fallen against him a few days ago during their dance lesson. The way she had tilted her face up toward him, her eyes fluttering closed. And it irked him that he couldn't read her. That he could not tell whether it was innocent on her part, or whether she was, in fact, a skilled seductress.

That was the problem with her in general. The fact that she had tricked him as she had done when she had come to work for him meant he did not trust anything she did or said now. They were allied of a necessity, and he believed what it suited him to believe, but he also believed it entirely possible that she might have ulterior motives.

He was all right with that, as long as he was fully cognizant that it might be the case.

In order to be fully cognizant he had to keep his lower extremities out of the equation.

Everything was prepared for the trip down to the city. He had arranged to have his penthouse prepared, so the two of them could spend the night there after the ball ended.

He had asked that his staff arrange to have any personal items she might need brought there and installed for her.

He was now waiting in the antechamber of his family home, and she was late.

He looked down at his watch, then looked up at the stairs, filled with impatience. Surely, arriving at an appointed time was not difficult. Liliana certainly had never had any trouble with it.

But then Liliana was an accomplished socialite, and he knew that Camilla was not.

Still, he had an entire team of people aiding in her preparations. Surely, it could not be that difficult.

He heard footsteps and looked up, and was shocked by the level of intensity that hit him hard in the stomach.

Because there she was, bare-shouldered, wearing a strapless gown that conformed to her lithe figure, until it reached her hips, where it fanned out in a glorious blaze of glittering gold. Her short hair was adorned with a simple golden band that was fashioned to look like a vine.

That vision of her as a goddess of some sort was only cemented by this. And suddenly, he did not care if they were late.

Her brown eyes were wide, and he could not read the emotion in them as she descended the staircase, her gown swishing around her with each movement.

When she reached the bottom of the steps, she looked at him with deep uncertainty. "Do you like it?"

"The dress?"

"I suppose so." Though she was keeping her tone flat, even, he could sense a vulnerability to her in that moment. One he found quite surprising.

"I like it on you," he returned.

She looked down, and he took her arm, surprised by the softness of her skin. He examined her profile, the strong shape of her jaw, the sweet, supple curve of her lip.

She was a fascinating woman. And more and more he could not fathom he had ever believed her ruse.

He simply hadn't looked.

It made him wonder what else he didn't see. It made him wonder what else he had closed himself off to.

But then he supposed there was no real point in lingering on those thoughts.

It didn't matter. He had her now. And he was going to get his part of the family fortune. Even if he was not going to have it all in its entirety. He would not be made a fool of by Diego. He would not allow his brother to win.

He might not be able to ensure his loss, but he could ensure he did not take it all.

And with Camilla on his arm tonight, he was likely to paint a very convincing picture of the entire scenario. It would be clear to anyone with eyes why he would have been tempted away from that pale, fragile woman he had found himself engaged to, drawn to this bright, vibrant creature.

She might not have the fame of Liliana Hart, might not possess a newsworthy family, but any man would be able to see why she was a temptation.

"The car is waiting," he said, leading them both out of the house and toward the limousine that was waiting for them.

She stopped. "That seems a bit expected," she commented.

"Please forgive me my expected limousine," he said. "The sad thing about events like this is we must endeavor to be expected. We must fulfill the expectations of those in attendance. Otherwise, there is precious little point in attending at all."

His driver opened the door for both of them, and they slid inside. Then, when they were safely ensconced, on the road and headed toward the city, she turned to him.

"Did your father do as expected?"

"No, my family has always made it their mission to do as little that was expected of them as possible. I have tried to be different. I was not taught the difference between right and wrong. Nobody attempted to teach me the value of integrity, and yet because of the deficit of it in my life I figured it out all the same. A man cannot live by his own rules, Camilla. A man must answer to a higher power. It is simply the way of it. If not, then he is bound to the whims of his own heart, his own desires. That ends in bad places. Dark places."

"Your father was cruel to you…"

His chest tightened, the words screaming in his head, begging to be released while his whole body tensed for a battle to hold it back. There was something about her. Something that made it seem so easy to share things he had never told another soul.

Perhaps it was because when he'd first spoken freely to her he'd seen her as a boy. A member of his staff. He'd barely seen her at all.

In the darkness of the car, he physically couldn't see her, and perhaps that was why he wanted to speak to her now. It was like confession. Whether or not it would be good for his soul, he couldn't say.

"It is not that. Yes, my father was cruel to me. He was cruel to everyone he encountered. But my father killed my mother, Camilla." The next words were torn, from somewhere deep inside him, with a pain he had no idea he still possessed the ability to feel. "It was not an accident."

Camilla was frozen, her heart turning brittle in her chest, cracking from the inside out. His father had killed his mother? It seemed impossible. Impossible words issued from the most beautiful lips. He was every inch Prince Charming to her Cinderella tonight, and yet, she had not felt a sense of enchantment when she had descended down the stairs toward him.

Instead, she had only felt a sense of dread, a sense of being deficient. Because she could never be the woman he had chosen for himself in the first place. She could never be that kind of sweet, delicate beauty she knew that men like him—all men—preferred.

But now she questioned that feeling. She had assumed, of course, that she was the only one carrying around dark feelings. She was the only one beset by misgivings of any kind. Because how could a man who looked so sublime in a custom-made tux be carrying around any sort of weight in his chest?

And yet, his was the greatest of all.

"How do you know?" she asked, her words muted.

"I saw it," he said, the words rough. "I saw him with my own eyes. You wonder how I can be so certain that Diego did not kill his wife. Because I spent my childhood with a man capable of such a thing. And while I think my brother is morally bankrupt, not unaffected by the life we led here at the *rancho*, I don't believe he's a killer. I looked into the eyes of a man who would do such a thing. I had been left to live with that man in the aftermath, while the local government bent over backward to cover it up, corruption and payoffs raining while Justice died a sad, horrible death alongside my mother. Diego is a villain. But he is not a killer."

"Did Diego see…?"

"No," he said, the words sharp. Hard. "I was the only one who was there that day. My father did not see it, either. I was frozen, up in a tree. I was…eight years old, I suppose."

She could tell that he remembered everything. From his age to his exact position in the tree, his specific vantage point. But that he was going out of his way to keep it vague. To keep it easy.

That he was doing what he had to do to protect himself.

"I had been playing out in the olive groves, and I heard the sound of approaching horses. A chase. A game, I thought at first, except when I realized it was my father and my mother I knew it could not be. My father did not play games. At least, not the kind that anyone but himself could win."

"Matías…"

"He shot her." There was a very long silence after that. The only sound in the limo the tires on the road. She said nothing. Could do nothing but simply sit and wait. She was…horrorstruck. She wanted to hold him and she knew she could not. Should not. He wasn't hers. And of course he never could be. But she wanted him to be. Oh, she wanted him to be now.

"She fell off the horse," he said finally, his tone distant, pained, "or, the horse fell, and there was screaming. I do not think it was the gunshot that killed her, but the fall from the horse. When I said she broke her neck falling from a horse…that was in the official report, and I know they were covering up some of what happened. But I do think there was truth in it. The way that the horse toppled over after." His words were hard, flat. "And I could not move. I was afraid that if I did he would kill me, too. I did try to tell the police. But the police chief said I was not to repeat that story. It was an accident. A terrible riding accident, as to be expected when people spent so much time with horses. An acknowledged risk, you see."

Camilla pressed her hands against her chest, as if that might do something to calm her thundering heart.

As if it might do something to dampen the horror she felt. "I'm so sorry. How could they do that to you? How could they do that to a child?"

"I don't tell you this to make you sorry for me. It is done. There will be no justice for my mother, and there never can be. All the evidence is long gone and buried. Every police officer involved in the investigation moved on, retired. And my father is dead. My father is dead, so he cannot be arrested. I hope, very much, that he burns in hell for what he has done. As it is, he was killed by something so mundane as a stroke while he was in the company of no fewer than three prostitutes. If that end would have brought him shame, I would have considered it a partial form of justice, but the man had no shame at all. And so, I can only hope there is justice in the afterlife for him. For he did not suffer enough in this life."

Her thoughts jumbled together, her heart full of immense pain. It was all starting to make sense. His need to redeem the *rancho*.

This place, the place where his mother had been killed, was a place of ghosts and demons for him. And she imagined that he was on a quest for redemption.

"And Diego…"

"I believe one of the more commonly held rumors. Which is that his wife caught him out in an affair and killed herself as a result."

"He must feel…awful."

"I don't know that he possesses the capacity," Matías said. "He's a vain, selfish man. And while I don't believe he would ever physically harm someone…he does it every day by living only to please himself."

They made the rest of the drive in silence, and when the limo pulled up to the front of the well-lit hotel, the previous conversation from the car temporarily fled her mind as she felt a growing sense of nerves over what lay ahead.

Shallow, trivial in many ways in light of all that Matías had told her. But she was only human, a human who was about to be put on display in a room full of people, and then put on display yet again in the papers. Online. The world over. Not because of any interest in her, but because of the interest in Matías and the entire Navarro family.

Matías exited the car and she stayed in her seat, her eyes fixed upon the entry doors that were standing open, people filtering in and out wearing all manner of evening finery. Long gowns glittering beneath the spotlights.

She saw a beautiful blonde make her way down the stairs, a formfitting gown highlighting her voluptuous figure, her hair left loose and blowing in the warm evening breeze.

For the first time in quite a while, Camilla missed her hair. Wondered if Matías would find her more beautiful if she hadn't cut it all off.

Then she frowned. She wasn't supposed to care what Matías thought. This wasn't about him. It was a business deal. She was the one who had said that. The one who had shaken hands with him as though they were in a board room. As though they had not been sitting in his family library, he coping with the betrayal of a fiancée, and she dressed as a boy.

The limousine door opened and Matías stood there, looming over her, tall, dark and perfectly dressed.

The sight of him took her breath away, and she was reminded why it was so difficult for her to keep the nature of the arrangement straight in her mind.

Because he was beautiful. So very beautiful and it didn't matter that she was not a lovely enough woman to catch his attention. At least, it didn't matter to her body.

It was shameful. The fact that she was not immune to him. That she would like to be disdainful of all his egotistical assertions that all women fell at his feet the moment they set eyes on him.

But she could not be disdainful because she was not immune in the least. And she was perilously close to falling at his feet.

So don't.

She held on to that stern, internal admonishment as she reached out to take hold of his hand. She lifted her chin, meeting his gaze, doing her best to appear confident.

Mercifully, she was wearing flat shoes, the nature of her long dress making heels unnecessary. They had an elegant, pointed toe and glittered gold just like her gown, and were easy to walk in.

With each step they took toward the ballroom her stomach tied itself in a slightly tighter knot.

She took a breath and imagined that instead of approaching a ballroom, she was approaching a barn. That all she would have to do was wrangle a two-ton animal, rather than dance before an audience of people who would be judging her, assessing her value.

She found that settling.

Horses were her confidence.

This was not.

And so she reminded herself who she was. That she could outride anyone here. That she possessed skills they could not possibly imagine. That she might, in fact, have a misstep tonight, but it would not change the fact that when it came to doing what she loved, no one could best her.

Somehow, that helped. Somehow, it infused her with a sense of confidence she had not known she could find here.

These men, these women, might well be the rulers of this domain, and she most certainly was not. But she had dominion over what she loved. And once she had completed this ruse with Matías, no one would ever be able to take it from her again.

She could withstand anything in order to ensure that. Anything at all.

She found herself holding her head higher, carrying her shoulders a bit straighter.

Matías put his hand low on her back and ushered her inside, and she felt that touch like lightning. She turned to look at him, her heart racing. No man had ever made her feel like this before. And a moment ago it had made her feel ashamed. It had made her feel as though she was simply one of the scores of women who had fallen prey to his charms before.

An inadequate one, at that. One who could not measure up in terms of beauty or grace.

But none of the other women that he had ever been with before would have matched her for horsemanship. Of that, she was confident.

And perhaps, a man would not find that to be an asset in a lover.

Just thinking the word made her stomach turn over.

Perhaps *he* would not. She was strong, she was athletic. She knew what her body could do, knew how to test the limits of her physical abilities when it came to doing ranch work.

She would be more than able to do the same in bed with a man.

Her face grew hot, her throat tight and prickly.

That burst of confidence had pushed her mind into strange territory. Or perhaps it was that hand on her body. Perhaps it was simply prolonged exposure to him. Perhaps it was everything. All the changes that had occurred in her life over the past few months.

And perhaps more than anything that time spent dressed as a boy and working at his *rancho*.

Being so aware of the fact that she was a woman when no one saw her that way. Being so aware that she was a woman when she could not behave like one.

And now she was thrust into this. The spotlight where her beauty, her femininity, was being highlighted in a way it never had been before. Where she was experiencing forced proximity with a man in a way that she had never done before.

Perhaps that was why her thoughts had gone to lovers and bedrooms.

She didn't want them to go there again.

She simply had to get through the night.

Then tomorrow she would focus on getting through that day. And the next. And the wedding day. And all the days after that until this ended and she got what she truly desired. Which was not Matías, but the ownership of the family *rancho*. The horses.

She simply had to keep sight of that end goal. That was all.

Matías swept her inside the beautiful, glittering hotel, and she marveled at the surroundings. The marble pillars, the glittering chandelier at the center of the room. And all the people swirling beneath it. Women in swirling pastel dresses, men in sharply cut suits.

To her, all men's suits looked roughly the same, but no man looked the way Matías did. They all looked domesticated, and somehow, putting Matías in a tuxedo only made him look more dangerous. Only highlighted the fact that in many ways, though he could move in this world freely, it was not *his* world.

He was like her in that way. Although, her ability to move within this space was up for debate and would continue to be until the evening was finished.

His fingertips brushed her arm as he abandoned her for a moment to procure glasses of champagne for them. Rough hands.

Working man's hands.

Yes, he might look the part of sophisticated businessman in this environment, but in reality he was part of the ranch. And it was part of him.

It was in his soul, in his blood, for better or worse, and now that she knew so much of the worst, she appreciated it on an even deeper level. Appreciated him, and his drive to possess it. To bend it to his will.

And now she knew the weight of his burden. The trauma he'd experienced and he'd come out the other side so…he cared so very much about what was right.

No one else knew the whole story. No one but her.

It made her feel…so strongly linked to him. To this man who was so different from her. So much more experienced.

But also…so much the same. He loved his land. He loved the horses.

She didn't want to feel anything for him, but she did. Oh, she did.

He handed her the glass of champagne and she took it in her left hand, lifting it to her lips, and it was then she noticed how her ring sparkled in the light. Her engagement ring. And she was not the only one who noticed the way that it caught the lights.

Suddenly, she felt at least fifty sets of eyes on her, and the discomfort from that chased away some of the feelings that had been wrapping themselves around her heart.

And it was only a moment before a couple made their way to Matías and herself, led by the petite, blonde wife and her much older husband.

"Matías," the woman said. "I daresay we did not expect to see you here tonight. Not after news of your broken engagement had surfaced. But it appears that you're here after all. And with a woman. A woman with a ring."

She looked at Camilla with an expression of speculation, her hands clasped together tightly, reminding Camilla of a praying mantis.

"Yes," Matías said, his tone smooth. "This is my fiancée, Camilla Alvarez. Her father was the late celebrated trainer Cesar Alvarez. I met her during a business venture and had quite the immediate connection."

"But up until last week you were engaged to Liliana Hart," the woman said as though Matías might have forgotten.

"I was indeed. I can only say that Liliana and I were clearly not suited, and she was the one who was brave enough to break things off before they became more permanent. I am thankful that Liliana followed her heart so that I was free to follow mine."

Matías nodded definitively, clearly pleased to let the conversation end on that note, and swept her away from the couple, taking her champagne glass from her hand and depositing it—along with his—on a passing tray. "I say we take this opportunity to share our first dance," he whispered, his lips close to her ear, his breath playing havoc over her skin, sending heat rioting through her body.

"Okay," she said breathlessly, her hands feeling slightly clammy.

"Knowing Señora Gomez, what I said to her will make its way into the paper nearly verbatim. I thought that was a good quote to offer up to the press. And a good chance for us to have our photograph taken."

He swept her into his arms, and this time, when they began to move, it was in time with music. The strains of the live quartet's song wound its way around them, but it wasn't what moved her. It was Matías.

Suddenly, she wished, if only for a night, that this were real. That the words he had spoken to that woman, so greedy for gossip and scandal, were true in some regard.

You don't want that. You don't want your life controlled by a man. You don't want to be bound to someone forever.

She didn't. Truly. But just for a while, it would be nice to be wanted. To be found beautiful.

She had spent so long not particularly feeling like she was any of those things. And this game they were playing touched the edges of those wounds.

She felt a pull between those old insecurities and new confidence that she hadn't known she possessed the ability to feel.

He made her want to know things. To test these new discoveries she was making.

To find out just what her body was capable of, in all areas. To discover why it mattered that she was a woman, and he was a man.

She had simply never wanted it before. Had never thought of it.

It made her want to laugh, really. The idea that he had somehow made her into a woman. And it was all a little bit silly, considering the symbolism. Considering the fact that she had literally been masquerading as a boy prior to his discovery, and then given this incredible makeover that turned her into a version of herself she didn't recognize.

"You are very quiet," he said, the words soft.

Matías was never soft, and the fact that he was being soft in this moment was notable.

"We're dancing. Should I be…noisy?"

"How are you liking the ball, Cinderella?"

"It's very nice. Though strange."

She adjusted her hold on him, moving her fingers across his broad shoulders. She wondered what it would be like to touch him without these layers of fabric between them. And for some reason the thought didn't even shock her. Because she was too busy being wrapped up in this magic spell.

"Why is it strange?"

"I have never been the center of attention in my entire life. My father loved me, very much, but I was a part of his crew. I was a part of the staff at the *rancho*. I think, in many ways, I was the son that he never had, but I'm not sure that I was ever truly his daughter."

"And your mother didn't care at all."

She bit her lip. He'd confided in her. Perhaps it would be okay to confide in him. She had been lonely for a long time. She was tired of that. Tired of feeling alone. "My mother was…*is*…only able to love herself, I think. She fancies herself in love with a parade of different men, but in the end she is never changed by them. In the end none of them can entice her to be faithful."

"Usually that doesn't mean you love yourself an extraordinary amount," he said slowly. "I would suggest it means she does not love herself very much at all. And doesn't know how to allow anyone else to do it, either."

She blinked. "Oh. I never thought of it that way." It was easier to think of her mother as selfish, unfeeling. Not wounded in some way.

"It was not your job to think of her that way. Not your job to be sympathetic. She is your mother, and she should have taken better care of you."

"Still," she said softly. "I think you're right."

"Often, the great and terrible tyrants in our lives are just as great a tragedy to themselves as they are to us."

"Except that your father was a greater tragedy to your mother."

He nodded slowly. "Yes. The women who love the men in my family do not come to good ends." She could feel a warning implicit in those words, and if she had not been feeling so much, such a large weight sitting on her chest, she might have said something sharp to lighten the mood. Might have argued with him, called him out on his ego for suggesting that a woman might fall for him.

But things had changed too much between them since they had gotten in the car tonight. And she knew more about him than she had earlier. More than that, she felt...

Somehow, the idea of being without him did not feel like freedom anymore, and that frightened her very much.

"I think we're drawing a lot of attention," he said. "It is that dress of yours."

"It is the ring on my finger," she returned. "And the fact that I'm with you."

"You're the most beautiful woman in this room," he

said. "They're all flowers. Pale, lovely, but insipid. You are the sun itself."

She felt her face growing warm, her breasts getting heavy, aching. She didn't know what to make of that. Didn't even know what it meant. What it might be preparing her for. And yet, she knew that was what it was. A preparation of some kind. For something more. Something from him. Something she didn't even have a name for.

Sex.

She shifted uncomfortably in his arms, and suddenly was very aware of that space between her thighs, of the ache there. Of the fact that she was aroused, and that she wanted him. Wanted him to touch her there. More thoughts that should shock her, and yet didn't. None of this did. She couldn't account for that. Couldn't account for who she was when she was in his arms. But it was something different. Someone different. A different creature entirely than she had been when she had first arrived at his *rancho*.

"I've never been called beautiful before," she said, and then cringed as the words left her mouth, because it was such a vulnerable thing to admit. To a man who was beauty incarnate. Who had to keep women off his property so they would not make fools of themselves around him.

The look in his eyes was so hot, it melted her. And when he spoke it was slow, steady and with such grave purpose she could not doubt him. "Perhaps it is simply because no one has ever taken the time to look," he said. "When you first arrived at my *rancho* I didn't look at you. I looked through you. But I am looking now. And I see you, Camilla."

His tone was so grave, his eyes so serious, and resting on her with a kind of intensity that she wasn't sure he could manufacture. But surely, it was all for show. Surely, this conversation was simply so he could paint the appropriate picture to the people around them.

Surely, it wasn't because she was truly beautiful. Surely, that wasn't why he continued to look at her, why his hand suddenly drifted down, lower on her back, and why he suddenly released his hold on her, and reached out to cup her chin with his thumb and forefinger.

Her lips felt like they were on fire, and she was suddenly so acutely aware of them she could scarcely breathe. She had never felt so very conscious of her face before, of every minute thing her expression might be doing. And when she realized how dry her mouth had become, when she slipped her tongue out to moisten her lips, it felt like a sexual act. Like an invitation.

One she would have said only a moment ago she had not even known how to issue. And yet apparently, she did.

Apparently, she did, because only a breath later, he closed the space between them, and claimed her mouth with his own.

CHAPTER TEN

IT WAS FOR SHOW, of course. That was why Matías had leaned down and pressed a kiss to Camilla's mouth. Not because it was so full and edible he could no longer resist it. Not because keeping his hands off her had been an exercise in futility from the moment he had seen her earlier. Not because he would rather kiss her than continue their entirely too honest brand of conversation.

Not because he was beginning to feel an impossible, immeasurable shift happening inside his chest that seemed to uncover parts of him that he had thought long destroyed.

A part of his soul he thought had bled into the earth and soaked into the ground along with his mother's life's blood on that terrible day.

This was for show. It was for the cameras. For the pictures that his grandfather would expect to see in the papers tomorrow. To go with that perfect headline he had spoken to Señora Gomez earlier in the evening.

Yes, that was why he pressed his mouth to hers. That was why he parted those delicate, sweet lips with his tongue and thrust deep inside her mouth, gripping her chin hard as he angled her head so that he could taste her deeper, take greater advantage of her inexperience, of the involuntary gasp she made, so that he might gorge himself on her.

It was all to give the impression of a man consumed by passion. It was not because he was a man consumed by passion, that was impossible. He was Matías Navarro, and he was consumed by nothing. He controlled each and every impulse, had dominion over all that he was, all that he wanted.

He did nothing more than what he chose to do. He was not a man like his father, ruled by temper. Or like his brother, steeped in debauchery.

He was *not* seduced. He never had been. He had always done the seduction. And the fact that she was trembling beneath his touch indicated that he was doing the seducing yet again. And if he was shaking, as well, it was only because of adrenaline. Because of arousal. Because his body was readying itself for an intimate act that would never eventuate. Not with her.

Though, he was having difficulty remembering why now.

When he pulled away from her, he remembered. Her lips were flushed with her arousal, her eyes glassy, but it was the look of wonder in them that hit him square in the gut.

The innocence there.

If there was any part of him that was pretending she was not a virgin, he could no longer pretend. He was not a man who had ever allowed himself to entertain the idea of taking a woman's virginity. That was the territory of villains like his brother, and the fact he wanted Camilla, even though he did not intend to make their union permanent, appalled him. It had been different with Liliana. He had intended to offer her a commitment that would last. To do the honorable thing. To offer her his name, his protection. She was like a hothouse flower. She would not only require protection, require being coddled, but she would expect and demand it.

Camilla would never submit to such a thing. She was wild, untamable. She was nothing like Liliana and all her pale, quiet beauty. Camilla was the sun, but she was also a storm. Uncontrollable. Unmanageable. She would tear through the *rancho*, tear through his life and tear through her own with all that same vigor and carelessness that she had employed when she had cut off all her hair and posed as a boy to get hired on by him.

He would never be able to tame her, never be able to leash her, and of course, he didn't want to.

But she had all that reckless spirit and it was not compatible to his life. Still.

Right now he wanted to crush her beneath him, spread those thighs and bury himself inside her.

But he could not. He would not.

"Wow," she breathed, that sweet, innocent reaction touching him in places he should not allow.

"Do not look at me like that."

She blinked. "Look at you like what?"

"Like you're looking at me right now," he returned. "Like I have taught you something new. It will look strange in a picture."

He tacked that last part on quickly, and he felt guilty when she looked like she had been struck.

"Sorry."

"Don't be," he said. "You have done nothing wrong."

Except reached inside him and changed something around. Moved parts of himself so that sacred spaces that had long been covered were exposed.

It was only a kiss. There was no reason to apply so

much to it. One would be forgiven for thinking *he* was the virgin given that response.

"You said I did."

"I only meant…you cannot look at me as though that was your first kiss. We are supposed to be a couple."

"But it was," she said softly.

His groin tightened, his stomach tense. "Do not tell me things like that, Camilla."

"Why not? You told me all those dark things about your past. Surely, this isn't a deeper revelation than that."

Again, she produced a kind of clear, real honesty in him he could not fight. "When you tell me things like that I am tempted. Tempted to teach you everything those eyes tell me you do not know. Tempted to make sure that I am not only your first kiss but also your first lover. And the lover that you think about every time thereafter. The lover you compare all other men to."

He was certain that that would scare her. Certain that that was a bridge too far for his innocent beauty. She would not want those things. She was fearsome, a warrior, but she was not worldly. She had been protected from the advances of men like him. She didn't have to say that for him to know it was true. Had she not been, she would have been kissed many times already. Would have been far from untouched.

She deserved her first time to be with a nice man. A man who would honor that gift. A man who was careful with things, rather than breaking them.

"What if I want you to?" she said softly. "What if I want you to teach me those things?"

"You do not know what you ask for," he said.

"I do. I am not so sheltered that I don't understand the way things are between men and women. And I…

I will not fall in love with you. I'm independent. I was born with a fierce spirit. I'm like my father. I have the gift of speaking to horses. I have the gift of strength and solitude. I am not meant to be tied down. So you have no worries on that score. Not for me."

"Your father married your mother. He fell for someone who betrayed him immeasurably over the course of his life. Why do you assume that because you're like him you're immune?"

"My father was bound to my mother because of me. And he was bound to stay married because of his faith. He could have sought an annulment, I suppose, because of her behavior, but he did not. It suited him. To keep that marriage. I think, in the end, he knew that a real marriage was not for him anyway. He wanted to spend long hours out on the *rancho*. He did not want to throw dinner parties. He did not want to spend his time catering to a wife. Any more than I want to spend my time catering to a husband. Do you think that I want to get dressed up and go to parties like this all the time? No. I would rather wear jeans. And I would rather ride horses. I would rather wear boots than these glittering gold shoes, no matter how beautiful they are. But just because I want those things does not mean that I'm immune to the desires of a man's touch. And I want yours, Matías. I crave yours."

She was bold, even in this. He was reminded of that first meeting. When she had spoken to him with such force, and he had imagined that it had come from the brashness of youth. Now he knew. It was simply the fire inside her. Some might call it an unearned confidence. But he found it to be a singular, beautiful gift.

She was no seductress. She was looking at him with frankness, with open desire. She was not gazing at him through her veiled lashes, fluttering her eyes at him. No. There was no shame. If there was embarrassment, it was simply because she was afraid of rejection. But there was no game being played here. She wanted. And so she asked. It was a fascinating thing to see. And it was...

Intoxicating.

To have a woman look him in the eye and swear she would not fall in love with him. To have a woman ask for what she wanted.

To want this creature that could offer him nothing in terms of skill in the bedroom. Who could not do tricks and would likely have no idea of what to do with his body once he took his clothes off for her.

That novelty should not appeal to him, and yet it did. Just as he had said, the temptation to educate her was real. The temptation to brand her as his. To burn his mark into her skin.

Perhaps he should be appalled by such an impulse and yet he could no more fight against it than he could fight against her honest, open request.

"You must tell me," he said, "little one." He braced his hand on the back of her head, holding her steady as he looked into her dark eyes. "That you want me to take your virginity. That you want me to take you back to my penthouse here in Barcelona. You want me to taste you, touch you. That you want me inside your body. You must say those things to me, so that I know for sure you understand what you ask."

"Remember," she said, those pouty lips curving upward. "I am not fourteen. I am a woman."

"When it comes to experience with men, you are barely that. You must ask, *mi tesoro*, so that I know that this is what you want."

"I want to," she said. She swallowed hard, that fine

throat working as she did. "I want for you to make love to me. I want you to take my virginity." And then she did something he did not expect. She curved her fingers around the back of his head, holding him tight as he was holding her. "I want you inside me." And then she kissed him, with all the boldness of a harlot, licked his lips with the seductive attention of a Siren. Then when she drew back, she blushed like an innocent.

And he was lost.

"Very well," he rasped, his voice a stranger's. "I will give you what you desire. But we will finish tonight. We will finish this together, and when we leave, we will leave it behind."

"What do you mean?"

"Here," he said, looking around the room, "we are an engaged couple. Here, we are engaging in a performance. Once we are in my bedroom, it will simply be Camilla and Matías. There will be nothing outside of that. It will not be a business transaction. Do you understand?"

"Yes," she whispered.

"No," he said, "I don't think you do. I do not require you to be this glittering creature. I require nothing of you beyond yourself. That is who I want in my bed tonight."

She ducked her head. "I'm not sure that you've met her before."

"Then I feel, *mi amor*, this would be an excellent time for you to introduce me."

It was those words that stuck with her. Those words that propelled her through the evening. That empowered her as she danced with him, each song powerful and deep, like something more intimate than it was, because of the shared knowledge of what was going to take place later.

He wanted her. He had said so. Her as she was, not her as this elegant creature that had been fashioned by a team of people. Not her, the one who had come to him in disguise.

The her that perhaps not even she knew. That she had shown to no one.

And it terrified her. Because she was suddenly so certain that in many ways she had spent all of her life burying some desires of hers down deep.

Her father had given her a great many things. He had given her the freedom to do as she pleased as long as she stayed within the boundaries of the *rancho*. He had given her a kind of freedom from her mother's expectations by allowing her to be the opposite.

But there had been no place for her to explore that other part of herself. The part that was very much a woman and wanted to be with a man. The part that wanted to be beautiful. To feel lovely.

They managed to make it through the entire evening, and she marveled at the way that Matías dealt with the people around him. He was a chameleon. Able to be charming and firm in the same conversation. To speak hard truths, and then smooth them over with a smile.

He was not a man that anyone wanted to defy, and she had a feeling that it had nothing to do with his family name or their formidable reputation, but everything to do with the magnetism of the man himself.

He was unlike anyone she had ever known. And she had a feeling that would always be the case.

Had a feeling that after this was over she would remember him forever. She would carry a small piece of him with her.

It felt…romantic in many ways. At least the right kind of romance for a woman like her. A woman who wanted nothing more than her freedom. Who wanted nothing more than to feel desired when she wished to, and to have total agency in her life at other moments.

When he swept her out of the ballroom, and back into the limo, she was afraid she might have left her stomach behind. Her anticipation had been growing stronger with each passing moment, but now that it was time, she found herself getting nervous. Found herself feeling that confidence slipping away again.

The limo pulled up outside the penthouse, and she looked up, her heart pounding hard at the base of her throat. "I didn't bring anything with me," she said.

"I've taken care of everything," he said.

"Have you?" she asked.

"Yes. You do not have to fear anything. Just follow my lead."

"Will there be music?" she asked.

"You will not be following a song," he said, brushing his fingertips to her lips. "You will be following me."

It was such a strange assurance, quietly spoken, and should be dissonant from the mouth of a man who was just so very masculine and dangerous as Matías was, and yet she believed him.

That while she was with him, while she was his, he would care for her.

No one had ever assured her of such a thing before. She hadn't realized she had wanted it until now.

"Even a toothbrush?" she asked, not wanting to reveal the vulnerability that she felt.

"Oh, yes," he said, "everything has been provided for you."

"And a nightgown?"

He chuckled, then grabbed hold of her chin, holding her face steady. "You won't be needing one."

Then she found herself being swept out of the limo and into the antechamber of the lovely, antiquated apartment building. They swept through the lobby and down to an elevator at the very end of the marble-carved room.

He pulled out a key card and swiped it, then they stepped inside. "This only goes to my floor," he said.

"You have your own floor?"

He shrugged. "I'm a man with specific needs. Privacy is one of them."

"I see," she said, suddenly feeling a lead weight in her stomach. "For when you bring women here," she said.

"I never claimed to be a saint, Camilla," he said, leaning against the door of the elevator, those deft fingers working the knot on his bow tie, letting it fall loose. "I have had lovers. Many of them. Not when I was engaged to Liliana. And not since meeting you. But yes. It suits me to have luxury accommodation in various places in the world for that reason."

"Just very strange. To think about, I mean. I've never touched another man. And you've touched…"

"Trust me," he said, a smile tipping the corner of his lips. "You will benefit from my experience."

"I'm sure I will," she said.

But that didn't mean jealousy didn't burn hot and fierce in her stomach, like a particularly vicious acid.

She had never kissed another man. Never wanted another man. But this man wanted easily. He wanted for no other reason than a face was beautiful, or a body pleasingly shaped.

It wasn't a flaw, she supposed, but it was certainly something.

The elevator doors swept open when it reached the top floor, and he pushed away from the door, leading her out into an apartment that was shockingly modern against the ornate backdrop of the lift.

"This is what you were talking about," she said, thinking of what he had said about the decor at the *rancho*.

"Yes," he said. "Most of my properties look more like this." He indicated the stark black-and-white design, the touches of chrome and other sorts of things that screamed masculinity in a very basic way.

She squinted. "You didn't do the decor," she commented.

"No," he said. He began to undo the cuffs on his shirt. "How did you know?" He slipped his jacket off and let it slide down onto the sleek leather couch that was positioned at the center of the room. Then he began to work the buttons on his white shirt.

"It doesn't look particularly like you. It just looks like someone was told to design a room for a man. Any man. One who doesn't particularly like frills. It's very generic."

He laughed. "And you think, perhaps, the ornate florals and powder blues of the *rancho* are more to my taste?"

She laughed. "I do. Because they have history. Because they're part of you. Whether you wanted to be or not."

Something in his face went hard, his mouth setting into a grim line. "I think that's quite enough talking."

And then she found herself being caught up in his strong embrace, pulled forward, his mouth hard and hot on hers as he devastated her with a savage kiss.

When he moved away from her she was breathing

hard, and then he took a step back, unbuttoning his shirt the rest of the way.

His body was…well, it was as classically masculine as their surroundings. But much, much more compelling. All strong lines and incredible muscle, dark hair covering that taut, bronzed skin.

She had never seen a man who looked quite like him before.

"Yes?" he asked.

"I'm just…staring," she said.

"Why are you staring?"

"Because you're…you're beautiful," she said before she could stop herself.

It was an incredibly gauche thing to say, but at the moment she felt that she was incredibly gauche and there was no way around it. She was inexperienced. Nonexperienced.

Had never even kissed a man until tonight, and she was about to do everything with him. Let him see her, let him touch her. See him, touch him. It was intoxicating, exhilarating and terrifying.

She wanted it. And she wanted to remember what he had told her earlier. Wanted to embrace who she was. Not who she was pretending to be. Not who she had dressed up as, either to get hired at the *rancho* or to get ready for the ball tonight.

And that meant committing to not being embarrassed when she said things like that. That he was beautiful. She was going to enjoy this. All of this. Claim it for herself. Because she supposed, that was the flipside to all that experience. He had had this experience before. It was not foreign to him. It wasn't new. Which meant that it was so much more for her than for him. She wanted to embrace that. Relish it.

"You're beautiful," she said again. "Truly."

Then, bolstered by that thought, she took a step forward, and she pressed her palm flat against his chest. He was so warm. Hot. She could feel his heartbeat raging against her touch. And that bolstered her, too. The fact that he wasn't unmoved by this. The fact that she did tempt him. Did test him. The fact that she created the same response in him as he created in her.

And no matter that her mother had always told her men were led around by their members. She chose to believe that it mattered still.

Her mother had taught her very few things, but that was one of the things she remembered. And along with that, she remembered her saying that men wanted sex and women wanted attention. And so she had imagined that if she ever came to this moment she would be in a situation of unequal desires. That she would crave attention, and he would simply crave touch.

But she knew, standing there looking at him, looking at the fire in his eyes, listening to the desires of her own body, that their desires were one. That they were united in their need tonight.

She didn't simply want attention. She wanted him. Needed him.

"I don't know what I'm doing," she said softly.

"I do," he said. "You don't have to know the steps. You simply have to follow my lead. And I will not let you fall."

Her heart swelled, those words, that promise, echoing through her.

Then he reached around behind her and grabbed hold of her zipper tab, drawing it down the center of her back. The bodice fell loose, the dress falling around her hips. Then he grabbed her hand and pulled her forward, and she stepped away from the glittering fabric, standing before him wearing nothing but glimmering, lacy underwear that she knew did very little to cover her body. She was not wearing a bra, because the dress had possessed built-in support, and so her breasts were bare to him, her nipples tight beneath his inspection.

She knew that he could see her dark curls at the apex of her thighs through that flimsy, light-colored lace. She knew that she should be embarrassed, but she wasn't. Because he wanted her. He wanted this. And just like with the dancing he had promised to lead. Promised to help make sure her steps didn't falter. She trusted him. Trusted him to do what he said, even if she had no reason to. But he was Matías. He was everything. He was the fulfillment of fantasies she hadn't even known she possessed. He was every secret desire she had always been afraid to put words to. He was the man that made her feel happiest to be a woman.

And for however long she could have him, she would. Oh, she would.

"Beautiful," he said, his dark eyes sharp, intense, as they looked at her mostly naked form.

She didn't wish for her long hair then. She didn't even wish for the gown. She had never felt more wholly female, perfectly feminine, than she did in that moment.

He reached out, and he dragged one of those callous thumbs over her tightened nipple. She gasped, drawing away from him because it was so shocking, so sensational.

"Teach me," he said, his voice rough. "Teach me what you like. Tell me when something feels good to you. Though I might embarrass myself."

"How?"

He chuckled, shaking his head. "Such an innocent."

He reached out, wrapping his fingers around her wrist, and drawing her hand toward the front of his pants. She gasped when she felt him there, hard, masculine and much larger than she had expected him to be.

"When a man wants a woman very, very much it becomes difficult for him to control himself. I would like to stay hard for you. I need to last for you. So that you can have as many orgasms as you want. So that I can pleasure you, over and over again before I finally take my own pleasure. And if I do not maintain my control, that may be difficult."

"Because you can only...you can only...*once*?" Her lack of experience was slightly mortifying, but they were naked together so she supposed being coy now was just silly.

"I can only come once in a certain amount of time. You, on the other hand, will not be similarly limited."

"That's...very interesting."

He leaned in, the tendons in his neck standing out, tension clear in every line of his body. "How is it you don't know about this? Haven't you talked to friends? Overheard men talking at the *rancho*?"

"I was the boss's daughter. They were very careful around me. And as for friends... I have horses. Which is informative enough regarding procreation but not regarding um...sexual...pleasures."

"But you must be somewhat familiar with pleasure," he insisted. "Haven't you explored your body on your own?" She shook her head. "And I haven't... I don't think I've experienced the pleasure you're talking about before," she said, feeling her face growing hot.

"You don't think you've had an orgasm?"

"No."

"Then you haven't," he said firmly. "If you had, you would have known."

And then on a growl, he lifted her up off her feet and pressed her against his body, kissing her, hard and deep, one hand pressed firmly against the center of her shoulder blades, the other cupping the back of her head.

The hair on his chest was rough, and it abraded her nipples, but it was not an unpleasant sensation.

It was…well, it was perfect. It was everything that she loved about their contrast. He was so hot, so hard, rough and intense. He matched her softness. Her smoothness. In the tentative feeling inside her.

And he coaxed something else out of her. Her recklessness. A wildness that she had not known existed.

Everything she had felt when on the dance floor with him, that sense of flying, freedom, was amplified now. And there was an edge to it. Something sharp, something sweet. A sense of desperation, but also something leisurely. As if she could hold on to this desperate, building feeling forever and ever. Hold off whatever storm was encroaching.

Because those rough hands skating over every inch of her curves, that large palm coming down to cup her butt as he pulled her more firmly against his body, allowing her to feel his heart and arousal up against her stomach, was such a heady, magical thing that she never wanted it to end.

Then he moved both hands to her hips, drawing them down to her thighs, and he lifted her up off the ground completely, wrapping her legs around his waist, bringing the vulnerable center of her up against all that hardened masculinity.

She gasped, a burst of pleasure breaking inside her, a wave of sensation pulsing between her legs.

And she wondered if that was it.

"Not yet," he said as if reading her mind. He dragged his lips down her throat, kissing the tender skin there, before licking the edge of her collarbone, and down farther to her breast, drawing one nipple into his mouth as he rocked his hips forward, sending another shock of sensation through her.

He squeezed her bottom, pulling her forward as he arched his hips again, and she gripped his shoulders, her fingernails digging into his skin as that small, pulsing sensation bloomed, expanded and became a never-ending storm inside her. That earlier feeling had only been a preview. A small taste of what was to come. This was endless. It was incredible. She never wanted it to stop, and yet she wasn't afraid she could withstand much more. He wanted this to happen to her multiple times over the course of the evening? She would never survive. Ever. It would break her. Destroy her. She was certain.

She gasped, and then went limp in his arms, resting her head against his shoulder, and he held her fast, moving through the open floor plan toward a door off to the left. He kicked it open, and then deposited her on a large bed at the center of the room.

She was still feeling languid and boneless from the force of her release, far too aroused and satisfied to feel any nerves about what might come next.

When he lowered himself down onto the bed, her heart leaped into her throat, her entire body on edge.

But then he looked at her, and she remembered his promise. That he would not let her fall. That he wouldn't let her steps falter.

He hadn't promised not to hurt her. She imagined that even with all of her years of riding horses it was going to hurt a bit, but he had promised that in the end it would be right. And she clung to that. She didn't need for it to be painless. She just needed it to be.

He moved his rough hand down her stomach, beneath the waistband of her panties and down between her thighs where he found her aroused and ready for his touch.

She wasn't embarrassed for him to know. How much she desired him. How ready her body was for his invasion.

He pressed two fingers down tightly, bracketing that sensitive bundle of nerves there, making her shiver, making her shake. Making her long for another release, which she would have imagined impossible only a moment before.

She shivered. "I want you," she whispered.

"Do you want me?" he asked, his dark eyes burning intensely into her own. "Do you, Camilla? Or do you simply want the pleasure that you know I can give you?"

"I don't know," she said, her voice trembling. "The kind of pleasure you can give me, I mean. I don't know anything about it at all. But I knew the minute that I saw you that there was something about you. Something about you that called to something in me. I just knew that you changed something inside me. And I wanted so badly for that not to be true. I wanted so badly to want nothing more than to simply be there with the horses. To simply gain back what the family lost. It was all I was supposed to do. All I was supposed to care about. And then there was you. There was you and this need inside me. And it wasn't there before. So yes, Matías, I want you."

She felt incredibly vulnerable, more naked than she had a moment ago. Even with his hand between her legs, she had not felt this vulnerable. But now she had admitted that. That her desire had appeared, manifested itself in her life at the same time that he had exposed a level she had not known possible. And yet, it also felt worth it. It also felt real.

So much deeper, so much stronger, than any other relationship she'd had. Than that nonexistent one with her mother as long as she could be a cute accessory, and then thereafter had ceased to exist. And even to her father, who had loved her, but who had also molded her into the image of what he had wanted. A companion to stay with him on the *rancho*. A daughter who behaved more like a son. This thing with Matías was like none of that. It was stripped bare of any artifice. Of any kind of calculation or manipulation. It was simply about the two of them. And about desire.

She ignored the tightening around her heart, focused on the need in her stomach. Because that was simpler. She could still make that about him. That heaviness gathering between her thighs. She could still make it about him and be safe. But anything in her chest. No. She couldn't risk that.

"Tell me you want me," he said, moving his fingers up slightly, squeezing that sensitive bundle of nerves again, before sliding them back down, not allowing himself to delve into her crease, not allowing himself to touch where she ached for him the most.

She bucked her hips, trying to force his touch to become yet more intimate.

He chuckled, his hold remaining fast. "Be a good girl," he said. "And tell me that you want me." He leaned in, his lips nearly touching hers. "When you wish to break a horse, you must first show it who its master is.

And I think you will find that I am the master of your body, *mi amor*."

She shivered, trying to muster up some kind of rage at that statement. Wanting to tell him that she was the master of her own body, of her own future. Wanting to tell him that he could not play such games with her.

But instead, only a whimper came out of her lips, and she bucked her hips even more intently, desperate now. For more. For his touch. For his possession, whatever that might mean.

"Patience," he said. Then he nipped her bottom lip before kissing her deep, hard, and shifting his hand so that his thumb was pressed up against her, one finger plunging deep inside her.

She gasped. The invasion was both welcome and unfamiliar, and it took a moment for her body to acclimate. But then...she wanted more. Oh, how she wanted more. She wanted all of him. Every last bit. Every hard, breathless inch.

"Matías," she said, the words coming out choked, desperate.

But she had already purposed that there would be no place for pride here. Had already committed herself to honesty. And as he worked his finger in and out of her desperate body, as he slid his thumb over and over her body, she gave herself up to it. To him. Surrendered herself completely, pleasure finding her this time on a short, sharp scream. Her body pulsed around his finger, her release like a storm, no less powerful for the fact that she'd had her first one only moments before in his living room.

She had surrendered her pride to him. And she did not regret it. But she did want something in return. On trembling limbs she rose up to her knees and pushed her panties down her thighs, stripping them off and throwing them off the edge of the bed, so that she was completely naked before him. There really was no point in being shy when she'd come apart in his arms twice, not when he had already had his fingers buried inside her.

She pushed lightly at his shoulder, and he went down on his back, not resisting her touch. Then she bent down, pressing a kiss to his bare shoulder, to his chest, to that place where his heart raged beneath that solid wall of muscle. Then she kissed his stomach, that hard, ridged abdomen that made her body weak with need. She paused, appraising the bulge in his pants. That was uncharted territory. But she would never be able to reclaim anything if she lost her boldness now.

A smile curved her lips and she let her fingertips drift across that cloth-covered arousal. "I think that I know a great deal more about horses than you," she said, biting her lip as she squeezed him. "And perhaps a bit more about mastery."

"Do not challenge me, Camilla," he said. "You're playing with fire."

"Good. I've always liked to live dangerously."

"You might get burned."

"Perhaps," she said, moving both hands to his belt and beginning to work through the loops. "I want to be burned."

She worked his pants down his lean hips and exposed his arousal to her hungry gaze. He was gorgeous. Intimidating, certainly, but he made her mouth water. Made her body feel hollow, aching to be filled. And she knew exactly with what.

But first…

But first.

She leaned down, boldly sliding her tongue over his

hardened length. He swore, raising his hand and fisting her short hair. It hurt, but she pressed on. She tilted
her head, taking him deep into her mouth, relishing
that musky, masculine flavor on her tongue, his heat
and hardness.

Everything.

She wrapped her fingers around his base and continued to move her tongue over him, savoring him as
if he were a delicacy.

"Enough," he said roughly, reaching down and lifting her up by the waist, bringing her down so that she
was straddling him as though she was about to ride,
her center connecting with his body. "I need you," he
said, his voice rough.

And that was enough. It was all she needed. She
rocked backward slightly, holding on to his arousal and
guiding it to the center of her body.

He swore, then reached over to his nightstand
quickly. "Condom," he said through gritted teeth. He
produced a plastic packet and held it out to her. "Put
it on me."

Another challenge. She wasn't going to back down,
either.

She tore the packet open with shaking fingers, and
thence resituated herself, fumbling for a moment before
rolling the latex down over his length. Then she moved
back into her previous position, struggling slightly to
find the angle, and then lowering herself down slowly,
biting her lip to keep from crying out as he stretched
her in new and unfamiliar ways, inch by tantalizing
inch.

There was no dramatic tearing pain, and she cred-
ited her years as a horsewoman with that, but it was
strange. New and different and not entirely pleasur-

able. But he was big, and she imagined that was difficult to get used to.

But then, as she seated herself fully onto him, a sensual thrill shot through her. Not just because of how it felt, but because the idea of getting used to him—to this—meant being with him…more.

She would have months with him. To do just this. To feel him deep inside her, to have him beneath her, naked and gorgeous. To explore his body, taste him, lick him wherever she wanted.

It made her feel powerful.

It made her feel free.

And then she began to ride him. She pressed her hands on his chest, her eyes meeting his as she rose up, and then went back down, as she explored that ancient rhythm, her body honed and fit from years of outdoor labor.

A ripple of pleasure worked its way through her body, that slight discomfort being replaced by a deep, intense satisfaction. And when her orgasm began to build inside her again, she knew what it was. She knew what to chase. She rolled her hips forward, seeking out that completion that she had already experienced twice before.

Then suddenly, she found their positions reversed, found herself on her back, Matías looming over her, dark and intense, his teeth gritted.

The air rushed from her body, and she felt…small. Fragile.

Completely out of control, as opposed to the way she had felt a moment before.

He captured her arms and lifted them up over her head, holding them tight with his hand, both wrists captured in his iron grip.

His thrusts were harder, setting a rhythm she could not anticipate or control. She was the one being written, and she had no experience of such a thing.

She also had no choice but to surrender to it.

She let her head fall back, and she allowed him to be her master.

The erotic thrill of such a thing shocked her. The joy in her helplessness something she had not anticipated.

She rocked against him, then wrapped her legs around his lean hips, moving along with his every thrust, meeting him each time.

And then he began to shake, then he began to tremble, and that mask of his, all that control, fell away and for one moment, one fleeting glance, she saw him as he was. Stripped completely bare of everything in its entirety as he shook and shuddered out his release.

But she only had a moment to watch, only a moment to enjoy before she gave herself up to her own pleasure, before she lost herself completely, clung to him as her internal muscles pulsed around him, as he shook in her arms and as she trembled in his. And when the storm passed, the only sound in the room was their labored breathing. It felt right. It felt like home. Like the wind through the olive groves. Familiar somehow, even though she had never experienced anything like it before.

Then he looked at her, like he might need her.

And it was no longer the pleasure in her body that commended her sole focus, but the pain in her heart.

She squeezed her eyes tightly shut and wished that it would go away.

CHAPTER ELEVEN

Matías watched Camilla sleep for a couple of hours before he went into the kitchen and rummaged around in the fridge for a tray of meat and cheese. He brought the charcuterie back into the bedroom and sat on the edge of the bed, waiting. She stirred, and then looked at him with sleepy eyes.

"Hello," he said, his voice roughened by the long hours spent in silence.

"Is it morning?" she asked, rolling onto her back, drawing her arm up above her head.

She was naked and making no move to cover herself. He didn't mind.

"Technically."

"It's still dark out," she said, pushing herself into a sitting position.

Her hair, artfully styled before he had taken her to bed, was now sticking straight up at the center, the golden crown she had been wearing discarded during their lovemaking. She looked like a beautiful, fallen fairy.

"Yes," he said, "it is. But I was hungry." He placed the food in front of her. "I thought you might be, too."

She eyed the cheese. "I suppose I am. But…"

"Don't worry about anything. We can stay here for

as long as we like tomorrow. Or today, as the case may be. There is nothing pressing for us to attend to. You should eat. Because I expect for you to build up your strength. Because I want you again."

He supposed he ought to feel guilt, perhaps. As he had defiled a virgin last night, something he had never done before, and he intended to do it again before the sun rose.

He did not feel guilt. It was blessedly absent. Possibly because of the color in her cheeks that spoke of her pleasure, or maybe because the sounds she had made as she had found her release still echoed in his ears. Whatever the reason, he felt surprisingly content, all things considered.

Considering that he would be getting married in a week's time. Considering that his original fiancée had been stolen and he disliked very much being manipulated in the way that he was, he felt very content indeed.

That could perhaps be because he had a warm and very willing woman in his bed. And he liked that very much indeed.

She drew her knees to her chest and picked up a piece of cheese, nibbling at it, and he watched the movements of her mouth, the very sensual slide of her tongue against the food. He wanted it against his skin again. But he would give her time.

"Tell me," he said, "about all of the plans that you have once we are finished here."

It would do him good to remember that there were plans for the end of all of this.

"My plans?" She swallowed the mouthful of cheese and looked at him quizzically. "Just…to go back to my *rancho*. To train my horses. I don't have any desire to compete. I would rather stay closer to home. But I should like to continue to train racehorses."

"That will put us in competition," he commented.

She tilted her head to the side. "I suppose it will. But then, our fathers always were."

"Yes. But I believe their relationship was a bit different."

Her cheeks turned a dusky rose color. "Perhaps."

"Do you have plans to expand the operation?"

She blinked. "I don't know. Right now I simply want to get back to what I know. It has been… It has been such a difficult few months. I can't even explain it. Or maybe I can. Just…feeling as though the rug was pulled out from under my life completely. As though I was left standing on nothing. Just falling, endlessly. My father died, and I have barely had a moment to grieve him properly. Because at the same time I lost my home. I lost my horses."

"And you did what you had to in order to keep them. To find them again."

She shrugged. "It was the only power I had. The only possible thing I could reclaim. There was nothing else. No way that I could get ownership of the ranch back on my own. No way that I could bring my father back from the dead. But I knew where you were. And I knew… I knew that you had the horses. I knew that you had Fuego. And I thought…if I could keep that connection maybe I could keep from going completely insane."

"You seem quite sane to me."

"That's up for debate, I suppose. Not very many women would chop off all of their hair on the spur of the moment and decide to try to get a job disguised as a boy."

"What made you think of that?" he asked. "It was quite inventive."

"I begged for a job. When your staff was there taking the horses away I begged to allow me to go with them. And the man who was leading Fuego away told me that you didn't hire women. So…it seemed the logical thing to do. At least, in my mind."

"I suppose there aren't very many people who would think to do that."

"Yes," she agreed. "Which is why it might be a stretch to call it *logical*."

"You're inventive. You're resourceful, and you're very brave." He pressed his thumb against her lower lip, looking at the longing in her eyes. It called to him. To a deep, empty place in his soul. "I know what it's like to feel alone, Camilla." Again, he found himself confessing to her. Only ever her. At first he had thought it was because she was unimportant. Because she wouldn't remain in his life, and so it didn't matter. But after what they'd shared, he could no longer pretend she didn't matter. "When my mother died the sense of isolation that followed was profound. I was the only one who knew that my father was responsible. No one else would believe me. My brother and I were never close, but that drove an even deeper wedge between us. We were just boys, but in many ways we had to become men far too soon."

"And you became a good man. While your brother…"

He swallowed hard. He thought of Diego as a child. All angry and defiant and impossible to talk to. He had been angry at him for a long time, because he'd imagined they'd shared the same upbringing, and that he'd had every chance to do the same with his life that Matías had. But Diego didn't know all of Matías's secrets. And it hit him then it was very likely he didn't know the whole story of Diego. "I don't know that he ever had a chance."

"But you did. And if you did, then I suppose he could have, as well."

He hesitated, suddenly not so certain of that. Suddenly not so sure of anything. He didn't like that. Didn't like relativism as a whole. He preferred things black-and-white. It was how he lived his life. "Sometimes I think people are put together differently," he said. "It is the best explanation I have."

"Perhaps you have more of your mother in you," she said softly.

"Perhaps," he said, the word rough, pulled from him.

"Is that the real reason you don't hire women?" she asked softly. "Is it because of your mother? Is it because you don't want women working on the *rancho*? Doing that kind of work?"

"My mother wasn't killed by a horse," he said. "She was killed by my father. The horse being spooked was his fault."

"Still." She placed her soft hand on his forearm. He felt something shift inside his chest, and he didn't like it. Didn't like it at all. The ways in which she rearranged him. Things inside him that he had so carefully placed where he wanted them. "I think that might be why."

"When I dream, it's all screaming. Horses and women."

The words sounded black and blank, and hopelessly pathetic. He didn't talk about this. Not to anyone. Not ever.

"Matías," she said softly, wrapping her arms around him, resting her cheek against his chest. "You had to be strong and good, so much more than anyone else, because you were the only one who could be. It's not fair."

She was trying to…comfort him. He could not remember the last time anyone had done that. If they ever had. Probably, his mother had done it, but he couldn't remember. All he remembered was the fighting. All he remembered was his mother hiding from his father. All he remembered was hiding from all of it.

"When Fuego kicked you…" Those words broke off, and he found himself unable to speak. His throat was tight. His lungs burned. He waited. Waited for the wave to pass. For the pressure to release. "It reminded me of when she died," he choked out. "Even if they don't mean to, they're large animals, and they can cause so much harm."

She stroked his arm as though he were a pet and not a man and he couldn't even muster up any anger over it. "It's amazing to me that you want to continue working with horses. That you want to keep the *rancho*. All things considered. I know why. At least, I know what you told me. About wanting to be the one that controls it. About wanting to redeem it all. But…no one would blame you if you decided you didn't want any of it."

That had been his intention in his twenties. His fortune elsewhere. Why he had left Spain and centered his business in London. But he had found that there was no getting away from his past. And that the farther he got away from his home, the farther away he went from the *rancho*, the more his dreams plagued him.

"That place has become a mission," he admitted. "Unfinished business, in many ways. Once it's all settled, I don't intend to spend too much time there."

"You're so good at it, though," she said, continuing to caress him with those lovely fingers. "I can't imagine you simply disappearing into a desk job. It isn't you."

"Maybe it is," he said, reaching down and putting his finger beneath her chin, tilting her face upward. "Perhaps I prefer this," he said, looking around the penthouse. "Perhaps I prefer evenings spent at galas to quiet evenings in rural libraries. Perhaps I prefer spending my days in glass and steel skyscrapers to dusty arenas."

"You don't." She said those words with such confidence that he wanted to laugh at her, except he could not because her dark eyes were so serious. So sincere. She reached up, grabbing hold of the hand that was beneath her chin, and drawing it down. She smoothed her thumb over his palm, her eyes never leaving his. "I can tell, because of your hands. You don't have the hands of a man content to work at a computer. Content to work at a desk. These calluses are thick, worn in from years of work. It's your heart. Right here. This is what you choose to do when you're not doing the thing you must do to increase your fortune. A man who does ranch work in a casual capacity is not going to have hands like this." Then she shocked him, placed his hand against her breast, a slow smile curving her lips, deep satisfaction etched into her expression. "You have just the kind of hands that I like."

"Tell me, then," he said, feeling driven to know the answer all of a sudden. "If I am the kind of man you like, then why didn't you do this with any of the other men who worked on your father's *rancho*? Why didn't you end up with them when you could have?"

"Because they weren't you. That was the missing piece. Rough hands were never going to be enough."

He was so aroused he could hardly think anymore. But before he took her again, he needed to know something. "Tell me," he said, "your dream. Your biggest dream."

When all of this was over and he set her free again, he was determined to see it done. The Alvarez *rancho* would be returned to her ownership, and he would be sure that her mother had no claim on it. Would be sure that it was entirely for Camilla.

He was going to give her Fuego, as well, in addition to the rest of the horses. He was determined on that score, too. Yes, the horse would have been an amazing asset for his own ranch, but he knew now that the animal had to go with Camilla. There was no other option.

But anything else, whatever else she desired, he was determined to ensure she had it. He would not be a man who left a woman broken. Not as his father had done.

He would ensure that whatever he had taken from Camilla tonight, he would restore it as best he could.

She looked blindsided by that question, confused. "Just the *rancho*," she insisted.

"That is something you already had. Is there anything more you want? Anything?"

She looked down. "No. I can't think of anything else. All I want is my normal life back. I couldn't... I couldn't begin to want anything else."

He had a feeling that she was lying, but whether to him or to herself he didn't know. And he was past the point of talking. Because her skin was soft and sweet beneath his touch, because her nipple had grown hard beneath his palm and his own body was growing hard in response.

He took the plate of meat and cheese and set it aside

and pulled Camilla into his arms. "Whatever you want," he said, "I will see that it is yours. You have my word."

The word of a Navarro had never meant much. But Matías was determined to change that.

He was determined to change it for her.

CHAPTER TWELVE

THE DAY OF the wedding began like any other day, which surprised Camilla to a degree, as the entire thing loomed large in her mind. There was no reason to be nervous, and she knew that. She and Matías had been over this, and over it and over it. How it would all go, how long it was going to last.

It was not going to be a terribly formal affair.

She had been presented with a small selection of gowns earlier in the week, and she had chosen one that best suited the outdoor event.

She had a feeling it was very different to the dress that Liliana would have selected, but it was right for her. Simple, white and with clean, elegant lines.

Though, as Matías had pointed out, a bit wickedly— while holding her arms above her head, his hips locked against hers as his weight pressed her down into the mattress—she was no longer a virgin, and therefore, did not have to wear white.

She had scoffed at him and said that the symbolism of the white dress had long since gone out of fashion.

And then he had kissed her and done something with his tongue that had made it impossible to think. And after she'd had to concede—to herself—there was no point in pretending that she was anything near a virgin now. One week spent in his bed and he had introduced her to a great many sensual delights.

Just thinking about that made her face hot. But not from embarrassment. Nothing the two of them did together embarrassed her. And she wasn't anywhere near finished with him.

She was already weaving fantasies about how they might continue this once their *arrangement* was finished.

Their ranches were only a few hours apart. It would be possible for them to continue seeing one another while carrying on separate lives. He could see to his business, and then when he had the chance he could come and visit her. They could sleep together. She could show him the house that she loved so much. Take him out back to the gardens, to the fountains, show him all the beautiful mosaics there. Take him on a ride through the trees, to the base of the mountains.

These were foolish fantasies, and she'd never in her life been prone to such things. But then she'd never wanted a man before. Had never been so…consumed— obsessed even—with another person. His body. His mind. His soul.

They had so much in common.

Well, except for the whole playboy international billionaire thing. But his soul. His soul matched hers in so many ways. Fiercely independent. Wanting to make his own way.

Except, much more than she, Matías was driven by demons from his past. She knew it, even if she couldn't understand them all.

At night he slept fitfully. And she stayed by his side, her hand on his chest. Sometimes she stayed awake and simply watched him, as if somehow holding vigil beside him as he wrestled with his past pain even in his dreams, she could provide some kind of support.

He made her *want*.

It was an endless well of want, not one that simply began and ended in the bedroom, but one that seemed to go on and on. In the evenings, when she was sated in the physical sense, there was still something else that lingered. Something that gnawed at her, nagged at her. Something that tugged at her heart and made her physically ache.

She did her best to ignore it, because she felt that only insanity sat at the end of that path.

But now it was time for the wedding. And somehow, she had expected the sky to fall before then. But it had not. Instead, when she had woken early that morning, Matías was already gone. Probably off doing chores on the *rancho*, and there was nothing unusual about that, though often they woke together.

But then she set about to readying herself for the event. The wedding would take place in the late afternoon, followed by a dinner and dancing. Mostly, people from the village had been invited. Distant relatives. And of course, Matías's grandfather would be making the trip, even though his health made it very difficult.

That made Camilla feel as though a weight was settled on her chest. Matías's family was a source of such pain to him, she was angry that his grandfather was intruding on their day. Except, the day would not exist if not for his grandfather. Truly, he was the cause of it. It was more. He was the reason they were doing this.

And she knew that. Truly she did. But sometimes, that twinge around her heart made it difficult to fully internalize. To fully believe. Because it felt like more. Even though it shouldn't, it did.

There were things about it that felt so very real. So real they hurt.

She looked at her reflection in the mirror, now more used to this glossier version of herself.

She was wearing a veil that reached the ground, blended together with the soft, gauzy fabric of her dress. Her lipstick was dark, drawing attention to her mouth, matching the dramatic winged eyeliner that the stylist had put together for her.

She felt beautiful. But it had nothing to do with the makeup. Nothing to do with the dress. And everything to do with the past week spent in Matías's arms.

He never made her feel like he wished she were another woman.

She had worried for a time that he would prefer Liliana. Had worried that he was fantasizing about the petite blonde while they were in bed together. But it become clear quickly that he had a deep appreciation for her athletic body. And all the things she could do with it. She might be inexperienced, but she was physically able, and he took great advantage of that.

Much to both of their delight.

That made her smile. Smile as Maria, the housekeeper, handed her the simple, deep crimson bouquet. Continued smiling as she walked down the stairs of the house and into the foyer.

"Everything is set up outside," the older woman said. "And they will be ready for you in a moment. I will signal you when it is time."

She couldn't believe the moment had arrived. And yet, it seemed like an entire lifetime in the making. As if all of this, her relationship with Matías, had been destined to be from the beginning.

This wasn't real. It wasn't. What was real had been

that first time they had made love. That was Matías and Camilla.

This was for the audience. This was for his grandfather. And she had to remember that. Had to try to find the practical woman she was, buried underneath the makeup. Beneath the bridal gown that made all this feel like a beautiful waking dream when she knew full well it was a simple business transaction.

Maria rushed outside and Camilla took a deep breath, pressing her hands against her stomach.

"Well," came a voice from behind her. "Don't you make a radiant bride."

She turned, and her heart hit her sternum hard. For the man standing in front of her was not Matías. He was tall, darkly handsome and resembled her fiancée just enough that she knew exactly who he was.

He possessed the same sort of magnetism, the same height and breadth. But there was something menacing about him. Something that went beyond dangerous. Something deadly.

"Diego, I presume," she said.

"You make this sound very like an overdramatic soap opera," he drawled, moving closer to her. "I must say, I am impressed with my brother's resourcefulness. Often, his scruples prevent him from claiming certain victories. I myself have never understood why he'd limit himself the way he does."

"I'm not entirely sure what you're talking about," she said. "Matías is my lover. He has been. Liliana's defection was only a good thing for us."

She did not know where she was drawing the strength to come at him like this. Except, it was the story that she and Matías had agreed on, a distortion of the truth to show the world why he was choosing to marry her, and it was not his day to wed beautiful, pale Liliana.

Because if it was, her heart would have broken into a million pieces and shattered on the ground.

She would rather this—this temporary union that might turn to nothing in the end—than watch him marry another woman. A marriage he had meant to be forever, leaving no chance for them to have anything more later on.

"It is a very nice story," Diego said. "But I already read it in the paper. You know, my brother fancies himself a good man, but he is not so different from me. He simply draws lines around moral dilemmas as he sees fit. And I have never seen the point of doing so. He decides that certain actions are *right*, and certain actions are *wrong*. He has decided that his motivation for inheriting the *rancho* is higher than mine, and therefore, he must win at this game. I require no motivation of myself beyond my need to win. To be satisfied. I don't need to pretend I am being *good*."

"Is that why you took Liliana?"

A smile curved one side of his mouth upward. "She was simply a means to an end. Like everything else."

"Did she go with you of her own free will? Or did you kidnap her?"

He chuckled. "Oh, I kidnapped her. But she was convinced quickly enough to marry me. I just had to have her throw out that lie to Matías so he wouldn't come searching for her. He's not very trusting. He believed so quickly that she would betray him. It's a character flaw, for sure. If I were you, I would watch out for that later on. If he were to walk in now, I imagine he would have a lot of follow-up questions for you. Particularly if he were to walk in when you were in my embrace."

Diego took another step toward her, and Camilla took a step away. "Don't come anywhere near me," she said. "You're a villain."

He laughed. "To you. But a villain is his own hero. I read that somewhere once. I quite like it. Although, I am not overly concerned with being either. I'm simply concerned with winning."

"Well, Matías and I are getting married today. So you're not going to win."

"Am I not? Because I will get my share of the family fortune. If I choose to press the issue with my lawyer, I will probably end up with a stake in my brother's company." That dark gaze turned cruel. "And he has had to settle for second best when it comes to wives. Yes, I think my victory, while not total, was handily enough done."

The door to the house opened again, and Maria waved her on. "It is time," she said.

"I had better go take my place in the audience, then," Diego said. "But rest assured and remember this. My brother might talk about being good. He might talk about doing the right thing, and in the end he might do the right thing by you, whatever that means. If it looks like a permanent marriage, or an attempt at commitment. But he will not love you. That is something the men in our family are incapable of."

Then he left her standing there, feeling diminished. Her heart feeling torn in two. He had not said anything she hadn't already thought to be true. Hadn't dropped any grand revelations on her. And still, he had accomplished everything he had set out to do. He had sent her out into the blinding sunlight on shaking legs. Had planted doubts inside her when before she had been quite content walking toward that while knowing that in the end, this would end as nothing.

But now Diego's words were swirling inside her, painful, horrendous. And she realized it was reality. He had made it impossible to pretend that this was going to end as a fairy tale. He had made it impossible for her to cling to that last shred of fantasy, which she had to admit to herself as she made her way toward the site of the wedding, she had been doing.

But then she came to the head of the aisle, and all the guests stood and turned, and she saw Matías standing there, dark, handsome and certain.

So very like his brother, and yet not.

And she realized that none of it mattered. Because there was only one choice to make. There was only one direction she was going to walk.

Toward Matías. No matter what.

CHAPTER THIRTEEN

IT HAD BEEN shocking to see his brother and Liliana in the crowd at the wedding.

Matías had a feeling that *shock* had been Diego's intent.

Matías had made it his mission to keep his older brother away from Camilla through the entirety of the reception, and during the farewells that evening.

Though he had a feeling that if Diego had intended to approach her at any point, he would have done so. But he had not, which was actually no less unsettling.

Liliana, for her part, had looked beautiful, but pale. Drawn.

Her face adorned with no makeup, as she had often done, her long hair left loose, her curves highlighted by the flowing, lavender gown that she was wearing.

Diego never took his hands off her, his dark eyes sharp every time he looked at her.

It was a strange dynamic, and one that surprised Matías. Because he had imagined his brother would care nothing at all for his new wife. Had imagined that he had simply seduced her away from Matías in order to win at this ridiculous game they were playing to gain their grandfather's possessions. But there was something there. Something dark and tense. He commented as much when he and Camilla were finally alone. Headed back to his penthouse in Barcelona for their wedding night.

"She loves him," Camilla said softly.

"What the hell are you talking about?" Matías asked. "Don't you think that by now she has seen what manner of man he is?"

"Unfortunately, I think she knew from the beginning. I... I had a conversation with Diego before the wedding," she said, twisting her hands together.

"Were you going to tell me if I had not brought him up?"

"Possibly not. The whole thing made me nervous. He was clearly trying to intimidate me. Trying to scare me away. But he has never met me. So he did not know that was a losing proposition."

"I almost feel sorry for him," Matías said. "What did he say to you?"

"He confirmed that he *did* kidnap Liliana. Their marriage, however, is legal, so whatever happened after that, she consented to it. He talked her into it, he says. I imagine there was blackmail involved. But... I see the way she looks at him. I spent a good portion of the ceremony looking. I don't think she wants to be rescued," Camilla said softly. "Though I'm not entirely certain she's happy."

"How could she be happy with a sociopath? How could she love him?"

"Oftentimes these things don't make sense," Camilla said, her voice hard. "And why do you care? Just for her happiness? Or are you wishing that you had married her today?"

Frustration roared through him and he growled, pinning Camilla up against the wall in the penthouse. "I don't give a damn about Liliana. At least, not beyond her safety. Of course I don't want my brother holding her against her will, but as she traveled with him, and obviously married him, and has not fled him, I think it's safe to say that's not what's happening. I don't want her. I want you."

"Well, you seem awfully concerned about her."

"And you seem jealous," he said, taking a step back.

"I *am*," she confirmed.

He looked at his wife, standing there in the flowing white gown. His *wife*. She was his. Legally. A binding agreement. And suddenly, he wanted, more than anything, to hold her to that. To hold her to him. Wanted to do what Diego had done. To take her away, to hold her captive. To make her his, however that looked, whatever that might mean. Suddenly, being right, being good, didn't seem half so important as it had before.

Only having her.

And he could see just how thin that line that separated himself from Diego, Diego from his father, and his father from their grandfather, really was.

It was in his DNA, whether he wanted it to be or not.

"I married *you*," he said, his voice hard.

"Yes," she hissed. "And the inescapable truth is that if Liliana had been available you would have married her."

"Why do you want a fight?" he asked, moving nearer to her, closing the distance between them and wrapping his arm around her waist. "I can think of much better uses of our time."

He consumed her then, capturing her mouth with his own and pouring all of his frustrations, all of the intense, crushing feelings in his chest, out onto her. His pulse was pounding angrily, mirroring the heat and fire moving through his veins, the hardness, the desire coursing through his groin.

He wanted her, but that was not all.

No, it was not all. He was not a stranger to sexual desire, but this was entirely foreign to him. This was sexual desire mingled with something else. A need so fierce, so ferocious, that he thought it might destroy them both.

If he acted on it, certainly they would both go up completely in the conflagration. But if he did not act on it, he didn't think he would survive it.

He was all out of control. That control that he prided himself on, that he was so convinced made him a good man. A better man than his brother, better man than his father.

All of his certainty was gone. Every last bit. All that remained was need. Need for Camilla, for his wife. His bride. The woman he had spoken vows to, in front of his townspeople, in front of his grandfather.

They might have an understanding. They might have an agreement that was supposed to make things clear, that was supposed to make them easy, but right now it felt anything but.

Again, in this moment, they were nothing more than Camilla and Matías. The world outside them didn't exist.

Here, in his penthouse, this place that was his and his alone, she belonged to him only. Here, he had his bride on his wedding night. And whatever the future held for them, whatever the reasons for this marriage, he intended to claim this night for them. For himself.

Suddenly, he could wait no longer, his patience growing thin. He grabbed hold of the flimsy fabric of the bodice of her dress and tore it wide, letting the material fall loose around her waist.

She sucked in a shocked breath. "That was a beautiful dress," she said, faintly admonishing, but she did not pull away from him, neither did she look as scandalized as she was attempting to sound.

No, her eyes were dark, filled with desire. He could see that she was as tested for control as he was. That she was as hungry for this as he was.

That he was not alone in his desire.

And that only made the monster inside him growl even louder.

"Yes," he agreed. "It was a pretty dress. But your body, *mi tesoro*, is the most beautiful prize of all. Anything that gets in the way of that... I'm afraid I cannot allow it to be."

As if to prove his point he grabbed hold of the lacy bra that covered her breasts, concealed them from his view, and he tore it away from her body, as well, leaving those high, perfect breasts exposed to him.

He lowered his head, taking one perfect nipple between his lips and sucking hard. He was starving for her. And it did not matter that he had been with her every night that week. It did not matter that he had sated himself on her whenever he desired since that first night he'd had her. It was as if it had been years. As if he had been kept from her.

Perhaps it was simply that she was his wife now. No matter that neither of them intended for it to be permanent. Perhaps it had changed things somehow. Made him more possessive. Made all of this somehow more.

It seemed impossible, and yet, with all that heat and fire pounding through his body, he wondered. If somehow, she truly had become part of his flesh as they had spoken those words to one another at that altar. If somehow, there was a sacred bond here that could not be manipulated, that could not be fooled.

He dismissed those thoughts as he ripped the dress the rest of the way from her body, and took her panties with it, leaving her beautiful, golden form entirely exposed to him.

He examined those slim, perfect curves, her taut, toned belly, her womanly hips and shapely thighs. That glorious thatch of dark curls between them.

She was beautiful. A work of art. And she was his. All his.

He was still fully dressed, still wearing the suit he had worn to the wedding, and he quite liked that. This woman, completely naked before him while he remained fully clothed. It made him feel powerful. Gave him some semblance of control in the moment.

And it also made him hungry for more. To expose her to an even greater degree, to exert that power.

To do something to deal with that yawning, endless ache in his chest, and the rest of his body.

"You are mine," he said, words coming out on a growl. He picked her up, her lithe form soft and warm in his arms. "You are mine, and no other man's. Is that clear?"

"Yes," she said, the word hushed. For the moment at least, he seemed to have tamed her. He was not sure how to feel about that.

"And if my brother were to come in trying to carry you off, I would chase him to the ends of the earth before I let him keep you. I hope that is clear." He gripped her chin, holding her face steady, looking into her eyes. "I would chase that bastard to hell to bring you back to me. Do you understand? He would not be allowed to lay one finger on you, and if he did, it would be the last thing he did. He would lose that hand, and then he would lose everything else dear to him. Everything."

Honesty. Always with her it was that damned, unguarded honesty and he did not possess the strength to fight it on any level. Not now.

She shivered in his arms, and he wondered if perhaps he had gone too far, and then he decided he didn't care. Not at all. Not in the least.

If he was possessive, then so be it. If he was untamed, then so be it. If he was no better than any of the other men in his family, then he supposed he would have to accept that, not fight it. Not anymore. Not with her.

It simply was.

Suddenly, he understood the nature of that violence that coursed through Diego's veins. He understood that rage in his father. Because he felt it now all the same. It wasn't anger. It was something different. It was big. And it was hot, and it was something that owned him, body and soul. A possessiveness that he could not fight.

Possessiveness he *would* not fight, here and now.

He set her down on his couch, positioning her toward the back of it as he knelt on the cushions, spreading her thighs wide. And then he examined her femininity, all of that gleaming beauty, and the pearl that was the center of all her pleasure. "Beautiful," he growled, stroking his fingertips over her sensitive and responsive flesh. "And all for me."

"I am not the one who was supposed to marry someone else today," she panted. "I am not the one who deserves to be caught up in such a fit of possessiveness."

He tightened his hold on her thighs. "This is not about what either of us *deserves*," he said, his voice rough. "This is about what *is*. About what I'm going to take. I will have all of you, my bride. I hope you understand that."

"And you need to know, my husband," she returned, "that it is understood that if there is any doubt in your mind as to what you would do if Liliana came in here tonight and said that she wished to leave Diego, that you will keep your hands off me, that you will stand up and walk away from me now. Because you are not the only one who is possessive."

"If she came in here, what would you do?" he asked.

"I would fight her for you," she returned, that stubborn chin tilting upward. "Because I fight for what's mine. You know that I do. If I have to cut my hair off and change my identity, I will do it. But I fight for what's mine."

If she had been another woman it might have been tempting to be offended to be compared to her horses, to have that same sort of possessiveness given over to him. But it was not another woman. It was Camilla. And knowing the fierce possessiveness with which she regarded those animals, he did not think he deserved more. But rather, he suspected he deserved a lot less.

"And if she were to come in here," he said, "I would scarcely notice, because she is not the woman that I want. You are the woman that I want."

Understanding that when he said that, he knew there was a cost to it. Because if things had gone as planned, he would have full ownership over the Navarro family estate. If Diego had not taken Liliana, then all of it would be his. He would be in the clear.

But then he would not have Camilla.

Somewhere in the depths of his mind he was reminded of words that felt similar. A Bible story. A king offering his queen whatever she desired, even if it was half of his kingdom. And he realized then that if given the choice now, that was the trade he would make. It was the trade that had been made through no choice of his own, but it was what he would do if the need presented itself. If the choice were on offer again.

Half of his kingdom. With no hesitation.

"I have no desire for anyone but you," he reiterated, leaning forward, drawing his tongue across that sensitive bundle of nerves, wringing from her as much pleasure as possible with his lips, his tongue, his fingers. Working her body until she was boneless, breathless and spent, until the last vestiges of her release began to dissipate.

Then he picked up her boneless body and carried her into his bedroom.

"Mine," he growled, pressing a kiss to her lips. "My wife."

He pressed her down into the mattress, settling between her thighs. Typically, Camilla preferred to be the one doing the writhing. At least, that was how she preferred to begin their encounters. But not tonight. Tonight the possession was his. Tonight he was in control. Utterly and completely.

She also enjoyed pleasuring him, something that he was not averse to. Usually.

But again, tonight, he would not allow that. Tonight he would not surrender that to her. Tonight he would extract all of the control, all of the pleasure from her that he could.

He slid his hand beneath her hips, cupped her soft, perfect rear and lifted her up off the bed, angling her just so, so that he could thrust into the hilt.

He growled, realizing a moment later that he was bare, that he had not put a condom on. He was tempted, so tempted to press that. To keep doing this with nothing between their bodies. To spill himself inside her when he found his release, and damn the consequences.

It was that same, feral part of him that wanted to possess her completely.

But he would not. He would not do that to her. She wanted her freedom when all this was over. And it was that, that knowledge, that slowed his hand. That helped him hold on to his sanity. And only that.

"I must protect you," he said thickly, withdrawing from her body and making his way to the nightstand, grabbing a condom and sheathing himself quickly. "I'm sorry."

He thrust back into her, not bothering to clarify whether or not he was sorry he had entered her without protection in the first place, or whether he was just sorry that he had to get it.

He wasn't sure which thing made him sorrier, frankly.

Likely that he had to get a condom and he would rather feel her, all that silky heat, surrounding him.

He gritted his teeth, trying to maintain his control as he rocked his hips backward, then thrust home, pleasure almost blinding him as he did so.

He closed his eyes tight, sparks bursting behind them as he lost himself completely inside her.

There had never been anyone like this. There had never been anything like this.

She didn't just make him feel pleasure, she made him feel pain. Didn't simply satisfy him, she opened up on the heels of that satisfaction. Made him want in ways he hadn't expected to ever want before.

The build of his release was almost violent, was deadly, far too intense. And when it captured him, it didn't just send a burst of pleasure through him, it wrenched his chest open. He gritted his teeth, growling as his orgasm rocked him, pressing his forehead to hers and kissing her, deeply, fiercely, begging her, in Spanish and in English, to come along with him. It was the first time he had not ensured that she was satisfied more than once before he found his own release, but he had not had the control tonight. He had not possessed that kind of restraint.

He rolled his hips, grinding himself against her, and then finally, she gave him her pleasure. She pulsed around him, squeezing his arousal, pulling a few more spasms of pleasure from him as her own orgasm rocked her.

And when it was done, she clung to his shoulders, shaking, crying.

Her tears hit him with all the violence of a closed fist. Because his Camilla did not cry. She was strong, and she was lovely. That warrior goddess of his fantasies. She was weeping now, weeping like a child, because of something he had done.

"Camilla," he said, gripping her face, holding it steady, looking into those luminous dark eyes, gazing at her tearstained face. "Have I hurt you? What have I done?"

She shook her head. "Nothing," she said. "You haven't hurt me at all."

"Why are you crying?"

She sobbed, her entire body shaking. "Because," she said. "You didn't hurt me, you bastard. You made me fall in love with you."

"What?" he asked, drawing back.

"I'm in love with you, Matías. Oh, how I love you."

CHAPTER FOURTEEN

Camilla knew that she had made a grave mistake, and yet, she wouldn't go back and change it even if she could. She couldn't lie to Matías, not anymore. The relationship had started out a lie, and she would be damned if it continued one. He had asked her what she wanted. Not that long ago, he had demanded to know. Well, now he would know. She wanted him. She wanted this. Forever. No matter the cost.

"I love you," she repeated. "I didn't mean to. I wasn't supposed to. I was supposed to love the *rancho*, the horses and nothing more. I was supposed to want nothing beyond that. Nothing bigger than that life. Because that life was everything. At least, that life was everything to my father. And I love it, Matías, don't get me wrong. If I didn't, I never would have put myself at such a risk to come and work for you. But it's not everything. Not now. You are."

"This cannot be, Camilla," he said, his voice rough. "You cannot love me."

"I have never asked your permission to do anything, Matías. I'm hardly going to ask your permission for this. I don't need it. I don't want to. It just… It is." She had never been so certain of anything in her entire life.

Never been so certain of anything more than she was certain of this burning, deep conviction in her soul.

She would risk anything for this. For him. There was no pride in hiding away and denying feelings. She had too much experience watching someone else fall into that trap. Into that lie. That was her father's life. Shrinking everything down so that he could never be heard.

Wanting nothing beyond what he had in front of him. Nothing more than the *rancho*.

And she supposed her father had found a way to be happy in that. They'd had a good life. And he had never longed for the wife who wouldn't stay with him.

But Camilla did not want that life. She did not want a life reduced in order to avoid pain. She did not want a life where she could have Matías, where he was alive, where he was within reach, if she would only go after him.

She would exhaust every avenue before she accepted that.

She had always seen her mother as flighty. As unfeeling. Running continually, unavailable to her father.

But now she wondered. She wondered if Cesar Alvarez had ever gone after his wife, or if he had simply let her leave.

If he had simply assumed that love was beyond their reach.

Camilla was not going to do that. Not with Matías. It was too important. He was too important.

"I love you," she repeated. "I didn't know that I wanted this. I didn't know that I wanted more than a life on the *rancho*. But I do. You asked me once, Matías, what I needed to be happy. And I have decided that I need you."

"You little fool," he said, the words almost despairing, as much as they were enraged. "You could have had a life that made you happy, if you had not decided that you wanted me in it."

"Why can't we be together? You were going to have a wife. You were going to have Liliana. You had committed to that. So why can't you have me?"

"Because I have seen where it ends," he said, exploding now. "It ends in brokenness. It ends in despair. For everyone involved. And I will not be part of that."

"Why wouldn't it have ended in despair with Liliana?"

"Because I—" He cut those words off.

"Because you felt nothing for her. But you feel *something* for me. Admit it. You care for me, Matías, and if it isn't love, it could be someday."

"I will admit no such thing," he said. "This is not love. This is an abomination. It is a lack of control, a lack of control that I swore to myself I would never experience. And here I am, at the very end of everything, because of you. Liliana would have been safe because she didn't challenge me. Because she didn't make me feel so much like I might understand the man that my father was."

"Do you honestly think you would hurt me? You have never once threatened me. Ever. You have never demonstrated any such tendencies, and I'm not going to believe now that that's the reason that you can't be with me."

"There is a thin line between love and hate. Between passion and destruction. And I never appreciated that fully until tonight. Until I could not control myself with you. Until I had to fight every last one of my impulses to keep from going and killing Diego, not because he was standing there with Liliana, but because he was within reach of you. Knowing that he went and spoke to you tonight…that he was alone with you… I don't know myself when I'm with you, Camilla, and if I can't control myself… I fear that is a man neither of us wants to know."

"You think you're going to break me?"

"I know it's possible."

"It's not. It isn't."

He advanced on her, then reached out, pressing his palm against her throat, beneath her chin. She lifted her fingers to his, curving her fingers around his knuckles, forcing his hold tight.

"You think that I should be afraid of you?" she asked. "You think that you might harm me? Do you see how I trust you?"

He growled, tightening his hold on her and pushing her back against the wall, something in his gaze sharp, desperate. "You test me, because you don't know better."

He released his hold and turned away from her, walking away. "There are ways to break people that have nothing to do with the physical body. You can break them in a thousand different ways, and believe me, Camilla, I have seen it. My father killed my mother that day, but he broke her long before. He broke her by denying her the one thing that she wanted. His love. It's the way that he tried to break all of us." He let out a long breath. "In a home like that, you have two options in the end. You either decide that you don't need love, or you die from the lack of it. I learned to live without, and I can't ask you to do the same."

"You think it would kill me?"

"Not physically."

"You think you would make me that miserable?" she implored.

"I know it," he bit out.

"We have months to work this out," she said. "This doesn't have to be the end. We can figure out what will work between us. I know that we can."

"No," he said, his tone bleak.

"Yes," she insisted. "I love you, but I'm not asking you for anything in return. I'm asking that you try. Let's try. The two of us. We can make something better, you and I. Better than what we had. Than what we saw. I'm not my mother. But I'm not my father, either. I'm not going to allow the one that I've said was you, the one that I have decided that I love, to walk away from me without a fight. I will be damned if I do, Matías. You're mine, and I'm not going down without a fight. You're right. I'm not Liliana. I will fight for you. Perhaps that's why I scare you. Because you know that she would've let you hide away. That she would never have demanded your love. But I am. I'll work for it. You don't have to give it now. But I will win it someday."

"No," he said again. "This is the end."

"It can't be. Matías, you know that it can't be, because if it is then Diego will get that stake in your company. And you won't get the *rancho* at all."

"It is the end." He picked up his phone, and she just watched, in shock as he dialed. "Grandfather," he said, his tone almost casual, as if he wasn't calling the old man past midnight. "I regret to inform you that my marriage is not going to work out. Camilla and I are going to seek an annulment. On the basis of fraud. I lied to her, you see. I led her to believe that our relationship was real, when it was not. It never was." His horrible, blank gaze was rested on her as he spoke those words. And somewhere, down deep, she knew that he was only doing this to harm her. To make her leave him be. To make her walk away. But knowing that didn't make it less painful. "Yes, I am aware of what that means," he said. "I'm aware that it means I'm forfeiting all that could be mine to Diego. I'm aware that it means I'm walking away from the inheritance. I only ask for one thing. I want the horses that were purchased from Cesar Alvarez. They are assets of the *rancho*, but I wish to return them to Camilla for her trouble. Otherwise, I will return to running my business, and Diego will have control of the Navarro assets. Whatever that might entail."

There was a pause. And then Matías nodded once definitively. "Then we have a deal."

He hung up. "The horses are yours," he said, his tone completely void of emotion. "The *rancho* will be Diego's."

"No," she said, crumbling inside. He was giving all of this up rather than being with her. All of it. He was committing an extreme act to get away from her, and if anything could possibly speak more to the fact that he didn't love her, that he wanted to escape her, she didn't know what it could be.

She had not expected this. Of all the things she had expected, it had not been this.

"It was never my intention to hurt you," he said. "I thought that I made it very clear what was to happen between the two of us. But obviously, I did not make it clear enough. We will not work. This will not work. I will return you to your family *rancho*. All of your assets should be returned to you. And then we can go on as though this never happened. As though we never met."

He began to get dressed, walking away from her, moving to the front of the apartment. She stood, frozen, numb, watching him prepare to go. "That's it? You're leaving tonight?"

"Yes," he said. "I'm going to go deal with a few business matters, the first of which being the restoration of your *rancho* to your ownership. You will not have to see me again."

"But what if I want to?" The question was small, and there truly was no pride at all left in it. There was none left in her entire being.

"It does not matter what you want," he said. "This is what must be."

And then Matías Navarro walked out of the penthouse, and out of her life.

Camilla Alvarez was certain she had experienced the lowest moment anyone possibly could. The death of her father, followed by the loss of the ranch, the loss of the horses.

But she had been wrong.

The most painful loss of all was the loss of her heart.

Her heart that had just told her she would never see him again.

And sadly, she believed it.

Matías had gotten on a plane to London directly after leaving Camilla in the penthouse. He had worked at a punishing pace for days, completely unnecessarily from his office there. He had not needed to go there. He had not needed to leave the country at all, not to deal with transferring ownership of a ranch back in Spain. But this was not about business. It was about needing to get distance between himself and the woman who had bewitched him in great and terrible ways.

He had never been for her. Ever. He had never meant to mean something to her. In fact, he had imagined she would be the last woman on earth who would fall in love with him.

Those words echoed in his mind. She had fallen in love with him.

How many times had he told her that he did not hire women because they only fell in love with him?

How many women had said they loved him in the past? Countless. But it had been nothing like this.

When he'd sent them away they had pouted. They had cajoled. They had been annoyed. But they had not been wounded.

Camilla had been *wounded*.

She loved him. She truly did. She might have been the only person in all the world who ever had. He had sent her away.

There'd been no other choice. Not really.

If he had kept her, he would only break her. It had hit him when he'd realized that he...that he understood his father. His brother. That the unhinged, uncontrollable things in them he'd always despised lived inside him, too.

Control was everything. A lack of it was destructive. And love was...it was a force that couldn't be tamed. It was a hurricane.

That was what love was. Being broken apart.

He swallowed hard. Then he stood from his desk and made his way over to the sideboard, grabbing a bottle of whiskey and pouring himself a generous tumbler full before knocking it back.

Love was pain. And nothing more.

He had never intended to revisit this kind of pain on himself. Not again.

He shook his head and looked around the pristine office space. This was his. And perhaps, Diego would end up with a small amount of shares in the company. That would irritate him, but it would hardly give his brother any control. Of course, anything Diego touched had a tendency to get turned into fire and brimstone.

But then, so be it.

He had that thought before he had entered her body for the last time, that he would give her anything, even half of his kingdom.

Apparently, he was not averse to giving away the entire thing.

He still couldn't believe he had done it. That he had cut ties with her quite so definitively. That he had made such a bold statement to his grandfather.

That he had given it all away.

It was late, and he did not expect it when his secretary called into his office phone line.

"Someone is here to see you, Mr. Navarro," she said in her cut-glass English accent.

Penelope was at home, not in the office, but if somebody wanted to be let in, the call still went to her even after hours, and she could control entry into the office building from her computer.

"Who is it?" he asked.

"He says he's your brother."

Matías swore. Of course. He should have known that he couldn't avoid that snake for long. He would know by now that he had won. And he would want to gloat.

"Let him in."

Matías stood from his desk again and poured another measure of alcohol. By the time Diego walked in he was standing there with two glasses in his hand and a smile on his lips.

"You would only smile when offering me a drink if it was poisoned," Diego said, producing a flask from inside his jacket. "I'm good."

His brother was smiling, but Matías could see that

something had begun to fray around the edges of his personal brand of dark charm.

"To what do I owe the displeasure?"

"I heard that you had forfeited our little game," Diego said.

"Because it quit being a game to me."

"Oh, I see. So it was still a game when I stole Liliana right out of her bedroom, but it's not a game now. Fascinating."

"Liliana said that she wanted to be with you," Matías pointed out. "I was hardly going to rescue a woman who didn't wish to be rescued."

"Yes," Diego said. "She did tell you that. Because I'm blackmailing her. Her father is not the upstanding citizen that he appears to be, and Liliana was quite shocked to find out the Hart family name was not built on the pristine foundation she had once thought. A tragedy all around."

"Not for you, though."

"Indeed," Diego said. "I have met very few tragedies that I didn't want to exploit. And this was no different. However," he said. "I think it is time we finish this."

"I agree," Matías said. "And you've won."

"No," Diego said. "*Abuelo* has won. At least, if we allow him to." His brother rubbed his chin thoughtfully then took a drink from his flask. "So, you wish to discontinue this, to call your marriage a sham and be done with it. I wish to do the same."

Matías could only stare at his brother. Shocked at the words he'd just spoken. "Why?"

"I suspect for the same reasons you do," Diego said, taking a drink from his flask. "The game got away from you, didn't it?"

"Has it gotten away from you?"

"Liliana Hart," Diego said, "was supposed to be the simplest and softest of targets. I have watched her for years while doing business with her father. Sheltered. Meek, or so I thought. She is such an innocent, Matías. You have no idea. At least, she was."

Matías could scarcely believe what he was hearing. Because by all accounts it appeared that perhaps his brother—his brother he would have said had no heart at all—had fallen in love.

And if he knew Diego at all, he also knew that his brother would not be able to accept it.

It was a strange thing, imagining that such a soft, pale creature would appeal to Diego. But then he supposed that stood to reason as much as anything else in this messed up world.

As much as the ways in which Camilla had destroyed him from the inside out.

"So, neither of us play?" Matías asked. "That's what you're proposing?"

"Yes," Diego responded. "I already called Grandfather and told him that Liliana was divorcing me."

"Is she?"

"I have already put her on a plane back to America. Along with all of the evidence of her father's misdeeds so that she has no fear I will use it against her."

"We are in a similar place, then. As I have sent Camilla away. Back to her family *rancho* and have just finished procuring documents for her to sign that will restore her ownership."

Diego laughed darkly, then he reached out and grabbed hold of the whiskey tumbler in Matías's hand. He took a drink, quick and decisive.

"I thought you were afraid that was poisoned," he pointed out.

"At this point, I feel it would be all the same either way."

Matías shrugged and took a sip of his own whiskey. "You may not be wrong."

"I have always found it astoundingly simple to take what I want," Diego said, looking merely confused. "Why was it not with her?"

"You're not going to like my conclusion."

"Oh, probably not."

"Love." The moment he said it he knew it was true. But not about Diego. About himself.

Matías loved Camilla. And the real issue wasn't so much that he was afraid he might break her, but that she might break him. That she might destroy him, utterly and completely.

"I've already tried love," Diego said. "Against my better judgment."

He was speaking of his first wife, Matías knew. "It ended badly."

"Yes," Diego said slowly, "though not in the way that people think."

"I knew that already."

The two brothers stared at each other for a moment. They had never been close. The way they had grown up had simply made it impossible. A wedge had always been driven between them, first by their father, and then later in life by their grandfather.

Suddenly, Matías wanted to fix it. If he could fix nothing else, he wanted to fix this.

It had occurred to him last night that he was much more like Diego than he had ever allowed himself to believe, but now he felt that might mean something different than he had originally thought.

"I know that our father killed our mother," Diego said, his tone grave.

"Dios." Matías breathed it, as a curse or a prayer, he didn't know. "Why did you never say?"

"I don't know how to talk about such things," Diego said. "And he...threatened me. And as a boy I was too frightened to stand against him. I am a coward, Matías, and I have to live with that."

"You were a child, not a coward."

Diego went on as though Matías hadn't spoken. "And I know that...that I am broken. Just as he was."

"No," Matías said, suddenly finding it much easier to deny it when the words were coming from his brother's mouth rather than from somewhere deep inside himself. "You're not. He was. *Abuelo* is. We can be something else."

"Can we?"

"Does Liliana love you?"

Diego shook his head. "I don't think so."

His brother was lying. Matías could see that. Though whether to himself or to Matías, he didn't know.

"Camilla says she loves me. And I feel that... I feel that if she can love me then perhaps I'm not broken."

"The concern," Diego said, his voice rough, "becomes breaking them."

"Yes," Matías agreed. "But I wonder...if love is the difference."

Diego chuckled. "That is the one thing I can confidently say our father and grandfather do not possess at all. Though that highlights other failures of mine, sadly."

"No one ever taught us how to love, Diego," Matías said. "They taught us to be ruthless. They taught us to play these games. To be cold, unyielding men who cared for nothing beyond our own selfish desires."

"I would say they taught us everything we should have tried not to be. And you," Diego said, "have certainly come the closest."

"I still didn't have love. So I'm not sure if it made any difference in the end."

"Is it too late now? Do you think it's too late to have it now?"

He remembered what Camilla had said. About how she would not be like her father. How she wouldn't let go of what they had until there was no other path. Until she was certain there was no more hope.

"It's never too late," he said. "I have to believe that. And then, even when it is too late, I feel that you have to keep trying. Beyond hope. Beyond pride or reason. Because love has no place in any of those things. Love is something entirely different."

"When did you become such an expert?" Diego asked.

"I'm not," Matías said. "But I know about pride. I know about failing. I know about loss. I know about selfishness. I know about anger. And nowhere, in any of that, did I find peace. Nowhere was there love. I can only assume it's this thing," he said, grabbing hold of his chest. "This thing that feels foreign. This thing that I don't know at all. This thing that has taken me over, body and soul. And… I wanted. I would've given it all up for her. We were both acting fools for this, and we were willing to give it up for them. Would our father have ever done that?"

"No," Diego said without hesitation.

"No," Matías agreed.

"Well, then," Diego said. "Perhaps we are not broken after all."

Matías agreed. Perhaps they weren't broken. And perhaps, he would not break Camilla.

Losing her would break him, though. As the loss of his mother had done. But it was a risk he had to take. Because the alternative was life without her.

And that was no life at all.

CHAPTER FIFTEEN

CAMILLA STEPPED THROUGH the front door of the ranch house, feeling the uneven tiles beneath her bare feet. Finally. It was what she had longed to do ever since she had lost this place all those months ago. It was all she had dreamed of. And yet, for some reason, the stones did not feel as warm or welcoming as she had imagined they might. For some reason, it did not feel like home.

"Because home is where the heart is," she said, the words falling flat in the empty room.

And sadly, Matías Navarro was her heart. Her soul. Her everything.

She had been out riding, and while she had most definitely found some pleasure in it, it had not been the deep, unmitigated joy she had once known when she was on the back of a horse. It was different now. She was different.

She was something more than she had been. And it galled her, because of course these simple things no longer provided her with the expansive feelings of happiness that they once did.

Her life had taken on a deeper, richer dimension. And with that had come deeper, richer pain. And it tinged everything. Even this victory. Even having Fuego back out in the fields.

She had not expected Matías to do that. She was *angry* at him for it. He should have kept the horse. Because…at least then it would have been easier to pretend that he really did feel nothing for her. Nothing beyond a sense of honor. A sense of duty and a need to do the right thing.

Giving back all the horses, most especially Fuego, felt like the actions of a man who cared. And she would rather not have to feel that he might. It was too hard. It hurt too bad. She just wanted to believe that initial feeling she'd had when he had sacrificed everything to get rid of her.

Now, as the weeks had passed, she was beginning to see it differently. She was beginning to wonder if it wasn't as she had first thought.

If he wasn't so desperate to get away from her, but if he was that afraid. So afraid of what might happen if he gave them a chance, that he had been willing to give up everything to protect her.

The idea that he was protecting her from himself made her ache. Because of course, she feared nothing when it came to Matías. Nothing but never being with him again. That was the real fear.

Her real, true fear.

She walked into the kitchen and grabbed an apple, then made her way back outside. She was too restless to spend the afternoon in the house and there was nothing to do in there anyway.

Work was the only answer.

She left her shoes on the front porch and walked down the dusty drive out into the sun. She closed her eyes, trying to recapture her joy in these simple pleasures. In the feel of the dirt beneath her bare feet, in the taste of the apple—sharp and crisp. But there was just nothing. It was all hollow. All desperately sad.

She was sad. All the way down.

She remembered that last time she and Matías had been together. When he had entered her first without a condom, and then thought better of it.

How terribly small and selfish it was of her that she wished a baby had resulted from that. So that she had something to tie her to him. Someone to keep her company.

But it had not. And anyway, she should be relieved by that.

She wasn't. The paperwork had been sent back to her, and the *rancho* was hers. She had signed all the appropriate documents. And still, she felt unsettled. Unfulfilled.

But she knew that there was more to life now. More to life than horses and ranches. More to life than simply protecting yourself from loss.

There was love. Oh, there was love. Deep, all-consuming love that hurt as much as it did anything else.

She sighed heavily and walked out toward the stables. And then her heart jolted when she saw a man standing there. Tall and broad. He was wearing the kind of hat *caballeros* liked to wear, and he had on jeans. A work shirt.

Still, there was no mistaking the man himself. He didn't need a suit to be him. Perfectly, undeniably him. *Matías.*

It didn't seem possible. But there he was. Standing right out there in the hot sun, dressed like a ranch hand.

"What are you doing here?" she asked.

"I came to see about a job," he responded.

"I'm sorry," she said. "I don't hire international billionaire businessmen."

"Why is that?"

Her throat tightened, her heart squeezing. "Because I always seem to fall in love with them."

She turned away from him, horrified when tears began to well up in her eyes. She didn't want to give him any more of her weakness. She'd been willing to fight to the end, but the end was long past, and now it was simply pathetic.

"That's strange," he said, his voice dark. "That isn't the reason I thought you might give."

Her body stiffened. "What reason did you imagine?"

"I thought it was perhaps because they were unable to prevent themselves from falling in love with you."

She put her hand over her mouth, trying to regain her composure. Trying to get a foothold. "I don't think that's the case," she said, shaking her head and straightening her shoulders, walking away from him resolutely. She was not going to allow him to play games with her. Not anymore.

"It is," he said. "Camilla, it is very true. But I was too much of a coward to admit it. I have been... I have been trying to sort through all of that. Over the past weeks. And I've come to the conclusion that... I am nothing more than a little boy, hiding in a tree and hoping that the dark things don't find me."

That made her heart crumple. She couldn't resist him then. Not with that.

She turned to him. "You're not a little boy."

"Listen to me," he said, the words tinged with desperation. "My world as I knew it ended forever the day that my father killed my mother. I think it killed something in me, as well. Or at least wounded it desperately.

I couldn't get the image out of my head. Of what he had done to her. Watching Diego's disastrous attempt at a first marriage only convinced me even more that I could never have such a relationship myself. That I could never let go of my control. But then there was you. And you're so strong. You don't fit any mold of anything that I thought I might find. Of anything I thought I might need. You are strong in ways that I could never hope to be."

"That's not true," she said.

"Yes," he said, "it is. You have never faltered. You told me that you loved me, in spite of the fact that I gave you no indication I love you back. In spite of all that I told you about me and my life. In spite of everything you had seen of a marriage growing up. In spite of the betrayal of your mother. You told me that you loved me. You set your pride aside, and any fear, and you laid it out there. You were the one. You have always been. Brash. Fearless."

She shook her head. "I'm not fearless, Matías. I was overwhelmed by fear, overcome by it that night, but I couldn't hold it back. I couldn't. Because I've seen what happens when you do. When you let love walk away so that it doesn't make a fool of you. I would rather be a fool. Ten times over. And I… I have been. I've felt like nothing but a fool these past weeks. A brokenhearted one at that."

"That's not fair," he said. "What I did to you. You did not deserve it."

"Were you so afraid? For me? *Of* me?"

"Yes," he admitted. "Both. I was afraid of what I might do to you. But more than that, I was afraid of what letting myself love you might do to me if I wanted you, but then could not keep you. If I somehow turned into my father the minute that I released my hold on that control. The minute I admitted that you were more important than air... Well, what would happen if I felt threatened?"

"You would let me go," she said. "And shower me with gifts. You proved that."

"I did," he said, his words torn from him. "But I didn't realize then, I wouldn't let myself admit that, that I loved you already. That love was already there, and it made all of the difference."

"What do you mean?"

"Remember we talked about how your mother loved herself more than she loved your father. More than she loved any of the men she has taken up relationships with."

"Yes," she said.

"My father loved himself more than he loved anyone in his own life. My grandfather is the same. He doesn't love Diego and me the way a grandfather should love his grandsons. He didn't love his own son the way that he should have. And my father certainly didn't love our mother or love us. It is not a decision in your head that keeps you from harming those around you. It's self-lessness. And that only comes from one place. It comes from love. It comes from loving someone more than you love yourself. From the desire to see them happy even if you're miserable. And I... I felt that for you. Even as it tore me apart to send you away. That is not a testament to my own strength, or to my own goodness, but to you. To the fact that you reached inside me and found something there I didn't think existed. That you make me want something I didn't think I could want."

"Matías," she said, closing the distance between them and kissing him, fiercely, ferociously. "I love you.

And I think... I think you are a good man. I think that you are better than your name. Than the legacy of your father and your grandfather."

"I should hope so. Because I actually do need the job on your ranch."

"Do you?"

"Well, we shall see how it goes, but Diego and I have both forfeited the game."

"What do you mean?"

"He has told our grandfather his marriage has ended, and I already announced to my grandfather I was divorcing you. And so, neither of us is married. Neither of us has fulfilled the terms of my grandfather's will. We refuse to play."

"Why did Diego do that?"

Matías sighed heavily. "For the same reason I did. For love. Because in the end we would rather do the right thing for the women we love than the right thing for ourselves, and I believe that's the first time either of us have ever felt that way."

"Has he told Liliana?"

Matías shook his head. "Not when last we spoke. But it was my conversation with him that made me realize I had to come to you. That I had to try."

"I love you," she said again. "I love you. More than myself."

"And I love you more than myself. And I will do so for the rest of my life, as long as there is breath in my body."

"I trust you."

He smiled, those simple words obviously touching something deep inside him.

"You are everything I need," he said, dropping a kiss on her lips. "You are strong, but you are fragile. Beautiful. My wife, and my stable girl."

She laughed. "I believe, my dear, that you might end up being my stable boy. After all, I am the owner of this *rancho*."

"So you are. I shall have to comfort myself with my billion-dollar industry."

"Well, if it won't keep you warm at night, I promise that I will."

He picked her up, holding her tightly in his arms. "Well, that, my lovely wife, I do believe."

And this time, when she passed over the threshold of her house, she truly felt like she was home. Because her heart was with her. And she was in his arms.

EPILOGUE

MATÍAS STEPPED OUT onto the balcony at the Navarro *rancho*, overlooking the fields before him. And he smiled when he saw his wife, riding up the path on the back of Fuego, who she had brought out to stay with them for the weekend.

She was still wild, that woman, even after several years of marriage. And he would have her no other way. He lived to watch her ride. To watch her race.

It had taken some convincing but he had finally talked her into acting as the jockey for Fuego and the two of them had had a few very successful years. Until she'd had to take time off for her pregnancy. And then for the next one.

"Papá."

He looked down at his son, who was standing there staring up at him with wide, dark eyes. His mother's eyes.

"Yes, Cesar?" he asked, bending down and picking the little boy up, holding him in his arms.

"Is *Mamá* coming back soon?"

"Yes," Matías said. "She's on her way for supper. You know how she likes to ride in the afternoon."

"Me, too," said his son.

Matías knew that was true. Because it was in his blood. Just as it was in Camilla's.

During dinner they ate on the terrace and Matías held baby Amelia on his lap while Cesar peppered Camilla with questions about each and every horse. A routine evening. One he loved more and more with each passing day.

But not half as much as he enjoyed what transpired after dinner. After the children were in bed. Tonight he and his wife sat outside in the warm air, a fire lit in the ring in front of them the only light besides the stars.

She kissed him passionately, switching positions so she was straddling his thighs. "I think tonight," she said, "I would like to have you out here."

"Something you won't be able to do when Diego and his family arrive," he pointed out.

His reconciliation with his brother had occurred after they'd both decided to quit playing their grandfather's game. And it turned out the old man had been so entertained by being outmaneuvered by his grandsons that he'd ended up gifting the estate in equal parts. And then had kept on living. Much to everyone's surprise.

"Which is why I must make the most of it now," she whispered against his lips.

When they were sated he carried her up to bed, and held her in his arms.

And when he dreamed it was only of her.

* * * * *

MY BOUGHT
VIRGIN WIFE

CAITLIN CREWS

CHAPTER ONE

Imogen

IN THE MORNING I was to marry a monster.

It did not matter what I wanted. It certainly did not matter what I felt. I was the youngest daughter of Dermot Fitzalan, bound in duty to my father's wishes as women in my family had been forever.

I had always known my fate.

But it turned out I was less resigned to it than I'd anticipated when I was younger and far more silly. And when my wedding had not loomed before me, beckoning like some kind of inevitable virus that nothing could keep at bay.

There were no home remedies for my father's wishes.

"You cannot let Father see you in this state, Imogen," my half sister, Celeste, told me briskly as she swept in. "It will only make things worse for you."

I knew she was right. The unfortunate truth was that Celeste was usually right about everything. Elegant, graceful Celeste, who had submitted to her duty with a smile on her face and every appearance of quiet joy. Stunning, universally adored Celeste, who had the willowy blond looks of her late mother and to whom I had forever been compared—and found lacking. My own lost mother had been a titian-haired bombshell, pale of skin and mysteriously emerald of eye, but I resembled her only in the way a fractured reflection, beheld through a mist, might. Next to my half sister, I had always felt like the Fitzalan troll, better suited to a life beneath a bridge somewhere than the grand society life I'd been bred and trained for.

The life Celeste took to with such ease.

Even today, the day before my wedding when theoretically I would be the one looked at, Celeste looked poised and chic in her simple yet elegantly cut clothes. Her pale blond hair was twisted back into an effortless chignon and she'd applied only the faintest hint of cosmetics to enhance her eyes and dramatic cheekbones. While I had yet to change out of my pajamas though it was midday already and I knew without having to look that my curls were in their usual state of disarray.

All of these things seemed filled with more portent than usual, because the monster I was set to marry in the morning had wanted her first.

And likely still wanted her, everyone had whispered.

They had even whispered it to me, and it had surprised me how much it had stung. Because I knew better. My marriage wasn't romantic. I wasn't being chosen by anyone—I was the remaining Fitzalan heiress. My inheritance made me an attractive prospect no matter how irrepressible my hair might have been or how often I disappointed my father with my inability to enhance a room with my decorative presence. I was more likely to draw attention for the wrong reasons.

My laugh was too loud and always inappropriate. My clothes were always slightly askew. I preferred books to carefully vetted social occasions where I was expected to play at hostessing duties. And I had never convinced anyone that I was more fascinated by their interests than my own.

It was lucky, then, that my marriage was about convenience—my father's, not mine. I had never expected anything like a fairy tale.

"Fairy tales are for other families," my severe grandmother had always told us, slamming her marble-edged cane against the hard floors of this sprawling house in the French countryside, where, the story went, our family had been in residence in one form or another since sometime in the twelfth century. "Fitzalans have a higher purpose."

As a child, I'd imagined Celeste and me dressed in armor, riding out to gauzy battles beneath old standards, then slaying a dragon or two before our supper. That had seemed like the kind of higher purpose I could get behind. It had taken the austere Austrian nuns years to teach me that dragon slaying was not the primary occupation of girls from excruciatingly well-blooded old families who were sent away to be educated in remote convents. Special girls with impeccable pedigrees and ambitious fathers had a far different role to fill.

Girls like me, who had never been asked what they might like to do with their lives, because it had all been plotted out already without their input.

The word *pawn* was never used. I had always seen this as a shocking oversight—another opinion of mine that no one had ever solicited and no one wanted to hear.

"You must find purpose and peace in duty, Imogen," Mother Superior had told me, time and again, when I would find myself red-eyed and furious, gritting out another decade of the rosary to atone for my sins. Pride and unnatural self-regard chief among them. "You must cast aside these doubts and trust that those with your best interests at heart have made certain all is as it should be."

"Fitzalans have a higher purpose," Grand-Mère had always said.

By which, I had learned in time, she meant money. Fitzalans hoarded money and made more. This was what had set our family apart across the centuries. Fitzalans were never kings or courtiers. Fitzalans funded kingdoms they liked and overthrew regimes they disparaged, all in service to the expansion of their wealth. This was the grand and glorious purpose that surged in our blood.

"I am not 'in a state,'" I argued to Celeste now, but I didn't sit up or attempt to set myself to rights.

And Celeste did not dignify that with a response.

I had barred myself in the sitting room off my childhood bedchamber, the better to brood at the rain and entertain myself with my enduring fantasies of perfect, beautiful Frederick, who worked in my father's stables and had dreamy eyes of sweetest blue.

We had spoken once, some years ago. He had taken my horse's head and led us into the yard as if I'd required the assistance.

I had lived on the smile he'd given me that day for years.

It seemed unbearable to me that I should find myself staring down so many more years when I would have to do the same, but worse, in the company of a man—a *husband*—who was hated and feared in equal measure across Europe.

Today the historic Fitzalan estate felt like the prison it was. If I was honest, it had never been a home.

My mother had died when I was barely eight, and in my memories of her she was always crying. I had been left to the tender mercies of Grand-Mère, before her death, and my father, who was forever disappointed in me, but still my only remaining parent.

And Celeste, who was ten years older than me. And better at everything.

Having lost my mother, I held fast to what was left of my family, and no matter if that grip often felt a good deal more like a choke hold I was performing on myself. They were all I had.

"You must look to your sister as your guide," Grand-Mère had told me on more than one occasion. Usually when I'd been discovered running in the corridors of the old house, disheveled and embarrassing, when I should have been sitting decorously somewhere, learning how to cross my ankles and incline my head in sweet subservience.

I had tried. I truly had.

I had watched Celeste come of age before me, elegant and meek in ways I envied and yet failed to understand. She had done it all with grace and beauty, the way she did everything. She had been married on her twentieth birthday to a man closer in age to our father—a hereditary count who claimed the blood of famed kings on both sides, stretching deep into Europe's gloried past. A man who I had never seen crack so much as the faintest smile.

And in the years since, Celeste had presented her ever-glowering husband with two sons and a daughter. Because while I had been raised to do my duty and knew what was expected of me—despite the dark thoughts I had about it in private while dreaming of Frederick's blue eyes—Celeste had *bloomed* in her role as countess.

It was hard to look at all that blooming, I thought

uncharitably now. Not the day before I turned twenty-two, came into my fortune, and—not coincidentally, I was well aware—married the man of my father's choosing, who I had never met. My father felt a meeting was unnecessary and no one argued with Dermot Fitzalan, least of all the daughters he used as disposable pawns.

Happy birthday to me, I told myself darkly.

I would celebrate with a forced march down the aisle with a man whose very name made even the servants in the manor house recoil in horror.

A man I knew all manner of terrible things about.

A man widely regarded as a devil in the flesh.

A man who was not even the member of some or other gentry, as I had expected my eventual husband would be, given my father's celestially high opinion of himself and all he felt his vaunted pedigree—and thus mine—demanded.

In contrast, Celeste's husband, the dour count, had a title that ached with age—but had very few lands behind it. Or any money left over after all those centuries of aristocratic splendor, I had heard them whisper.

And this, I knew, was why my father had chosen a man for me who might have lacked gentility and pedigree, but more than made up for both with his astonishing wealth. Because this would surely add to the Fitzalan reach and financial might.

Genteel Celeste, so gentle and fragile, had been married carefully to a title that would sit well on her perfect brow. I was hardier. I could be sold off to a commoner whose coffers only seemed to swell by the year. In this way, my father could have his cake and eat it, merrily.

I knew this. But it didn't mean I liked it.

Celeste settled herself on the other end of the settee beneath the windows in my sitting room, where I had

curled in a miserable ball this gray January day as if
my brooding could make time stand still and save me
from my fate.

"You will only make yourself ill," she told me, prag-
matically. Or at least, that was how I interpreted the
way she gazed at me then, down the length of the aristocratic nose she shared with our father. "And nothing
will change either way. It is a wasted effort."

"I do not wish to marry him, Celeste."

Celeste let out that lilting laugh that I normally
thought sounded like the finest music. Today it clawed
at me.

"You do not *wish*?" She laughed again, and I wondered if I imagined the hardness in her gaze when it
faded. "But who, pray, told you that your wishes mattered?"

I noted the year in as grim a tone as I could manage. "Surely my wishes should be consulted, at the very
least. Even if nothing I want is taken into account."

"Fitzalans are not modern, Imogen," Celeste said
with a hint of impatience, as I knew my father would.
Though he would not *hint*. "If what you want is progress and self-determination, I'm afraid you were born
into the wrong family."

"It was hardly my choice."

"Imogen. This is so childish. You have always known
this day would come. You cannot possibly have imagined that *you*, somehow, would escape what waits for
every Fitzalan from birth."

I turned that over and over in my head, noting it felt
more bitter every time. More acrid.

The way she said *you*, with what sounded a great
deal like scorn.

And the way she'd said *escape*, as if the very notion was fantastical.

It suggested she was neither as effortless nor as *joyfully blooming* as I had always imagined. And I didn't know quite how to process that possibility.

I shivered, here in these gloomy rooms built to impress fellow Norman invaders centuries ago en route to their sacking and pillaging of England, not to provide any semblance of comfort for the descendants of those invaders. I stared out the window at the deceptively quiet countryside spread out before me. The gardens that rolled this way and that, dead now, but still scrupulously maintained and manicured. I pretended I didn't know that the front of the house was decidedly less tranquil today as the family and guests gathered to cheer me on to my doom.

Celeste and her family in from Vienna, our shriveled great uncles from Paris, the impertinent cousins from Germany. My father's well-fed and sly business associates and rivals from all over the planet.

Not to mention the terrifying groom. The monster I was expected to marry in the morning.

"What is he like?" I asked, my voice cracking.

Celeste was quiet so long that I dragged my gaze from the window to study her expression.

I don't know what I expected. But it wasn't what I saw—my sister's mouth tilted up in the corners, like a cat in the cream.

An unpleasant jolt walloped me in the gut, then shivered through me. I endeavored to shake it off. Or better yet, ignore it.

"Are you sure you wish to know?" Celeste asked, after another long moment of nothing but that self-satisfied half smile that boded all manner of ill, I was sure.

It shuddered through me like some kind of fear. "I am not certain that anything is gained by approaching an arranged marriage with an excess of knowledge about a man you must come to terms with, one way or another, no matter what you know ahead of time."

"You did not marry a monster," I retorted.

Though when I thought of the count and that expression of his that suggested he had never encountered a scent he did not abhor and never would, I wondered if the term *monster* might not have a variety of applications.

That smile of hers, if possible, grew ever more smug and made that shuddering thing in me all the more intense.

"He is not like anyone you have met, Imogen. It is impossible to prepare for the impact of him, really."

"I don't understand what that means."

Again, that tinkling laugh. "I must remind myself you are so young. Sheltered. Untouched, in every possible way."

"You were younger when you got married. And presumably, equally untouched and sheltered."

But the way she looked at me then made my heart stutter in my chest. Because if her sly, faintly pitying expression was to be believed, my half sister was not at all who I had believed her to be all this time.

And if Celeste was not Celeste…it was almost as if I forgot who I was, too.

The truth was, I didn't know what to make of it. I shoved it aside, thinking I'd take it out and look at it again when I could breathe normally again. Sometime in the dim future when I was married and settled and had somehow survived the monster who was already in this house, waiting for me.

"I feel sorry for you," Celeste murmured, after a moment, though her tone did not strike me as the sort one would use if that was true. "Truly, it isn't fair. How can a naive little thing like you be expected to handle a man like Javier Dos Santos?"

Even his name struck dread through the center of me. I told myself it had to be dread, that thick and too-hot sensation. It hit me in the chest, then spiraled down until it lodged itself low in my belly.

That, I told myself, was a measure of how much I loathed and feared him.

"I thought you hated him," I reminded my sister. "After what he did to you…"

I remembered the shouting. My father's deep voice echoing through the house. I remembered Celeste's sobs. Until now, it had been the only example I'd ever seen of something less than perfection in my half sister—and I had blamed the man who was the cause of it. I had held him responsible for the commotion. The jagged tear in the smooth inevitability that was our life here, so securely beneath our father's thumb.

More than this, I remembered the one glimpse I'd had of Javier Dos Santos in person. After another bout of screams and sobs and the sort of fighting I'd been taught Fitzalans were above, I had plastered myself to the window over the grand front entrance where I could hide myself in the drapery, and I had gazed down at this monster who had threatened to tear my family apart.

It had been years ago, but my memories remained as vivid as if it had happened yesterday.

He was dark like sin. A stain against the stones. His hair was glossy and black, so dark it looked nearly blue and reminded me of nothing so much as a raven's wing.

His face was cruel and hard, so harsh it took my breath away. He had been made of muscle, hard and dangerous, a striking counterpoint to the genteel men I had been raised with. He was not elegant. He was not graceful.

He had no right to my beautiful sister, I had thought fiercely.

A sentiment my father had echoed in no uncertain terms. Celeste, he had bellowed throughout the manor house, was meant for better.

But it seemed Javier Dos Santos was good enough for me.

"Of course I do not hate him," Celeste said now, with more of that laughter that seemed to suggest I was very young and foolish. I didn't care for it, but I couldn't work out how to ask her to stop. "Where do you get such ideas?"

"From you. When you screamed that you hated him, and would hate him forever, and would never cheapen yourself by succumbing to the kind of dime-store forgiveness—"

"Here is what I can tell you about Javier," Celeste said, cutting me off. And pronouncing his name as if it was a meal. "He is not like other men. You should know this, going in. Throw out any preconceptions you might have."

"The only man I know is Father. A handful of priests. And your husband."

I had not meant to say those words the way I did. *Your husband.* As if I was pronouncing some kind of judgment.

But Celeste settled farther back against the settee as if she was relaxing. As if this was the moment she could finally retreat from her usual strict perfection and render herself boneless. "Javier is virile. Animalistic, even. He will take what he wants, and worse, you will happily debase yourself to give it to him."

I frowned. "I have no intention of debasing myself. Much less happily."

Celeste waved a hand. "You will. He will demean you, insult you, and likely make you cry. And you will thank him for it."

My heart was pounding so hard it made me feel dizzy. My throat was dry, and my tongue felt thick in my mouth. And that dread seemed to pulse in me, hotter and wilder by the second.

"Why are you telling me these things? The day before I must marry him?"

If Celeste was abashed, she didn't look it. At all. "I am merely trying to prepare you, Imogen."

"I already think he is a monster. I'm not certain why you think talk of debasement and insults would improve the situation."

"You will have to watch that tongue of yours, of course," she said, almost sadly. "He won't put up with it. Or the way you run about heedlessly as if you are one of those common women on a treadmill somewhere, sweaty and red-faced."

Because she was naturally slim and beautiful, of course. She assumed that anyone who had to work for perfection didn't deserve it.

It had somehow never occurred to me before that this description might apply to me, too.

"You are very lucky, then, that you were spared this," I said softly. "That I am here to carry this burden for you. For the family."

I had never seen her look as she did then. Her face flushed with what I could only call some kind of temper. Her chin rose. And her eyes glittered. "Indeed. I count myself lucky daily."

I found my hands on the hem of my pajama top, fiddling with the fine cotton as if I could worry it into threads. Betraying my anxiety, I knew.

And as strangely as my sister was behaving today, she was still my sister. The only person who had never punished me for asking questions.

This was why I dared to ask the one thing that had worried me the most since my father had announced my engagement to me over Christmas dinner.

"Do you think…?" I cleared my throat. "Will he hurt me?"

For a long moment, Celeste did not speak. And when she did, there was a hard look in her eyes, her lips twisted, and she no longer looked the least bit relaxed.

"You will survive it," she told me, something bleak and ugly there between us. "You will always survive it, Imogen, for better or worse, and that is what you will hold on to. My advice to you is to get pregnant as quickly as possible. Men like this want heirs. In the end, that is all they want. The sooner you do your duty, the quicker they will leave you alone."

And long after she swept from my room, I stayed where I was, stricken. And unable to breathe. There was a constriction in my chest and that heavy dread in my gut, and I couldn't help but think that I had seen my half sister—truly seen her—for the first time today.

It filled me like a kind of grief.

But I was also filled with a kind of restlessness I didn't understand.

That was what got me up and onto my feet. I dashed the odd moisture from my eyes with hands I knew better than to keep in fists. I started for the door, then imagined—too vividly—my father's reaction should I be found wandering about the house when it was filled with important wedding guests, clad only in my pajamas with my hair obviously unbrushed.

I went into my bedroom and dressed quickly, pulling on the dress the maids had left out for me, wordlessly encouraging me to clothe myself the way my father preferred. Not to my own taste, which would never have run to dresses at this chilly time of year, no matter that this one was long-sleeved and made of a fine wool. I paired the dress with butter-soft knee-high leather boots, and then found myself in my mirror.

I had not transformed into elegance during my vigil on the settee.

Curls like mine always looked unkempt. Elegance was sleek and smooth, but my hair resisted any and all attempts to tame it. The nuns had done what they could, but even they had been unable to combat my hair's natural tendency to find its own shape. I ran my fingers through it as best I could, letting the curls do as they would because they always did.

My hair was the bane of my existence. Much as I was the bane of my father's.

Only then, when I could say that in all honesty I had at least tried to sort myself out into something resembling order, did I leave my room.

I made my way out into the hall in the family wing, then ducked into one of the servants' back stairs. My father would not approve of his daughter moving about the house like one of the help, but I had never thought that he needed to know how familiar I was with the secret passages in this old pile of stones. Knowing them made life here that much more bearable.

Knowing my way through the shadows allowed me

to remain at large when there was a lecture brewing. It permitted me to come in from long walks on the grounds, muddy and disheveled, and make it to my own rooms before the sight of me caused the usual offense, outrage, and threats to curtail my exercise until I learned how to behave *like a lady*.

I carefully made my way over to the guest wing, skirting around the rooms I knew had been set aside for various family members and my father's overfed friends. I knew that there was only one possible place my father would have dared put a man as wealthy and powerful as Javier Dos Santos. Only one place suitable for a groom with such a formidable financial reputation.

My father might have turned Javier from the house ten years ago, but now that he was welcome and set to marry the right daughter, Dermot Fitzalan would spare him no possible luxury.

I headed for what was one of the newer additions to the grand old house, a two-story dwelling place appended to the end of the guest wing where my grandmother had lived out her final days. It was more a house all its own, with its own entrance and rooms, but I knew that I could access it on the second level and sneak my way along its private gallery.

I didn't ask myself why I was doing this. I only knew it was tied to the grief I felt for the sister it turned out I barely knew and that dread inside me that pulsed at me, spurring me on.

I eased my way through the servant's door that disappeared behind a tapestry at one end of the gallery. I flattened myself to the wall and did my best to keep my ears peeled for any signs of life.

And it was the voice I heard first.

His voice.

Commanding. Dark. Rich like dark chocolate and deep red wine, all wrapped in one.

Beautiful, something in me whispered.

I was horrified with myself. But I didn't back away.

He was speaking in rapid Spanish, liquid and lovely, out of sight on the floor below me. I inched forward, moving away from the gallery wall so I could look over the open side of the balcony to the great room below.

And for a moment, memory and reality seemed tangled up in each other. Once again, I was gazing down at Javier Dos Santos from afar. From above.

Once again, I was struck by how *physical* he seemed. Long ago, he had been dressed for the evening in a coat with tails that had only accentuated the simmering brutality he seemed to hold leashed there in his broad shoulders and his granite rock of a torso.

Today he stood in a button-down shirt tucked into trousers that did things I hardly understood to his powerful thighs. I only knew I couldn't look away.

Once again, my heart beat so hard and so fast I was worried I might be ill.

But I wasn't.

I knew I wasn't.

I watched him rake his fingers through that dark hair of his, as black and as glossy as I remembered it, as if even the years dared not defy him. He listened to the mobile he held at one ear for a moment, his head cocked to one side, then replied in another spate of the lyrical Spanish that seem to wind its way around me. Through me. Deep inside me, too.

With my functional Spanish I could pick up the sense of the words, if not every nuance. Business concerns in Wales. Something about the States. And a fiercer debate by far about Japan.

He finished his call abruptly, then tossed his mobile onto the table next to him. It thunked against the hard wood, making me too aware of the silence.

And too conscious of my own breathing and my mad, clattering heart.

Javier Dos Santos stood there a moment, his attention on the papers before him, or possibly his tablet computer.

When he raised his head, he did it swiftly. His dark eyes were fierce and sure, pinning me where I stood. I understood in a sudden red haze of exposure and fear that he had known I was here all along.

He had known.

"Hello, Imogen," he said, switching to faintly accented English that made my name sound like some kind of incantation. Or terrible curse. "Do you plan to do something more than stare?"

CHAPTER TWO

Javier

I WAS A man built from lies.

My faithless father. My weak, codependent mother. The lies they had told—to each other, to the world, to me and my sisters—had made me the man I was today, for good or ill.

I allowed no room in the life I had crafted from nothing for lies like theirs. Not from my employees or associates. Not from my sisters, grown now and beholden to me. Not from a single soul on this earth.

And certainly not from myself.

So there was no hiding from the fact that my first glimpse of my future bride—the unfortunate Fitzalan sister, as she was known—did not strike me the way I had anticipated it would.

I had expected that she would do well enough. She was not Celeste, but she was a Fitzalan. It was her pedigree that mattered, that and the sweet, long-anticipated revenge of forcing her father to give me the very thing he had denied me once already.

I had never done well with denial. Ten years ago it had not taken me to my knees, as I suspected Dermot Fitzalan thought it would. On the contrary, it had led me to go bigger, to strive harder, to make absolutely certain that the next time I came for a Fitzalan daughter, their arrogant, self-satisfied father would not dare deny me.

I had expected that my return to this cold, gloomy mausoleum in the north of France would feel like a victory lap. Because it was.

What I did not expect was the kick of lust that slammed through me at the sight of her.

It made no sense. I had been raised in the gutters of Madrid, but I had always wanted better. Always. As I'd fought my way out of the circumstances of my birth, I'd coveted elegance and collected it wherever I could.

It had made sense for me to pursue Celeste. She was grace personified, elegant from the tips of her fingernails to the line of her neck, and nothing but ice straight through.

It had made sense that I had wanted her to adorn my collection.

The girl before me, who had dared try to sneak up on a man who had been raised in dire pits filled with snakes and jackals and now walked untroubled through packs of wolves dressed as aristocrats, was...unruly.

She had red-gold hair that slithered this way and that and stubborn curls she had made no apparent attempt to tame. There was a spray of freckles over her nose, and I knew that if I could see them from this distance, it likely meant that my eyes were not deceiving me and she had not, in fact, bothered with even the faintest hint of cosmetics in a nod toward civility.

On the one hand, that meant her dark, thick lashes and the berry shade of her full lips were deliciously natural.

But it also showed that she had little to no sense of propriety.

She was otherwise unadorned. She wore a navy blue dress that was unobjectionable enough, with classic lines that nodded toward her generous figure without making too much of it, and leather boots that covered her to her knees.

I could have forgiven the hair and even the lack of cosmetics—which suggested she had not prepared for her first meeting with me the way a woman who planned to make the perfect wife would have.

But it was the way she was scowling at me that suggested she was even less like her sister than I had imagined.

Celeste had never cracked. Not even when she'd been denied what she'd so prettily claimed she wanted. Oh, she'd caused a carefully prepared scene for her father, but there had never been anything but calculation in her gaze. Her mascara had never run. She had never presented anything but perfection, even in the midst of her performance.

The fact it still rankled made it a weakness. I thrust it aside.

"Surely that is not the expression you wish to show your future husband," I said quietly. "On this, the occasion of our first meeting."

I had heard her come in and creep along the strange balcony above me the butler had told me was a gallery. Not a very good gallery, I had thought with a derisive glance at the art displayed there. All stodgy old masters and boring ecclesiastical works. Nothing bold. Nothing new.

Until she'd come.

"I want to know why you wish to marry me." She belted that out, belligerent and bordering on rude. A glance confirmed that she was making fists at her sides. *Fists.*

I felt my brow raise. "I beg your pardon?"

Her scowl deepened. "I want to know why you want to marry me, when if you are even half as rich and powerful as they say, you could marry anyone."

I thrust my hands—not in anything resembling fists—into the pockets of my trousers, and considered her.

I should have been outraged. I told myself I was.

But the truth was, there was something about her that tempted me to smile. And I was not a man who smiled easily, if at all.

I told myself it was the very fact that she had come here, when our wedding was not until the morning. It was the fact she seemed to imagine she could put herself between her grasping, snobbish father and me when these were matters that could not possibly concern her. Daughters of men like Dermot Fitzalan always did what they were told, sooner or later.

Yet here she was.

It was the futility of it, I thought. My Don Quixote bride with her wild hair, tilting at windmills and scowling all the while. It made something in my chest tighten.

"I will answer any questions you have," I told her magnanimously, trying my best to contain my own ferocity. "But you must face me."

"I'm looking right at you."

I only raised a hand, then beckoned her to me with two languid fingers.

And then waited, aware that it had been a long time indeed since I had been in the presence of someone… unpredictable.

I saw her hands open, then close again at her sides. I

saw the way her chest moved, telling me that she fought to keep her breath even.

I learned a lot about my future bride as the seconds ticked by, and all she did was stare down at me. I learned she was willful. Defiant.

But ultimately yielding.

Because when she moved, it was to the spiral stair that led her down to the stone floor where I stood.

Perhaps not yielding so much as curious, I amended as she drew near, folding her arms over her chest as if she was drawing armor around herself in order to face me.

I took a moment to consider her, this bride I had purchased outright. This girl who was my revenge and my prize, all in one.

She will do, I thought, pleased with myself.

"I suppose," I said after a moment, in the cool tone I used to reprimand my subordinates, "you cannot help the hair."

Imogen glowered at me. Her eyes were an unusual shade of brown that looked like old copper coins when they filled with temper, as they did now. It made me wonder how they would look when she was wild with passion instead.

That lust hit me again. Harder this time.

"It is much like being born without a title, I imagine," she retorted.

It took me a moment to process that. To understand that this messy, unruly girl had thrust such an old knife in so deftly, then twisted it.

I couldn't think of the last time that had happened. I couldn't think of the last person who had dared.

"Does it distress you that you must lower yourself to

marry a man so far beneath you?" I asked, all silk and threat. "A man who is little more than a mongrel while you have been deliberately bred from blood kept blue enough to burn?"

I could not seem to help but notice that her skin was so fair it was like cream and made me...hungry. And when her eyes glittered, they gleamed copper.

"Does it distress you that I am not my sister?" she asked in return.

I hadn't expected that.

I felt myself move, only dimly aware that I was squaring my shoulders and changing my stance, as if I found myself engaged in hand-to-hand combat. I supposed I was.

"You cannot imagine that the two of you could be confused," I murmured, but I was looking at her differently. I was viewing her as less a pawn and more an opponent. First a knife, then a sucker punch.

So far, Imogen Fitzalan was proving to be far more interesting that I had anticipated.

I wasn't sure I knew where to put that.

"As far as I am aware," she said coolly, "you are the only one who has ever confused us."

"I assure you, I am not confused."

"Perhaps I am. I assume that purchasing my hand in marriage requires at least as much research as the average online dating profile. Did you not see a picture? Were you not made aware that my sister and I share only half our blood?"

"I cannot say I gave the matter of your appearance much thought," I said, and I expected that to set her back on her heels.

But instead, the odd creature laughed.

"A man like you, not concerned with his own wife's appearance? How out of character."

"I cannot imagine what you think you know of my character."

"I have drawn conclusions about your character based on the way you allow yourself to be photographed." Her brow lifted. "You are a man who prefers the company of a very particular shape of woman."

"It is not their shape that concerns me, but whether or not other men covet them." This was nothing but the truth, and yet something about the words seemed almost…oily. Weighted. As if I should be ashamed of saying such a thing out loud when I had said it many times before.

Though not, I amended, to a woman I intended to make my wife.

"You like a trophy," she said.

I inclined my head. "I am a collector, Imogen. I like only the finest things."

She smiled at me, but it struck me as more of a baring of teeth. "You must be disappointed indeed."

Though she looked as if the notion pleased her.

I moved then, closer to her, enjoying the way she stood fast instead of shrinking away. I could see the way her pulse beat too fast in her neck. I could see the way her copper eyes widened. I reached over and helped myself to one of those red-gold curls, expecting her hair to be coarse. Much as she was.

But the curl was silky against my fingers, sliding over my skin like a caress. And something about that fell through me like a sudden brush fire.

If I was a man who engaged in self-deception, I would have told myself that was not at all what I felt.

But I had built my life and my fortune, step by step in the face of only overwhelming odds, on nothing short of brutal honesty. Toward myself and others, no matter the cost.

I knew I wanted her.

She reached up as if to bat my hand away, but appeared to think better of it, which raised her another notch or two in my estimation. "You have yet to answer the question. You can marry anyone you like. Why on earth would you choose me?"

"Perhaps I am so enamored of the Fitzalan name that I have hungered for nothing but the opportunity to align myself with your father since the day I met your sister. And you should know, Imogen, that I always get what I want."

She swallowed. I watched the pale column of her neck move when she did. "They say you are a monster."

I was so busy looking at her mouth and imagining how those plump lips would feel wrapped around the hungriest part of me that I almost missed the way she said that. And more, the look on her face when she did.

As if she was not playing a game, any longer.

As if she was actually afraid of me.

And I had dedicated my life to making certain that as many people as possible were afraid of me, because a healthy fear bred respect and I did not much care if they feared me so long as they respected me.

But somehow, I did not wish this to be true of Imogen Fitzalan. My bride, for her sins.

"Those who say I am a monster are usually poor losers," I told her, aware that I was too close to her. And yet neither she nor I moved to put more space between us. "It is in their best interests to call me a monster, because who could be expected to prevail against a creature of myth and lore? Their own shortcomings and failures are of no consequence, you understand. Not if I am a monster instead of a man."

Her gaze searched my face. "You want to be a monster, then. You enjoy it."

"You can call me whatever you like. I will marry you all the same."

"Again. Why me?"

"Why does this upset you?" I didn't fight the urge that came over me then, to reach over and take her chin in my fingers and hold her face where I wanted it. Simply because I could. And because, though she stilled, she did not jerk away. "I know that you have spent your life preparing for this day. Why should it matter if it is me or anyone else?"

"It matters."

Her voice was fierce and quiet at once. And emotion gleamed in her lovely eyes, though I couldn't discern what, exactly, that sheen meant.

"Did you have your heart set on another?" I asked, aware as I did so that something I had never felt before stirred to life within me. "Is that why you dare come to me with all this belligerence?"

It was because she was mine, I told myself. That was why I felt that uncharacteristic surge of possessiveness. I had not felt it for a woman before, it was true. Despite how much I had wanted Celeste back in the day and how infuriated I had been when I had lost her to that aristocratic zombie of a count she called her husband.

I had wanted Celeste, yes.

But that was a different thing entirely than knowing she was meant to be mine.

Imogen was mine. There was no argument. I had

paid for the privilege—or that was how her father planned to spin this match.

He and I knew the truth. I was a wealthy man, my power and might with few equals. I took care of my sisters and my mother because I prided myself on my honor and did my duty—not because they deserved that consideration. And because I did not want them to be weak links others could use to attack me.

But otherwise I had no ties or obligations, and had thus spent my days dedicating myself to the art of money.

The reality was that Dermot Fitzalan needed my wealth. And better still, my ability to make more with seeming ease. He needed these things far more than I needed his daughter's pedigree.

But I had decided long ago that I would marry a Fitzalan heiress, these daughters of men who had been the power behind every throne in Europe at one point or another. I had determined that I would make my babies on soft, well-bred thighs, fatten them on blue blood, and raise them not just rich, but cultured.

I had been so young when I had seen Celeste that first time. So raw and unformed. The animal they accused me of being in all the ways that mattered.

I had never seen a woman like her before. All clean lines and beauty. I had never imagined that a person could be…flawless.

It had taken me far longer than it should have—far longer than it would today, that was for certain—to see the truth of Celeste Fitzalan, now a countess of petty dreams and an angry old man's promises because that was what she had wanted far more than she had wanted me.

But my thirst for my legacy had only grown stronger.

"If there was another," my confounding betrothed said, a mulish set to that fine mouth and a rebellion in her gaze, "I would hardly be likely to tell you, would I?"

"You can tell me anything you like about others," I told her, all menace and steel. "Today. I would advise you to take advantage of this offer. Come the morning, I will take a far dimmer view of these things."

"It doesn't matter what I want," she threw at me, pulling her chin from my grasp.

I assumed we were both well aware that I allowed it.

"I never said that it did. You are the one who came here. Was it only to call me names? To ask me impertinent questions? Or perhaps you had another goal in mind?"

"I don't know why I came," Imogen said, and I could tell by the way her voice scraped into the air between us that she meant that.

But there was a fire in me. A need, dark and demanding, and I was not in the habit of denying myself the things I wanted.

More than this, she was to be my wife in the morning.

"Don't worry," I told her with all that heat and intent. "I know exactly why you came."

I hooked my hand around her neck, enjoying the heat of her skin beneath the cover of those wild curls. I pulled her toward me, watching her eyes go wide and her mouth drop open as if she couldn't help herself. As if she was that artless, that innocent.

I couldn't understand the things that worked in me. To take her, to possess her, to bury myself in her body when she looked nothing like the women that I usually amused myself with.

But none of that mattered.

Because I already owned her. All that remained was the claiming, and I wanted it. Desperately.

I dropped my mouth to hers.

CHAPTER THREE

Imogen

HE WAS KISSING ME.

The monster was kissing me.

And I hardly knew what to do.

His mouth was a bruising thing, powerful and hard. It should have hurt, surely. I should have wanted nothing more than to get away from all that intensity. I should have tried. But instead, I found myself pushing up on my toes and leaning toward him…

As if I wanted more.

He cradled the back of my head in one hand and moved his lips over mine.

And I *wanted*. I wanted…everything.

I had dreamed of kisses half my life. I had longed for a moment like this. A punishing kiss, perhaps. Or something sweet and filled with wonder. Any kind of kiss at all, if I was honest.

But nothing could have prepared me for Javier Dos Santos.

Nothing could have prepared me for this.

I felt his tongue against the seam of my lips, and couldn't help myself from opening up and giving him entry. And then I thought I would give him anything.

And even though I understood, on some distant level, what he was doing to me—that his tongue was testing mine, dancing here, then retreating—all I could feel was the heat. *The heat*. Something greedy and wild and impossibly hot, thrilling to life inside me. What I had called dread had melted into something else entirely, something molten. It wound around and around inside my chest, knotted up in my belly, and dripped like honey even lower.

And still he kissed me.

His arms were a marvel. Heavy and hard, they wrapped around me, making me feel things I could hardly understand. Small, yet safe. Entirely surrounded, yet sweet, somehow.

Still Javier's mouth moved on mine. He bent me backward, over one strong arm. His heavy chest, all steel planes and granite, pressed hard against mine, until I felt my breasts seem to swell in response.

It was like a fever.

The ache was everywhere, prickling and hot, but I knew—somehow I knew—I wasn't ill.

He bent me back even farther and there was a glory in it. I felt weightless, too caught up in all that fire and honey to worry whether or not my feet still touched the ground.

And then I felt his fingers as they found their way beneath the hem of my dress, a scandalous caress that made my heart stutter. Yet he didn't stop. He tracked that same sweet flame along the length of my thigh, climbing ever higher.

My brain shorted out. The world went white-hot, then red-hot, then it became nothing at all but need.

His hand was a wonder. Not soft and manicured, like the hands of the very few men whose hands I'd shaken at some point or other, but hard and calloused. Big, and brutally masculine.

He traced some kind of pattern into my skin, and then laughed against my mouth when I shuddered in response.

His taste was like wine. It washed through me in the same way, leaving me flushed, giddy.

And then his fingers toyed with the edge of my panties, until I was sure I stopped breathing.

Not that I cared when he angled his head, taking the kiss deeper. Hotter.

While at the same time, his fingers moved with bold certainty to find my soft heat.

And then, to my wonder and shame, he began to stroke me, there below.

His tongue was in my mouth. His fingers were deep between my legs, and I couldn't remember why I had ever thought this man was a monster. Or maybe I thought he was a far greater monster than I'd ever imagined.

Either way, I surrendered. And my surrender felt like strength.

It was like some kind of dance. Parry, then retreat. His mouth and his hand, one and then the other, or both at once.

Before I knew it, that fever in me was spreading. I shook, everywhere. I could feel my own body grow stiff in his arms and I felt myself edging ever closer to crisis.

I would have pushed him away if I could. If I could make my hands do anything but grip the front of his shirt as I shook and stiffened and spun further and further off into that blazing need.

I lost myself somewhere between Javier's hot, hard mouth and his pitiless hand between my legs. I lost myself, and I followed that shaking, and I hardly understood why I was making those greedy, shameful noises in the back of my throat—

"Come apart for me, Imogen," he growled against my mouth, as if he owned even this. "Now."

And there was nothing in me but heat and surrender. I exploded on cue.

And I was only dimly aware of it when Javier set me away from him. He settled me on the lip of the table behind us, ran his hands down my arms as if he was reminding me of the limits of my own body, and even smoothed the skirt of my dress back into place.

I was tempted to find it all sweet, however strange a word that seemed when applied to a man so widely regarded as a monster. A man I still thought of in those terms. But there was a tumult inside of me.

My head spun and everything inside me followed suit. I couldn't focus. I couldn't breathe. I couldn't make sense of what had happened.

And when my breathing finally slowed enough that I could think beyond it, Javier was waiting there. He stood in the same position he'd been standing before, his hands thrust into the pockets of the trousers I knew at a glance had been crafted by hand in an atelier in a place like Milan or Paris.

His might seemed more overwhelming now. I had a vague memory of the stable boy's dreamy blue eyes, but they seemed so insubstantial next to Javier's relentless masculinity. I felt it like a storm. It buffeted me, battering my skin, until I felt the electricity of it—of him—as if he had left some part of himself inside me.

I told myself I hated him for it.

"You look upset, *mi reina*," Javier murmured. I understood the words he used—Spanish for *my queen*—

but stiffened at the dark current of mockery in it. "Surely not. I am certain someone must have prepared you for what goes on between a man and a woman no matter how hard your father has worked to keep you locked up in a tower."

I was not one of the sacrificial maidens ransomed out of this place in centuries past, despite appearances. I might have lived a sheltered life, but that life came with abundant internet access.

Still, I followed an urge inside of me, a dark insistence I didn't have it in me to resist.

"I prepared in the usual way," I told him. "Locked towers might work in fairy tales. They are harder to manage in real life, I think."

And when his dark gaze turned to fire and burned where it touched me, I only held it. And practiced that half smile I had seen on my sister's face earlier.

"I will assume you mean that your preparation for marriage took place under the careful tutelage of disinterested nuns as they discussed biology."

I channeled Celeste. "Assume what you like."

Right there, before my eyes, Javier…changed. I had thought he was stone before, but he became something harder. Flint and granite, straight through.

I couldn't tell if the pulse that pounded in me then—in my wrists and my ears, my breasts and between my legs—was fear or something else. Something far more dangerous.

All I knew was that I wanted whatever Celeste had appeared to have on my settee. I wanted that confidence. I even wanted her smugness.

Because it seemed to me that was some measure of power.

I didn't want to be what they called me. The lesser Fitzalan sister. The unfortunate one. Not here. Not now.

I didn't want this man—who had broken me wide-open in ways I didn't know how to explain without, as far as I could tell, so much as breaking a sweat—to know how inexperienced I was. I didn't want to give him my innocence, particularly if he thought it was his by right.

Just once, I thought defiantly, I wanted to feel so-phisticated.

Just once, I wanted to be the sleek one, the grace-ful one.

I wasn't sure I could fake my sister's effortlessness. But I knew that my smirk was getting to him. I could see it in all that stone and metal that made his face so harsh.

"All the better," Javier growled at me, though he didn't look anything like pleased. "You should know that I am a man of a great many needs, Imogen. That I will not have to tutor you how best to meet them can only be a boon."

I didn't believe him. I didn't know what it was that whispered to me that he minded a great deal more than he was saying, but I knew it all the same.

Or you want *to know it*, something whispered in me, leaving marks. *You want to affect him, somehow, after he took your breath away like this.*

I didn't want to think such things. I found myself frowning at him instead.

"Careful," Javier said with a soft menace that made me feel molten and shivery all over again. "If you do not want an example of the sort of appetites I mean, here and now, I'd suggest you go back wherever you came from. There is a wedding in the morning. And an entire marriage before us in which, I promise you, you will have ample time to learn what it is I want and expect. In bed and out."

And then I felt twisted. As if there was something wrong deep within me. Because the fact he was dismissing me stung, when I knew I should have been grateful for the reprieve. I flushed again, but this time it felt more like poison than that same impossible, irresistible heat.

I was only pretending to be like Celeste—and the look on Javier's harsh face suggested that I wasn't doing a particularly good job. I was certain that if he touched me again, I would never be able to keep it up.

And no matter that there was a part of me that shimmered with longing. That wanted nothing more than to feel his hands on me again. And more.

So much more.

I knew I had to take the escape hatch he had offered me—or lose myself even further.

Possibly even lose myself for good.

I slid off the table to find my feet, and fought to keep my expression from betraying how tender I felt where his hand had been between my legs. It felt as if my panties were somehow too tight, as if I was swollen, and I hardly knew how to walk on my own.

Yet I did. I managed it.

I skirted around him as if he was on fire, convinced that I could feel that blistering heat of his from feet away. Convinced that he had branded me, somehow. And entirely too aware of his glittering, arrogant gaze.

But I had a long night ahead of me to fret over such things.

I only understood that I expected him to reach out and take hold of me again when he didn't. And when I made it to the spiral stair and ran up it as fast as I could on my rubbery legs, the clatter of my heart inside my chest was so loud I was surprised he didn't hear it and comment on it from below.

I made my way along the second-floor gallery, aware of his gaze on me like a heavy weight—or some kind of chain binding me to him already—but I didn't turn back. I didn't dare look back.

Maybe there was a part of me that feared if I did, I might go to him again. That I would sink into that fire of his and burn alive, until there was nothing left of me but ashes.

When I slipped back beneath the tapestry and into the servants' walkway, there was no relief. It was like I carried Javier with me, in all the places he had touched me and, worse by far, all the places I only wished he had.

It was as if I was already half-consumed by that fire of his I both feared and longed for.

But I would die before I let him know that he had taught me more in those wild, hot moments than I had learned in a lifetime.

The reality was, I thought about what a wedding night with this man might entail and I…thought I might die, full stop.

I knew that was melodramatic, but I indulged in it anyway as I made my way through the shadowy recesses of my father's house. Why had I gone to Javier in the first place? Why had I been so foolish? What had I imagined might happen? I wanted to sink into a bath and wash it all away, let the water soothe me and hide me. I simply wanted to be back in my rooms again, safe and protected.

Because a deep, feminine wisdom I hadn't known resided there inside me whispered these final hours before my wedding might be the last bit of safety I would know.

I knew too much now, and none of it things I'd wanted to learn. I had found a magic and a fire, yes. But now I knew how easily I surrendered. I knew how my body betrayed me.

I knew, worst of all, that I wanted things I was terribly afraid only Javier Dos Santos could give me.

And I wasn't paying sufficient attention when I slipped out from the servants' hall. I was usually far more careful. I usually listened for a good few minutes, then used the carefully placed eyeholes to be certain that no one was in sight before I slipped back into the house's main corridors.

But Javier had done something to me. He had used my own body against me, as if he knew what it could do better than I did. He had made me feel as if I belonged to him instead of to myself. Even with all this distance between us, clear on the other side of the rambling old manor house, I could feel his hands on me. Those powerful arms closed around me. His harsh, cruel mouth while it mastered mine.

That was the only excuse I could think of when I stepped out and found myself face-to-face with my father.

For a long, terrible moment, there was nothing but silence between us and the far-off sound of rain against the roof.

Dermot Fitzalan was neither tall nor particularly physically imposing, but he made up for both with the scorn he held for literally every person alive who was not him.

To say nothing of the extra helping he kept in reserve for me.

"Pray tell me that I have taken leave of my senses." His voice was so cold it made the ancient stone house feel balmy in comparison. I felt goose bumps prickle to life down my arms. "I beg you, Imogen—tell me that I did not witness an heiress to the Fitzalan fortune emerge from the servants' quarters like an inept housemaid I would happily dismiss on the spot."

I had imagined myself brave, before. When I had taken off on a whim and found the man my father had chosen for me. When I had tangled with a monster and walked away—changed, perhaps, but whole.

But I realized as I stood there, the focus of my father's withering scorn as I so often was, that when it counted I wasn't the least bit brave at all.

"I thought I heard a noise," I lied, desperately. "I only ducked my head in to see what it was."

"I beg your pardon." My father looked at me the way he always did, as if the sight of me was vaguely repulsive. "Why should a lady of this house, a daughter of the Fitzalan line, feel it is incumbent upon her to investigate strange noises? Are you unable to ring for assistance?"

"Father—"

He lifted a hand. That was all.

But that was all that was needed. It silenced me as surely as if he'd wrapped that hand around my throat and squeezed. The hard light in his dark gaze suggested it was not outside the realm of possibility.

"You are an enduring disappointment to me, Imogen." His voice was cold. Detached. And I already knew this to be so. There was no reason it should have felt like an unexpected slap when he took every opportunity to remind me how often and comprehensively I let him down. And yet my cheeks stung red as if he'd actually struck me. "I do not understand this…willfulness."

He meant my hair. He meant those curls that had never obeyed anyone. Not him and not me, certainly. Not the relentless nuns, not my old governesses, not the poor maids he hired to attack me with their formulas and their straight irons to no avail.

"You might almost be pretty, if distressingly rough around the edges, were it not for that mess you insist on flaunting."

My father glared at my curls with such ferocity that I was almost surprised he didn't reach out and try to tear them off with his hand.

"I can't help my hair, Father," I dared to say in a low voice.

It was a mistake.

That ferocious glare left my hair and settled on me. Hard.

"Let me make certain you are aware of how I expect this weekend to go," he said, his voice lowering in that way of his that made my stomach drop. "In less than twenty-four hours you will be another man's problem. He will be forced to handle these pointless rebellions of yours, and I wish him good luck. But you will exit this house, and my protection, as befits a Fitzalan."

I didn't need to know what, specifically, he meant by that. What I knew about my father was that whenever he began to rant on about the things that *befit* a member of this family, it always ended badly for me.

Still, I wasn't the same girl who had foolishly wandered off in search of my husband-to-be. I wasn't the silly creature who had sat on my own settee staring out at the rain and dreaming of a stable boy. She felt far away to me now, a dream I had once had.

Because Javier Dos Santos had branded me as surely

as if he'd pressed hot iron against my skin, and I could still feel the shock of it. The burn.

"What do you suggest I do?" I asked, with the sort of spirit I knew my father would find offensive. I couldn't seem to help myself. "Shave it all off?"

My father bared his teeth and I shrank back, but it was no use. My back came up hard against the wall. There was nowhere for me to go.

And in any event, it was worse if I ran.

"I suspect you are well aware that I wish no such thing, Imogen." If possible, my father's voice dripped with further disdain. "I take it you imagine that your marriage will provide you with some measure of freedom. Perhaps you view it as an escape. If you know what is good for you, girl, you will readjust that attitude before tomorrow morning. Your new husband might not be of the blood, but I assure you, he expects total and complete obedience in all things."

"I never said—" I began.

My father actually smiled. It was chilling. "In fact, Dos Santos is nothing but a common, rutting creature who handles any and all conflict with the deftness you might expect from an uncivilized beast. I shudder to think how he will choose to handle these displays of yours."

I thought I had a good idea of how he might handle them now, but I dropped my gaze, terrified that my father might see all that need and fire Javier had taught me, written all over me. And because I didn't want to see the malicious glee I knew would be stamped all over my only living parent at the notion my husband would *handle* me.

I tried not to miss my mother as it did no good. But in moments like this I couldn't help myself. I knew that if she'd lived, she wouldn't have defied my father, either, but at least I'd had no doubt she loved me.

"Silence at last?" my father taunted me. "That will not help you, either. The die is cast, I am afraid. You will spend the rest of this day and evening locked in your rooms. But do not imagine you will have the opportunity to retreat into those books you love so much, unnatural as you are. I will send in your attendants and mark my words, Imogen. I do not care if it takes from now until the moment the ceremony begins tomorrow, but you will look like a proper Fitzalan for the first time in your life, I swear it. You will tame that mess you call hair. You will do something with your face, for a change. You will be manicured and pedicured and forced to look like the pride and joy of this house no matter what it takes."

"Father," I tried again, "none of this is necessary."

"You cannot be trusted," he seethed at me. "You are an embarrassment. I have never understood how a child of my loins could come out so slovenly. Quite apart from those curls, look at how you walk around my house knowing full well we have important guests who expect the Fitzalan name to connote nothing but grace and elegance, handed down over centuries." His scornful glare swept me from forehead to toes, then back again. "You look as common as he is."

That was the worst insult my father could think to hurl at me.

And the part of me that wished I could please him, no matter how well I knew that was an impossibility, recoiled.

But I didn't say a word. I stood there, letting him skewer me in every way possible, because it wasn't as if there was any way to stop him. There never had been.

When he was done, he straightened, though he already stood as if there was an iron pole where his spine should have been. He adjusted the cuffs of his jacket indignantly, as if my slovenliness was contagious.

"Go to your rooms at once," he told me, as if I was a small child. Which was how I felt when he looked at me. "You will sit there and you will await your attendants."

"Yes, Father." I tried to sound obliging and obedient.

He reached over and grabbed my arm, his fingers closing painfully over my biceps. But I knew better than to make any sound of protest.

"You have less than a day remaining in this house," he hissed. "Less than a day remaining to conduct yourself appropriately. And I warn you, Imogen. If you attempt to embarrass me further, you will not like how this wedding ceremony goes. Remember that all I require is your presence at the ceremony. It is utterly irrelevant to me if you are capable of speaking or even standing."

He left me there, marching off without so much as a backward glance, because he was certain that I would obey him. He was certain—and he was right.

I knew that none of his threats were idle. He would roll me into my own wedding ceremony strapped down to a stretcher if he wished, and not one guest would raise an eyebrow. I wasn't a person to them. I wasn't *me*. I was a Fitzalan heiress, nothing more and nothing less, and it was my father's right to do with me what he pleased. The guests here were as interested in my feelings on what happened in my life as they would be in the thoughts of any piece of livestock.

I could feel the fingerprints Father had left on me, bruising up on my arm already. I ducked my head down, frustration and fury making my eyes water, as I headed toward my rooms.

As ordered.

But the things my father had said to me had, perhaps, the opposite effect of what he'd intended.

Because I had been so focused on Javier. On the fact he was meant to be a monster. I had been so worried about marching myself down the aisle and straight on into my own doom.

I hadn't spent nearly enough time thinking about the fact that monster or not, Javier could only be an improvement on the monster I would be leaving behind.

I might never be free, but I would be free of my father.

And if the price of that was an unpleasant evening of attempts to beat me into submission and make of me the perfect Fitzalan bride to honor my father's vanity, I could only believe it was worth it.

CHAPTER FOUR

Javier

I WASN'T ENTIRELY surprised that my blushing bride was nowhere to be seen at the tedious drinks affair Dermot Fitzalan threw that night.

After all, this was not the kind of wedding that got written up in the gossip pages or excessively photographed for the Style sections of various magazines across the globe, rife with planned events and excessive opportunities to celebrate the romantic idiocy of the marrying couple. My wedding was not a performance.

It was a contract and Imogen was incidental. I had paid for access. For a connection to the kings across time who lived in the Fitzalan name. For the pièce de résistance to add to my collection.

"Have you come with no family of your own, Dos Santos?" asked one of the wolves gathered for this occasion that I doubted anyone would call joyous. He was an overly titled idiot who had spent the last few moments risking his continuing health by standing too close to me and making a great show of looking around the room while he did it. He had obviously wished me to ask what he was doing. I had not. "What kind of man attends his own wedding solo?"

I raised my glass, but made no attempt to wrestle my expression into anything approaching polite. "A man who is well aware that he is making a business acquisition, which I am perfectly capable of doing without an entourage."

The other man brayed with laughter, and I was already bored. I left him without another word, making my way through the high-ceilinged room that had been set up to host this supposedly genial cocktail hour ahead of what promised to be an even duller banquet. I knew Fitzalan was showing off, the way he always did. The guests were meant to be in awe of this historical monument he called a house, me most of all. I was meant to be cowed into reverence by the medieval flourishes and the history in every ostentatious antique.

I was meant to feel small.

Sadly for Fitzalan and his self-regard, I felt quite the opposite.

I couldn't get my bride-to-be and her wild, wholly irreverent red-gold curls out of my head.

Imogen Fitzalan was not at all what I had been expecting and I could not recall the last time anything had surprised me. Much less a woman. Women tended to blur together for me, in truth. Those who approached me hungered for my wealth, my power, and were willing to trade their bodies for a taste of it. And who was I to refuse these generous offers? I accepted them, I enjoyed them, and then I promptly forgot them.

I had always known that I intended to marry a woman who could give my children the only thing I could not buy for them myself: blue blood.

But until that day came, I had always been perfectly happy to revel in the demands of the common red blood that coursed freely in me. It was a heavy pulse in me even now, surrounded by the pale blue aristocrats on all sides and the sort of ancient, theatrical objects cluttering every surface that I knew were meant to trumpet the value of their owner. I was surrounded by the worst sort of wolves, yet I was thinking about sex. All thanks to the bride I had expected would be a cold, prim virgin unable to make eye contact.

I wasn't sure what to do with the surprise I felt. I wasn't sure I liked it.

I made my way to the windows that overlooked the gloomy gardens out back as the fog rolled in to cap off another miserable French day. I preferred the bright heat of Spain, the warmth of my people, and the rhythm of my native language. I nursed my drink as I watched some of Europe's wealthiest men circle each other warily as if violence might erupt at any moment, when I knew very well that was not how men like these attacked. They preferred a stealthier approach. They came at their enemies through hostile takeovers and cruel buyouts. They wielded their fortunes like the armies of lesser men.

They didn't scare me. Not one of the men in this room had created what was his with his own hands. I was the only one here with that distinction.

It meant I was the only one here who knew what it was to live without these privileges. To grow up hard and have nothing but myself to rely on.

And that meant they had a weakness, a blindness, that I did not.

I was smiling at that notion when Celeste swept into the room on the arm of the animated corpse who had made her a countess. The decrepit aristocrat she had chosen over me.

I waited for that kick that I recalled so well at the

sight of her. I had called it lust, back then. Lust and fury, need and madness.

But I knew it better now. Or I knew myself. It had been a kind of covetousness, the way I lusted after the finest cars and the most luxurious residences in the best locations. I had wanted Celeste, desperately. I had imagined she would be the crown jewel of my collection.

Yet tonight, as I saw her operate the room like the shark I hadn't realized she was ten years ago—despite that flat gaze and the smile she leveraged like a weapon—that kick was missing. Was it that I was a decade older now? Perhaps I had seen too much to be turned around by a gracefully inclined neck and too many pretty lies. Or was it that I had finally tasted something sweet today and wanted more of it instead of these bitter dregs of once proud family lines?

If they are bitter dregs, what are you? a harsh voice inside me asked. *As you are here to drink deep of what little they have to offer.*

I didn't know the answer. What I did know was that this evening wearied me already. It could have been any night on any continent in any city, surrounded by the same people who were always gathered in places like this. The conversation was the same. Measuring contests, one way or another. In the dangerous neighborhoods of my youth, men had jostled for position with more outward displays of testosterone, but for all the bespoke tailoring and affectations, it was no different here. Learning that had been the key to my first million.

And still all I could think about was Imogen. That ripe mouth of hers that looked like berries and tasted far, far sweeter. And better yet, her scalding softness that had clung to my fingers as she'd clenched and shook and fallen apart.

I had tasted her from my own hand as she sat before me on that table, attempting to recover, and now it was as if I could taste nothing else.

I'd forgotten about Celeste entirely when she appeared before me, smiling knowingly as if we shared a particularly filthy secret. As if we'd last seen each other moments ago, instead of years back.

And as if that last meeting hadn't involved operatic sobs on her part, vicious threats from her father, and a young man's blustery vows of revenge from me.

In retrospect, I was embarrassed for the lot of us.

"How does it feel?" she asked in that husky voice of hers that was so at odds with all her carefully icy blond perfection. But that was her greatest weapon, after all. Hot and cold. Ice and sex. All those deliberate contradictions at once, that was Celeste.

I eyed her entirely too long for it to be polite. "Are you suddenly concerned with my feelings? I somehow doubt it."

Celeste let out that tinkling laugh of hers, as if I had said something amusing. "Don't be silly, Javier."

"I can assure you I have never been 'silly' a single moment in my life. There is little reason to imagine I might start now. Here."

I did not say, *with you*.

"You and I know how this game is played," she told me, managing to sound airy and intimate at once. "There are certain rules, are there not? And they must be followed, no matter what we think of them. I must commend you on thinking to offer for poor, sweet Imogen, the dull little dear. But it will all work beautifully now."

"I have no idea what you're talking about."

"You were wise to wait," she continued gaily, as if the harsh tone I used was encouraging. As if this was an actual conversation instead of a strange performance on her part. "For men with bloodlines as pristine as the count, there can be no stain upon his heirs. Not even a stray whisper. But I have already done my duty and given him spotless children without the faintest bit of scandal attached to their births. Why should he care what I do now?"

I stared at her. So long that the sly, stimulating smile faltered on her lips.

"You cannot imagine that you hold the slightest enticement for me, can you?" I asked with a soft menace I could see very well hit her like a blow. And she was lucky that I knew very well that no matter how disinterested the crowd around us might have seemed, everyone was watching this interaction. Because everyone knew that a decade back, I had made a fool of myself over this woman. "Is your opinion of yourself so high that you honestly believe I would so much as cross a street for you? Much less marry another woman for the dubious pleasure of becoming close to you in some way? I am interested in the Fitzalan name, Celeste. The blood of centuries of kingmakers. Not a single faithless woman I forgot the moment you made your decision ten years ago."

But this was Celeste, who had never faced a moment she couldn't turn into a game—and one in which she had an advantage. Though I was certain I saw a hint of uncertainty in her gaze, it was gone in an instant.

And then I was assaulted with that laughter of hers that had haunted me long after I had left this very house way back when. And not because I had longed to hear it again—ever—but because it was the soundtrack of my own, early humiliation. One of my very few losses.

"You do what you must, Javier," she murmured

throatily at me. "Play hard to get if your pride requires it. You and I know the truth, do we not?"

And, perhaps wisely, she did not stick around to hear my answer.

But when they called us into the formal dining hall for the banquet sometime later, I made my way over to Fitzalan and curtly told him that I would not be joining him at the table.

"I beg your pardon," the man said in his stuffy way. I couldn't tell if he looked more affronted or astonished—and this could have been as much because I had approached him without express invitation as what I'd said. "Perhaps you are unaware, Dos Santos, but you are the guest of honor." In case I had failed to pick up on that little dig, that suggestion I didn't know enough to realize the dinner was supposedly for me, he inclined his head in a show of benevolence that made my jaw clench. "You are the one getting married in the morning. It is customary for you to take part."

I forced myself to smile, though it felt raw and unused. "I suspect you will all enjoy yourselves more if you can talk about me rather than to me."

And I only lifted a brow when the other man sputtered in obvious insult.

Not because it wasn't true. But because a man like Dermot Fitzalan was far more offended that anyone might dare call him out on his behavior. Especially if that "anyone" was a commoner like me.

I didn't wait for his response, which no doubt insulted him all the more. I left the crowd without any further awkward discussions, then I made my way through the great house, not sure where my feet were taking me. My thoughts were a strange jumble of Celeste, then and now. The Fitzalan family and how Imogen fit into it, so different was she from her father and sister.

And I even thought about my own family, who it had never occurred to me to invite to take part in this spectacle.

My mother had never taken to the new life I had provided for her. She viewed it all with suspicion and saved the worst of that suspicion for me—especially because of the deal we'd struck. Namely, that I would support her only if she gave up her former life and habits entirely. No opiates. No drink. Nothing but the sweet prison of my money.

"Why must you have a wife such as this?" she had demanded the last time we spoke, when I had subjected myself to my usual monthly visitation to make sure neither she nor my sisters had backslid into habits that would—sooner or later—send the wrong sort of people to my door.

I would pay for their lives as long as they kept them quiet and legal. I would not pay to get them out of the trouble I'd insisted they leave behind in their old ones.

They had all flatly refused to leave Madrid. I had only convinced them to leave the old, terrible neighborhood after a criminal rival had murdered my father— years after I had cut him out of my life because he'd refused to quit selling his poison.

It had taken longer than that for my mother and sisters to kick their own seedy habits. And none of us pretended they'd done it for any but the most mercenary reasons. They all wanted the life I could give them, not the life they'd had—especially not when they might find themselves forced to pay for my father's sins if they stayed there.

But that didn't mean they liked it. Or me.

"The Fitzalan girl is an emblem," I had told my mother, sitting stiffly in the house I kept for her and my sisters. I would not have discussed my marital plans with her at all, but had run out of other topics to discuss with these people who hated me for bettering them. "A trophy, that is all."

"With all your money you can make anything you like into a trophy. What do you care what these people think?"

My mother had a deep distrust of the upper classes. My father had trafficked in too many things to count as the local head of a much wider, much more dangerous operation—and she had always been in peril herself because of it—but she knew that world. On some level she would always trust the streets more than the fine house I had provided for her.

Just as she trusted the desperate men who ruled there more than she ever would me.

"My children will have the blood of aristocrats," I had said. "There will be no doors closed to them."

My mother had made a scornful sort of noise. "No one can see another person's blood, Javier. Unless you spill it. And the only people who worry about such things are too afraid to do such things themselves."

My sisters, by contrast, had praised the very idea of a Fitzalan bride for their only brother, because they believed that if they pretended to be kind to me, I might confuse that for true kindness and increase my generosity.

"It will be like having royalty in the family!" Noellia had cried.

"She might as well be a princess!" Mariana had agreed rapturously.

My sisters had taken to my money with avid, delirious greed. They had not disagreed with me in years. On any topic. Because they always, always wanted more. And the longer they lived lavishly at my expense, the less they wanted to find themselves tossed back into the dank pit we'd all come from.

Or more precisely: the pit from which I had clawed my way, with all of them on my back.

I had made the same bargain with all of them. I would finance their lives as long as their pursuits never embarrassed me or caused so much as a ripple in the careful life I'd built.

We had always been family in name only. My father had used us all in different ways, either as mules or distractions or accomplices. We were all tainted by the man who had made us and the lies he'd told us.

And worse still, the things we'd done back then, when we'd had no other choices.

Or what I had done to get away from the tragedy of my beginnings.

Of course I hadn't wanted them here, surrounded by so many of Europe's hereditary predators, each and every one of them desperate to find something—anything—they could use to weaken my position in any one of the markets I dominated.

I wandered the Fitzalan house for a long while. Eventually I found myself in the library, cavernous and dimly lit this night. The roof up above was a dome of glass, though rain fell upon it tonight with an insistent beat that made me almost too aware of its potential for collapse. It felt too much like foreboding, so I focused on the books instead. On the shelves that lined the walls two stories high, packed tight with volume after volume I had never read. And had likely never heard of, for that matter.

I was not an educated man. There had been no time to lose myself in books when there were worlds to be won. And yet I felt it tug at me, that insatiable thirst for knowledge that I had always carried in me. Knowledge for knowledge's sake, instead of the kind of intelligence I had learned to assemble to carry into boardrooms and stately homes like this one, so I might best whoever I encountered.

There were times I thought I would have killed for the opportunity to immerse myself in these books men like Dermot Fitzalan had grudgingly read at some or other boarding school in their youth, then promptly forgot, though they always considered themselves far more educated than the likes of me.

Men like him—men like all those who gathered around that dining table even now, no doubt trading snide stories of my barbaric, common ways—preferred to build beautiful monuments to knowledge like this library, then never use them. I didn't have to know a single thing about Dermot Fitzalan's private life to know that he never tarried here, flipping through all these books he had at his disposal simply because he wished to improve his mind. Or escape for an hour. Or for any reason at all.

Meanwhile, I still remembered the first library I had ever entered as a child. We had been rich for our neighborhood because my father ran product, but still poor in every meaningful way. There had never been any cozy nights at home, reading books or learning letters or tending to the mind in any way. Anything I knew I had been forced to pry out of the terrible schools I'd been sent to by law, often without any help from teachers or staff. And any bit of information, knowledge, or fact I'd uncovered in those sad places had been a prize to me.

The library in the primary school I had attended had been a joke. I knew that now. But what I remembered was my sense of awe and wonder when I had walked into a room of books, however paltry the selection or small the room. I hadn't understood that I could read whichever of them I chose at will. It had taken me years to trust that it wasn't another trick like the ones I knew from home. It had taken me a long time to truly believe I could take any book I liked, read it elsewhere, and return it for another without any dire consequences.

Here in this hushed, moneyed place that was palatial in comparison to the libraries in my memory, I pulled a book with a golden spine out from the shelf closest to me, measured the weight of it in my hand, then put it back.

I drifted over to one of the tables in the middle of the floor, set up with seating areas and tables for closer study. The table nearest to me was polished wood, gleaming even in the dim light, and empty save for three uneven stacks of books. I looked closer. One was a pile of novels. Another was of nonfiction, the narrative sort, in several languages. The third, the shortest, was of poetry.

"May I assist you, sir?" came a smooth, deferential voice.

I looked up to find one of the staff standing there, looking apologetic the way they always did. As if they wanted nothing more than to apologize for the grave sin of serving me. I had gotten used to service after all this time, but that didn't make me comfortable with it.

"I am enjoying the library," I said, aware that I sounded as arrogant as any of the men I had left to toast my humble roots in the banquet hall. "Does the family prefer it to remain private?"

"Not at all, sir," the man before me replied, unctuously. He straightened. "The Fitzalan collection is quite important, stretching back as it does to the first recorded history of the family in this area. The most ancient texts are protected, of course, in the glass cases you may observe near the—"

He sounded as if he was delivering a speech from a museum tour. A very long speech. I tapped my finger against the stack of books nearest me. "What are these?"

If the man was startled that I had interrupted him, he gave no sign. He merely inclined his head.

"Those are for Miss Imogen," he said. When I only stared back at him, he cleared his throat and continued. "Those are the books she wishes to take with her into her, ah, new life."

Her new life. With me.

The servant left me shortly thereafter and I told myself that it was time to go back to my rooms. There was business waiting for my attention the way there always was, and I had better things to do than linger in a library.

But I couldn't seem to move. I stared at those three stacks of books, and it was as if her taste flooded me all over again.

Imogen. Red-gold and wild. Tilting at windmills from all sides.

Because I knew without a shadow of a doubt that had I married Celeste the way I had wanted to do ten years ago, she would not have come to me with a collection of books. Just as I knew that while there was very little possibility that Celeste had spent any time in this library of her own volition growing up, it was a certainty that Imogen had.

There was no reason that should have washed through me like heat.

I picked up the first book of poetry on the stack before me and flipped it open, not surprised that it fell open to a well-worn page. My eye was drawn to a poem that someone—and I was certain I knew who—had clearly liked so much that she'd underlined the things that had struck her most.

"'For here there is no place that does not see you,'" I read, with two lines drawn beneath it in blue ink. "'You must change your life.'"

I closed the book again and left it there, that odd heat still surging in me.

And when I finally started back toward my rooms, I found that I was far more intrigued with this business arrangement of mine than I had been before I'd arrived here.

I had wanted a Fitzalan wife. And I prided myself on getting what I wanted, by any means necessary. When I had decided at a mere eight years old that I would get out of the stark war zone of my youth, I had done whatever I needed to do to make that happen. I had lied to liars, cheated the cheaters, and had built my own catapult before I rocketed myself straight out of my humble beginnings. It had required a ten-year wait to bend Dermot Fitzalan to my will the way I had done, but I had never wavered.

I had wanted the Fitzalan blood. The Fitzalan consequence and breeding. All the aristocratic splendor that went with a connection to these people and the nobility they hoarded like treasure. I had wanted all of it.

I still did.

But I also wanted Imogen.

CHAPTER FIVE

Imogen

I DIDN'T KNOW how most weddings were meant to go.

I had no idea how they were conducted out there in the world where people made their own choices, but mine was not exactly the festival of emotion and tearful smiles I'd been led to expect by entirely too many bright and gleaming online wedding sites. Or reports from my friends at the convent, whose glittering nuptials had been spread across glossy magazine inserts all over the globe—and as such, had been far too crass and common for my father to permit me to attend.

Not that I had truly imagined it would be otherwise.

I had been presented in my father's rooms first thing, after a long evening and another long morning—already—of what one of my attendants had euphemistically claimed was my opportunity for *pampering*.

If this is pampering, I'd thought a bit darkly as they'd worked on me as if I was the Christmas goose, *I'm glad this is the first I've had of it.*

But soon enough it had been time to parade me before the only person whose opinion mattered. I had been marched down the hall of the family wing to my father's sitting room and presented. He had been taking his usual breakfast and had deigned to lower the corner of his newspaper, the better to glare at me as he took in my appearance.

He glared at me for a long time.

The attendants he'd ordered to handle the problem that was me had done their duty. I was buffed and shined and beaten to a glow. But the true achievement was my hair. They had straightened it, time and again. They had poured product on it. They had ironed it and brushed it and had blown it out, more than once, so ruthlessly that it still hurt. Then, not to rest on their laurels, they had painstakingly crafted the kind of sweeping, elegant chignon that my sister made look so elegant and easy.

It had taken hours. I felt…welted.

"I see I should have taken you more in hand years ago," my father said acidly, as if my transformation was somehow as upsetting as my usual appearance was to him. "Why have you roamed about in your usual state of disarray all this time if it was possible for you to look like this?"

I didn't think that was a real question. I could still feel yesterday's bruises on my arm, reminding me of the many virtues of silence, but he continued to glare at me until it occurred to me that he meant me to answer it.

"Well, sir, it took hours," I said, awkwardly, given my scalp still ached and the movement of my jaw needed to form words made it worse.

"Yet you felt the reputation and honor of your family did not merit putting in these hours at any other point in your life." My father shifted his glare to the attendant at my side, dismissing me with a curl of his lip. "See to it she does not mess herself up as she is wont to do.

I want there to be not so much as a single hair out of place at the ceremony, do you understand?"

"Of course, sir," the attendant murmured, also not looking at me.

Because what I thought about the discussion did not signify. To anyone.

And that, naturally, comprised the entirety of the fatherly advice I received before my wedding.

When I was escorted back to my rooms, they were buzzing with activity. My things were being packed by one set of attendants while another set was responsible for dressing me, and no one required my input on these matters. I let them herd me into the wedding ensemble that had been chosen without my input, muttering to each other as they sewed me into the gown I knew my father had paid a fortune for, as it was nothing short of an advertisement for his power.

But then, Javier had also paid a fortune for this, I assumed. So I supposed it was best if he, too, got his money's worth in the form of a proper bride. Even I knew that what mattered on occasions like this was perception. No one in this house cared if I was happy. But they likely all cared deeply that I *look* happy. As well as elegant and effortless and *fully a Fitzalan*, the better to honor the blood in my veins.

They might whisper about the ways I was lowering myself. They might titter about *lying down with the dogs*. They would talk among themselves about the variety of ways money was neither class nor nobility and amuse themselves with their feelings of superiority every time they looked at Javier, who could buy and sell them all. A few might even tut sympathetically about the sacrifice I was making.

But if I dared show so much as a hint of trepidation, they would turn on me like the jackals they were.

When I was dressed in acres of sweeping white and draped in fine jewels that proclaimed my father's consequence and taste to all and sundry, my attendants sat me on the bench at the foot of my bed and ordered me not to move. I had been sitting there stiffly, certain I would somehow spill something on myself without actually having anything to spill, when Celeste appeared.

My father felt bridesmaids were gauche—or he was unaware and/or uninterested in the fact I'd actually made friends at school—but I supposed it didn't matter anyway, as Celeste filled all those roles for me.

I sighed a little as she came into the room, careful to maintain my painfully perfect posture, lest I inadvertently wrinkle something. Or make my hair curl. Celeste looked beautiful, as always, and she certainly didn't look as if it had taken hours upon hours and an army to achieve it. She wore a dress in another, warmer shade of white that only enhanced all her blond beauty.

"I'm supposed to be the bride, but I think everyone will be looking at you instead," I said, and smiled at her.

She smiled back. But I couldn't help thinking it took her too long.

"You've made the guests quite curious, you realize," she said, her voice so light and merry I forgot about how long it might have taken her to smile. "How mysterious, to hide away the night before your own wedding. What on earth were you doing? Engaging in some last-minute contemplation and prayer?" She shook her head at me as if I was a silly, hopeless creature she'd happened upon in the gardens and had rescued out of the goodness of her heart. "I hope you weren't continuing the same futile line of thought as yesterday."

"I was enjoying an enforced battery of spa treatments, courtesy of Father." I held up my hand so she could behold the manicure. It wasn't my first manicure, of course, but the women had done more than simply try to shape the ragged nails I had presented them. They had built me new ones, long and elegant enough to rival Celeste's. "I had no idea that so-called pampering could be so painful."

"A wedding is the last day where a girl should look like some kind of dreadful *tomboy*, Imogen," Celeste said with one of her carefree laughs that somehow landed strangely on me. I told myself it was the unnatural way I was sitting there, like some kind of wooden doll. "But don't worry. I can still see the real you in there. A little bit of makeup and pretty nails doesn't change the truth of who you are."

That should have made me smile, surely. But for some reason, instead, it raked over me as if the words had an edge.

An edge I found myself thinking about a little too much as she conferred with my attendants and determined the time had come at last to transport me to my fate. Because once I started thinking of such things, all I could see was that edginess. Celeste looked beautiful, certainly, but she was holding herself as if all her bones had gone brittle in the night.

And when she returned to my side, it again took a moment for her to summon her smile. I didn't let that fact drift away this time, and saw that no matter how she curved her lips, it did not reach her eyes.

A hollow pit seemed to yawn open in my belly.

But I didn't say a word as she motioned for me to rise to my feet and I obeyed. Because I only had one sister. And if she thought as little of me as everyone else in my life, did I really wish to know it? This was the only family I had left.

That hollow pit had teeth, I found. But I endeavored to ignore it.

"Have you seen my groom?" I asked as she linked her arm through mine and led me toward the door, her steps measured and purposeful. "I'm hoping he might have changed his mind."

I was joking, of course. And yet the look Celeste gave me then was...odd. It was as if I'd somehow offended her.

"One thing you should know about Javier, Imogen, is that he never changes his mind," she told me, no hint of her usual laughter in her voice. And no attempt at the light and airy tone I associated so strongly with her. "Never. When he is set upon something, when he has made up his mind, nothing else will do."

That settled uneasily in my gut, right there in that same hollow place, but I didn't question her on it. The brutal way she was holding herself next to me, so rigid and sharp, and the way she looked at me kept me quiet.

And besides, I could still feel the way Javier had touched me. Kissed me. Turned me utterly inside out without it seeming to affect him in the least. While I was still boneless at the very thought—though it was the next day.

I tried to conceal the shaky breath I let out then, but the sharp look Celeste threw my way told me I hadn't fooled her.

She seemed to soften a bit beside me then. Another thing I opted not to prod at. Something else I didn't want to know.

Downstairs on the main floor of the house the great ballroom had been transformed into an elegant wedding venue. My father waited for me at the doors. He swept a critical glance over me when Celeste presented me to him, then slipped inside herself.

"Let's get this over with quickly," he said gruffly, looking down his nose at me. "Before you revert to type."

And without any further conversation, and certainly no inquiries into my state of mind or feelings about this momentous occasion, he nodded to the servants to fling the doors wide. Then he led me down the center of the room.

I had dreamed about this, too. A wedding. *My* wedding. I had spent years imagining how it would feel. What I would do. How magical it would all seem, even if it was an exercise of strictest duty, because it meant the next stage of my life was about to begin.

But *magical* was not the word that came to mind today. I gazed out at the assembled throng of people my father deemed important, all those greedy-eyed men and the haughty women they had brought with them as decoration. The members of my own extended family, those cousins and relations who I wasn't sure I'd recognize out of context, who were entirely too impressed with themselves to do more than stare back at me as if I was inopportuning them by marrying in the first place.

I was tempted to pretend my mother was still alive. And here. And just out of sight, beaming with a magic all her own…

Because there was precious little magic in this room today. And maybe I was the empty-headed, disappointing creature everyone seemed to think I was, because the lack of it surprised me. I suppose I'd imagined that if I was going to dress up like this and play the part of a fairy-tale bride, everyone else might do the same.

But the way the guests all eyed me as if I was nothing more than a piece of meat laid out for their consumption, I thought we might as well have forgone this ceremony altogether, signed a few papers in the presence of an authority somewhere, and been done with it.

I was trying my best not to let any of my thoughts show on my face when my gaze slid—at last—to the center of the makeshift aisle my father had placed between the tables and the man who waited at the head of it.

And it was as if everything else simply...disappeared.

Every time I saw him I was struck anew. This time was worse than before, not least because I felt the impact of him in so many different places. My breasts felt heavy. My stomach was a knot. In between my legs, I was soft and hot at once.

And Javier could tell.

I knew he could.

He watched me approach as if he had already claimed me in every possible manner. As if this was nothing but a formality. Inevitable in every way.

Something about that hummed in me. Like a song.

I forgot about this crowd of mercenaries and snobs, none of whom I would ever have invited to anything had it been up to me. I forgot about the strange way my sister was behaving, all edges and angles when I had expected at least a modicum of sisterly support. I even forgot about my father, who gripped my arm as if he expected me to fling myself out of the nearest window.

None of that mattered. Not while Javier watched me come to him, dressed for him, his gaze like lightning and the storm at once.

As if he had commanded me to do this thing for the simple reason it pleased him.

As if this was nothing more than an act of obedience.

I didn't know why that word somersaulted through me the way it did. Like a sweet little shiver that wore its way down into the depths of me, deep into places I hadn't known were there.

When I had never wanted to obey anyone, and no matter that I'd had no choice in the matter for most of my life. My father. The nuns. The attendants who were less servants than prison wardens. That was the trouble with the way Javier looked at me. That light in his dark eyes made me imagine the kind of obedience that I might choose to give him.

That faint curve to his hard mouth made me wonder what he might give me in return.

We reached the head of the aisle and my father swiftly handed me over to Javier, as if he dared not risk a delay.

My fate, I thought as Javier's hands wrapped around mine. *My doom.*

This monster I had to hope was truly a man, somewhere behind his harsh exterior.

A man who I knew without the slightest shred of doubt would be inside me, and no matter if he was a monster to his core, before I saw another dawn.

I hardly heard a word of the ceremony. The priest intoned this and that. We made our responses.

But nothing was real to me. It was all a kind of dream until Javier slid that heavy gold band onto my finger, as if it was an anchor.

"You may kiss the bride," the priest said severely, as if, were it left to him, he would rid the world of kissing altogether.

But I didn't care about the opinions of a priest I would never see again. Because Javier was pulling me toward him with the same easy confidence my body remembered all too well, bending his head—

And I was filled with a sudden panic.

Did he really want to do this here? What if I responded to him the way I had yesterday? Right here, where everyone could see me... Where my father could watch as I fell apart and shamed him...

I shuddered at the notion. And I saw a corner of Javier's hard, cruel mouth curl as if I'd amused him.

"Be strong, Imogen," he ordered me. "It is only a little while longer until you will leave this house and be entirely in my hands."

"That is not exactly a relaxing thought," I murmured in reply.

That curl deepened, only slightly.

And then he claimed my mouth with a sheer ruthlessness that nearly took my knees out from under me.

He gave no quarter. He made no allowance for the fact we were in public.

Javier, it was instantly clear to me, didn't care who saw me tremble in his arms.

And when he finally raised his head, there was no mistaking it.

He was smiling.

That was what stayed with me as the guests applauded anemically, and the servants swept in to begin serving the wedding breakfast. His ruthlessly male, deeply satisfied smile.

I expected Javier to leave me so he could make his rounds, talking the usual dry business men always did at these things. As far as I knew it was the point of them. But instead, he stayed beside me. So close beside me, in fact, that I could feel the heat of him.

It sank deep beneath my skin, then into my bones,

as if he was that restorative bath I hadn't had last night. Though I did not have to study the man who stood with me—the man I had married, which I couldn't quite take in—to understand that he was nothing so easily comforting as a warm bath.

He was something else altogether.

"Are you very hungry?" Javier asked.

I found the question perhaps more startling than I should have. I chanced a look at him, feeling that same shivery thing wind its way through me, making my knees feel weak. Because his gaze was so direct, so dark and confronting. His nose was a harsh blade, his mouth that hard line, and I felt scraped raw.

And unable to look away.

"No," I managed to say, after taking much too long to stare at him. "I am not hungry at all."

"Then I see no reason to participate in this circus."

I didn't really process what he said, because he wrapped his arm around my back. That heavy arm of his, all roped muscle and lean, leashed power, and I... floated off somewhere. There was nothing but the wild buzz in my head, Javier's arm around me, and that shivery thing that became a flush, working its way over me until I thought that intense heat between my legs was actually visible. Everywhere.

But I came back to reality with a sharp crack when Javier steered me directly toward my father.

"Fitzalan." Javier nodded curtly, which was not the way people normally greeted my father. They tended toward obsequious displays of servility. But that was not Javier. That was not the man I'd married. "You will wish to say your goodbyes to your daughter."

My father drew himself up into the human equivalent of an exclamation point, all hauteur and offense. He gazed at Javier, then turned that same gaze on me.

I flinched. Javier did not.

"I am afraid I am not following you," my father said in the same distant, appalled voice he used when forced to have a conversation with the servants instead of merely issuing demands.

I thought that really, I should have jumped in to assure Javier that my father was not about to launch into any protracted farewells. That had I slipped off without a word he would likely have had no idea I'd gone.

But I couldn't seem to operate my mouth. I couldn't seem to form any words.

And Javier's arm was around me. It was all I could focus on.

I looked away from whatever strange, male show-down was happening between Javier and my father, and found my gaze snagged almost instantly. It was Celeste. She was sitting at one of the tables next to her husband, paying no attention to whatever conversation the count was having with a selection of other European nobles who looked as close to death by heart attack and advanced age as he did. She looked as effortlessly gracious as always, not a single glossy hair out of its place.

It was the look on her face that struck me. It was so…

Bitter, a voice inside me supplied.

And she wasn't looking at the count. Or my father. Or even me.

She was looking at Javier.

I didn't have time to process that, because Javier was moving again, striding away from my father and leaving me no choice but to hurry to keep up or be left behind. Or, more likely, dragged.

"Are we truly leaving our own wedding breakfast?"

I told myself I was breathless from the sudden sprint, that was all.

"We are."

"I didn't think that was allowed."

My breath caught when he stopped, there on the other side of the great doors that led into the ballroom. Because we were suddenly something like alone, out here in the grand foyer that my father always said had offered gracious welcome to a host of Europe's aristocrats. It was a shock after all the eyes that had been on us inside.

And it was even more of a shock because I was suddenly even more aware of how...difficult it was to be near this man.

My palms felt damp. There was that awful, betraying flush that only seemed to sizzle against my skin. There was heat in all the most embarrassing places.

And still I could only seem to manage to stare at the man who had married me as if I was mesmerized. I thought perhaps I was.

"Listen carefully, Imogen," Javier said sternly, but his tone didn't start any alarms ringing in me. There was still all that mad electricity in his gaze. And that hint of a potential curve in one corner of his mouth. "You are my wife now. Do you understand what that means?"

My heart began to pound, hard. "I think I do."

"Clearly you do not."

He reached over and smoothed his hand over the glossy surface of my chignon, grimacing slightly. No doubt because my hair had been shellacked so many times it was now more or less a fiberglass dome.

"This hair," he growled. "What have you done to it? I prefer your curls."

I blinked at that, aware that if he hadn't still been touching me, I would have assumed I was dreaming. No one liked my curls. Not even me.

Especially not me.

"My father wanted me to look the part today," I managed to say despite my confusion. "He has very specific ideas about how a proper Fitzalan heiress is meant to look."

Javier dropped his hand from my head, but it was only to take my hand. The hand where he had slid that heavy ring that I was sure I would never grow accustomed to. He looked at the ring a moment, then he looked from the ring to the place on my arm where my father had grabbed me yesterday. My attendants had done what they could to cover the marks, but he was so close now. I was sure he could see them.

His hard mouth turned grim. And his gaze when it met mine seemed to shudder through me, so intense was it.

"Your new life begins now," he told me in the same dark, gruff way. "You are a Dos Santos wife, not a Fitzalan heiress today. You need no longer concern yourself with the petty concerns of the man who raised you. It does not matter what he likes, what he wants, what he allows."

He toyed with my hand in both of his, almost idly—though I knew somehow that nothing this man did was truly idle.

"This is true of the whole of the world," Javier told me gravely. "It has nothing to do with you. There are no laws, no leaders, no men of power anywhere that you need consider any longer. You are above all of that."

"Above...?" I echoed, as caught up in his intensity as I was in the way he traced my fingers and warmed my hand between his.

"You are mine," Javier told me, that dark gaze like a new vow, hard on mine. "And that, Imogen, is the beginning and end of everything you need to know, from this moment on."

CHAPTER SIX

Javier

I COULDN'T LEAVE that old pile of self-satisfied stone fast enough.

Or its equally smug inhabitants.

We could have stayed for what would likely have been an interminable wedding breakfast, of course. I could have subjected myself to more condescension. I could have stood in that room, choosing not to let myself get offended by every sanctimonious or outright snobbish comment aimed in my direction. I could have pretended I didn't see the way Celeste watched me, as if she still somehow believed that I would waste all these years and all this time chasing after her when she had made her choice.

But I saw no point in playing those games. I already had what I wanted.

I had already won.

A Fitzalan heiress wore my ring as I had told Dermot Fitzalan one would, sooner or later. Nothing else mattered. Nothing in this old house, at any rate.

I had won.

That Dermot Fitzalan had clearly put his hands on what was mine did not surprise me. Men like Dermot wielded their power in every petty way they could. But it was a rage for another time, beating in me like a pulse.

If I gave in to it here, I feared I would raze these stone walls to rubble.

And I didn't know what to do with the notion that the woman at my side—my prize, my wife—was clearly so used to her father's behavior that she not only hadn't commented on it, she didn't look particularly cowed by it, either.

I took Imogen's hand in mine and started toward the grand entrance, ordering the servants to bring my car around as I moved. One thing men like Fitzalan always did well was train their staff to perfection, so it did not surprise me to find my car waiting when we stepped out of the house and, more, another car idling behind it with all of our bags.

I had left instructions, but even if I had not, there was no way all of Imogen's belongings could have fit into a Lamborghini Veneno. Even if they could, the point of a Lamborghini was not the hauling of baggage, as if it was some kind of sedate, suburban SUV.

I handed her into the sports car that was more a work of art than a vehicle, and then climbed into the driver's seat myself, taking pleasure in the way her wedding gown flowed all over the bucket seats and danced in the space between us. It threatened to bury us both in all those layers of finery.

I wouldn't mind if it did.

I liked the dress in the same way I liked the ring I'd put on her finger. I like signs. Portents and emblems. I liked the optics of a Fitzalan girl at my side, dressed in flowing white with my ring—*mine*—heavy on her finger. I could see faces at the windows inside and knew that those same optics weren't lost on our audience.

I had won a major victory and no matter how they looked down on me, these stuffy, inbred aristocrats knew it. In fact, I thought the snobbier they were to my face, the more aware they likely were that my money and its reach had surpassed them in every possible way.

I was a nobody from the gutters of Spain, and yet I was the one the world still bowed to. They were ghosts holding fast to a past few remembered any longer.

But I remembered. And I had done the unforgivable. I had used all my filthy money to buy my way into their hallowed little circles. I had dared to imagine myself their equal.

They would never accept me, but I didn't need acceptance.

I had what I wanted. The past in the form of the lovely aristocrat beside me, and the future we would make together with my influence.

I drove off from the Fitzalan manor house, allowing the car to growl and surge forward like the high-powered, predatory beauty it was. But as I drove it down the lane, half of my attention was on Imogen, who was leaving her childhood home behind her. It would have been normal if she'd shown a bit of trepidation. Or emotion.

Something complicated, even, to match those marks on her upper arm.

But she didn't look back.

I made it to the landing strip where my plane waited for us in record time, exhilarated by all the power and speed I had in my hands again. Especially after these dreary days locked up with ponderous old men who talked about long-gone centuries as if they'd personally lived through them.

It was Imogen I was focused on as we climbed out of

the car near the plane, however, not the haunted remains of what had once been Europe's most powerful families.

"You look as if you have seen a ghost," I said as I helped her—and all the filmy layers of her wedding dress—out of the car. I tried to imagine what might upset a sheltered creature like this. "Do you miss your late mother, perhaps?"

She looked a little pale, it was true. Though I couldn't tell if that was an emotional reaction on her part after all, or if it was that damned makeup slapped all over her face, hiding those freckles I liked so much, despite myself.

When I looked closer, however, her copper eyes were sparkling.

"I miss my mother every day," she said. "But that was *fast*."

In that same demure voice she had used at our wedding ceremony. The one that made me almost wonder if the half-wild creature who had turned up in my rooms yesterday had been nothing more than a figment of my clearly oversexed imagination.

I was wondering it again when she smiled at me, big and bright enough to make me very nearly forget all the ways they had muted her for the wedding. "I think I like fast."

I felt that directly in my sex.

"I am glad to hear that. I believe I can promise you fast."

I was not only speaking of cars, but I wasn't sure she took my meaning. She reached over and ran her fingers lightly over the sensually shaped hood of the Lamborghini, then jerked them away. And her smile turned guilty.

"I'm sorry. I shouldn't have touched it."

"You can touch it whenever you like."

"Oh. Are you sure? Only, I was under the impression that most men are very picky about who they let touch."

"They are perhaps choosy about *how* they are touched," I said in a darkly amused voice I made no attempt to hide. "But if you show me a man who claims to be overly picky about where a beautiful woman places her fingers, I will show you a liar."

She curled the fingers in question into a fist, and swallowed hard enough that my gaze drifted to that neck of hers I longed to taste.

When her eyes met mine again, she seemed almost... shy. "Are we still talking about your car?"

I felt my mouth curve. I didn't want to answer that. "If you like."

"I think I may have given you the wrong impression yesterday," she said in a rush, as if it had been difficult for her to get the sentence out. "I don't know why I came to your rooms in the first place. And it certainly wasn't my intention—"

"We will have nothing but time to revisit what happened in my rooms," I told her. "Not a single detail will be overlooked, I assure you."

She looked nervous, and another man might have taken pains to put her at her ease. But I was enough of a bastard to enjoy it.

"Oh. Well. I mean, I think you might have come to a certain conclusion..."

Her voice trailed away as I took her hand again, and I liked that. I liked the way her pulse beat wildly in the crook of her neck, there where I could see it. I liked the heat of her hand in mine and the smoothness of her manicured fingers twined with my hard, calloused ones.

I wanted to be inside her more than I wanted my next

breath. I wanted her beneath me, above me. I wanted her in every position I could imagine, and I was a creative man. But they had turned her into a stranger with all that makeup and alien hair.

I didn't like it at all.

"I had intended to jump straight into the sweet satisfaction of consummation," I told her as I led her toward the plane's folded-down stairs.

And I made a split-second decision as we moved. I had planned to take her to my penthouse in Barcelona. It was not the place I considered my true home, but it had seemed to me to be more domestic and private than other properties I had. But she was naive and she was mine. There were marks on her shoulder and they had rendered her unrecognizable. And I wanted things I couldn't quite name.

I followed an urge I hardly understood, and decided I would take her home instead.

"It is not a long flight to the Mediterranean, I grant you." I sounded stiff and strange. I knew it was because I had made a revolutionary decision—when no one was usually granted access to my private island but me. "Still, I thought there would be ample time to take my first taste of wedded bliss."

I could feel her tremble. It was another show of those nerves that lit me up from the inside out, like heat and triumph all at once. Because I liked a little trepidation. I was not an easy man, nor a small one. And Imogen might have indicated that she had already rid herself of her innocence, but I could tell by all these jitters that she had not gotten much experience out of the bargain, no matter who she had been with.

I shoved away the little twist of something darker and stickier than simple irritation that kicked around in me at that thought. Of Imogen spread out beneath another man's body, allowing him inside her…

She was mine. The thought of another's fingers all over her…rankled.

But I was not in the habit of showing my emotions. To anyone. Even myself, if it could be avoided.

"Do you have some objection to the marital bed?" I asked her instead as I allowed her to precede me up the stairs and into the jet. I even attempted to keep my tone…conversational.

I couldn't see her face then. But I saw the way she froze, then started again almost at once, as if she didn't want me to see her reaction any more than I wished to show her mine. I saw how hard she gripped the railing in one hand, and the way she bent her head as she wound as much of the fabric of her heavy dress around her free hand as she could.

I didn't have to see her face to watch the way she trembled. Again. Still.

"I have no objection," she said over her shoulder, in a voice that didn't sound quite like hers. As if her nerves were constricting her throat.

I waited until we had both boarded the plane. I spoke to the captain briefly about the change in flight plans, and when I made my way back into the sleek lounge area, it was to find Imogen seated on one of the leather couches, prim and proper and still awash in all that white.

I threw myself down on the couch facing her, stretching my legs out so that they grazed hers. And then waited to see if she would jerk herself away. Because she was a girl raised to suffer through her duty no matter what, and it had occurred to me that she might very well consider the marital bed one of those duties.

I didn't care to interrogate myself about why, exactly, that idea was so unpalatable to me.

When she didn't move her legs away from mine—when instead she sighed a little bit and stayed where she was—it felt a great deal like another victory.

And the creeping flush that turned her ears faintly pink told me she knew it.

"It looks as if they spent a great deal of time making you into a mannequin today," I said after a long moment spun out into another. "This was certainly not for my benefit. Is this how you prefer to present yourself?"

She took her time raising her gaze to mine, and when our eyes met, hers were cool. I found I missed her wildness. "My father takes his reputation very seriously. You have been saddled with the disappointing Fitzalan daughter, who, I am ashamed to say, requires the aid of a battalion of attendants to look even remotely put together. I assumed you knew."

I didn't think she looked ashamed. If anything, I would have described her as faintly defiant somewhere behind all that composure.

"Remember what I told you, please. The only disappointment that need concern you now is mine. And I am not disappointed."

I saw her work to keep her face still. Polite and composed, which I knew in her world meant wiped clean of anything but that slight smile. Still, there was emotion in that copper gaze of hers that I couldn't quite read.

"My father does not share your taste, it appears. He insisted that for once in my life I represent the family appropriately." She reached up and patted that smooth helmet of a chignon they'd crafted for her. It didn't move. I doubted a blowtorch could move it. "The main point of contention, as ever, was my hair. It offends my father. He has long been under the impression that I will it to curl for the express purpose of defying him."

I studied her as the plane began to taxi for our take-off. She looked as elegant as I could have wished. She looked pulled together and carefully curated, the jewel of any collection, even mine. I had no doubt that every man in that ballroom today who had sneeringly referred to her as the lesser of the two Fitzalan sisters had kicked himself for his lack of vision. She looked like what she was: the lovely daughter of an extraordinarily wealthy and powerful man who had been raised to be adorned in gowns and stunning pieces of jewelry. A woman who would function as decoration and an object of envy, whose pedigree was as much in the way she held herself as in the decidedly blue blood that ran in her veins.

She looked perfect, it was true.

But she did not look like Imogen.

She did not look like my Don Quixote bride, who carried windmills in her smile and an irrepressible spirit in her wild red-gold curls.

I wondered how I would have felt about the vision before me now if I hadn't seen the real Imogen yesterday. Would I have been satisfied with this version of my Fitzalan bride? Would I have accepted this smooth version of her, no edges or angles? Would I already be inside her to the hilt, marking my claim upon her tender flesh?

I couldn't answer that. But I did know this: the woman sitting before me looked entirely too much like her sister.

I wanted the Imogen who was nothing at all like Celeste.

And I opted not to look too closely at why that was.

"You say I have not disappointed you," Imogen said as the plane soared into the air, then turned south to cross France, headed toward Majorca and the Balearic Islands off the coast of Spain. "And I appreciate the sentiment. But you're looking at me as if I'm every bit the disappointment my father always told me I was."

"I'm staring at you because you do not look like yourself at all."

"Are you an expert, then?"

"I did meet you before the wedding, Imogen. Perhaps you have already forgotten."

Her ears pinkened yet again, telling me clearly that she hadn't forgotten anything that had happened yesterday. Neither had I.

"I'm not sure why you think that was an example of me looking more myself." She gave the impression of shrugging without doing so. "Perhaps it was yet another costume. The many faces of Imogen Fitzalan."

"Imogen Fitzalan Dos Santos," I corrected her, all silken threat and certainty. I considered her another moment. "Are you planning to maintain *this* costume?"

Her expression was grave. "I shouldn't think so. It took quite a long time. And several battalions of attendants, as I said."

"This I believe."

I stayed where I was, lounging there as the plane hurtled along, my arms stretched out along the back of the sofa. I did not dare move—because if I did, I was quite certain that I would stop caring all that much about what was the real Imogen and what was not. I would put my hands on her and that would be that.

I was not a man given to denying myself much of anything. So I wasn't entirely sure why I didn't go ahead and do it.

I suspected it had something to do with those marks on her arm and the fact I could not—would not—make myself yet another brutish male she would have to suffer. That was not at all what I wanted from her.

I nodded toward the rear of the jet instead.

"I have no interest in claiming a mannequin," I told her, not certain I recognized my own voice. "Your bags have been taken into one of the staterooms. I suggest you use this flight to wash away all traces of—" I let my gaze move over her hair, her face "—this."

"'This,'" she repeated. She made a sound that I thought was a laugh, though her expression was clear of any laughter when I raised a brow at her. "Which part of *this*? Do you want me to re-chip my nails? Unexfoliate my skin?"

"Do something with your hair," I told her, aware that I felt very nearly…savage. It was need and lust mixed up with that possessiveness I didn't quite know how to handle, much less that softer thing I couldn't name. "It doesn't suit you. And I cannot see your freckles."

"That is for your benefit," she replied, quick enough that I felt the lick of it in my sex again, the reappearance of that defiant girl I had met after all. "Surely everyone knows that the sight of a stray freckle on the nose of one's carefully vetted and purchased bride might scar a man for life."

"Wash it all off," I ordered her quietly. "Or I will come back and do the washing myself, and I'm not certain you will enjoy that as much as I know I will."

There was no mistaking the bright sheen of heat in her gaze then, no matter how quickly she dropped it to her lap. For a moment, I thought I could feel flames leap and dance between us, taking up all the oxygen in the cabin.

"That won't be necessary," she said, addressing her lap. Because, no doubt, she imagined that was safer. "I may play the part of a helpless female, Javier, but I assure you I can handle a simple shower."

CHAPTER SEVEN

Javier

I WATCHED HER go in a great cloud of white—moving as quickly as I supposed a person could on an airplane without actually running—and sat where I was for a beat or two after I heard the door to the stateroom open and then shut. Emphatically.

I pulled out my mobile, scrolling through the nine or ten million things that needed my attention immediately, but set it down again without retaining anything. I could feel her, still. Her taste was in me now, and I wanted more.

I wanted so much more.

Even though I had just told her that I wasn't going to help her wash off her bridal costume unless it was necessary, there was a part of me—a huge part of me—that wanted to head back there anyway.

It had never occurred to me that the other Fitzalan daughter would get to me in this way.

I had assumed, in fact, that she would not. Rumors had always suggested that she was awkward and shy, unused to the company of men. I had expected a shy, trembling flower. I had assumed she would require patience and a steady hand and I had been prepared to give her both to get what I wanted.

"The best-bred ones are always crap where it counts," one of the braying jackasses last night had informed the whole of the room as I'd claimed my drink and cautioned myself against swinging on any of the genteel crowd. Not because it wouldn't have been entertaining, but because it would only prove their wildest speculation about my monstrous, animalistic tendencies to be true and I refused to give them such satisfaction. "They make it such a chore. Best to get a few brats on them as quickly as possible and move on to more tempting prospects."

He had not been speaking to me directly. I was not sure he had even been aware I was in the room. The man in question had been a group or two away, perfectly happy to spout such a thing next to the ratchet-faced woman I could only assume was his unhappy wife. The chore herself, in other words.

All the men in the group had laughed. None of the women had.

And I understood this was how things worked in such circles. I understood that the unpleasant submission of wife to husband was a part of what made their world go round, and they all made the best of it. Because there were lands to think of. Inheritances. Bloodlines and legacies.

Easy enough to lie back and think about the comfortable future. Easy enough to suffer a little in order to gain so much in return.

If I understood anything, it was that particular math.

But I was not one of those blue-blooded aristocratic horror shows, a fact they had taken great pains to make sure I understood this weekend. And understand I did. I understood that they would hate me forever because I could take what they wanted, I could claim it as my own, and I could laugh at the notion that it mattered how little they thought of me.

Just as I could dismiss the notion that I needed to treat the aristocratic wife I'd gone to such trouble to buy the way they would have, if she'd been theirs.

I did not need my wife to be my partner, the way I knew some wives were to their husbands, each of them committed to the continuation of their family's influence. And I'd watched my parents sell out each other—and us—too many times to believe in love. But if there was one thing I knew I was good at, and took pride in the practicing, it was sex.

I had been certain that in this, at least, I would manage to work a bit of magic, no matter how repressed and overwhelmed my convent-trained wife appeared.

But that was before Imogen had appeared in my rooms and let me taste exactly how sweet she was. How soft, how hot.

And now I had no doubt at all that whatever else there might be between us, we would always have that deliciously wild heat and everything that came with it.

Windmills all around.

Steady, I ordered myself. There was no point rushing things now when I had waited ten years to get here.

I picked up my mobile again, and forced myself to concentrate on my business. And when I looked up from putting out fires and answering the questions only I could, hours had passed. The plane was landing.

And the woman who walked out of the back of the plane to meet me was the Imogen I remembered. The Imogen I wanted.

Gone was the wedding dress and all its gauzy, bridal splendor. In its place, the first Senora Dos Santos wore another dress like the one she'd had on yesterday when

I'd first caught sight of her. Three-quarter sleeves and a hemline no one in their right mind would call provocative. Another pair of glossy, polished leather boots.

But what got my attention most was the hair. Her glorious hair, curling this way and that. I could see that it was still damp, so it looked darker than its usual red-gold, but I hardly minded. Not when I could see the curls I already thought of as mine and, even better, those freckles scattered across her nose.

"Much better," I told her.

"I'm glad you approve," she said, and though her tone was nothing but polite, I found myself searching her face to see if I could locate the edge I was sure I had heard. She looked out the windows. "Where are we?"

"This is the Mediterranean," I said, gesturing out the window at the deep blue surrounding us. "Or more properly the edge of the Balearic Sea, somewhere between Menorca and Sardinia."

She came and sank down on that sofa across from me again. "I've seen pictures of the Mediterranean, of course. But I've never been before."

"I was given the impression you haven't been anywhere."

"My role is to operate as an ornament," Imogen said, without any particular bitterness. "Not to travel the world, collecting experiences. I've had to make do with pictures on the internet."

"I am not at all surprised that your father feared that if you left, you wouldn't return to his tender mercies."

Imogen gazed at me, a faint, sad curve to her lips. "Do you know, I never tried to leave. I'm not sure he was the one who was afraid. He might not have been much in the way of family, but he was the only one I had and I suppose that meant more to me than it should have."

I didn't know why that touched me. I hated that it did. It was one thing to enjoy the fact that we had chemistry, and all the things that could mean for the marriage ahead of us and the sort of sex I had not been looking forward to doing without.

It was another entirely to feel.

Especially when those feelings tempted me to imagine I could relate in any way to a girl who had been raised wrapped up tight in cotton wool and convent walls when I had never been protected or sheltered from anything. On the contrary, my parents had often used me to help sell their poison.

I had learned how to mistrust everything by knowing full well no one could trust me.

"I have an island," I told her coolly, determined that there be no trace of those unwelcome *feelings* in my voice. "It is not very big. But I think it will do nicely enough."

Her gaze moved from the deep blue of the water below to me, then back again, and I could see the trepidation written all over her, stamped into her skin, and yet her anxiety didn't thrill me as much as it had before.

What I could not seem to get straight in my head was why I had presented my island to her in the fashion I had. My own words seemed to hang there in the cabin as the plane lowered toward the ground. Had I truly dismissed it—called it *not very big*? The private Mediterranean island that I had long used as my primary home? It was the one place on the planet I could be sure there would be no eyes on me unless I allowed it. Unless I expressly invited it.

Which I never did.

When I had stood in that house with Imogen's father and all the stuffed shirts he called his contemporaries, there had not been a single part of me that had felt in any way inferior. The very idea was laughable. But let Imogen gaze at me, her freckles uncovered and her curls unleashed because I had demanded she reveal herself to me, and I was undermining myself.

Until this moment, I hadn't known I had such a thing in me.

To say I loathed it was an understatement.

I let that betrayal of myself simmer in me as the plane touched down. I said nothing as we disembarked, allowing Imogen to take her time down the metal stairs, making noises of pleasure as she went.

Because, of course, the island I called La Angelita was—like everything in my collection—a stunning thing of almost incomprehensible, unspoiled beauty. In every direction was the sea, flirting here, beckoning there. The island was barely ten miles across, with the ruins of an old villa of some sort on one end, and high on the cliffs at the other, my own version of a manor house.

Except mine was built to bring the island inside instead of keeping the dour northern French weather out. I had insisted on wide-open spaces, graceful patios, arches beneath red-roof tiles so that everything was airy and expansive. Notably unlike the depressing blocks of flats I'd been forced to call home as a child.

I was proud of this place and the way I'd had it built to my exact specifications. I showed it to very, very few. My own family had never merited an invitation.

It was possible, I thought as I swung into the Range Rover that had been left for my use by my staff, that

I was experiencing a most uncharacteristic attack of nerves myself.

Except Javier Dos Santos, Europe's most feared monster, did not have *nerves*. I did not suffer from any kind of performance anxiety. If I had, I would likely have remained in the neighborhoods of my youth, working a dead-end job if I was lucky. Except young men in those neighborhoods were very rarely *lucky*. They usually ended up dying as my own father had, victims of their own greed and circumstances, slinging poison until it killed them one way or another.

"What a lovely spot," my wholly unaware new wife said, beaming around in all the Mediterranean sunshine as if she hadn't the slightest idea what she was doing to me. I supposed it was possible she didn't, though that suggested she was far more innocent than she had told me she was. "How often do you make it here?"

"La Angelita is my primary residence."

"You mean it's your home."

That was what I called it, but only to myself. The word *home* had too many associations I shied away from. Too many *feelings* attached. "That is what I said."

Her smile only widened at that. It made me...restless.

By the time we drove up to the house itself, sprawled there at the highest point of the island to capture the sweeping views in all directions, I was certain that I had made a terrible mistake. I should have taken her to Barcelona as planned, where I could have been far more certain there was nothing of *me* to be found. I had properties in every major city across the globe, and even more than that in tucked-away, hard-to-reach places. There was a beach in Nicaragua that I had been meaning to visit for some time, for example, to bask in the lack of crowds. There was a mysterious rain forest in Uganda, a spectacular oasis in Dubai.

I should never have brought her *here*.

Especially when I pulled up to the front of the villa and my brand-new wife turned to me, her eyes shining, as if I had given her a gift.

"This is *wonderful*. I thought I would be marched off to some dreary place like my father's house. Somewhere in the pouring rain, very grave and serious and cold, where I would have the opportunity to contemplate the occasion of my marriage in daily sober reflection in the bitter chill. This already seems much better than that."

"Far be it from me to keep you from sober reflection of any kind."

She was still smiling. "I suspect I'll enjoy all kinds of reflection a great deal more in all this *sunshine*."

"I do not know how you are used to spending your days," I heard myself say as if I was auditioning for the role previously played by her own officious father. "But the first thing you must know about your new life, Imogen, is that I am not a man of leisure. My primary occupation is not finding ways to live like a parasite off the interest of family investments without ever having to lift a finger. I work for my living. I always have and, I promise you, I always will."

I expected her to be offended at that, but instead she gazed at me with a thoughtful expression on her face. "Does that mean I am expected to work, too?"

I scowled at her. "Certainly not."

"That's a pity. I have always wanted to."

"Let me guess." My voice was too harsh. She didn't deserve it. But I noticed that she also didn't seem to react to it, particularly. It was almost as if she was so used to being badly treated that she hardly noticed it at all, and I couldn't say I liked that, either. But I didn't stop. "It has long been your heart's dearest dream to find yourself working in a factory, is it? Backbreaking hours on a factory floor, canning, perhaps? Doing boring, repetitive work, where mindless perfection is required hour after hour after hour? Or let me guess, you would prefer something in a field somewhere? Hideous physical labor among the crops, perhaps. Or there is always the oldest of all professions."

"You are mocking me, of course," she said, in such a calm voice that something I hadn't felt in a decade shifted inside of me, then shot out oily tentacles. *Shame.* I'd last felt it when I'd burned all bridges with my father and used the fire to propel me out of his world, once and for all. "Though now that you mention the oldest profession, you should probably know that the most famous Fitzalan widow of the twelfth century was rumored to have been quite the mistress of her field. I'm sure it was terribly scandalous at the time. Now it's just a story my father likes to tell."

"Even if I wished to put you to work tomorrow, what could you do?" I asked her, still unable to stop myself, and still not sure why I was angry in the first place—and her matter-of-fact talk of ancient prostitutes in her family line only made it worse. "By your own admission you have been trained to be a quiet, genteel decoration, nothing more."

She said nothing for a moment, and I was too aware that we were still sitting in the drive as if frozen there. The sun danced over her, catching those freckles and the gold in her curls. My jaw ached, I was clenching my teeth so hard.

"I am more aware than you could ever be of my own limitations," Imogen told me quietly. With a dignity that felt like a slap. "I know that there is no possibility that I will ever find myself working in a factory. But perhaps I could contribute to the welfare of those who do. There are supposed to be advantages to this much wealth and privilege. Would it be the worst thing in the world if I tried to use them for good?"

I didn't know what I would do if I stayed where I was, caged up in that Range Rover. As if I had somehow shut myself in a box and couldn't find my way out. I slammed out of the vehicle, then stormed around the front of it, my gaze hard on Imogen's.

I opened her door and took her hand as she exited, because she might know her limitations, but I had studied mine. I had determined that of all the things that might trip me up or get in my way in the world I chose to inhabit, manners would not be one of them. I knew which fork to use. How to address whoever might be standing in front of me. How to tie my own damned tie. That was what I had done with the ill-gotten money I'd stolen from my father when I'd left his particular den of iniquity. I'd learned how to look like the man I wished to become.

Then I'd become him.

I was aware that in the places people like Imogen frequented, acts of chivalry were considered the very height of manners. The difference between me and those who practiced it—because the act was what mattered, and the more public the better—was that not one of them had any respect for this woman.

And I was terribly afraid I had more than was wise.

I led my wife into my house, aware of something primitive that beat in me, forcing me to examine it with every step. I had never been possessive like this before. I hardly knew what to make of it.

"I don't suppose you have a library?" she asked me as we crossed the first atrium, where the sun and breeze brought the sea inside. I could hear the hope in her voice.

Just as I could hear how hard she had worked to strip the sound of it from her words.

It pierced me. It was as if she had taken one of the ceremonial blades that hung as decoration on my walls and thrust it straight through me. I thought of those three stacks of books on the table in her father's library. Telling me things about her I wasn't sure I wanted to know.

I didn't understand why it felt like this. As if I could see her, straight through her, and yet was somehow showing her entirely too much of me.

I was not a man who needed to be known. I was more than happy to remain a mystery. I actively courted it, in fact. And at the same time I didn't want to think of Imogen in my house the way she'd been in her father's. Hiding in out-of-the-way places like that library, steering clear of her father's ego and cruelty. And I certainly didn't care for the comparison.

"Yes," I said stiffly. "There is a library. But most of the books in it are in Spanish."

If I expected that to dim her enthusiasm, I was sadly mistaken. If anything, she brightened. "I need to work on my Spanish. I'm not quite fluent yet."

And that was too much. I had an unsolicited vision of Imogen, with her red-gold curls and those sparkling eyes, crawling over me. Naked. And whispering sex words in Spanish. *Mi pequeño molino.*

I didn't think then. My hands did the thinking for me. Before I knew what was happening, they were pulling her to me.

"There is only one word you need to know in Spanish, Imogen." I bent my head. Her lips were a temptation almost beyond imagining. Ripe and sweet, and this time I already knew how good she would taste. "*Sí*. All you need to learn is *sí*. Yes, my husband. Yes, Javier. *Yes*."

I could feel her tremble. But it wasn't fear. I could tell that from how pliant she was, there between my hands. But if I had been in any doubt, her copper eyes glowed.

I crushed her mouth to mine, as if in a fever.

I didn't care that we were in the wide-open foyer of my house. My staff was paid handsomely for their discretion. But that was the last thought I gave the matter.

I feasted on her. Her mouth was plump and ripe and *mine*, and I had married her, and the fact I was not yet inside her was like torture.

I could feel the pulse of it in my neck. My gut. And in my sex most of all.

I lifted her up, high against my chest, then pulled her thighs around me so she could lock her ankles in the small of my back. I didn't break the kiss, carrying her with me as I moved, my arms wrapped around her to keep her from falling even as she held on to my neck.

I found the first available surface, an incidental table against the nearest wall, and propped her on the edge of it. I kept her at an angle, moving my hands down to find their way beneath that skirt with an urgency I had no desire to temper.

And still I kissed her, deeper and more wild with every stroke. I could taste the addicting heat in her. I could taste every small cry she made in the back of her throat. I could smell the shampoo and soap she had used in the shower on my plane, and they struck me as impossible aphrodisiacs.

There was no time left. I felt mad with the need to claim her. Now.

It was like a drumbeat pounding in my head, and everywhere else besides.

I hooked my fingers on the scrap of lace I found beneath her dress, and tore it off. She made a noise of surprise against my mouth, but my fingers were in the soft heat between her legs, and I felt her turn molten.

I felt clumsy and something like desperate as I fumbled with my own trousers, shoving them out of the way, and letting the hardest part of me spring free at last.

I shifted, and picked her up again, notching the head of my sex against her heated furrow. I angled my head, taking the kiss deeper, thrilling in her uninhibited response to me and those greedy little noises she couldn't seem to stop making.

I didn't understand why this woman got to me the way she did. I didn't understand the things she had made me feel. But I told myself none of that mattered, because there was this.

I gripped her bottom, positioned her perfectly, and then slammed myself home.

And everything changed.

Imogen cried out. Her body, which had been pliant and soft, stiffened.

And I knew.

She was so tight around me it was something like a dream—and I knew.

I muttered a curse and clamped down on the vicious need stampeding through me, bringing myself under control.

"You are a virgin," I bit out, vaguely surprised that I was even able to speak.

Her eyes were slick with unshed tears. Those fine,

ripe lips of hers looked vulnerable. Her hands had somehow ended up in fists against my chest.

But still, she tilted up her chin and met my gaze, her
curls tumbling over her shoulder as she moved. Because
this was Imogen.

"Of course I'm a virgin," she said, and though her
voice was scratchy, there was no mistaking the challenge in it. "I was under the impression that was what
you paid for."

CHAPTER EIGHT

Imogen

IT HURT.

Oh, how it hurt.

I had meant to tell him, despite my bravado back at my father's house. But I hadn't. And then he had kissed me, sweeping me into his arms, and everything had been so thrilling, so wild—

I felt betrayed that had turned to this. To pain, though the sharpness was fading. But there was still this impossible...*stretching*.

I could feel him inside me. And that part of him, it seemed, was as mighty and powerful as the rest of him.

"You told me you were not a virgin." Javier's voice was the darkest I had ever heard it. Strained, almost. Gritty and harsh, but that seemed the least of my worries. "You made certain to tell me you had given your innocence to another."

It struck me as more than a little ridiculous that we were having a regular conversation. Like this. Both of us half-naked and parts of us *connected* in that too real, still heavy and unsettling way. I thought that all things considered, I'd very much like to cry. Though I refused to dissolve in front of him. I refused to prove that I was every bit the too-sheltered convent girl he already thought I was.

"I didn't actually *say* I'd slept with someone else," I pointed out.

We were so *close*. I wanted to shove him away from me even as he continued to hold me in the air, wrapped around his big body. And at the same time I wanted to move even closer to him, though I didn't think that was even possible.

And I had no idea why I couldn't catch my breath. I told myself it was the way he continued to stretch me from the inside out. I didn't know if it was the picturing it that made my throat go dry, or the actual sensation.

Javier's expression was far too intent. His dark eyes glittered. "This seems as good a time as any to tell you that I cannot abide lies. Of any kind. Ever. You would do well to remember that, Imogen."

I wanted to tell him what he could do with his dire warnings, but he was inside me and I was…*wide-open* in ways I could hardly process.

"I wanted you to think I had slept with someone, yes," I corrected myself, and then hissed out a little breath when he moved, there below, where I felt exposed and too soft and split open and shivery.

He didn't move much. He pulled the littlest bit out, then slid in again, and I shifted in his firm grip, irritably, to accommodate him.

He still held me up and it was odd to think about that. That he could be so strong that he could continue to hold me like this, my legs wrapped around him and all of my weight propped on his hands.

And on that other part of him, I supposed.

When I flushed a bit at that, he moved again. Still,

only that very little bit. He did it once, then again. And again.

"Why would you tell me something like that?" Javier did not sound angry, exactly. His voice was too rich. Too dark. It was as if his voice was lodged inside me, too. "It was never my intention to hurt you, Imogen. And now I have. I wonder, does this fit into the story you have in your head? The barbarian commoner who took you like an animal and hurt you on your own wedding night?"

My breath was doing funny things. And he hadn't stopped that odd little rocking of his. "I don't have any stories in my head."

"I told you how I feel about lies. They say I am a brute, do they not? A monster? Did you want to make sure there could be no debate about that? Do you plan to report back that I am actually far worse than you'd imagined?"

"I don't know what you... I would never... I didn't mean for this to happen."

But I didn't know if that was true. Had I meant it? After all, I hadn't told him any different and I was the only one who knew the truth. If there was someone to blame for my discomfort, I was very much afraid it was me. I might not have had much experience—or any, come to that—but I had only met him yesterday and he'd had his hands between my legs with dizzying speed.

I had known the moment he swept me into his arms today where he was headed, hadn't I? The destination might have been fuzzier in my mind. Gauzier, perhaps. But I'd known where we were going.

Maybe he's right, a terrible voice inside me whispered. *Maybe you* wanted *the pain*.

I couldn't tell if the wave of sensation that washed through me then was heat or shame, frustration or need, and I wasn't sure I cared. I moved against him instead, making my own kind of rocking. And something was different then. Something had eased a little, deep inside me, and so I shifted again.

And that time, the wild sensations that swirled around in me were somehow a part of that feeling that stretched me. A part of it and yet something else, too. Something infinitely hotter.

Something that seemed to reflect in Javier's eyes as well.

He gripped me harder. And then he began to move. Or more to the point, he moved *me*.

He lifted me up, then settled me back down on that insanely hard part of him, and waited. When I only sighed a little, then sneaked my hands back up around his neck again, his eyes gleamed.

"I do not wish to play into your stereotypes," he murmured, lifting me and settling me again. Then again. "There are any number of ways this marriage can and may yet be terrible, *mi esposa*, but it will not be because I am a monster in this way. I will not brutalize you in bed. That is the very last thing I would ever wish to do while inside you."

He lifted me up, and put me down again, and every time he did it there was…*more*. More heat. More sensation.

More greed, stampeding through me like some kind of sudden rain shower. I wanted to dance in the storm. I angled myself closer, heedless and needy and amazed, so I could rub the tips of my breasts against the hard wall of his chest.

I did it once, not sure why I wanted to do such a thing

until the mad sensation of it made me shudder. I did it again, and he laughed.

Then he picked up his pace.

And I had meant to say more. I had meant to somehow explain the decision I had made. Why I hadn't told him that I was a virgin and why that didn't count as the kind of lie I shouldn't have cared if I told him or not.

But I couldn't concentrate on anything except that glorious heat inside of me. *Him.* The thickness, the length. The way he seemed to fit me perfectly, over and over and over.

I began to feel that same crisis. I began to pant and shake. And all the while he held me as if he could do it forever, thrusting into me over and over again as if I had no purpose on this earth but this. Him. *Us.*

And when I finally broke, it washed over me like another kind of storm, intense and endless. I sobbed out his name, tipping my head forward to bury my face against his neck.

But Javier wasn't done. He shifted me back against the table, angling me so he could hold me against him with one strong arm and brace himself against the wall with his other hand.

And when he thrust into me then, I understood he had been holding back.

This was deeper. Harder.

So wild I wasn't entirely sure I would survive. So hot and glorious I wasn't sure I wanted to survive.

I had already exploded into too many pieces to count, but something about his ferocity lit that fire in me all over again, tossing me from one great crisis straight into the arms of another.

And this time, when it hit me, I screamed.

I felt him pulse within me as he let out a deep groan

I only wished was my name, and then he dropped his head to mine.

I had no idea how long we stayed there like that. Panting. Connected.

And for my part, anyway, completely changed.

But eventually, Javier pushed himself away from me. He reached down to release himself from the clutch of my body, and I didn't understand how I could feel… empty. When I had never known what it was to feel *filled* before.

I watched him, half in embarrassment and half in fascination, as he tucked himself away into his trousers again. Then he tugged me off the table and onto the floor, my dress falling down to cover me as if he'd planned that, too.

He didn't say a word. He studied my face for a moment and I regretted the sunlight that poured in from all the open spaces in this house of his, no doubt showing him things I would have hidden if I only knew how. He slid his hand to the nape of my neck, set me in front of him, and propelled me through the sprawling, open house that way.

I should have objected. I should have told him I didn't require that he march me about as if his hand was a collar.

But I was too busy concentrating on putting one foot in front of the other when I felt as if I was made out of froth and need and might shiver to pieces again at any moment. I was surprised I could walk at all. I felt giddy. Silly.

And that didn't change when Javier brought me into a huge, sprawling set of rooms I understood at a glance were his. And likely also mine, though my brain shied away from that, as I had never shared a room—or a bed—with anyone in my life. I couldn't understand how it worked. I'd seen a thousand images of couples tangled around each other, of course, but I couldn't imagine how *I* would settle like that, with arms heavy over me, or my face pressed against someone's back, or…

It was possible I was panicking.

I forced myself to breathe as Javier led me over to a set of the floor-to-ceiling windows that made up the outside walls of this room. This house. Up close, I saw they were actually sliding doors. Javier nodded toward the series of sparkling blue pools outside, each reflecting the blue of the sky above and the sea beyond, and it seemed some kind of dream to me after such a cold, gray January at my father's house. After all the cold, gray Januaries I'd endured there.

It was a gift. It fell through me like the sunlight itself, warming me from the inside.

"The top one is the hottest," he told me, and there were things in his voice I didn't understand. Dark, tangled things. Intimate things. I shuddered. "Go sit in it and soak."

"I didn't bring a bathing costume," I heard myself whisper.

His hand tightened at the nape of my neck, just the slightest bit. Just enough to assure me he felt every shivery, shuddery thing that worked its way through me. "You will not require one, *querida*."

It didn't occur to me to disobey him. He pulled open the heavy sliding door and I walked through it of my own volition. The breeze was warm, or I was warm, and I breathed it all in, deep. I went over to the side of the first, highest pool, and busied myself unzipping boots that seemed too clunky and severe for all this Mediterranean sunlight. He had done away with my panties, another thing I couldn't quite think about directly without blushing, so I pulled off my dress, unhooked my bra, and then went to the edge of the pool. I could see the steam rising off it in the air that could only be the slightest bit cooler. I didn't question it. I eased my way in, sighing a little as the heat enveloped me.

And only as I sat there did I understand the true beauty of these pools and the careful way they had been arranged. Because as I sat, I couldn't see the other pools I knew were there, laid out on different levels here on this cliff high above the water. I could only see the sea.

I thought I had never seen anything so beautiful in person, with my own eyes. There was the sun up above, the blue sea wherever I looked, and the sweet January air that I suspected might be considered cool to those who lived in this climate year-round. But it felt like some kind of prayer to me.

And when Javier slid into the water next to me, I was tempted to imagine that prayer had been answered. I didn't look at him. I was afraid to look at him, I understood, because he was so big and *male* and I could still feel where he'd been inside of me.

And looking at all his flesh, stretched out in such an unapologetically male fashion beside me, might... change me.

We sat in the hot water overlooking the endless stretch of blue for a forever or two. The water soaked deep into my bones, or so it felt. It made me feel as boneless as he did. Maybe it was the sun, washing over the both of us and making me feel all kinds of things I never had before.

Light. Airy. As if I was made of the sunlight and the deep blue water, infused with all that glorious warmth.

As if I were connected to the bright pink flowers that crawled up the stone walls of the villa, or the almond tree blossoms, or even the sweet scent of jasmine that danced on the breeze.

"Your life has been lonely, has it not?" he asked after a long while. "Is that why you pretended you weren't a virgin? To confuse the issue?"

And I should have felt ashamed, I thought—but I was too boneless and warm, suspended in all that sunlight and blue.

"Lonely compared to what?" I turned to look at him, my breath catching. And that place between my legs pulsing with fascination. And hunger. "What of your life? You had no friends or family at your own wedding. Are you lonely?"

He eyed me as if I had grown fangs there before him. "I do not get lonely."

"Well, neither do I."

"You told me you miss your mother every day."

The air went out of me at that, but I managed to smile at him anyway. "Yes, but that is no more than another part of me. A phantom limb. I miss her, but it doesn't make me lonely. It reminds me that I loved her." And that she had loved me the way my father had never managed to, but I didn't say that. "I thought you lost your father, too."

"I did." There was an arrested look on his face then. "But I do not miss *him*, Imogen. If I miss anything, it is the father he never was."

I didn't know how long we merely gazed at each other then. I only knew that somehow, I felt more naked than I had before. When Javier moved again, rising from the pool, I wasn't sure if I felt a sense of loss or relief.

"Come," he said from behind me, and I felt as glutted on sunshine as I did shaky and exposed, but I obeyed him.

It was not until I climbed from the pool that I realized that I was showing myself to him. Fully naked, as I had felt in the water. I stopped at the top of the stairs and froze, though the alarm I surely ought to have felt seemed dulled, somehow, as if the sun had taken that, too.

Or that look in his dark gaze had.

Javier had wrapped a towel around his lean hips and something about the contrast between the bright white of the fabric and his olive skin made a different kind of heat tumble through me. And his dark gaze blazed as it moved over me. I felt the heat of it in the fullness of my breasts, the flare of my hips.

He did not speak as he came toward me, then wrapped me carefully, so carefully, in a towel of my own. His expression was grave, that gaze of his intent.

And he made me shudder. Simply by tucking me into the embrace of that towel, then smoothing a few curls back from my face, with a kind of quiet heat that spiraled through me like reverence. And then again when he ushered me over to a table, saw that I was seated with a courtesy that made me ache, and only then raised a finger to beckon his servants near.

I hadn't known I was hungry until the table was covered, piled high with all sorts of delicacies I knew must be local to the region. Cheeses and olives. Marvelous salads made of wild, bright-colored produce. An aromatic chicken, steeped in spices. Almonds and various dishes. I hardly knew where to look. What to taste first.

The food seemed like a part of the sun, the sea. Javier himself. As if there was not one part of this new world

I found myself in that wasn't different from the one I had left behind, down to this meal before me with all its sweet, bright colors and savory combinations instead of my father's routine meals made to cater to his vanity in his trim physique, never to tempt him in any way.

Here, with Javier, everything was a temptation.

Especially Javier himself.

He sat across from me, the acres of his bare chest as lush and inviting as the food between us, all mad temptation and sensory overload.

And this man had bought me. Married me. He had taken me from my father's house, and then he had taken me in every other meaning of the term. He had brought me out of the rain, into the light. And now it seemed I found every part of him as sensual as his hands on my body or his hard, cruel mouth and the wicked things it could do against mine. Or that impossibly hard heat of him, surging deep inside me.

He leaned back in his chair, lounging across from me, and I discovered that watching him eat was almost too much for me to bear. Those big, strong hands that I now knew in an entirely different way. Even his teeth, that I had felt graze the tender flesh of my neck. I felt goose bumps dance up and down my arms, then down my spine, and all he did was tear off a crust of bread and dip it into a saucer of olive oil.

Javier was beautiful. Rugged and demanding. He was harsh and he was beautiful and I knew, now, what it was to have him deep inside me.

And I understood that I would never be the same. That I was changed forever, and even if I didn't know quite what that meant—even if I wasn't sure how it would all play out or what it meant to be married at all, much less to a man so different from my father or my sister's husband—I knew that there was no going back to the girl I'd been on that window seat a mere day before, staring out at the rain and dreaming of a safe, sweet stable boy I had barely met.

Here, now, sharing a table with a man like Javier in all the seductive sunlight, it was clear to me exactly how I'd been fooling myself.

There were girlish dreams, and then there was this. Him.

And even as I shivered inside, the shiver turning into a molten heat there where I was still soft and needy, I was glad I knew the difference.

"Let me know when you have eaten your fill," Javier said almost idly, though there was something about his voice then.

Stirring. Intense. As if he knew full well why I couldn't quite sit still.

"Why? Do you not have enough?"

A flash of his teeth. Another man's smile, though in Javier, all I could see was its menace. As if I had insulted him.

"Do I strike you as a man who goes without, Imogen?"

"I only meant… Well, it is an island."

Javier's mouth kicked up in the corner in that way it did, so rarely. His real smile, I knew. Not that other thing he deployed as a weapon.

And this was wired to that molten heat in me, because all I could feel was the fire of it.

"I want to make sure you have your strength, *querida*," he murmured, which did not help the fire at all. If anything, it made it worse. Because I could see the same bright flame in his gaze. "As we have only just begun."

CHAPTER NINE

Imogen

"TODAY WE FLY to Italy," Javier announced one morning weeks later, without warning. "You may wish to prepare yourself for a touching reunion with your family."

He sat, as he always did, at that table out on the terrace overlooking the pools and the endlessly inviting ocean where he preferred to take his breakfast each day. The morning was bright and clear, and yet as I sat there across from him I felt as if I'd been tossed back into the shadows, cold and gray, I thought I'd left behind in France. I must have made some kind of noise, because Javier set aside one of the many international newspapers he scanned each morning and raised his dark brows at me.

"We will be attending a charity ball in Venice. It is an annual opportunity to fake empathy for the less fortunate, something at which your father excels." He studied me for a moment. "Do you have an objection to charity, Imogen? I seem to recall you mentioning you wished to make it the cornerstone of your existence."

I realized I was gaping at him and forced my mouth shut. It was ridiculous that I was reacting like this. There was no reason at all to feel that he had...broken something, somehow, by announcing that we had to leave this place. Particularly for the sort of event that I knew would thrust us both back into the world I had done such a great job of pretending no longer existed these past weeks.

A world that included my father.

I didn't want to leave. I wanted to stay like this forever. The days had rolled by, sunlight and deep blue, the sea air and the soft, sweet breeze.

It was the first holiday I had ever been on in my life.

And yes, of course, I knew it wasn't truly a holiday. Javier worked each and every day. I would have worked myself, had there been something for me to do, but every time I asked he shook his head and then told me to amuse myself as I pleased. So I swam in the pools. I braved the sea on the afternoons when the temperature edged toward hot. I took long, rambling walks down to the ruins on the far end of the island and back, basking in the sunshine and solitude that felt a great deal like freedom.

And anytime he wasn't working, Javier was with me.

Inside me.

All over me, and me all over him, until I could no longer tell the difference between this day or the next. Between his hand and mine, clenched together on the coverlet as he surged inside of me.

I learned how to kneel down and give him pleasure with my mouth. I learned how to accept his mouth between my legs in return. I learned how to explore every inch of his fascinating body with my hands, my mouth, my teeth. We ate the food that always seemed to be taken directly from the heart of all the brightness and calculated to be as pretty as the sun-drenched island around us, and then we rolled around more.

He called me adventurous. He called me *querida*.

I called him my husband, marveled that I had ever thought him a monster, and every day I wondered how any person could be expected to hold so much sensation inside. I could scarcely imagine how my one, single body could contain all these things I felt. All these joys I dared not name.

I didn't want to leave.

I didn't want to return to that cold, cruel world I had left behind without so much as a backward glance, or anything that reminded me of it. I didn't want to start what I knew would be the endless circuit of balls and events that comprised the bulk of the high-society calendar. I had been raised to make that calendar the center of my life. From events like the Met Ball in New York that made the papers to the aristocratic private house parties all over Europe that were only murmured about later, behind the right hands. I had allowed myself to forget that part of my value was appearing at these things, dressed to communicate my husband's wealth and might.

If it were up to me, these weeks on La Angelita would have been a permanent relocation. I wanted us to stay here forever, wrapped up in each other, as if everything else was the dream.

But somehow, I knew better than to say it.

Because this is not his *dream*, a foreboding sort of voice whispered in me, like a blast of cold air down my spine.

"I have always wanted to see Venice," I managed to say.

I even forced myself to smile. To meet that considering gaze of his.

"You are not so convincing."

"I am drunk on the sea air and all this sun." *And you*, I thought, but knew better than to say. Because in all these halcyon days of sex and sun and nights that never seemed to end, there had been no talk of emotion. No whisper of the things I had been raised to consider the province of other, lesser people. "I will have to sober up, that is all."

"I have business that requires my sobriety. You will have nothing to do but party, which certainly doesn't demand any teetotaling should you oppose it. Though I suppose the party itself is your business."

I felt some of the magical glow that had been growing in me by the day stutter a bit, and I resented it. I rubbed the stuttering spot between my breasts and resented that, too.

"If parties are my business, I'm afraid you're going to be deeply disappointed. There were not many parties in the convent."

"Which is why you were sent to that finishing school to top off your chastity with dreary lessons in how to bow, and when, and to whom. You know this very well." Javier set his newspaper aside entirely then, and regarded me for a moment that dragged on so long I almost forgot there had ever been anything but the stern set to his hard mouth and the way his gaze tore into me. "If there is something you would like to tell me, Imogen, I suggest you do so. I have no patience for this passive-aggressive talking around the issue you seem to enjoy."

"There is no issue. I have nothing to tell you."

"Did you think that you would stay on this island forever? Locked away like a princess in a fairy tale? I know I have a fearsome reputation, but I do not believe I have ever tossed a woman in a tower, no matter the provocation." That curve of his mouth caused its usual answering fire in me, but today it felt like a punishment. "I do not believe I have to resort to such things to get what I want. Do you?"

He did not have to resort to anything to get what he wanted from me. I gave it to him with total, obedient surrender. And happily.

And it hadn't occurred to me until now that he wasn't as swept away as I was. That this was all...his design.

I had to swallow hard against the lump in my throat then.

"This is no fairy tale." It cost me to keep my voice light. "For one thing, Fitzalans are not princesses. We have long been adjacent to royal blood, but very rarely of it. Royals are forever being exiled, revolted against, decapitated. Fitzalans endure."

I felt as if I'd been slapped awake when I hadn't realized I'd fallen asleep. When I'd no idea how deeply or long I'd been dreaming. It had been weeks since I'd spared a thought for my father and all the ways I was likely to disappoint him. Or since I'd worried about Celeste and the way my favorite—and only—sister had looked at me on my wedding day. Or how she'd looked at Javier as we'd left the manor house.

I didn't welcome the return of these preoccupations.

Or, for that matter, the fact that it had been weeks since I had given a single thought to the state of my hair and its defiance of all accepted fashion dictates. I clipped it up or I let it curl freely, and that was all the attention I gave the curls that had so dominated my previous life. I hadn't thought about how badly I played the part of a graceful, effortless Fitzalan heiress. I hadn't thought about how different things would be now that all the snide society wives could address me directly instead of merely whispering behind their hands as I walked behind my father in my slovenly way, with the dresses that never quite fell right and the hair that never obeyed. I hadn't thought at all about the many ways I stood in my more accomplished, more beautiful sister's shadow, not for weeks, and now it was likely I would have to do it all over again.

And this time, where Javier could watch and judge the two of us side by side.

I didn't like thinking about it. My stomach rolled at the very notion. I glared down at my coffee and told myself there was nothing wrong with my blurry eyes. Nothing at all.

"We will be attending one of the most famous charity balls of the season," Javier said, his voice darker than it had been before. Darker and somehow more intense. "I was asked to donate a staggering amount of money, and my reward for this act of charity is that I am forced to attend the ball. We will all put on masks and pretend we do not recognize each other when, of course, we do. It is all very tedious. But this time, I will at least be spared the endless advances of the unmarried. And the unhappily married."

I shifted in my chair, still blinking furiously at my coffee.

I had gotten too much sun on my nose, causing even more freckles. I knew my shoulders were in no better state. The sun had brought out more gold and red in my hair, and more curls besides. I tried to imagine myself swanning about a Venetian ballroom, surrounded by women like Celeste. Elegant, graceful women. Silky smooth, sleek women who never worried about dripping their banquet dinners down the front of their gowns, or tripping over the hems of their dresses as they strode about in their impossibly high heels.

I had been to the convent, yes. And I had spent those years in what was euphemistically called finishing school, too. My friends and I regaled ourselves with memories of the absurdities we'd suffered there almost daily in the group chats that kept us connected, shut off as we were in our very different lives. But all the schooling in the world couldn't make me over into Celeste, no matter how many hours I'd spent walking around with a heavy book on my head to improve my posture.

"You are the very definition of a silk purse made from a sow's ear," my father had snarled at my debutante ball. Right after I'd tripped and nearly upended the punch bowl and the table it had been set upon.

That had been the first and last time I had been let loose in aristocratic society, aside from my wedding.

And now this. Where I would bring shame not only upon my father, which I did so often it hardly signified, but on Javier.

This man who knew how to make me sob with joy and need. Who broke me wide-open with more pleasure than the human body should have been able to bear, and yet he did it again and again, and I not only bore it—I craved it. The man who did not want to hear the words that bubbled up in me, so I moaned them out instead in a meaningless, wordless tune.

The very thought of humiliating him the way I knew I was more than likely to do made me want to curl up into a ball. And sob for a few hours.

"Or perhaps you are only comfortable with this marriage when it is conducted in private," Javier said, snapping my attention back to him. "Out of sight. Off on an island no one can access but me. Hidden away where no one can see how far you have fallen."

I blinked at that. Because he sounded almost…hurt. "I don't… I don't want…"

But something had gone horribly wrong. Javier pushed back from the table, rising to his feet and tossing his linen serviette onto the tabletop. He glared down at me in much the same way he had once stared up at me in my father's house. With commanding, relentless fury that should have burned me alive.

And I felt exactly the same as I had then.

Frozen. Paralyzed. Intrigued despite myself.

And in no way immune from that fire.

"You are happy enough to glut yourself on my body," he growled down at me, an expression I didn't recognize on his harsh face. Again, I was tempted to believe that I'd hurt him. *Him.* "You are insatiable. No matter how much I give you, you want more. When you call out for God, I believe you think I am him. But that does not mean you wish to show the world how much you enjoy your slumming, does it?"

He could not have stunned me more if he had overturned the table into the nearest pool and sent me tumbling after it. I felt myself pale, then flush hot, as if with fever. "That's not what I meant at all. I'm not the one who will be embarrassed, Javier. But I'm almost positive you will be."

His mouth was a flat, thin line, but in his gaze I swore I could see pain. "Yes. I will be humiliated, I am sure, when the world sees that I truly married the woman I intended to. That I procured the last Fitzalan heiress. You will have to try harder, *mi reina*, if you want me to believe the stories you tell to hide your true feelings."

I found myself on my feet across from him, my heart kicking at me. I felt panicked. Something like seasick that everything had twisted around so quickly. That I had possibly wounded him, somehow. "I'm not telling you a story."

He said something in guttural Spanish that I was perfectly happy not to understand. Not completely.

"You must have heard what they call me," I continued, holding myself still so he wouldn't see all the shaking I could feel inside of me. "The disappointing Fitzalan sister. The unfortunate one. It was never a joke."

"Enough." He slashed his hand through the air, still staring at me as if I had betrayed him. "We leave in an hour. I have a phone call to make. I suggest you use the time learning how to control your face and the truths it tells whether you are aware of it or not."

He left me then. He stormed off into the villa, and I knew there'd be no point following him. When he disappeared into the wing he kept aside as his office, he did not emerge for hours, and he did not take kindly to interruptions. I had learned these things the hard way.

But today, everything felt hard. I stood where I was for a long time after he'd gone.

That does not mean you wish to show the world how much you enjoy your slumming, does it? he had demanded.

Slumming was the sort of word my father used. It felt like poison in me, leaving trails of shame and something far sharper everywhere it touched. And it touched every part of me. And, worse, corroded the sweet, hot memories of our high blue, sun-filled weeks here.

My eyes blurred all over again.

It had never crossed my mind that Javier even noticed what people like my father thought of him, much less how they might act when he was around. He hadn't seemed the least bit interested in the guests at our wedding, or the things they might have said about him. He hadn't even bothered to stay for the whole of the wedding breakfast, dismissing them all as insignificant, I'd thought.

Yet he'd thrown out that word, *slumming*, as if he was far less impervious to these slights than I imagined.

I moved out of the sun, as if that could somehow retroactively remove my freckles, and stood there in the cool shadows of our bedroom. I tried to calm my breathing. That wild beating of my heart. But I was staring at that vast bed and I was...lost.

Javier had been intense these past weeks. More than intense. He was demanding, in bed and out. Focused and ferocious, and it sent a delicious chill down my spine and deep into the softest part of me just thinking about it. He turned me inside out with such regularity that I hardly knew which was which any longer. I'd stopped trying to tell the difference.

And now we had to leave here. I had to parade all these things I felt in front of the whole of the world and, worse by far, my own family.

I squeezed my eyes shut, but that didn't help, because then all there was to do was *feel*. And sometimes I told myself that Javier must feel the things that I did. Sometimes I dreamed that he felt as torn apart, then made new, every time we touched.

I wrenched my eyes open again. In the harsh light of day, when I was out on another walk or tucked up beside the pools with one of the Spanish books I was steadily making my way through, I knew better. I had been the virgin, not him. He was a man of vast experience—as I had seen for myself when I searched for him online.

Javier could have anything he wanted. Anyone he

wanted. *The only thing he ever wanted from you*, a nasty little voice inside me whispered, *was your surname.*

Because all the rest of this, I was forced to admit to myself as I stood there—staring blindly at the master bed where I had learned more things about myself than in all my years at the convent—Javier had already had a thousand times over. With women the whole world agreed were stunning beyond measure.

And one of them had been Celeste.

My knees felt wobbly, or maybe it was that my stomach had twisted so hard it threw me off balance, but I found myself sinking down onto the bench at the end of the bed.

Sometimes I told myself sweet little fantasies that Javier might feel as I did, or might someday, but if I was honest, I'd known that was unlikely. I'd pretended I didn't know it, but I did. Of course I did.

Because the only time I had seen any hint of feelings in him was just now.

Now, when we were finally stepping out into public together. Now, when he would have to parade the lesser Fitzalan sister before the world. Maybe it wasn't surprising that our first outing would be to a costume ball. I'd read entirely too many books that used masks and costumes to terrible advantage. Why should this be any different?

Because this was an arranged marriage, plain and simple.

I had spent these weeks in some kind of a delirium. A daydream. Sex and sun and the gleaming Mediterranean—who wouldn't be susceptible?

But Javier had not been in any such haze. Javier had known exactly what he was doing.

He had married me for my name. My fortune, and

not because he needed money, but because he was now a part of the Fitzalan legacy.

He had married a pawn, but I had made the cardinal sin of imagining myself a wife in truth. Somehow, in all these weeks, my actual situation had not been clear to me. This was an arranged marriage, and the arrangement was not in my favor.

Javier had not promised me love. He had not promised me honor. And crucially, I realized as I sat there, feeling like the child I had never thought I was until today, he had never promised me fidelity, either.

If Javier noticed my silence—or any of those feelings I was afraid I wasn't any good at hiding, though I tried my best—he gave no sign.

He spent the flight to Venice on his mobile and seemed as uninterested in the fairy-tale city that appeared below us as we landed as he was in me. I pressed my face to the window, not caring at all if that made me look gauche. Or foolish. Or whatever word I knew my father would have used, if he had been there to see my enduring gracelessness.

But I didn't want to think about my father. Or any of the things that waited for me tonight. All the ways my foolish heart could break—I thrust them all aside.

We were delivered to a waiting boat and that was when my treacherous heart flipped over itself, as if this was a romantic journey. As if any of this was romantic.

I knew it wasn't. But Venice was.

The haughty, weathered palazzos arranged at the edge of the Grand Canal. The piers with their high sticks and the curved blue boats. The impossible light that danced on the dome of Santa Maria della Salute.

Gondoliers on the waterways and pedestrians on the arched bridges.

Venice was like poetry. Arranged all around me, lyrical and giddy at once.

The private water taxi delivered us to a private island in the great lagoon.

"Another private island?" I asked, then wished I hadn't when all I received in return was that darkly arched brow of his and that dark gaze that still looked pained to me.

"I prefer my privacy," Javier replied. Eventually. "Though this is not mine. It is a hotel."

I blinked at the pink stone building that rose before me and the rounded church facade that gleamed ivory beside it. There were gold letters on the stones, spelling out the name of some or other saint. "Why are there no other people?"

Javier angled an arrogant sort of look down at me.

And I understood then. He had bought the place out. Because of course he had.

He was Javier Dos Santos. How had I managed to forget all that meant?

I felt flushed straight through as we walked across the empty courtyard, following the beaming staff up from the water and into the hotel itself. This was not like his villa, so open and modern at once. I was struck by the age of the rooms, and yet how graceful they remained, as if to encourage guests to revel in all their mystery and grandeur. And yet it was far more welcoming than my father's residences, all of which had always erred on the side of too many antiques. Cluttered together, simply because they were pieces of history that broadcast his taste in acquisitions.

Our footsteps were loud on the floors. The staff led

us to a sprawling suite that encompassed the whole of the top floor, and I told myself it shouldn't feel like punishment when Javier disappeared into the designated office space. Especially since he didn't glance back.

But I summoned a smile from somewhere, because I wasn't alone.

"You have some time before you need to begin getting ready for your evening, signora," my attendant told me in deferential Italian. "Perhaps you would like some light refreshment?"

My smile hurt. "That would be lovely."

I watched as she left, wondering what I looked like to her, this woman who attended the fabulously wealthy and astronomically celebrated occupants of this suite. She must have seen a thousand marriages like mine. Did it begin here, I wondered? Was she rushing down to the kitchens to snigger about the freckled, mop-headed wife who had somehow found herself with a man like Javier Dos Santos in a hotel he'd emptied of all other guests because he preferred the quiet?

But I was making myself crazy. I knew it.

I moved across the grand salon where my attendant had left me, then out through the shutters to the balcony that ran down the length of our suite. And though the air was bracing, especially after all those weeks on the island, I made my way to the edge and leaned against the railing to watch the winter sun turn the sky a pale pink.

If Venice had been pretty in the light, it was magical at dusk.

I breathed in, then let it out, and I thought I felt a kind of easing deep inside.

The city was otherworldly before me, spread out as it must have been at the feet of all the women who had stood on this balcony before me. So many lives, begun and ended right here. All those tears, all that laughter. Panic and fear. Joy and delight. Down through the ages, life after life just as it would continue on after me, and somewhere in the middle of all of it was me.

What was the point of working myself up into a state?

My problem was I kept imagining that I could make my marriage what I wanted it to be when that had never been in the cards, and I should have known that. I did know that.

The day before my wedding I had dreamed of the sweet blue eyes of a stable boy because that was some kind of escape. The day after my wedding I had been punch-drunk on the things my new husband could do to me, the things he could make my body feel, and I had lost myself in that for far too long.

The truth of the matter was that I was a Fitzalan. And no matter if I was the lesser one, I was still a Fitzalan. The women in my family had been bartered and ransomed, kidnapped and sold and held captive across the centuries.

And if my fierce old grandmother had been any indication, not a one of them had dissolved in the face of those challenges. On the contrary, Fitzalan women made the best of their situations. No matter what.

Fitzalans have a higher purpose, Grand-Mère had always said.

There wasn't much I could do about my curls or my clumsiness, but I could certainly work on my attitude. It was perhaps the only thing that was truly mine. Javier had called the party I was headed to tonight my business, and I had been silly to dismiss that.

He wasn't wrong. I had spent years in finishing school learning all the ways an aristocratic wife could use her role as an accessory to her husband to both of their advantage.

"Your greatest weapon is the fact no one expects you are anything but window dressing," Madame had always told us. "Use it wisely, ladies."

And that was why, when I was dressed in my mask and gown and was led out into the main hall to meet Javier that evening, I was ready.

I'd had them pull my hair back into another chignon, though this one did not pretend to be smooth. My curls were obvious, but I thought if they were piled on top of my head it would look more like a choice and less like the accident of birth they were. My inky-black gown had been made to Javier's exacting specifications, my attendants had assured me, clasped high on one shoulder and cascading down on an angle to caress my feet. The mask itself was gold and onyx, and I couldn't deny the little thrill it gave me to see it on my face when I looked in the mirror.

Better by far, however, was Javier's stillness when he saw me, then the gruff nod he gave me.

It told me the same thing I'd told myself while I'd stood outside in the cold and gazed at the fairy tale of Venice laid out before me in the setting sun. Javier might feel nothing for me at all. I needed to accept that. But he wanted me with at least some of the same desperation I felt in me.

It was more than I'd been raised to expect from my marriage. I told myself it would be more than enough.

Because it had to be enough.

"I am ready," I told him. When he held out his arm, I slid my hand through it. And I angled my head so I could look up at him. Then wondered if my breath would always catch like this at the sight of him, even more

overwhelming than usual tonight in his dark black coat
and tails. "This will be our first society event as a married couple. You must have imagined how it would go."

I could see his dark eyes behind his mask. And that
mouth of his, hard and tempting, that I would know
anywhere.

"I have."

"Then you must tell me exactly how you see it all
in your head, so that I can be certain to do my part."

His gaze was a harsh, glittering thing. He was
dressed all in black, including his mask, and yet the
way he looked at me made me think I could see all the
bright colors of the Mediterranean. "Your part? What
is your part, do you imagine?"

"My part is whatever you prefer, of course. You can
use me as a kind of weapon to aim however you like.
You have no idea how indiscreet men like my father
are around people they think are too far below them
to matter."

His hard mouth curved slightly, though I did not
mistake it for a smile. "I know exactly how they treat
people like me, Imogen. And I do not need weapons to
handle them. I am the weapon."

"Then it seems we have an arsenal."

When he only watched me in that same stirring and
vaguely threatening way, I lifted my chin as if I was
preparing myself for a fight. With him.

Even though I knew we were both aware I would
never, ever win.

"And if I say all I want from you is decoration?" His
voice was silk and menace. It wound around me like
the ties he'd used to secure me to that bed of his, one
memorable night. "Silence and submission and a pretty
smile on your face? What then?"

"You bought me, Javier," I reminded him, and it wasn't until I heard the edge in my own voice that I understood there were all manner of weapons. And that I didn't need his permission to wield them. "I can be whatever you want me to be. I thought that was the point."

CHAPTER TEN

Javier

IF SHE MENTIONED the fact that I'd bought her one more time, it might send me over the edge—and I chose not to question why that was when it was true. I had. And would again. There was no reason at all to resent the way she threw it at me like some kind of challenge.

I didn't like the fact that I was so close to the edge as it was, and we hadn't even made it to the ball yet.

And it didn't help that Imogen looked good enough to eat.

Her hair was more gold than red after our time on La Angelita, even tucked back into a complicated, curling mystery she'd secured to the back of her head with some or other gleaming thing my fingers itched to remove.

She looked like every dream I'd ever had about the wife I would one day win. Or, yes, buy. She was elegant, masked in a way that showed off the aristocratic bones of her face and draped in the finest black that clung to her generous figure in ways that made me ache. She looked gracious beyond measure and far, far out of the league of a drug dealer's son who'd been raised in a gutter. She was as beautiful as she was unreachable, as befit a woman with blood so achingly blue.

Imogen was exactly the wife I wanted on my arm at this or any other society event. She would exude all that Fitzalan superiority without even trying and my dominance would continue unabated and unchallenged from all these men who fancied themselves better than the likes of me.

And she was standing here in front of me talking about what I'd paid for her, as if this union of ours was nothing but the oldest profession in action on a grand scale.

I told myself I was outraged at the insult. When wealthy men hired prostitutes, they were called escorts. And when they bought wives, it was not called a purchase, it was deemed a wise marriage. To think about my choices in any other way suggested I was still in the gutter, despite all my accomplishments.

I assured myself I was furious, but that hardly explained the heaviness in my sex.

The same heaviness that had become my obsession.

The very last thing I wanted to do was take her out of this hotel I'd emptied for my own privacy when it would have been far more entertaining to experiment with that privacy. I wanted to undress her, right here in the cavernous lobby. I wanted to worship every silken inch of her fine, soft body in the filthiest way imaginable. Starting with my mouth.

But there was work to be done. There was always work to be done. Charity balls were only merry social occasions when a man's donations were relatively minor. For me, they were necessary appearances that had to look social and offhanded when they were anything but.

That beguiling, demanding need for her scraped at me with a raw force that was nothing short of alarming, because Imogen was the first woman I'd ever met that I couldn't get enough of—but I ignored it. I had no choice but to ignore it tonight. I kept her arm linked in mine and I led her down to the boat that would take us to the ball, and if my jaw ached from clenching it, that was at least a different sort of ache from the one currently driving me mad.

"I knew it would be beautiful here," she said softly, standing at the rail as the boat cut through the waves, though the night air was cool and whipped at her curls. "But I had no idea it would be *this* beautiful. I had no idea it was possible for anything to be this beautiful."

I moved to stand next to her at the rail, my gaze on the water of the lagoon. And then the canals of Venice before us, inky and dark. Very nearly brooding, this time of year. "I keep forgetting how sheltered your life has been."

"I have been nowhere," she said simply, and I thought it was the lack of bitterness in those words that cut me the most. "I have seen nothing outside the walls of the convent or that dreary finishing school. Not in person, anyway. And it turns out that you can watch a thousand things on the internet, read as many books as you can get your hands on, and they still won't prepare you for reality."

That word bit at me. *Reality.* Because I knew that on some level, no matter her protestations, she had to be embarrassed that she'd been forced to lower herself to marry a man like me. Of course I knew it. It was one of the defining truths of my life, and it didn't matter that she hadn't said such a thing to me in so many words. I knew it all the same. And I had never felt inferior in her father's house, but it was amazing how easily I slipped into that space when it was only Imogen. When she was the one who looked at me and made me feel that odd sensation I had never felt before—that slippery, uncomfortable notion that I would never get as far away from my wretched origins as I wanted.

It rose between us like a ghost.

And it was a feeling I should have been used to. I was. Still, when it came from Imogen, it made me ache in a new way. I couldn't say I liked it.

Even so, I couldn't keep myself from reaching over to one of the curls that had already escaped. I tucked it behind her ear with a gentleness I knew made me a stranger to myself.

"You mean Venice, of course," I murmured, that stranger firmly in charge of me now. Was I...*teasing* her? Was I a man who...*teased*? I never had been before. "Or the legendary Mediterranean Sea, perhaps. Not the great many more prurient things a person could read about or watch online, if they wished."

Her gaze met mine, filled with a laughter that I shouldn't have liked so much. I couldn't figure out why I *cared* so much about this woman who came apart in my hands so easily and yet imagined she could fashion herself into some kind of weapon, mine to command.

I didn't want any part of that. The very notion made me have to fight to hold back a shudder.

I told myself it was rage.

Though I knew full well it was connected instead to a hollow place in me that recalled an eight-year-old boy who had understood he would never be as important to those who should have loved and protected him as that poison they took to deliver them into oblivion.

But I refused to think about my parents. Not here. Not now.

There was still so much of the innocent about Imogen as she gazed at me, despite all I had done to claim her for my own. "Of course I mean Venice. What else could I mean?"

"Tell me more about what, precisely, you watched from the confines of the convent. All to better aid your education."

"Documentaries, mostly." Imogen smiled. And it was worrying, I thought in some distant part of me, how much I liked to see her smile. As if I craved it. As if I was a man who had ever allowed myself to crave anything when I knew full well it was the kind of weakness people like my parents lived to exploit. "About Venice, naturally, in all its splendor. And the Mediterranean Sea, too, now that you mention it."

"They will make a documentary about anything these days," I murmured.

I traced the edge of her mask, the place where the gold and onyx met the soft skin of her cheek. I meant to say something. I was sure I had planned it, even.

But there was something about the water. The echoes and the ancient buildings around us and the particular, peculiar magic of this submerged city, and I couldn't find the words. Or I could, but I didn't want to say them.

I didn't want to name the things that moved in me when I looked at her. Every time I looked at her.

And then we were landing at the palazzo where the ball took place, all gleaming lights and noise spilling out into the winter night, and the moment was lost.

I told myself it wasn't disappointment that crashed over me as I led Imogen toward the entrance of the charity ball and handed off our winter coats. It couldn't be anything like disappointment as I waited for us to be announced, then drew her into the thick of the crowd, because that suggested a depth of emotion I didn't feel.

Because I did not *feel*. I refused.

I had spent all these weeks on the island making certain of this. I had forced myself away from Imogen when I wanted to stay. I had remained in my office for hours though I was distracted and, worse, uninterested.

I kept pretending I could think about something other than getting back inside Imogen, and I kept proving myself wrong.

Tonight appeared to be no exception.

Once inside, I could see the business associates I had come here to meet. Masks did nothing to hide the power that certain men seemed to exude from their very pores no matter what they did to conceal their features. The ball was taking place on the ground-floor ballroom of the ancient palazzo, with mighty old pillars and chandeliers three flights up ablaze with light. There was an orchestra on a raised dais at one end, and enough gold everywhere to make the whole world gleam.

But I wasn't ready. I couldn't quite bring myself to let Imogen loose into this particular pack of wolves. And not because I feared them, but because I was the most fearsome wolf of all and I wasn't nearly done with her. I wished that the weeks we'd spent on my island, happily isolated and removed from all this, had been twice as long.

That felt like another betrayal of the person I had always imagined myself to be, and I wasn't sure I could speak. I was as close to terrified as I'd ever been at what might come out of my mouth if I tried.

Instead, I swept my lovely wife out onto the dance floor. I held her in my arms, gazed down at those perfect lips of hers that I could taste anytime I wished, and told myself my head swam because there were too many people here. It was hot. Noisy.

But she tipped back her head and smiled at me.

And I understood that it wasn't simply that I didn't recognize myself around this woman.

She had made me a liar. A liar with far too many feelings.

Worse, I did nothing with this realization but accept it. And dance.

"I never thought…" Imogen's voice was breathy. Her eyes gleamed brighter than the blaze of lights all around us. "You are a marvelous dancer."

"You sound slightly *too* surprised."

"It's only that I would never have dared imagine you dancing. You're too…"

I felt my brow rise. "Beneath you?"

"Elemental, I was going to say."

What was it about this woman? Why did she turn me into this…sniveling creature who advertised his own weaknesses at the slightest provocation?

"I taught myself," I said. Stiffly, but I said it.

It had been part of those early years, when I'd decided to make a guttersnipe a gentleman. And there was a part of me that expected her to laugh at the notion of a monster practicing a waltz. I might have joined in. But she didn't laugh.

"I took comportment and ballroom dancing lessons. First with the governesses at home, then in the convent. And it was not until I was in finishing school that Madame told us that proper dancing was merely another form of battle."

I studied her face as it was tipped up to mine.

"Battle? I was unaware that finishing school was so…aggressive."

"We find our weapons where we can, Javier."

Her soft voice echoed in my ears long after the song

ended, and I was forced to take a step back. To allow her to loop her arm through mine again. To do what I knew I must, rather than what I wanted.

And it occurred to me, with an unpleasant sort of jolt, that I couldn't recall too many instances of doing what I wanted. Rather than what I must.

I had more money than I could ever spend. It would take commitment and effort to rid myself of my wealth. It would take years. Decades.

And yet I still behaved as if I was that kid in the sewers of Madrid. I still expected that at any moment, the authorities might step in and take it all away from me. Denounce me for my father's sins and throw me back where I came from.

I knew better than anyone that we were all of us nothing but self-fulfilling prophecies. And still I allowed those same old obsessions to own me. To shape me. To determine my every move.

I felt far closer to uncertain than I was comfortable with as we drew close to a group containing a man I couldn't help but recognize. He, too, was masked— but his mask was the sort that only drew attention to him, rather than making any attempt at concealing him from view.

"Hello, Father," Imogen said from beside me.

I don't know what I expected. I had seen and loathed those marks this man had left on my wife's skin. I had watched what passed for Fitzalan father/daughter interactions before. Most notably at our wedding, when for all the paternal emotion on display Dermot could have been handing me a large block of granite.

That stoniness was in evidence again tonight.

"It is such a pity that you could not take a little more care with your appearance on a night like this," the old man said, his voice bitter. Cruel. It took me a moment to realize he was speaking to Imogen. "It is your first introduction to society as part of a married couple. Surely you could have done something with your hair."

Imogen only smiled. "I did do something with my hair."

Fitzalan gazed at her with distaste. Then shifted his cold glare to me, as if he expected an apology. Certainly not as if he was giving me one. "I am afraid that no amount of correction has ever worked with this level of defiance. If I were you, I might consider a firmer hand."

Beside me, I felt Imogen stiffen, even though her expression did not change at all. It put me in mind of the sort of weapons she had mentioned. But more than that, Fitzalan dared to speak to me of a *firmer hand*?

I wanted to rip Dermot Fitzalan asunder, here where all the circling wolves could watch. And tear into him themselves when I left him in pieces.

But that was not how men like this fought. Well did I know it. I made a mental note to hit Fitzalan back hard, where he lived.

In his wallet.

And in the meantime, I would force myself to stand here and speak to him as if he did not deserve a taste of his own medicine. My fingers itched to leave their own dark marks on his skin to see how he liked it.

Somehow, though Fitzalan did not deserve it, I kept the true monster in me at bay.

"You are not me," I said coolly to this father who cared so little for his own daughter that he would send her to a marital bed with marks from his own hand. This pompous man who likely had done it on purpose, because it was the next best thing to actually branding Imogen as if she was truly property. "I believe this simple truth fills us both with gratitude, does it not?"

But I didn't hear his response. Imogen excused herself with that same serene smile and her head held high. And instead of attending to the conversation with this man I had cultivated for a decade or more and now had every intention of ruining—instead of taking pleasure in deceiving him or decimating him in turn, one or the other, as long as I came out the winner—I watched her go.

I couldn't seem to stop myself. I couldn't seem to force myself to pay attention to Fitzalan or the men standing with him. I was aware they were talking around me—possibly at me—but I didn't care the way I should have.

The way I always had in the past.

I watched Imogen instead. I watched the light reflect off her glorious curls from those dizzying chandeliers. I watched the easy, unselfconscious way she navigated through the crowd, aware she had no sense of her own grace.

As if I wanted to chase after her like some kind of puppy. Like the kind of soft, malleable creature I had never been.

Like a man besotted, though I knew that was impossible.

And worse, as if what I felt when she walked away from me was grief.

CHAPTER ELEVEN

Imogen

I LOCKED MYSELF in a bathroom stall in the elegant ladies' powder room, perching there on top of the cold porcelain lid and making no attempt to use it.

And then stayed there, where no one could see me.

Or stare at me. Or talk about me where I could hear the unkind note in their voices, yet none of the words, as a group of society women I knew I ought to have recognized had done as I'd found my way here.

Or make disparaging remarks about my hair. My dress. Whatever it was they found lacking in me.

It isn't that you're lacking something, a voice inside of me whispered. It reminded me of the low, husky way Javier spoke to me in the middle of the night when we were wrapped tight around each other in bed, fitted together like puzzle pieces in a way I hadn't been able to visualize before our wedding. And now craved the way I did everything else that involved touching him. *It's that you have the misfortune of being related to your sister while not actually being her.*

That had the ring of an unpleasant truth. And part of me wanted to stay where I was for the rest of the night, the pride and ferocity of the Fitzalan women be damned, because I was tired of all the comparisons. Especially when I was always coming out on the wrong side of them.

I wanted to stay hidden here, but I knew I couldn't. I had to gather myself together. I had to smile sweetly, serenely, while people compared me to my perfect sister. I had to pretend I was oblivious to the way people looked at me and the things they said to me or about me.

But I couldn't seem to make myself move.

That was when I heard the doors open, letting in a burst of sound of the ball outside. And more than that, a merry, tinkling laugh that I had known my whole life.

Celeste.

I surged to my feet, reaching over to throw back the lock and launch myself out of the stall and at my sister. She would know what to do. She always knew what to do. She had somehow gotten that gene while I had gotten…madly curling, obstinately red hair.

But I froze there, my hand on the lock.

Because I could hear what she was saying and I suddenly wished I was anywhere in the world but here.

"Did you see her lumbering furiously across the floor?" Celeste was asking her companions, all of whom tittered in response. "Storming off with that look on her face in the middle of the ballroom. As if she was planning to break out in some kind of brawl at any moment!"

I had no reason to be standing there, I told myself sternly. No reason at all not to reveal myself. But I still didn't move.

"Your sister does seem a bit *overwhelmed* by things, doesn't she?" asked another woman, in a syrupy sweet voice that I knew I could identify. If I wanted to identify it.

I didn't.

"Imogen is my half sister, thank you very much," Celeste said with a sniff. "I don't know what my father was thinking, messing about with that common trollop."

"I was under the impression Imogen's mother was a duchess or something," someone else murmured, managing to sound apologetic, as if they weren't sure about correcting Celeste even when they were right.

I squeezed my eyes shut. I could feel my hands curled into fists, but I didn't know who or what I wanted to hit. Or even how to hit. My stomach was a terrible knot and there was something too heavy to be simple pain at my temples. I might have thought I was sick, but I knew it wasn't as simple as that.

"Oh, she was the daughter of someone. The Viscount Something, I think. Who can keep track of all those endless British titles?"

That was Celeste speaking. Celeste, who I had always loved. Celeste, who I had trusted.

Celeste, who very clearly hated me.

There was something about that terrible notion that spurred me into action at last.

I shoved open the door and stood there, aware that my chest was heaving as if I'd been running. There was a wall of mirrors in front of me, which allowed me to see exactly how pale I'd become.

It also allowed me to lock gazes with my sister.

Half sister, I reminded myself bitterly.

If Celeste was surprised to see me, she didn't show it. She was dressed like a column of gold tonight, a color that drew attention to her sheer perfection. Her blond hair was elegantly styled in a sweeping updo that I only dared to dream about. She was tall and long and lean. She was the sort of woman who belonged on the covers of a thousand magazines, smiling mysteriously.

Though she didn't smile at me.

"Lurking about in bathrooms now?" she asked, and I couldn't tell if she had always looked at me that way. Or if, after those bright weeks with Javier, I could see all kinds of things in the shadows that I had never seen before.

It was amazing what a difference it made to be wanted.

Loved, something in me whispered, though I didn't dare call it that.

All I knew was that I'd never felt anything like it before. And that meant that this had always been bubbling in my sister. The way she was looking at me. That awful tone I'd heard in her voice. None of it was new. It couldn't be. And that meant...

"My mother, Lady Hillary to you, was the daughter of a duke," I said quietly, not wanting to accept what all this meant. "As I think you know."

"If you say so," Celeste said dismissively, and then made it worse by rolling her eyes for the benefit of her group of minions.

There was no more pretending. It didn't matter if Celeste had always been like this or if this was something new. She wasn't making any attempt to hide it.

"Are you just going to stand there, Imogen?" Celeste asked after a moment. That was when I realized I still hadn't moved.

"When I first heard you walk in, I thought I might come in for a hug," I said drily. "That seems to be off the table."

Her friends tittered again, but not with her, this time. It was likely childish that I felt that as a victory.

Celeste certainly didn't like it. Her perfect features flushed, and when she turned back to face me, it was as if I had never seen her before. Temper made her face twist.

And for the first time in as long as I could remember, she didn't look beautiful to me at all. I knew what beauty was now. I knew what warmth was. And I couldn't help thinking that I deserved better than spite in a bathroom stall, no matter who it came from.

"Eavesdroppers never hear anything good about themselves, or did you not learn that in all your years locked away in that convent?" Celeste let out one of those laughs. "You certainly didn't seem to learn anything else."

I thought about that look on her face the day of my wedding. I studied the look she wore now. And I remembered what it had been like ten years ago. Her dramatic sobs, loud enough to be heard all over the house, but more important, the fact she hadn't run outside to prevent Javier from leaving. Very much as if it was a performance designed to hasten her own wedding and her own exit from my father's house.

Maybe everything about Celeste was a performance.

But I played my hunch anyway. "Jealousy doesn't become you, Celeste."

This time, that peal of laughter she let out had fangs. I could feel it sink into me and leave marks. Yet I refused to react. Not even when she stepped closer to me, a mottled sort of red sweeping down over her neck to her chest.

"You foolish, absurd child," she said, her voice scathing and pitying at once. "Don't you understand what Javier is doing? He's using you."

I would die before I showed her how that landed on me like one of the walls around us, hard stone crushing me into dust. I stared back at her, lifting my chin, and it occurred to me in some dim part of my mind that I had been preparing for this for years. Hadn't I?

Because my feelings were hurt. There was no getting around that. But I couldn't say I was surprised.

"Yes, Celeste, he is. In much the same way your count used you to fill his coffers and provide him with heirs. Some might call this sort of thing mercenary, but in our family we have always called it marriage."

Something rolled through her. I could see it, ugly and sharp, all over her face.

"You mistake my meaning." Behind Celeste, her group of tittering friends had gone silent. The better to listen so that they might repeat it to the crowd outside, I knew. "The count married me for all the reasons you name, of course. That is simply practical. *Realistic.* But look in the mirror, Imogen. You know what I look like. Do you ever look at yourself?"

"My husband has yet to turn to stone, if that's what you mean."

But my heart beat too hard. Too wild. As if it already knew what she would say.

Celeste leaned closer so there could be no mistake at all.

"Javier could have had anyone's daughter. He is wealthy enough that even royals would have considered him in these progressive times. But he chose you. Have you never asked why?"

I wanted to say something that would hurt her, I realized. But before I could pull myself together enough to imagine what that might be, she kept going.

"He chose the ugly, embarrassing Fitzalan daughter when he is a known connoisseur of only the most beautiful women in Europe."

If she saw the way I sucked in a breath at that, she ignored it. Or worse, liked it.

"Don't you see?" Celeste's voice only grew colder the longer she spoke. Colder. Harder. "He is Javier Dos Santos. He possesses wealth greater than kings. He can do what no other man can, Imogen. He can flaunt an ugly duckling and pretend she is a swan. He can make even the disappointing Fitzalan heiress into a style icon if he so desires. He can do whatever he likes."

I made a sound, but it wasn't a sentence, and in any case, Celeste ignored me.

"Are you truly as simple as you act?" she demanded, pulling herself up to her full height. She shook her head at me, haughty and something like amazed at my naïveté. "It's a *game*, Imogen. Nothing but a game."

For a moment, I heard nothing else. I was aware that Celeste's friends were whispering among themselves. The water was running in one of the sinks. Someone opened the door and I heard the music again. But the only thing I was truly aware of was the scornful way Celeste had said that last bit.

Nothing but a game.

She smiled then, but this time I could see the pity in her gaze. And worse, what I thought was triumph.

"I am sure you find this cruel," she said with great dignity. "But in time, when you have resigned yourself to the reality of your position, I think you'll realize that I was only trying to be kind."

I knew, beyond any shred of doubt, that she was lying.

Or performing, anyway.

And then it didn't matter, because Celeste had always been better at both than me. She swept around, gathering up her skirts and her friends, and left me there to stew in what she'd told me.

And for some reason, I didn't break down when the door shut behind her. Instead, I thought of what it had been like to step off that plane on Javier's island after a lifetime, it seemed, of gray and gloom. I thought of the light. The blue.

I thought of the heat and fire I had found in Javier's arms. Again and again and again.

I took a deep breath, blew it out, and understood deep into my bones that I would rather steal a few weeks of fantasy with Javier whenever he had a mind to indulge himself than subject myself to all of Celeste's chilly, practical "reality."

I would rather be filled with almost too much sunlight to bear. I would rather have wild curls and freckles all over my shoulders. I would rather earn the contempt with which these people treated me than slink around trying to please them and only find myself in the same place.

And there was something about that that felt like liberation.

Because the glory of never fitting in, I realized in a sudden rush, was that I was never *going* to fit in.

And there was no one left to punish me for it.

No governesses. No nuns. My father had no more power over me. He had sold that right. And Celeste... didn't matter. I knew that Javier was determined and relentless enough to have chosen the Fitzalan daughter he wanted no matter what my father might have said about it. And he'd chosen me.

He could have had anyone, as Celeste had said. And he'd still chosen me.

Because he had, he was the only one who mattered.

I knew it was possible—even likely—that Celeste was right and Javier was playing some game. But I wasn't sure it mattered.

I was in love with him either way.

I didn't know a lot about love. Or anything about it, really. Grand-Mère had always banged on about *higher purposes* and *duty*, but *love* had never been a part of the Fitzalan experience. I had assumed that Celeste and I had loved each other the way sisters did, but it turned out I was wrong about that, too. And it was possible there was a part of me that would mourn the loss of a sister it turned out I never quite had and the family that might as well have been carved from the same stone as my father's manor, but I couldn't process that here. Not now.

Because I was in love with my husband.

I was *in love* with him.

And I knew that of the sins women in society marriages like mine could commit, this was perhaps the worst.

Just as I knew that the man who touched me so softly and held me so closely, who made me cry and sob and shake around him, would not want to hear that I loved him.

That didn't change the fact that I did.

And I might have been afraid of the things he made me feel. They overwhelmed me. They were sticky and dark, too much and too wild to contain. I could hardly believe they were real. Or that he was.

I was afraid that he would tell me it was only sex and I was unnecessarily complicating a simple business transaction. I was afraid that he would banish me, send me off to one of his other properties where he could keep me under lock and key and my feelings couldn't inconvenience him. I was afraid that he would laugh at me.

I was terribly afraid that Javier would never look at me again the way he had this morning, when he'd been deep inside of me and I'd thought I might die. That I had died. That I wanted to die. I was afraid I would never feel any of that again.

But I wasn't afraid of him.

And I had spent a lifetime locking myself up before anyone could come and do it for me. I had tried to minimize myself. Hide myself. Stuff myself in a box and be something I wasn't. No matter how many times I'd sneaked off down the servants' stairs, I'd always come back and tried to be what was expected of me.

I wasn't going to do it anymore.

I stepped up to the wide counter, ignoring the sinks before me and keeping my eyes on the bank of mirrors. I peeled the mask off my face and tossed it aside.

Then I reached up, tugged the clip from my hair, and threw it on the counter as well.

I shook my head, using my fingers to help pull out all the pins. I tugged and I pulled, and I tore down the hairstyle I'd considered a compromise. There would be no more compromises.

My hair fell around me, red and gold and curling wildly.

And it wasn't fear that moved in me then, I knew. It wasn't reality according to Celeste.

It was that power I hadn't been able to access, cringing in a bathroom stall.

It was that long, tough line of women who had come before me and survived, one after the next.

It was what had happened in those weeks with Javier. On that beautiful island, the place where I had learned that surrender was not weakness. That it could be a glorious strength.

I had fallen in love with my husband, and that changed everything.

Me most of all.

I didn't think it through. I didn't worry or prepare. I wheeled around, ignored the other women in the powder room who looked my way, and pushed my way back out into the ball.

I was tired of hiding.

Finally, I was tired of it.

I kept my head high, moving through the crowd as if I was made of silk. I paid no attention to the commotion I caused. I kept my eyes on my husband, finding him easily in the crush and then heading straight for him.

Javier, who I had considered a monster.

If he was a monster, I thought now, then so was I. If what it meant was that all these people, these circling wolves, considered us too different from them to matter. But I thought the truth of the matter was that this ball was filled with the real monsters, gorgons fashioned from snobbery and toxic self-regard, bitterness and centuries of living only to get richer.

I kept my gaze trained on Javier. The one man here who didn't belong. He was too…real. Even with a mask on, the truth of who he was seemed to fill the whole of the palazzo. As if everyone else—as if Venice itself— was little more than a ghost.

"You changed your hair," he said in that dark, stirring way of his when I made it to his side. It was the kind of voice that made me wish we were naked together, sprawled out in our bed, where none of this mattered. As if he heard that same note in his voice, he stood straighter. "I didn't realize this was the sort of party that called for different costumes."

"Imogen can always be trusted to do the most embarrassing thing possible," my father sneered from beside him.

I hadn't even seen him there. Because I was free of him, I realized. And it felt like an afternoon of La Angelita sunlight, here in the middle of a cold winter's night.

"My wife's hair—and indeed, my wife herself—cannot be embarrassing, Fitzalan," Javier bit out, with the kind of violence that usually never made it into ballrooms such as this. My father stiffened. My husband's dark eyes blazed. "She is *my* wife. That makes her, by definition, perfect in every way."

"Javier." I liked saying his name. I more than liked it. I waited for him to drag that thrillingly vicious glare away from my father. When it landed on me, it was no softer, but I liked that, too. "I love you."

I saw the way he froze. I heard the astonished laughter from my father and the terribly genteel men around him, none of whom would ever use that word. Or allow it to be used in their presence—especially not in public.

But I had decided not to hide. Not from anyone. Not ever again.

"I love you," I said again, so there could be no mistake. "And I've had enough of this nonsense tonight, I think."

I turned around like some kind of queen. I held my head high as I started across the floor.

And only breathed again when Javier walked beside me, taking my arm in his.

I told myself that come what may—and there was a

storm in those brooding dark eyes of his that already felt like thunder inside me, a reckoning I wasn't sure I wanted to face—I would never regret falling in love with my husband.

CHAPTER TWELVE

Javier

I FOLLOWED HER.

I had no choice.

Imogen had made a scene when she'd dropped her little bombshell, and if I let her walk away, they would say I had already lost control of my brand-new marriage. They would smugly agree with each other that it was only to be expected. *Blood will out*, they would assure themselves.

But if I truly didn't wish to lie to myself, I didn't much care what they said.

I cared more that the bomb she'd dropped was still going off inside me.

Again and again and again.

I did not allow myself to think about my hand on her arm. I ignored my body's automatic response to her scent. Or her firm, smooth skin beneath my palm that made me want to touch her everywhere.

I did not feel. I could not feel.

And no matter that I had already felt too much today already, when she had made it so clear she, too, was as ashamed of me as I was.

You do not wish to feel, something in me whispered

harshly. It was the truth. And I had built my life on truth, had I not? No matter the cost?

"Javier—" Imogen began when we stepped outside.

The music inside the ballroom played on, bright against the dark. Light from those chandeliers inside the palazzo blazed, dancing over the stones. But the temperature had dropped significantly, on the water and inside me, and our coats seemed little protection against the cold.

And my wife thought better of whatever it was she had been about to say.

I did not speak when I summoned our transportation and climbed on board. Or when I pried the mask from my face and sent it spinning into the water with a flare of temper I couldn't conceal. We floated back down the Grand Canal, but this time I did not marvel at the palazzos that lined our way. I did not congratulate myself on my climb from grimy flats in Spain to famous canals in Italy's most magical city the way I usually did.

Instead, I stood apart from Imogen and cautioned myself.

I needed to remain calm. Contained.

There had always been a monster in me, but it wasn't the one her father and his pack of wolves imagined.

Whatever this was—this need people had to hurl emotions around like currency, though I had thought better of Imogen—I had never understood it. I had always stood apart from it, gladly.

She had told me she loved me and it beat in me like a terrible drum, dark and dangerous, slippery and seductive.

And I wanted no part of it.

We made it all the way across the lagoon, then

docked at our hotel, and I still had not uttered a single syllable.

There were lights around the hotel's courtyard, making it look festive though it remained empty of any guests but the two of us, just as I had wanted it. I waved away the waiting hotel staff and accepted the blast of the January wind—slicing into me as it rushed from the water of the lagoon—as a gift. It would keep me focused.

It would remind me who I was.

"Do not ever do that again," I told her harshly when we had both climbed out of the boat. "It is not up to you to determine when we leave a place. Particularly not if I have business."

"You could have stayed if you wished. I didn't ask you to come with me, I merely said I was done."

She was different. Or she was herself, again—the creature I had beheld what seemed like a lifetime ago now in her father's house in France. She did not avert her eyes as I scowled at her. If there was any meekness in her at all, any hints of that uncertain innocence that had driven me mad on the island, it was gone.

Tonight Imogen was electrifying. Her curls cascaded around her shoulders like fire. Her eyes gleamed in the dark, inviting and powerful at once. She reminded me of an ancient goddess who might have risen straight from the sea in a place like this, gold-tipped and mesmerizing.

I wanted nothing more than to worship her. But that was what I had spent these last weeks doing, and what had I gained?

Protestations of *love*, of all things.

I was more likely to believe her a deity than I was to imagine her *in love*.

I started for the hotel and she was right behind me, hurrying as if she had any chance at all of catching me if I didn't allow it.

"Will you chase me all the way up to our rooms?" I asked her from between the teeth I couldn't seem to keep from clenching when I made it to the stately double doors that discreetly opened at our approach.

"Only if you make me chase you. When I was under the impression that the great and glorious Javier Dos Santos has never run from a fight in the whole of his life."

She was a few feet behind me, looking serious and challenging as she closed the last of the distance between us. She didn't look as if she'd exerted herself unduly running across the courtyard, despite the shoes she wore. Not my Don Quixote bride, who was perfectly happy to tilt at any windmill in sight.

Even if the windmill was me.

I strode inside, not sure what I was meant to do with the temper and din roaring inside of me. Not sure I could keep it locked away as I should, and equally sure I didn't want to let any of it out.

I told myself I didn't know what it was, that howling thing knotting loud and grim within me, but I did.

And I didn't want to feel any of this.

I didn't want to feel at all.

Imogen stayed with me as I made my way across the lobby and I cursed myself for having bought out the whole of the hotel, ensuring that this torturous walk took place in strained silence. I could hear Imogen's shoes against the marble floors. I could hear my own.

And I could hear my heart in my chest, as loud as the roaring sea.

We got into the elevator together and stood on opposite sides as if sizing each other up.

I didn't know what she saw, but I wasn't at all pleased to find she looked no less like a goddess in close quarters.

"What happened to you?" I asked her, too many things I didn't wish to address there in my voice.

"I was born a Fitzalan. Then I got married. Not much of interest happened in between."

What did it say about me that I was tempted to laugh at that?

But I already knew what it said. This had gone on too long, this wildfire situation I should have extinguished the first time I'd seen her in her father's heap of stone and history. I should never have brought her to La Angelita and, once I knew how it would burn between us, I should never have allowed us to stay as long as we had.

The responsibility was mine. I accepted it.

So there was no reason at all that I should have let my head tilt to one side as I beheld her there on the other side of the elevator, dressed in that sweep of deep black, the bright red-gold of her hair a striking counterpoint to the wall of gilt and flourish behind her.

"I think you know that I mean tonight. What happened at that ball?"

She didn't smile this time. And somehow that only drew my attention to her mouth and those berry-stained lips I had tasted time and time again. Yet I could never seem to get my fill.

"My sister suggested I face reality." I couldn't read that gleam in her copper gaze. "I declined."

I hadn't spared a thought for Celeste, I realized now. She would have been there, of course. Annual charity balls like this one were exactly the sort of places Celeste liked to shine. But if she had been there tonight, I had missed it entirely. What was a bit of shine when my wife was like the sun?

I was appalled at the train of my own thought.

"Your sister is the last person on earth I would expect to comment on reality," I said, perhaps more witheringly than necessary. "Given that her own is so dire and uninspiring."

The elevator stopped at our floor, opening directly into our paneled foyer. This time it was Imogen who moved first, sweeping through to the grand salon that made up the bulk of the sprawling hotel suite's public rooms and was even more ecstatically decorated than the hotel lobby, all statuary and operatic sconces.

She moved into the center of the room, leaving me to trail her as she had me down below. I stopped short when I realized that was what I was doing, following her about like some kind of...pet.

And when she turned back to face me, she still didn't look the least bit sorry for what she had done.

"You could have married her. You didn't. Why?"

It took me a moment to stop seething at the notion that I could be the pet in any scenario. And another to comprehend her meaning. When I did, I scowled.

"I believe we already covered this subject in some detail the night before our wedding. If the reality Celeste wished to discuss with you had something to do with me, you should already know she is in no way an expert on that subject."

"Javier. Did she love you?"

The way she asked that question suggested she knew something I didn't. And worse, I didn't get the sense that simple jealousy was motivating the question.

I could have handled jealousy, but I didn't know what *this* was.

"Your sister and I hardly knew each other." It was hard to speak when my jaw was clenched so tight and my hands wanted so badly to curl into fists. "And as time goes on I consider that a great blessing. You must know Celeste better than anyone, Imogen. Do you believe her capable of loving anything?"

She didn't tremble. Not exactly—and yet something moved over her lovely face. "No. I don't."

"But you must step away from all this talk of love," I cautioned her. Though my voice was little more than a growl. "It has no place in an arrangement like ours. It has no place in the kind of lives we lead."

It had no place this close to *me*, I thought, but did not say.

"I'm sorry you feel that way," my blithely disobedient wife replied, without looking the least bit apologetic as she said it. "But it doesn't change the fact that I'm in love with you, Javier."

That torment inside me knotted harder, deeper, and only grew more grim.

"Love is the opiate of the weak," I threw at her. "A gesture toward oblivion, nothing more. It is only sex dressed up to look pretty."

"You are the most powerful man I have ever met. And yet you let my father send you away ten years ago, which tells me you must have wanted to go. Then you came back and took the only daughter available. Not even the one you'd come for the first time."

I didn't know where she was going with this. I only knew I didn't like it. "You were a virgin, Imogen. I understand why this is difficult for you. Virgins are so easily confused."

"You didn't even know she was there tonight, did you?"

That took me by surprise. Another unpleasant sensation only she seemed capable of producing in me.

"No." I knew I shouldn't have said it when Imogen smiled as if I'd made some kind of confession. "Why do you continue to talk about your sister?"

"They whisper when they think I can't hear, but I do," my wife said in a soft, quiet way that only a fool would mistake for weakness. And I might have been acting the fool tonight, but I wasn't one. "They think you only married me to get to her. I assume she thinks so, too."

"I don't want her." I didn't mean to say that, either, but it was as if that furious growl came out of me of its own volition. "She got what she wanted and so did I. There are no second chances where I am concerned, Imogen. You are either the best or I am bored."

I didn't understand the way she looked at me then. Almost as if I was causing her pain. But she was still smiling, though it was the kind of smile I could feel like a blow.

"I don't care why you married me," she said after a moment. "I don't care if it was purely mercenary or if it was a means to an end like they all think. It doesn't matter to me. What matters to me is what's happened since."

My heart was beating in that strange way again, that insistent and terrible drum. I recognized it. It reminded me of when I was a child, hiding from my parents' demons in filthy hovels, surrounded by too many desperate people.

I shook the memory off. But the fury in me only grew.

"Once again, Imogen, you are confusing sex and passion for something else. But that something else does not exist. It cannot exist."

Her eyes gleamed and I didn't want to understand what I saw there. It made me perilously close to unsteady.

"I love you, Javier," Imogen said. She kept saying it. "I don't think it's something you can order away."

"You might think you do," I gritted out, my voice like gravel. All of me like gravel, come to that. I felt as if I was turning to stone the longer I stood here. "But I know that you do not."

"Don't I?"

"It is a lie, damn you. Love is a weakness. It is a fairy story people tell themselves to excuse the worst excesses of their behavior. Our marriage is based on something far better than *love*."

"Money?" Imogen supplied, and I found that defiance of hers grating tonight. "The fickle support of selfish old men?"

"Neither one of us walked into this marriage with any unrealistic expectations. That is more than any fool who imagines himself in love can say."

"But I want more than easily met expectations," Imogen argued, that gleam in her gaze intensifying. "I want everything, Javier. What's the point otherwise?"

I knew that there were counterarguments I could make. Or better still, I could walk away and end this conversation altogether. I didn't understand why I did neither of those things. Or why I only stood there as if I was rooted to the hotel floor, staring at this wife of mine as if I didn't know her at all.

When I would have said I knew everything there was to know about her. From the poems she read to the sounds she made in the back of her throat when the pleasure I gave her was too much to bear.

"I told you I cannot abide lies," I said, as if from a great distance. "Love *is* lies, Imogen. And I will never build my life on lies again."

She made a noise that could as easily have been a sob as a sigh. She swayed slightly on her feet, and I had to order myself to stay where I was.

My protection was earned, I thought gravely, not given out like candy or sold like street heroin. But it was better when I saw she wasn't toppling over where she stood, felled by the force of her inconvenient emotions. She was squaring her shoulders the way fighters did.

"Show me the lie," she said.

At first I didn't understand what she meant. But as I watched, she reached up and undid the clasp at her shoulder that held her dress on her body. And then, I could only stare in a mixture of astonishment and pure, mad lust as that beautifully inky dress slid down her lush body like a caress and pooled at her feet.

I stood as if I was merely another statue in this salon full of lesser Renaissance offerings. Imogen's copper eyes glowed with more than a mere invitation. I saw in their depths a knowledge I refused to accept.

"I was raised by criminals," I heard myself say as if the words were torn from me. "They trafficked in lies and poison, down in the dirt and the gutters. And love was just another drug they sold, a high that wore off before morning."

I watched as she took that in, waiting for the censure. The revulsion. I watched emotion move across her face like a storm, but she didn't recoil as I expected her to. Instead, she gazed at me with a kind of understanding that I wanted to deny with every breath in my body.

"We can play any game you like, Javier," my wildfire wife told me as if she was the one with years and years of experience. As if I had been the virgin on our wedding day, locked away in a stone house for most of my life, and therefore needed her patience now. "We can start with an easy one, shall we? When I lie, I will stop."

"Imogen."

It was an order, but she didn't heed it.

And I didn't know if I would survive this. I didn't know if I could. I wasn't sure what was worse—if she obeyed me, put her clothes back on, and stopped confusing me with the sight of all that glorious flesh...

Or if she didn't.

As I watched, she unwrapped the particular feminine hardware that held her plump breasts aloft. She reached down and hooked her fingers into the lace that spanned her hips. And I nearly swallowed my tongue as she rolled her panties down the long, shapely legs that I loved to drape over my shoulders as I drove into her. I watched as she kicked the panties aside. And then, still holding my gaze, she kicked off her shoes.

And then my wife stood there before me like the goddess I must have known she was from the very first moment I laid eyes on her on that balcony.

All of those red-gold curls tumbled over her, calling attention to the jut of her nipples and, farther down, that sweet thatch between her thighs in the same bright color.

"Is this a lie?" she asked, all challenge and defiance as she started toward me.

My mouth was too dry. My pulse was a living thing, storming through me and pooling in my sex.

She crossed the floor and stood before me. I could smell the soap she used in her bath and, beneath that, the warmth of her skin. And further still, the sweet, delirious perfume of her arousal.

I could feel my hands at my sides, fisting and then releasing. Over and over. But I didn't reach for her.

"Or perhaps this is a lie," she murmured, her voice hoarse and almost too hot to bear.

But then she put her hands on me, and taught me new ways to burn.

Especially when she ran her fingers over my abdomen, then down farther still, so she could feel the proof of my desire herself.

"What do you want?" I demanded.

I sounded like a man condemned.

"You," she replied, much too easily. "I only want you, Javier. I love—"

But I'd finally had enough.

I heard the noise that came out of me then, like some kind of roar. It came from such a deep place inside of me that I didn't know how to name it.

I didn't try.

I pulled her into my arms, crushing my mouth to hers.

There was no finesse. If I was an animal—if I was the monster they'd always said I was—this was where I proved it. I lifted her from the floor, hauling her into my arms. Then I carried her over to the nearest antique chaise and laid her out upon it. My own sacrifice, once an innocent and now my tormentor.

I followed her down, too far gone to concentrate on anything but my own greed and the way she grabbed my coat as if I was taking too long. And the way her hips rose to meet mine long before I had finished wrestling with my trousers.

There was no time. No playing. There was only this.

There was only the slick, deep slide into all her molten heat.

There was only Imogen.

"Is this a lie?" she whispered in my ear as I lost myself in the rhythm. The deep, sweet thrust in, then the ache of the retreat.

I didn't believe in love. I wanted this to be a lie. That was the only world I knew.

But it was hard to remember what I knew with Imogen beneath me, holding me as tightly and as fiercely as I held her. It was hard to remember my own name as she met me, spurring me on, wrapping her legs around my hips and arching against me to take me deeper.

And the first time she exploded, I kept going. On and on, until she was sobbing out my name the way I liked it.

Only when she convulsed around me a second time did I follow.

But it still wasn't enough.

When I could breathe a little again, I rose. I stripped off what remained of my evening clothes, and swept my still-shuddering wife up into my arms again. I carried her through the sprawling suite, not letting go of her when I reached the bedroom.

I threw her onto the bed and went down with her, and then, finally, I took back control.

Over and over.

I had her in every way I could imagine.

I tasted her, everywhere. I made her sob, then scream.

I took her into the shower and rinsed us both, then started all over again while the steam rose in clouds around us and the hot water spilled over us both.

I took her and I worshipped her. I imprinted myself on her.

And if there was a lie in any of the things we did, I couldn't find it.

There was pink at the windows when Imogen finally slept, smudges beneath her eyes as she sprawled where I'd left her after the last round. I sat on the side of the bed and forced myself to look away from all of that lush sweetness.

It took some doing.

She would not stop talking of love. She'd kept it up all night, charging that same windmill again and again.

Over and over and over.

And I had spent the whole of my adult life telling myself only the truth. Or trying. I could do no less now.

I was a man, not the monster they imagined I was. Or I believed I was. And no windmill, either. And if there was any creature on this earth who could make me believe in things I knew to be lies, it was this one.

And I could not have that.

I could not bear it.

That was how I, who had never run from anything, found myself out in the Venice dawn.

Running like hell from a woman with red-gold curls, an impossibly sweet smile that cut into me every time I saw it, a defiance that I wanted to taste, not crush—and no sense at all of how she had destroyed me.

CHAPTER THIRTEEN

Imogen

FITZALANS ENDURED.

That was what I told myself when I woke up that morning in Venice and found myself alone.

And without him there to insist on those truths he seemed to hate so much, I lied.

I told myself that he had gone out, that was all. Perhaps to conduct some business. Perhaps to exercise the way he liked to do in the early morning back on the island. I made up all kinds of excuses, but I knew. Deep down, I knew.

He was gone.

His staff arrived at noon.

I didn't put up a fuss. I didn't even ask any questions. I let them collect the bags and lead me out of the empty hotel. I didn't look back.

Nor did I ask where I was headed once they bundled me onto a plane. Not Javier's plane, I noted. Or at least not the one I had been on before. I stared out the window as we soared over Italy and I wondered where he was. Where he had gone to.

And when—or if—he might return.

I didn't know if I was relieved or hurt when we landed

back at La Angelita. I held my breath as the car pulled up in front of the villa, telling myself a thousand different and desperate stories about how he'd needed to rush back here, that was all. I would walk inside, past that table in the foyer that still made me blush every time I saw it, and he would be here to greet me with that tiny curve in the corner of his hard mouth...

But he wasn't there.

For the first week, I jumped at every noise. Every time I heard a door open. Every time the wind picked up. Every time a window rattled. I jumped and I expected to see him standing there.

But Javier did not return.

It was sometime into the third week that I found myself sitting in his library, surrounded by books that failed to soothe me for the first time in my life. I was rereading one of my favorite novels, but even that didn't help. I felt thick and headachy and on the verge of tears, all at the same time, and it got worse every day.

I told myself it was a broken heart, that was all. But identifying what was wrong with me didn't help. It didn't fix it. It didn't bring my husband back.

I sat in that library, I thought about the grand sweep of history that had led down through the storied history of the Fitzalan family to me. Here. Alone.

I found myself thinking about my sister and the life she led. How much worse would I feel if I had been married, claimed in such an intimate fashion, and then abandoned...by my sister's husband? By the pursed-mouthed count who never smiled or one of the many indistinguishable men of father's acquaintance just like him?

Despite the way the memories of the ball still smarted, I felt the stirrings of something like sympathy for her. Celeste hadn't had much choice in the matter of her marriage, either. What must it be like for her, shackled to the count until he died, with her unhappiness expected on all sides—and held to be wholly unimportant?

The truth was, I was lucky. I loved Javier. More, I couldn't help believing that he loved me, too, though he might not know it.

If marriage was forever, and I knew full well that this one was—that the kinds of marriages people like me had were always permanent, because they were based on all those distressingly practical things Celeste had mentioned and Javier had echoed—then it didn't matter how long Javier stayed away.

I didn't have to hunt him down. I had already said my piece in Venice.

All I had to do was wait.

The days rolled by, as blue and bright as ever. I found that I was less interested in being on holiday, and started to amuse myself in different ways now that there was no one here to tell me any different.

"I do not think that Senor Dos Santos would like you in his office," the worried butler fussed at me when he found me behind my husband's imposing steel desk, helping myself to Javier's computer and telephone.

"Would he not?"

"The senor is deeply concerned with his privacy, Senora. He does not like anyone in this space when he is not at home."

I beamed at the butler. "Then it is a great shame that he is not here to tell me so himself."

I busied myself as I saw fit. I couldn't put myself to work the way others might, it was true. But I could do my part, so that was what I did.

And if Javier had a problem with the way I was spending his money on what I held to be worthy charities, well. That was his problem. If he wanted to make it *my* problem, he would have to come back to this island and face me.

I filled my days with all that glorious Mediterranean sunshine. I walked through the budding olive groves, looking for signs of spring. I sat in the pools outside the bedroom when dark fell so I could gaze up at the stars and do my best to name them. I walked the length of the unspoiled beaches on all sides of the island, letting all that crisp sea air wash over me, into me.

I spoke to the ocean when no one was around to hear me. And I always felt it answered me in the relentless way the waves beat against the shore.

It told me stories of endurance, deep and blue and forever.

It was a full month since the ball in Venice when I woke as I always did. I stretched out in the vast bed where I lay alone at night and tortured myself with memories of those lost, beautiful weeks when I'd first come here. When I'd given Javier my virginity and my heart and he'd given me light. I blinked at the sunshine as it poured in through the windows.

And then, instead of rolling to my feet and perhaps going for a morning swim, I was seized with the sudden certainty that I was about to be sick.

Horribly sick.

I barely made it across the room and into the bathroom in time.

It was only when I had finished casting out my misery and was sitting there on the tiled floor with a cold washcloth against my face that it occurred to me my evening meal of the night before might not have been to blame.

I wore nothing but one of Javier's shirts that I had liberated from his closet so I could pretend he still held me. And I told myself it was close enough to him actually being here as I sat there on the floor, my back against the wall, and spread my hands out over my belly in a kind of half wonder, half awe.

I hadn't cried since that morning in Venice. Not since I had finally accepted the fact that Javier had left me, and had taken myself into the shower because I knew that there was no way he would simply abandon me to my own devices. Not after what he'd paid for me. I knew that his staff would turn up, sooner or later. I needed to be dressed and ready.

But first I had stood beneath the hot spray in that Venetian hotel, loved him, and cried.

These tears were different. There was still that same despair a month later, but it didn't quite take hold of me. Because beneath it was searing, irrepressible joy.

I knew that in my world babies were seen as insurance, not people. Heirs and spares and collateral damage. Too many children and the inheritance was diluted. Too few and tragedy could send all that wealth and history spinning off to someone else's unworthy hands.

But here, now, on the bathroom floor in a villa that was the only place I had ever been truly happy, I forgot all that. I pushed it aside.

"I don't care what they say," I whispered, a fierce promise to the new life inside of me. "I will always love you. You will always know it."

And when I was done, I climbed to my feet and washed my face until there was no trace of tears. Then I called for my attendant and told her what I wanted.

Two hours later, I received a delivery from the nearest chemist's, somewhere on the Spanish mainland. Fifteen minutes after that, I confirmed the fact that I was, in fact, having Javier's child. My child.

Our baby.

And when night fell on that very same day, the sun making its idle way toward the horizon while it painted the sky golds and pinks, I heard the same sort of noise I always heard. And as I always did, I looked up from my favorite chair in Javier's library, expecting to hear the wind or see one of the servants hurrying past.

But this time, he was there.

Right there in front of me after all these weeks.

And he looked murderous.

CHAPTER FOURTEEN

Javier

SHE WAS MAGNIFICENT.

The truth of that slammed into me like a hammer, one hit and then the next, and I had to fight to breathe through it.

Imogen sat with her feet folded up beneath her in an armchair and a thick book open in her lap. I had been standing in the doorway to the library for some time before she noticed me, so enthralled was she with her reading.

It was like torture. She worried her lower lip between her thumb and forefinger. Her skin was flushed from the sun and from the walks the staff had told me she took daily.

And because she was carrying my child.

My child.

She lifted her gaze and instantly made me wonder if she'd known I was there all along.

"Hello, Javier," she said, as if I had happened out for an hour or two. "I wasn't expecting you."

"Were you not?"

I didn't wait for her to answer. I hardly knew what moved in me then. Fury, certainly. Something like panic. And that same dark current of need and longing that had chased me all over the planet and had never let me escape.

She had haunted me everywhere.

And it was worse, somehow, now that we were in the same room.

"I gave up expecting you in the first week," she said, and what struck me was the tone she used. So matter-of-fact. Not as if she was trying to slap at me at all. Which, of course, made it sting all the more. "How long will you stay, do you think?"

"I am told you have news to share with me, Imogen. Perhaps you should start with that."

"News?"

She looked flustered. But I didn't quite believe it.

"Surely you cannot have imagined that you could ask my staff for a pregnancy test without my knowing of it." I stepped farther into the room, expecting her to shrink back against her chair. But she only gazed at me, those copper eyes of hers wiser than before. Or perhaps it was only that I noticed it more now. Now that I knew how completely she could take me apart. And had. "There's nothing you have done in this house that I have not been made aware of within the hour."

She lifted her chin to that challenging angle that I had imagined a thousand times. And that I had wanted to touch a thousand more.

"If you have complaints about the way I choose to donate to the charities of my choice, I'm always happy to sit down with you and discuss it."

"Is this how our marriage works? Is this how any marriage works, do you imagine?"

"If it doesn't, that would also require that you sit down with me. Face-to-face. And have an actual conversation." She lifted one shoulder, then let it drop with an ease I didn't believe. Or didn't *want* to believe, because nothing in me was easy. "It is so hard, I find, to conduct a marriage all on one's own."

I found myself circling her chair, much as I had circled this island again and again since I'd left her in Venice. I had flown all over the world, dropping in on my various business concerns wherever I went. But I always returned to Spain. And I always had to fight myself to keep from coming straight back to this island.

To Imogen.

"That depends, I think, on what marriage it is you think we are having." I was filled with that same dark fury I hadn't been able to shake in all these weeks— the fury I had begun to suspect wasn't fury at all, but feelings. "I bought you for a very specific purpose. I never hid my intentions. You are the one who changed the rules. You are the one who made everything—"

"Real?" she supplied.

"You don't know what real is," I hurled at her, and I could hear that I was spinning out of control. That quickly. That completely. But I couldn't stop it. "You have no idea what it is to grow up the way I did."

"No, I don't."

I was so taken aback by her agreement that I froze. Then watched as she rose to her feet, the light, summery dress she wore flowing around her. I was struck by the expanse of her legs and her bare feet with toes tipped pink. I couldn't have looked away from her if my life depended on it.

She had become no less of a goddess in the time I'd been away, and it was worse now. Because I knew she carried my child. I couldn't see it, not yet, but I knew.

It made her more beautiful. It made everything more

beautiful, and I didn't know how to handle it. Beauty. Love. Imogen.

This is what I knew: I wasn't built for happiness.

"I don't know the precise details of how you grew up, or every last thing your childhood did to you. I know the bare bones. I know what little you told me when you thought you could use your past as a weapon. And I'm never going to know more than that unless you tell me. Just as there are things you don't know about me that you never will unless you're here to ask. But it doesn't matter, because our marriage will last forever. That's the benefit of a business arrangement." She waved an airy hand that I didn't believe and wanted, badly, to take hold of with my own. Yet I refrained. "We have all the time in the world to tell each other everything, one detail at a time."

Yet it was the phrase *business arrangement* that I couldn't get past, not this light talk of *details* when I had already shared more with her than anyone else in this life I'd scraped together by force of my own will. *Business arrangement* was in no way an incorrect way to describe our marriage, and yet it scraped over me, then deep inside me, as if it was hollowing me out.

"Why am I not surprised that a few weeks of solitude and the threat of motherhood are all it takes?" I shook my head. "No more talk of love."

And it was not until my own, bitter words hung there in the quiet of the library between us that I realized how much I'd been depending on hearing more of those protestations she'd thrown my way in Venice.

Or how certain I'd been that she'd meant all those words of love I'd refused to accept.

Imogen's eyes blazed copper fire. "You have everything you want, Javier. The Fitzalan heiress of your dreams. A child on the way to secure your legacy. And right when I was tempted to get ideas about my station, you put me in my place. Mention the word *love* and that's a quick way to get a month of solitary confinement." She wrinkled up her nose. "I can't complain. I've spent a lot of time in far worse prisons than this."

"La Angelita is hardly a prison."

"I love you, you fool." But she sounded something like despairing. "It isn't going to go away just because you do."

"You didn't come after me."

I heard the harsh, guttural voice. And it took me a long, hard kick from my own heart to realize it was mine.

"Javier…" she whispered, one hand dropping to cradle that belly where my child already grew.

And something in me…broke.

"You have ruined me," I told her, as if I was accusing her of some dark crime. "You took my home. You took my heart when I did not think it existed to be taken. And you left me with nothing. You talk of prison? I have spent these past weeks flying from country to country, looking at every last part of my collection…and none of it matters. None of it is *you*. The whole world is a prison without you in it."

Her lips parted as if she was having trouble believing what she was hearing. "You can have any woman you choose."

"I chose you!" I thundered. "Don't you understand? All I ever wanted was to *collect*. To win. You don't have to feel anything to do these things, you just have to have the money. And I always had the money. That is why, whatever the thing is, I have the best of it. But then you stormed out of a bathroom in Venice ranting about love and nothing has been the same since."

"Because I love you," she said again, in that same *absolutely certain* way she had in Italy.

Those words had chased me around the world. And back to her side again.

"I don't know what that is," I told her, the emotion in my own voice nearly taking me to the floor. "But I do know that a collection is not a life. And I want to live. I want to know my own child. I want to raise him. Not the way my parents raised me, feral and grasping and out of their minds. And not the way your father raised you, shut up behind one set of walls or another. I want to *live*, Imogen. And I think that must be love because I cannot come up with any other name for it."

That had come out like another accusation, but she only whispered my name. And it sounded like a prayer.

Maybe that was why I found myself on my knees before her after all, my hands on that sweet belly of hers that I had tasted and touched, and now held the start of our very own family. The future. All the hopes and dreams I'd told myself I was far too jaded to allow.

"I cannot live with lies," I told her, tipping my head back so I could look up at all those curls. And her shining eyes. Her lips like berries, trembling now. "But I do not know how to feel."

"But you do." She held my face between her hands and made me new, that easily. "You call it sex. You dismiss it. But it isn't just sex, Javier. It never was."

"How would you know this? You have never had anyone but me."

"Because I know."

And again, she struck me as a creature far wiser

than her years. Far more powerful than the sheltered girl she had been.

I understood then.

She was all those things and more. She was everything I needed.

I had bought a bride, but she had given me life.

"I think I looked up to that balcony and lost myself," I told her, fierce and sure.

"I married a monster," she whispered in return, her face split wide by that smile of hers that made the floor seem to tilt beneath me, "but it turned out, he was actually the very best of men. And better yet, mine."

"Yours," I agreed. "Forever."

She sank down before me, wrapping her arms around my neck, and something inside me eased.

"Forever," Imogen said solemnly. "And you can leave me alone if you must, Javier. I am quite happy with my own company—"

"I have wandered the world alone and without you for quite long enough. I do not plan to do it again."

"I love you," she whispered.

There was a truth in me then. I had been denying it for a long time. And I couldn't pretend that it didn't unnerve me, but the truth of it haunted me all the same.

It had chased me all over the world. It had never let me go.

Just as she wouldn't, I knew. Marriages like ours were built to last.

And ours was far better than most.

"I love you, too, Imogen," I said in a rush.

But when she smiled, brighter than the Mediterranean sky outside, I said it again.

And found it got easier every time.

"I love you," I said as I fit my mouth to hers in wonder.

"I love you," I told her as I smoothed my hand the belly where our child grew, and pressed my lips her navel.

And then I showed her what it was to love her, inch by beautiful inch, all across that beautiful body of hers.

I loved her and I'd missed her and I showed her all the ways that I would never, ever leave her again, right there on the floor of the library.

And when she was shaking and laughing and curled up against me, her face buried in my neck as she tried to catch her breath, I understood at last.

The Dos Santos marriage was a love match, not merely good business, and it would confound them all. It would add to our legend. It would make me more powerful and it would make Imogen an icon, and none of that would matter half so much as this. Us.

The way we touched each other. The children we would raise together. The life that we would live, hand in hand and side by side, forever.

This was love. It had always been love. This passion was our church, these glorious shatterings were our vows.

And we would say them, every day and in every language we knew, for the rest of our lives.

* * * * *